Deep in the Valley

THE GRACE VALLEY TRILOGY, BOOK 1

DEEP IN THE VALLEY

ROBYN CARR

THORNDIKE
CHIVERS

This Large Print edition is published by Thorndike Press, Waterville, Maine, USA and by BBC Audiobooks Ltd, Bath, England.

Thorndike Press, a part of Gale, Cengage Learning.

The text of this Large Print edition is unabridged.
Other aspects of the book may vary from the original edition.
Set in 16 pt. Plantin.
Printed on permanent paper.

LIBRARY OF CONGRESS CATALOGING-IN-PUBLICATION DATA
Carr, Robyn.
Deep in the valley / by Robyn Carr.
p. cm. — (In the Grace Valley trilogy ; #1) (Thorndike Press large print romance)
ISBN-13: 978-1-4104-1622-3 (hardcover : alk. paper)
ISBN-10: 1-4104-1622-4 (hardcover : alk. paper)
1. Women physicians—Fiction. 2. Emergency physicians—Fiction. 3. City and town life—California—Fiction. 4. Country life—California—Fiction. 5. Large type books. I. Title.
PS3553.A76334D44 2009
813'.54—dc22   2009007945

BRITISH LIBRARY CATALOGUING-IN-PUBLICATION DATA AVAILABLE

Published in 2009 in the U.S. by arrangement with Harlequin Books S.A.
Published in 2009 in the U.K. by arrangement with Harlequin Enterprises II B.V.

U.K. Hardcover: 978 1 408 44228 9 (Chivers Large Print)
U.K. Softcover: 978 1 408 44229 6 (Camden Large Print)

Printed in the United States of America
1 2 3 4 5 6 7 13 12 11 10 09

For Kate Bandy, with gratitude for the many wonderful years of devoted friendship.

ONE

June stood in the shower a little longer than usual, preoccupied with a conversation she would have later in the day. She was the town doctor in Grace Valley, California, a post she had inherited from her father, Elmer "Doc" Hudson. Elmer was seventy-two and playing at retirement, which was a polite way of saying he didn't keep hours anymore but he stayed in his daughter's business all the time.

The need for another full-time doctor to serve the town was becoming more dire every day. June had already talked to several physicians, and so far there hadn't been a fortuitous match. But today John Stone, M.D., was going to interview. He was forty, had attended Stanford University and UCLA Medical, done his OB-GYN residency at Johns Hopkins, worked for eight years in a prestigious women's clinic, then done a second residency in family medicine.

He was made to order for Grace Valley. But was Grace Valley made to order for him?

She tried to picture him, a yuppie from Sausalito. He had probably passed through town while on a wine tasting tour and begun fantasizing about the good life here. The beautiful landscape — mountains, valley and ocean — seduced more and more transplants from the cities every year. Or perhaps he'd been on a family vacation, doing the bed-and-breakfasts up the coast. But no, she thought, maybe a rich friend from San Francisco had a huge summer place nearby, someone who didn't need to eke out a living from the town. John Stone couldn't have been drawn here for golf or sailing; there was nothing so refined as that around. Hiking and camping, maybe, but only for a true woodsman. So what's he doing here? He'd *say* he was looking for peace and quiet and beauty and safety, all of which were plentiful in Grace Valley. Apple butter, heirloom quilts, unlocked doors, front porches and pies cooling in kitchen windows. Country life. Decency and simplicity.

He probably wanted to get his kids out of the dirty city, away from drugs and crime. How would he react to the news that the Coast Ranges and the Trinity Alps were so full of marijuana growers that army helicopters frequently flew just over the treetops, searching? The regular raids in the deep mountain forests made the simple sport of hiking a dangerous endeavor for the newcomer, since you never knew which camps and trails were controlled by drug farmers. Cannabis remained the largest cash crop in California. It was an uncomfortable reality, and it was just up the road.

As for peace and quiet, June was looking for a little of that herself. Her reason for trying to hire another physician. Obviously.

She turned off the water and began to towel her hair.

June had chosen to practice medicine in the small town she grew up in, *knowing* the challenge of it, knowing it could be more exciting than a city emergency room. She understood the inconvenience all too well — she lived it — and the sometimes discomfiting intimacy of being close friends with your patients, a thing big-city doctors could afford to avoid. So far all the medical contenders she had spoken to were trying to escape the hard work, long hours, overstimulation and constant demand of their city practices. Each had ultimately decided this wasn't the place for them, for it was a trade-off, one kind of pressure for another, but no less exacting. It took a certain personality to take on the medical needs of a whole town.

The phone rang. She glanced at the clock: 6:15.

That was another thing. There was no such thing as being "on call." There was you. Period.

She reached for the phone, but the damn cordless didn't work. Out of juice. She'd forgotten to plug it in again. With a towel wrapped loosely around her, and hair dripping in stringy tendrils to her shoulders, she made a dash for the kitchen phone.

The presence of strangers in the living room caused her to yelp in shocked surprise and dive behind the kitchen counter. Then she slowly rose and peeked over the counter into her small living room as the phone rang on. Had she really seen what she had seen? Four people . . . a man, a woman, two teenagers — boy and girl. The woman had a horrible scar running down the left side of her face. It took June a second to realize it was an old wound; the family had not come for help with that. They sat on her sofa, nice as you please, not in any way alarmed by her state of undress.

The phone continued to ring as she peered over the counter.

"You the doctor?" the man finally asked.

10

"Um, yes. That would be me."

By their out-of-date clothing and questionable manners, June assumed they were from the backwoods — subsistence farmers or mountain people. Since Grace Valley sat at the junction of three counties, it was impossible to tell which one they might be from. She didn't recognize these folks; maybe they'd never before sought medical treatment.

"Got a problem with the boy, here."

June tightened her towel and reached for the phone. "Excuse me," she said to the family. "I'll be with you in just a moment." She slid down behind the counter again. "Hello?" she said into the phone.

"Hi there," her father said. "I thought I'd better call and tell you that some family from back in Shell Mountain stopped George Fuller along the road and asked for directions to your house."

"Well, what the hell was George thinking?" she whispered fiercely.

"I don't imagine George thinks much if he can help it."

"They're here! Let themselves in and took a seat in the living room while I was in the shower!"

"Mercy. Well . . . would you like —"

"I'm practically naked! I had to run to the

11

kitchen phone, wearing only a towel!"

Elmer cackled, a laugh that had a slight wheeze to it, pipe smoking having taken its toll. "I bet they hadn't counted on that."

"I'm going to kill George!"

Elmer could hardly speak, he was laughing so hard. "Right now . . . I'll bet . . . you wish . . . you'd plugged in that cordless phone for once."

Her father seemed to have some simple psychic ability, a talent that did not amuse June at the moment. "Dad, if you see George before I do, tell him I want him to *suffer* before he dies!"

"You really need a dog, June. Haven't I been saying so? You want me to come over?"

"What for? I can handle this now."

"Okay then. Is tonight meat loaf night?"

"If I survive the day," she answered, and hung up without saying goodbye. Elmer was going to get a kick out of this a lot longer than she would.

June made sure her towel was secure, then slowly stood and looked at the family. Dad wore a suit jacket that was probably thirty years old, and Mom wore a hat. They'd put on their Sunday best for a trip to the doctor, but it seemed like they'd had a hard journey. If the man hadn't said his boy needed a doctor, June would have thought

12

the woman was in some need; the scar that marred her face ran deep from her forehead to her chin, across a blind eye that drooped sadly. It looked as if she'd taken an ax in the head. It gave June a headache just to look at it, though obviously the wound was years old. A childhood accident, perhaps.

The boy must be in bad shape for them to come to her house. She saw he wore one boot and one clean sock. This did not bode well.

"Let me get dressed, then I'll look at your son. Stay right there, please."

So much for the peace and tranquility of country life.

Elmer used to see patients in their home. The office space wasn't an add-on suite or anything like that, just two rooms right in the middle of the house, built that way by the first town doctor. And when a patient had come to the house wearing only one shoe, it had meant the other foot was too swollen. June's training for spotting such things had begun in her childhood.

Her visitors were the Mulls; a family of very few words. June managed to learn the boy had been stepped on by a jenny — a female donkey. The flesh was torn and rotting, and there were an unknown number of broken phalanges and metatarsals. Country people usually did much better than this with their bone settings and poultices. Maybe the boy had some metabolic problem that affected his healing. She would see that he was checked for diabetes.

"You waited too long on this injury," June told the family, comprised of Clarence Mull, his wife, Jurea, and their children, Clinton, sixteen, and Wanda, thirteen. Clinton was a strapping, handsome youth. In Wanda June could see a beauty that might have been the mother's had she not been so tragically marred. Clarence and Jurea were not young parents; June thought they might be in their fifties. "You have broken bones in the foot, and tissue and muscle damage from walking on it. Not to mention the necrotic flesh around this gash. Didn't it hurt?"

The boy shrugged. "Yeah, it was pretty bad. But Ma —"

"It's my fault," Jurea said. "I was the one set it. And put on a poultice."

"And I bet you gave him some serious herbal remedies for the pain — his pupils are dilated. You should go easy on that stuff."

"Works good on the pain though, don't it?" she answered.

14

"Too good. It was possible for him to walk on a broken foot and maybe do worse damage. Did you get to my house in a truck or car?"

"Pickup," said Clarence.

"You think it could make it as far as either Ukiah or Eureka?"

He shrugged. "We're slow but steady."

June gently pulled the sock back over the blackened, swollen foot. "How slow?" she asked.

The boy answered. "Can't get her up over thirty these days."

"Well, I have a better idea," June said. "Let me get one of the deputies to give you a lift up to Rockport, to Valley Hospital. You need to see a specialist."

"I'll get him where he needs to go," Clarence said.

"We're in a hurry now," she emphasized, going for the phone. "You already knew that or you wouldn't have brought him here at six in the morning."

"You worried that foot is going dead?" he asked.

June glanced back at him. A backwoods mountain man who could interpret necrotic tissue into a dead, gangrenous foot? Maybe he was only expressing his own fears. Still . . .

"I'm telling you, if you don't get that boy to the hospital, he could lose his foot. Or worse. You wouldn't want that."

"Specialists. They come at a pretty high dollar?"

"Don't worry about the money, Mr. Mull. Things like that can be worked out. There's all kinds of assistance if you find you're a little short right now." She dialed the phone.

"I'm accustomed to paying my way."

"I'm sure you are." Then, into the phone, she said, "Ricky? This is June. I need a favor. A young patient of mine needs a lift to Valley Hospital to see a specialist. I'll give him the name and send him to the police department. Thanks in advance."

June wrote down the name of the hospital and doctor, and grabbed a full bottle of antibiotic capsules from her bag. She ran a tall glass of tap water, then handed the pills and water to Clinton and the paper to Clarence. When Clarence reached toward her, his coat sleeve rode up briefly revealing part of a tattoo that reached his wrist.

"Mr. Mull, losing the foot would be a tragedy, but an even greater tragedy would be to ignore an injury like this and have your son die of septicemia. You probably learned about blood poisoning in Vietnam. Don't ignore my advice about the specialist

16

and the hospital. Here are some antibiotics," she said to Clinton. "Take four immediately, then one every four hours until they're gone. Be sure to show the bottle to the doctor when you get to the hospital — and tell him how many you took. He may want to give you something else, okay? Do you know where the Grace Valley Police Department is? Would you like to follow me into town?"

"I guess we'll make it all right. It ain't far," Clarence said. And with that he stood and hefted his son, a boy at least six feet tall, into his arms and carried him out the front door. Clarence Mull was a huge, huge man.

The pickup, circa 1940, moved like its joints ached. When it had finally cleared June's long drive, she locked the door and dashed to her bedroom to change clothes. The Mulls were not simple unsophisticated backwoods mountain folk who didn't know better than to come to the doctor's home. Clarence hadn't wanted to take his boy to a place as public as the clinic. He might be a pot farmer. Or maybe a mentally disabled vet, suffering from paranoia. The hills were full of dropouts.

She changed out of her hastily drawn on sweat suit and into a pair of gaberdine slacks with nice creases down the legs, a silky blouse and a tapestry-patterned vest. She was interviewing today, after all.

Then she looked in the mirror and said, "Shit." She'd let her tangled hair dry on its own while she'd examined Clinton Mull, and what she had now was a wild, kinky, out-of-control mane. Sighing, she pulled it back into a knot and put a clip in it. She had never been good at things like hair.

Two

Tom Toopeek stood in front of his bathroom mirror, bare chested, and fastened his long, silky black hair into a ponytail. His wife of eighteen years, Ursula, pushed open the door and handed him a freshly ironed shirt.

"Tom, someone from the Craven house just called. One of the younger boys — I don't know which one. All he said was 'Daddy's real riled up.' But he didn't have to say anything more — I could hear. Gus is tearing up the house again. And probably most of the family."

Tom was already in his shirt by the time she finished. He pulled his gun and holster out of the bedroom closet and armed himself.

"Are you going to go straight out there?" she wanted to know.

" 'Course," he said, buckling the belt.

To the Craven house at dawn. One of these days he was going to be too late.

Ursula lifted a steaming mug from atop the bureau and handed it to him. He kissed her, took the cup and moved down the long hall, past the bedrooms that held his own sleeping children. His fifteen-year-old daughter, Tanya, stepped out of her room and blocked his passage. "Daddy, can't you arrest him?"

"I arrest him all the time, Tan," he said. "Come on, let me go . . . I'm in a hurry now."

"He's going to kill someone," she said to his back. "Someone needs to put him in prison!"

Ursula yelled, "I'm calling Ricky to back you up."

"No," Tom said. "Call Lee at home and tell him to meet me there. He's closer."

"You be careful, Tom! You be *so* careful! Gus would as soon shoot you as —"

"I'm not going to let him shoot me," he said impatiently. "Call Lee."

Gus Craven was the meanest son of a bitch in the valley. He had five sons, each of whom came close in age to one of the five Toopeek children; their oldest were both fifteen. They hadn't played together, of course, because Gus did all he could to keep his family isolated. The Cravens had a farm in upper Mendocino County near the Humboldt County line. It was a modest farm with a few crops, a few animals. It could be a good business, but Gus was a binge drinker and got tanked up regularly, beat the tar out of the whole family, tore up the house and had to be hauled off till he was sober. Then again, there were times when he knocked the stuffing out of his wife and kids and he hadn't had a drop. Just a genuine badass.

It was Tom's duty as police chief to try to stay one step ahead of old Gus so his daughter's fearful proclamation didn't turn out to be true. Tom was one-third of the Grace Valley Police Department. Ricky Rios and Lee Stafford, both thirty years old, young husbands and fathers, were his only deputies. The three of them worked all the time. Anyone who lived in the valley could call Tom or the deputies at home if they were needed when the police department was closed. Like this morning.

Tom drove as fast as he dared along County Road 92, but he didn't run the siren. He didn't want to give Gus any warning. Tom was going to get him out of there before Gus figured out that one of the boys had called for help. Gus had spent a few nights and weekends locked up for this kind of behavior, but generally it was just enough

21

time to cool him down and get him think-ing straight. It was never enough time to make him sorry. He plain wasn't ever sorry. This time, though, Gus would be gone awhile. Tom had warned him that they didn't need Leah to press charges. He'd charge Gus with assault and battery himself. It would be Gus's fifth official arrest on those charges, and he'd do time. Judge Forrest was getting sick of seeing the man come before the bench. Tom was getting fed up with Gus's failure to have his behav-ior modified by consequence.

Everyone in town hated Gus, bar none. Who knew why he was such a nasty man? He wasn't from the valley and no one knew his people. When the Craven family came into town to shop or go to church, most folks gave Gus a wide berth. They'd say hello to Leah and maybe the boys, but no one ever traded words with Gus on purpose. The worst thing about their terrible situa-tion was that Gus had come to the valley, bought that little parcel of land to farm and married a Grace Valley girl. Leah was one of theirs, and they couldn't seem to do anything for her.

Leah was only thirty-three and Tom re-membered her from school. She used to be friendly with one of his sisters. She had been a shy, pretty girl — and smart. How in the world Gus Craven got to her was an eternal mystery. He was seven years older and never, as far as Tom could remember, even halfway pleasant.

The farmhouse was sixty years old, and though solidly built, it had fallen into disrepair. The porch sagged, the paint was chipped, screens were torn. Inside was worse.

The sun was rising over the mountains, casting a long shadow. The lights were on, and Tom could see movement inside as he pulled up in the Range Rover. He headed around to the side of the house, parking in a less obvious position. At that very moment his deputy, Lee Stafford, drove up.

When Tom opened his door, he heard the sounds of domestic war pouring out of the windows: shrieking, hollering, running, crashing, slamming. Kids were screaming and crying, Gus was shouting and cursing, Leah was begging him repeatedly to stop. Tom pulled his shotgun out of the rack and checked that there was a shell in the chamber.

"Let's get him out of there," he said to Lee.

Both men, in perfect choreography, jogged up the porch steps. Lee pressed his back against the wall beside the front door while Tom kicked it. Tom always kicked if there was kicking to be done. He would never have his deputies, both younger than him by seven years, face harm's way in his stead.

Gus turned his rheumy eyes toward the door. He held his thirteen-year-old son by the hair, his other hand raised and ready to pummel him. Leah pulled back on his arm with no real hope of preventing his abuse. For a split second Tom had a rare thought; he wished Gus had been armed with a gun or knife so he could just shoot him and be done with it. He knew he could do it with a clear conscience. But just as fast, the thought retreated and was lost. Tom was, above all, a peace officer.

"Let the boy go, Gus," he said.

"This ain't your concern!"

Tom took two long strides into the room. It came into focus around him — the crunch of broken glass beneath his boots, the smell of booze and sweat and grease. The tinny odor of blood. He counted from the corner of his eye — one, two, three, four. "Leah, where is little Stan?" Stan was the youngest boy, only six years old.

She backed away from Gus. Her face was bruised and tearstained, and she wore a torn old nightgown. "He's upstairs. Hiding, I think."

"Which one of you sniveling little whelps called the Indian cop?" Gus asked, shaking the boy he still held.

"Gus," Tom warned. "You let that boy go and back away from him. Now."

"I been just looking for an excuse to sue you, Toopeek!" he yelled.

Tom let out his breath in what could pass for a weary laugh. *Sue?* He tossed his shotgun to Lee and walked almost leisurely toward Gus, while pulling his handcuffs from his belt. Gus's eyes grew round. In one swift motion Tom slapped a cuff on Gus's wrist, pulled his arm roughly behind his back, swept him off his feet and slammed him onto the floor, facedown. Gus grunted in outrage, a sound soon muffled against the worn carpet. The son he had held by the hair skittered away. Leah covered her mouth with a trembling hand, her eyes milky with fear.

Tom grabbed Gus's other wrist with a little more difficulty, what with his squirming and all. Once he was cuffed, hands behind his back, Tom held him there with a heavy foot on his back. "I warned you and Judge Forrest promised. This time you're going away, Gus."

25

"I ain't going nowhere! She won't press charges! None of 'em will!"

Tom wasn't sure whether or not Gus was as stupid as he sometimes sounded. The only time he ever had much to say was when he was drunk. Sober, he was glum and silent and seemed to direct his nervous family with eyes narrowed to slits, like Frank's. And just as Tom had that thought, he looked at the fifteen year old. He saw Gus's eyes, Gus's hate reflected there. Frank was a tall, gangly boy, but almost large and strong enough to give his father a real fight. Tom realized that this domestic nightmare was soon going to come to a head. Something was going to pop. Either Gus would finish off this poor family, or Frank would finish off Gus. It was just too volatile to drag on like this.

Tom jerked Gus to his feet. "We've been over and over this. No one has to press charges. I can press charges." He shuffled Gus to the door. "Let me get him settled in the car, then I'll come back and make sure no one is hurt real bad in here. Okay?"

Leah shook her head. "It's okay. I'll see after the boys."

"Don't you say one single word about me, woman! If you do —" Tom whacked him on the side of the head, palm open to shut him up. "Ahh! Police abuse! Police abuse!"

Lee holstered his gun and laughed outright. "Man, you got some balls, Gus."

"Yeah, I'll show you balls! Take these cuffs off me and we'll go a round in the yard, huh?"

"I wish," Lee said.

Tom and Lee dragged Gus away by the arms. Gus stumbled and swore and griped all the way to the Rover.

Tom was back in the house moments later. Leah held little Stan on her lap, wiping his tearstained face with a washcloth. Frank stood rigid, his back against the wall, arms crossed over his chest, a mighty bruise rising on his cheekbone. There's the legacy, Tom thought sadly. At least a couple of these boys would beat their wives and kids. Ironically, it could just as likely be the one most outraged by his father's violence.

"Leah, let me take you and the boys to the clinic. Have June look you over."

"I'm okay, Tom. I'll check over the boys, and if anyone needs to go, I can take 'em in. How long's he gonna be gone, Tom?" she asked.

"At least a few months. Could be up to a year. Judge Forrest is pretty sick of his excuses. Leah, you have to make a change here. You're running out of time." He glanced again at Frank, and Leah followed his eyes. "I know you know that."

She wore a helpless smile. "Where you think I'm going to hide five towhead boys?"

"You lack faith, that's all. Just call the social worker, get some ideas from her. There's programs you've never heard about, not just shelters at the edge of town. There are people who make helping battered families their life's work."

She laughed humorlessly. "It would be a life's work with me. Five boys, no money, no skills, and a husband who's taken a blood oath to kill me if I ever leave him."

Tom fished his wallet out of his back pocket and pulled out a card for Corsica Rios, County Social Services. Corsica lived just south, in Pleasure, but had many ties to the valley, including her only son, deputy Ricky Rios. She also had a great deal of experience with domestic abuse — personal and professional — and had raised Ricky as a single parent. "Just call her. Let Corsica tell you there's no help before you give up. Hmm?"

Leah held the card for a moment, staring at it.

"You must think awful of me," she finally said. "That I let him do this to my family."

Tom covered her small, pale hand with his

much larger one. "No, Leah. No one thinks you let him."

THREE

June drove right by the clinic when she got to town. She went to Fuller's Café, as she always did unless there was some emergency. Customarily, she picked up a coffee to go and a bagel or doughnut or pastry, made a little small talk with the regulars and *eased* into her day. But she was going to break custom today by adding a twist — she was going to kill George Fuller.

"Mornin', June," George called out as he poured her coffee into a large mug.

"George, have you lost your mind?"

"How's that?"

"What were you thinking, sending people to my house at six in the morning?"

He had a perplexed look on his face. June had gone all through school with George and was quite accustomed to that look, though she knew George wasn't completely dense. Well, he was obviously dumb about some things, but plenty smart about others.

"I didn't send 'em, June. They asked directions is all."

"Well, do you give directions to just any stranger in an old pickup who asks you for them?"

Again the look.

Tom Toopeek, June's best friend since childhood, left his conversation with two locals and wandered over to the pastry counter where June was engaged in ragging on George. Tom leaned against the counter, a faint smile playing on his lips. He held a ceramic cup that had The Law written on it. George kept that cup clean and handy for whenever Tom might wander in.

"It wasn't much more than the crack of dawn, and I was coming back from turning Buddy out to pasture when that old truck rattled up and the man — nice man if you ask me — says to me, 'Can you tell me how to get to Doc Hudson's house?' And I asked, 'Old Doc Hudson or young Doc Hudson?' And he said, 'June.' Nice as anything. Like you was old friends. Didn't look like his family was sick or anything, though that woman took a nasty crack in the face, didn't she? It was all healed up, though, so I knew she wasn't needing your services for that. I thought maybe you were expecting 'em. Was there trouble?"

"Oh no, George. There was no trouble! They just let themselves into my house while I was taking a shower!"

Tom chuckled but tried to mute it.

"Aw, June, I'm sure sorry about that. I had no idea —"

"My name's on the clinic sign, George. It's no miracle the man knew it!"

"Aw, June, jeez . . ."

"Well, don't tell people where I live unless you're absolutely sure I want them to come to my house! All right?"

"How'm I gonna know?"

"Well *call* me, George! Or just give them directions to the clinic and tell them we open for business at eight."

"Sure thing, June. I'm awful sorry. Here, you have a bear claw on the house." He reached into the pastry shelf and pulled out a huge sugary treat.

"Don't let it happen again," she said, mollified. More often than not she got her morning carbohydrate on the house anyway. It was smart to be in the good graces of the medic and the law. George only *looked* stupid.

"You can count on that, June."

George Fuller was actually a huge success in Grace Valley. His café brought in a good living; he had a big house, a nice family. His wife was pretty and smart. He sat on the town council most years, coached at the high school on and off and occasionally wrote letters to the editor that were thoughtful, even insightful. He'd gotten A's and B's in high school, as far as June could remember, but the occasions of him acting dumb as a stump were not infrequent.

"It must have given you a start, coming out of the shower to find you had company," Tom observed. The corners of his mouth were twitchy.

"You could say that. Especially since I was running for the kitchen phone, wearing my favorite towel."

His high, bronze Cherokee cheeks almost cracked. "What a way to start the day," he said.

"For them or for me?"

"I guess that could go either way." He didn't even attempt to conceal his wide, toothy grin.

"Did Ricky get that boy up to Rockport?"

"What boy?" Tom asked, startled.

"I called the department this morning and asked him to give a young patient of mine a lift to the hospital there. It was the boy from my living room. The parents and sister brought him. Mull family?"

Tom frowned as he searched his mental

catalog of local names. "I didn't realize. I was preoccupied. Lee and I were at the Cravens' at dawn, providing a little relief."

"Oh God, not again. Poor Leah."

"She's going to get a break now. I'm sure Judge Forrest will put Gus away for as long as possible."

"It can't possibly be long enough."

"Ricky said he was hanging around to run an errand for you, but he didn't say what. He was still waiting as of fifteen minutes ago. And I'm afraid I don't know of a Mull family."

It was not unusual for one of the deputies to be doing some errand for June or the clinic without Tom knowing the specifics. Sometimes there were patients who needed transportation, delivery of lab samples, pickup of blood or urgent need of supplies. Any number of things. The only way the clinic could exist was with the support of the local police.

"These people weren't from around here, Tom. They might be mountain people, or maybe subsistence farmers from another county. The father knew more than he let on, and I'm sure I saw the edge of a tattoo on his hand. Maybe he's a vet . . . or possibly even a dope farmer. And Mrs. Mull has that scar George mentioned — it runs down the right side of her face. She's terribly disfigured and probably vision impaired. If you ever saw her, you'd never forget her. But it's the boy who needs medical attention. He got stepped on by a jenny maybe two weeks ago, and his tissue's turning black around an infected gash. He's warm to the touch, and a few days could make it more than a foot he loses. I worry about them not showing up at the police department. It might mean they don't intend to go any further to get help for the boy."

"You didn't pass them on your way into town?"

"I went out to Mikos Silva's place to take his blood pressure," she said, shaking her head.

"The boy's a minor?" Tom asked.

"Sixteen. But still —"

"We'll take a look around."

"They're in an old pickup. They can't go more than thirty miles per hour in it, so they can't get far." What she didn't say was, "Please find them before they get away, disappear into the hills again."

This was not the first time someone in precarious health had ignored June's warning and advice, but she had never gotten used to it.

A rumble of chuckles from four old-timers at a table by the window distracted them. George leaned over the counter and tried to see out the front window. "What's doing?" he called to the men.

"Mary Lou Granger brought a box into the Presbyterian Church 'round fifteen minutes ago . . . and here comes Pastor's wife from the parsonage. She's got a nose like a hound. Can smell her husband alone with a woman from across town."

"Here she comes!" someone replied.

June and Tom gravitated to the front of the café and saw Mary Lou, an attractive young mother, maybe thirty years old, exit the Presbyterian Church in something of a huff. She wore fitted jeans and boots, and a sweater that didn't quite reach her waist. Her long, thick auburn hair swung across her shoulders in wide arcs. When she got to her station wagon she stopped, looked back over her shoulder toward the church, stomped her foot once in anger and finally got in the car.

"Wanna bet Pastor Wickham's got a nice red swatch across one cheek?" someone asked.

"He's as brave a preacher as we've ever had in this town," someone said. "Why, would *you* chance the wrath of Clarice

Wickham?"

"That's the very thing that drives him, I reckon."

The men all broke into laughter.

"You know, that really isn't funny," June said to Tom, referring to the womanizing pastor.

"Oh, I don't know. You have to keep your sense of humor. Have you seen him lately?"

"No, why?"

"He's taken off the rug. He now has — what are they called? Plugs?"

"Not really!"

"Really. His vanity is almost a reverent thing."

She chuckled in spite of herself. But then she said, "I don't think it would hurt to have a word with him, Tom. You, better than anyone, know how volatile and unpredictable these domestic situations can be. His roving eyes and slippery hands are going to cause some real trouble one of these days. What the boys say is true — Mrs. Wickham's wrath could do some actual damage. What if she gets her fill of his antics and flirtations? She seems a little . . . I don't know . . . high-strung."

"I know you're right in what you say, June. And maybe I should say something. It wouldn't hurt for him to know we know."

Tom shrugged. "Might even serve as a warning. But when I think about those hair plugs, I just don't think I could say something to him with a straight face."

June lifted an eyebrow. "I bet if he patted your ass and blew in your ear, you could."

Tom's eyes widened briefly. He cleared his throat, drained his cup and said, "You may have a point. I believe I'll take a drive. See if I can overtake the Mull family in their old truck."

When June Hudson was a little girl, she'd thought she would grow up to be her father's nurse. Even then she knew that Doc Hudson held the life of the town in his capable hands. She went off to college to become an R.N. This might have come to pass, but she was intercepted by a chemistry professor at Berkeley who recognized in her a special ability in the sciences. So, with the blessing of her father, she switched her major from nursing to pre-med.

During vacations and school breaks she worked with her dad. At Elmer's side it was more than family medicine she trained to practice, it was *country doctoring.* And there was a distinction. They often had to make do on less, by way of supplies and technologies, and frequently had to improvise to successfully treat a patient. It was more stimulating and challenging than any big-city specialty. What San Francisco doctor would be called out to the highway at 2:00 a.m. to try and hold together the victims of a car accident until a helicopter could be summoned? Or drive out to a logging camp to haul a man *and* his severed limb to the nearest emergency facility?

She returned to Grace Valley permanently twelve years later, a fresh-faced, idealistic young doctor. But in her time away, she had forgotten a few things about her town.

First, the people were slow to trust her — a new young doctor, a woman — even though they'd known her forever. She had to work beside Elmer for a few years, acting as his apprentice. It wasn't until she had performed a few of what the locals perceived as medical miracles that she was trusted enough to see a logger with his boots off. Even now, with Elmer mostly retired, there were still men who wouldn't bring their ailments to June until Elmer had seen them first and insisted. Half the time he saw them in the café or filling station or post office. Yet for most who lived in the valley, June was the official doctor. And she still relied heavily on her dad for professional and personal support. Since June's mother's death nine years earlier, they had been very dependent on each other.

Second, if you're going to stay in Grace Valley, live and work there all your life, then you'd better have picked out a husband in the ninth grade. What had she been thinking when she'd chosen this life, this town? That some handsome young bachelor would trip and they'd fall in love while she wrapped his ankle? June was thirty-seven now, and her two best friends were her dad and Tom Toopeek. She had close ties to her quilting circle, the Graceful Women, and kept up with friends from school. She wasn't exactly lonely, but she hadn't had a real date in about five years. Elmer seemed to think she was a virgin — a dubious if not ludicrous distinction. It wasn't true, thank God. But it was true she was now dangerously set in her ways. Perhaps too independent to become the prettier half of a couple. Still, she wouldn't mind a little romance.

Grace Valley had originally been a fishing and farming village. It sat on the corner of three counties, just barely more on the Mendocino side than Trinity and Humboldt. There was a small hospital in Rockport, a larger one in Eureka, and when June and Elmer had opened the clinic ten years ago, it had been considered an extravagance for a town of nine hundred. Now it was a necessity for a town of fifteen hundred and sixty-four . . . with Julianna Dickson about to make it sixty-five.

June parked behind the clinic, next to Charlotte Burnham's car. Charlotte, aged sixty, had been June's father's nurse. As nurses went, it would be hard to find one tougher or more efficient. Or grouchier. The only person Charlotte ever seemed to make a real effort to be sweet to was Elmer, even though her husband, Bud, fairly doted on her. June had been the doctor here for some time now, but Charlotte had never quite made the transition. Oh, she'd take orders, but she always treated June more like the girl who hung around her father's office than the boss. It was past annoying. June had enjoyed no act of vengeance so much as hiring Jessica Wiley, the bane of Charlotte's existence, to work in the clinic.

Charlotte was just making her way out the back door, shaking out a Marlboro, as June got out of her Jeep. There was no smoking allowed in the clinic. Charlotte would smoke the extra long cigarette, cough, get back to work, and need another one before long. There was a coffee can half full of butts beside the back step. June had begged her for years to quit.

"Having your spite smoke?" June asked.

Charlotte inhaled deeply. "I need it more today than usual," she replied shortly.

"Ah. Jessie dress up for you?"

"Wait till you see." She puffed again.

Jessica, age twenty, was the clerk-receptionist. Despite the fact that she had cut her formal education short by quitting school, she was the best office person June had ever had. A brilliant girl, resourceful and quick, she was also odd as a duck — a fashion extravaganza who never wore a dull outfit. June felt a surge of excitement as she entered the clinic. Stodgy Charlotte and avant-garde Jessica made for interesting days. They did not exactly get along like mother and daughter.

Or . . . maybe they did . . .

June knocked the caked mud off her boots and left them by the back door where the sun would dry them. Old Mikos Silva's place was on her way to the clinic, and she had stopped by to check his blood pressure. His idea of "taking it easy" was to sleep in till 4:30 a.m. and do only half his chores, so she'd had to slog her way out to the barn to find him. Old farmers like Mikos were typically afraid that if they sat down for too long, they might drop dead, doctor's orders notwithstanding.

She slipped on her clogs and headed for the front of the clinic. She would have said good morning, but she was frozen silent by the dizzying sight of Jessica's hair.

The girl was some kind of Goth, as she called herself. Black clothes, lots of piercings in oddball places, black nail polish and lipstick. There was no evidence she did any of the scary things her appearance seemed to imply — like take human sacrifices. But today she had reached a pinnacle. Her head was shaved but for the multicolored Mohawk plume that stood up proudly on top. Bold stripes — purple, blue, red, orange, yellow — waggled as she moved.

June wasn't sure how long she stared, but it was long enough for Charlotte to return to her post. June met her nurse's eyes and saw only grim misery. And a warning: *Don't give her the satisfaction.* When June looked into the small waiting room, she saw that all six eyes were focused on the colorful Mohawk, in slack-jawed, fascinated stares.

"I'll be just a few minutes," she said to the waiting room. "Good morning, Jessie. New do?"

Jessica looked up from her filing, smiled beautifully, for she was a beautiful girl, and nodded. The action set her many pierced hoops in motion — on ears, eyebrow, nose and places June didn't want to think about.

June picked up a stack of charts Charlotte had set out and made her way back to her office, her nurse on her tail. Charlotte closed the office door behind them.

"I'm at the end of my rope," Charlotte announced.

"Take it easy. It's only hair." June bit her tongue against the temptation to remark on Charlotte's own hair, a dark red with a purple hue that always looked two weeks overdue with its telltale quarter inch of gray against her scalp.

"You cannot let this go on!" Charlotte insisted.

"Charlotte, she's a very sweet, very efficient girl." June struggled not to laugh out loud. "She lends color to the place."

"How can her father allow this . . . this . . . *in-sanity?*"

Charlotte and Bud had raised six children, none of whom would have dared part their hair on the wrong side, much less shave and color their heads. But Jessica's father, Scott, a good-natured, broad-minded artist and widower of only forty-two, chose to let his daughter find her own way. June approved more of the latter parenting style, though she wouldn't dare admit that to Charlotte.

"What did *you* say to Jessie?" June asked.

"I am committed to not reacting."

"You have a lot of unnecessary stress over Jessica's clothing and hairstyles, Charlotte. Maybe you should talk to someone about it. Have you given any thought to seeing Dr. Powell about this?" Jerry Powell was the local shrink — a Ph.D. psychologist with a specialty in family counseling. He had relocated to Grace Valley in search of a quiet, peaceful life, after a stressful, twenty-year Silicon Valley practice.

"Why would I talk to that nutcase?"

Jerry Powell was probably an excellent counselor . . . with an unshakable belief that he had once been abducted by aliens.

"His beliefs are not so different from some of our own townspeople's," June pointed out.

"We don't any of us believe in spaceships, for God's sake!"

"Oh no," June laughed. "Not spaceships! Angels, buried treasure, Indian spirits, hidden caverns and Big Foot. But not spaceships."

Charlotte pursed her lips. "I think you're enjoying this," she said, and left June's office in a huff.

Jerry Powell took his coffee to his office, where he would wait for his first client of the day, Frank Craven. This was an emergency intervention — the boy had been in a fight at the school bus stop.

Jerry had lived in his three-bedroom rambler for just a few years, and while in one sense he would be a newcomer for at least twenty years, in another sense he was already accepted in Grace Valley. That was not to say he'd been pulled into the warm bosom of the town and cherished, but rather accepted as the San Jose shrink who'd admitted to Bay Area media about twenty years ago that he'd been for a ride in a spaceship. The Spaceship Shrink, they called him. Some, he knew, called him the Gay Spaceship Shrink, though no one in Grace Valley knew for sure whether he was gay or straight. There were undoubtedly lots of valley residents who thought he was delusional . . . but there were plenty of people who availed themselves of his services. He made a much better living in the little town than he'd ever expected to.

He had converted his garage into an office, and had a brick walk directed to the side door so that he wouldn't have to escort people through his living room and kitchen to their therapy sessions. Half the garage served as private office, half as waiting room, and he'd had a large picture window installed so he could see his clients as they pulled up to the curb in front of his little house. Through that window he saw the police car, a beige-and-brown SUV. Lee Stafford was at the wheel and Frank Craven was getting out.

Jerry might have been looking at himself thirty-five years earlier — skinny, lanky, feet as big as snowshoes, arms too long, hair badly cropped and askew, head down and gait clumsy. And not so different now, Jerry thought, for he was six foot five, wore a sixteen shoe and had never been able to manage his wavy blond hair. And though he tried to stand up straight, it was hard when nine-tenths of the world was under his chin.

"Come in, Frank, come in," he said, holding the door. "I don't think we've ever met. I'm Jerry Powell."

"The spaceship guy," Frank said sullenly and thickly through his swollen lip.

"The same. You've had a rough morning. Want some juice? Water? Soda?"

"Naw."

"Come back to my office, here. And if you change your mind, just say so."

Frank followed Jerry into the office. Jerry stood at the door and waited for him to choose a seat, either in the conversation area, where a couch was separated from two chairs by a coffee table, or in one of two chairs before the desk. But Frank stood just inside the door and waited. "Have a seat, Frank," Jerry said.

"Where?" he asked.

"Anywhere."

"Where?" he asked again, unwilling to select their seating.

"How about here?" Jerry suggested, indicating a chair in front of the desk.

The boy flopped down, slumping. "This going to take long?"

"Probably not. Let me just tell you a couple of things first. I'm going to make a few notes because I don't trust my memory, but they are completely confidential. Even though this visit was prompted by the high school assistant principal, I'm not required to tell him anything about our session. Okay?"

"I don't really care what you tell him," Frank said meanly. "He's a cocksucker."

"I am only obligated to tell him that you did, in fact, have your required meeting with me," Jerry continued, as though he hadn't heard the boy's comment.

"I had two choices. Expelled or counselor."

"Yes, well —"

"If it had been *suspended* or counselor,

I'd have taken suspended."

Jerry pulled a yellow pad onto his crossed knee and wrote April 17th at the top. "Why not take the option of being expelled? You like school?"

"Not really. But my ma wants me to go."

"But you could have an excuse . . . if you got expelled."

Frank started to pick a thread on his jeans. They were in pretty bad shape. Not only were they old, they were now dirty from having rolled in the dirt at the bus stop.

"Your mother's been through enough today, I suppose."

He looked up. "What do you know about it?" Frank wanted to know. There was such rage in his eyes. He was one angry kid.

"I know you got in a fight at the bus stop because someone said something about your dad being taken to jail and you were . . . what? Offended? Embarrassed?"

"How about pissed off?"

"Yeah?" Jerry asked.

"Yeah."

"Pissed off because?"

"Just because . . ."

"Do you want to tell me about it?"

"Naw. I'm over it now. It's finished."

"We gotta do something, Frank. We have fifty-five minutes to go."

He was met with silence.

"I'm not obligated to say anything to anybody about our time together, but that doesn't mean I won't want to."

Eye contact. Unhappy eyes.

"For example, if I thought you could benefit from more counseling, I don't have to say why, I just have to recommend. It could happen that way."

Unhappier eyes.

"So, let's talk. See where we are. Huh? At least tell me what it takes to get you to punch me out. What do I have to say to get slugged at the bus stop?"

"Man . . ."

"I'm patient. I get paid by the hour."

"Who pays for this hour?" Frank asked.

"In this case, county funds provided to the school district. When a kid gets in trouble and the school wants counseling, there are two ways to pay. The parents' medical policy, or the school. What's up, Frank? What are you so mad about?"

He squirmed a little, inhaled noisily through his nose like a bull and finally spoke. "How about if we make a deal? If I answer your questions for a half hour, you answer one question for me?"

This was a remarkably unoriginal barter. Jerry had this proposed to him regularly.

And he knew all the tricks. "Go," he invited.

Over the next thirty minutes he found out a lot about Gus's binges, the beatings, the rages and the regular visits made by the police. Jerry found out how much Frank hated his father, how much he loved but disrespected his mother, how fragile he was with his own rage and how frustrated he felt over his complete inability to protect his mother and younger brothers. Jerry wished he were hearing this story for the first time, wished it didn't happen this way so often. In the end he knew what he would do — try to get Frank to commit to an anger management workshop and a group for battered teens. But he'd have to tread slowly and carefully. And keep his part of the bargain.

"So," Frank asked, leaning forward in his chair. "What's the inside of a spaceship like?"

"Well, it looks like shiny metal, but it turns out to be something like glass," Jerry began.

FOUR

Christina Baker was sixteen and pregnant. Married, too, which gave her one advantage over many a pregnant sixteen year old. She was also anemic, underweight and probably depressed.

"Is the morning sickness over now?" June asked her.

"Oh yes. I haven't been sick in a long time."

"And you feel the baby move?"

"Uh-huh. For a couple of months at least. Gary is so excited, he can't stand himself."

But when she said that, she was unconvincing. Her blue eyes were flat.

June didn't really know Christina or her family. They came from down valley — another way of saying they were rural, lived off the beaten track. That could mean a farm, a shed, a collection of trailers, just about anything except mountains. That would be up valley. But it likely wasn't a farm. The girl wasn't in school and the handwriting on the new-patient paperwork belonged to Jessica. That would mean the girl couldn't read. It was surprising this was her first child. But to give them credit, her young husband had accompanied her; he was in the waiting room. Maybe they'd do better by their kids than was done by them.

"And Gary is helping you a little? Around the house and such? Because I'm worried about your weight and your anemia. It might be you're working too hard."

"It's not the house, it's me gettin' up at four in the morning to ride clear to Fort Seward with my mama and auntie to work at that flower hothouse up there. That's what's wearin' me down, but I can't do nothin' about it. We need the money."

"And where does Gary work?" June asked.

"He works timber . . . when he works. He's off right now."

June frowned. Off? He must have gotten fired, because logging was good at the moment. It was during the rainy winter months that loggers, construction workers and fishermen had trouble staying employed. In spring, everybody went to work.

"He do anything else?" June asked. "Besides logging?"

"Framing. Sometimes."

New construction was up, too. People were flooding to small, out-of-the-way coastal, valley and mountain areas, giving up on the big, dirty cities in search of the quiet, clean country life. How else could Grace Valley account for almost doubling its population in ten years?

"That is quite a drive you have to take. I'm more than happy to see you through this pregnancy, Christina, but did you know Dr. Lowe is right on your way to Fort Seward? You could probably make appointments on the way to or from work."

"I know. But I heard you was real good."

"Oh really," June said, smiling in spite of herself. How stupid to smile at that, she thought. This girl didn't know what good was. Still, it gave June enormous pleasure to know she was liked. "That's nice." And she looked back at the chart. Christina was not healthy and should see a specialist. June had high hopes of hiring John Stone, which would resolve so many similar problems.

"I'm going to see that you leave here with an extra supply of vitamins, Christina. I want you to double up and try to put on a little weight."

"Gary don't much like chubby girls," she said.

"Well, if Gary wants to be a daddy, he'd

better develop a taste for them. That baby needs nourishment."

"Yes, ma'am, I know it."

This was the part of country doctoring that was so hard. Grace Valley was a quaint village with some special shops and a few restaurants that drew people from other towns — people who drove nice cars. Most merchants did well here, and relocated yuppies who didn't seem to need money had moved in and raised the standard of living even more. Their taxes were welcomed by the schoolboard and roads department. Plus there were some successful farms, orchards, vineyards and ranches around the valley. But there was plentiful abject poverty, as well. Poor people who might not be seen in the Vine & Ivy, a quaint restaurant and gift shop at the edge of town. But June saw them. They didn't shop at The Crack'd Door — an upscale gallery that had opened six years before — but she could run into them anywhere, even her own living room at dawn. You could look at the houses in town, the bed-and-breakfasts that had opened since the late eighties, the local tasting rooms, some of the new architecture, and begin to think of this place as upscale country. An affluent village. But there was an underside here, not visible to the casual eye, that concerned only the police, medical and social welfare people: battered women living in isolation on rundown farms; a roadhouse called Dandies that was not quaint and did not welcome tourists.

And any new doctor June brought into this clinic had better understand the two faces of this town.

When she took Christina's chart to the front of the clinic, she saw that the young girl had been her last patient for the morning. The waiting room was blessedly empty.

"You have plans for lunch?" Charlotte asked.

"Just to avoid George Fuller."

"I heard he sent some people out by your house at six in the morning and they caught you naked, just gettin' out of the shower," Charlotte said.

"My God! This town is amazing! Why do we bother with a newspaper?"

Charlotte shrugged. "For good fiction, I imagine. Bet you wished you'd plugged that cordless phone in for once, don't you."

"Has my father been here?" June demanded, shocked.

"No, but your aunt Myrna called . . . and asked could you come out to lunch today, and if you can, would you bring her some more of that blood pressure medicine."

It was remarkable to June that, living in a town where everyone knew everyone's business, her aunt didn't realize that her blood pressure pills were placebos. Myrna was in astonishingly good health.

June had been out to Myrna's a lot lately, evidence that her aunt was bored or lonely or restless. Myrna, aged eighty-four, was hardly housebound. She drove a 1967 Cadillac all over the place, including to weekly poker with Elmer, Judge Forrest, Burt Crandall and Sam Cussler. Myrna was the oldest player and most frequent winner.

"Call her and tell her I'll be right out," June told Charlotte. "I need a change of scenery. And tell her I'll bring scones from the bakery." June began to walk away.

"Didn't you already have a bear claw today?" Charlotte asked.

June stopped, looked back over her shoulder and peered at her nurse. Charlotte was past pleasantly plump, and June had never known her to be slender. She, on the other hand, was whip thin, one of those pathetic creatures who'd drunk supplements to put on weight in high school. Yet Charlotte kept track of June's food intake as though she had an eating disorder. June lifted her eyebrows questioningly.

"You won't always be young," Charlotte

said, and turned her back on June.

June sat in her Jeep behind the clinic, door open, and wrote down in a little notebook she kept in her bag a few questions she wanted to ask John Stone, a few things she wanted to remember to tell him.

"My heavens above," she heard a man say, and she jumped in surprise. There, leaning against her opened door, was Jonathan Wickham. He pounded his fist against his chest. "Look at you! What's the occasion?"

She didn't know what he was talking about at first, but then remembered she had dressed up just a little. Gaberdine slacks with creases as opposed to jeans and boots. Skirts and dresses were fine for city docs, but out here, when a call might come from a logging site or farm, it was more sensible to be prepared than to slip in the mud wearing a thin-soled slipper and end up with your skirt over your head.

"Oh, that's right," she said. "I'm interviewing a potential new doctor this afternoon. What's that on your cheek, Jonathan? Looks like you got slapped."

He frowned, touched his palm to his cheek, then realized she was probably kidding, and smiled at her.

Jonathan was one of those men who had a

shot at being handsome, and spoiled it with ridiculousness. He was tall and slim, a bit over six feet. His labors were spiritual as opposed to physical, so his body was not muscular, but neither was he frail. He had a strong chin, square jaw and slightly rosy cheeks. His teeth were strong and straight, but unfortunately for him, his smile always seemed forced. And then there was that little problem with baldness. As was typical, if he'd just let it go, it would be so much better. But no, he had to try hair pieces, wigs, and now these foolish plugs.

"Well, you look ravishing," he said to June. "You would tempt the very saints."

"That's great, Jonathan, so long as I don't tempt you." She turned the key and started the ignition.

"Ah, June, I am but a mortal —"

"Didn't I see Mary Lou Granger storm out of the church this morning . . . right after Clarice stormed in? It almost seemed as though they might've had a disagreement."

He had to think about this for a moment, and June realized that Tom was right. It *was* hard to look at those silly plugs and keep a straight face. Jonathan was such a notorious flirt, and so bad at it, too. But there was something about June's demeanor, she knew, that held him at bay, as though he knew, instinctively, that if he ever touched her, she'd break his arm.

"I can't recall what that might've been about," he said. "Probably some misunderstanding."

"Probably," she said, putting the Jeep in reverse. "Jonathan, I have to get going. I'm running late. Was there something special you needed, or are you just casting out compliments to see if you catch anything?"

He laughed, backed away from the car and said, "You know me too well, don't you? I was on my way to the clinic to ask for a handout. I'm all out of that cream you gave me for the dry skin."

She pulled her door closed and draped an elbow out the open window. "You can go in and ask Charlotte, or you can come back later. I have errands."

At that moment Charlotte came out of the clinic, her purse hanging from her arm, and caught the tail end of what June said.

"Come back later," she told the pastor.

"I could . . . ah . . . maybe little Jessie could —"

"Jessie isn't allowed to hand out medicines, Pastor. Better not —"

"I'll just go see how she's doing . . . haven't seen her in —"

"No!" both women barked, and his palms went up as if to ward off their protests. He slowly turned and made his way back across the street. June and Charlotte made eye contact briefly, but neither moved out of the clinic parking lot until he was all the way across the street, safely ensconced in his church. And then Charlotte did something rare. She turned around and locked the back door. Anyone who walked in the front door of the clinic, where Jessica would probably be sitting at the reception desk, would be in full view of the street, the café and the church.

June and the nurse made eye contact again and both nodded in agreement.

Pastor Wickham and his family had been in the valley less than a year, and his reputation was getting worse by the day. This seemed to greatly amuse the old men at the café, but June thought that several women, and she for one, were getting just a little tired of it.

Charlotte routinely went home for lunch, where she could eat with Bud, and they could both smoke in peace. If June was gone, which she almost always was, that left Jessica alone in the clinic to answer phones and eat her packed lunch.

This was very much to her liking. If anyone knew how she occupied herself, they might think more than her hair was strange. She would go into June's office and find a medical book, usually *Gray's Anatomy* but sometimes *Disease and Microbiology.* She spent about forty-five minutes reading and looking at pictures while she slowly nibbled away at her peanut butter and pickle sandwich.

No one knew. Since Jessica had dropped out of high school and had no diploma, she was sure the fact that she read complicated science textbooks with lunch would only make people laugh. Her father understood that it wasn't a dislike of school, per se, that had caused her to drop out, but feeling so out of place.

Here, in June's clinic, Jessica felt at home.

The bakery was operated by Burt Crandall and his wife, Syl. When Burt had returned to Grace Valley after the Korean War, he'd wanted a business of his own so he could stay. Since he didn't farm or fish, he knew he'd have to be a merchant of some kind or else leave for a town with some industry. He'd wanted the gas station, but it wasn't for sale, so he opened a bakery, without having the first idea how to bake. But you'd never know it from tasting. Burt supplied everyone in town, including the café and the Vine & Ivy, and a good many eateries in surrounding towns.

The bell jangled as she walked in.

"Hey there, June. I heard you flashed some little old mountain people this morning," Burt remarked, a wide grin on his face.

"You know me," she said wearily. "Just can't keep my clothes on."

He laughed happily, a high-pitched giggle, really. His teeth were too big for his mouth and his good nature brought them into frequent prominence. He was thin all over except for his round paunch, like a barrel on legs.

His wife, however, was built like a little beach ball — five feet tall and round as an apple. Right on cue, Syl came through the swinging door from the back. She carried a large tray full of fresh cookies. "Burt, leave that girl alone. June, you just pay him no attention. And take some cookies while they're warm." That said, Syl went back to the ovens.

"Give me four scones and hold the bullshit," June said to Burt.

"Oh, you going out to Myrna's? Tell her I baked these special for her. You know, June, you ought to have a dog, warn you if someone's letting themselves in your house."

That was a dead giveaway.

"My father used to be the most discreet person in the valley. And now I think he has just about the biggest mouth."

"He's been fishing too much. Fishermen — big-mouthed liars, that's what they are. Plus I think keeping all those secrets he had to as a doctor ate a hole straight through him and now he just can't shut up. That's what I think." Burt put the scones in a box while June dug out her money. "He still has a poker face, though, old coot."

"Says the pot."

"Tonight's meat loaf night, isn't it? Why don't you take some dinner rolls with you. Elmer likes these potato rolls."

"Burt, don't you think there's something wrong with living in a place where people know what you're eating for dinner?"

Burt grinned and popped four dinner rolls into a white bag. "Naw, honey, I don't worry about that. I take comfort in it." He handed her the bag and she reluctantly smiled, but she did not go for her purse. Damned if she'd take his bull and pay him for it, too. "What I think is worrisome is running around naked in front of strangers," he stated. Then he laughed so hard a little tear gathered at the corner of his right eye.

June snatched the bag out his hand. She gave him a warning glare as she left, but she could hear his laughter long after the bakery door closed behind her. She got into her Jeep. "Serve him right if he popped a vessel," she said to herself, and headed for the gas station.

The garage door was down and the shade on the window at half-mast. June pumped the gas herself, and while her tank filled, she thought about the situation. *This* was going to change. People were moving to the valley and they didn't understand these old ways. The station was Sam Cussler's and he worked when it suited him and fished when he wanted to. He might have locked the station, but then again, it might be open. Since people were driving more foreign cars, Sam was doing less mechanical work. The pumps were left running, and if you needed gas, you pumped it yourself, then scribbled the amount you took on a slip of paper and stuffed it in a box with a slot that hung on the post by the pump. Once in a while, probably when he needed bait, Sam would go around and collect.

"Hey, young woman," he called, coming out the side door with a tackle box and fishing pole. "You caught me. I was just slipping away."

"I didn't see your truck," June said.

"I gave it to George's boy to run some errands."

"You want a lift to the river?" she asked.

"Naw. I'm gonna worry Windle Stream, right back of Fuller's Café. I don't know if I'll catch anything, but I'll avoid work, which is my main occupation. Heard you got yourself caught naked by some family from back in Shell Mountain. Some people George sent out to your place."

Sam Cussler was a good-natured man, with a deep tan, pink cheeks and twinkling eyes, a full head of lush white hair and a thick white beard. If he were round, he'd resemble Santa, but though he was probably seventy, he had the physique of a much younger man — tall frame, muscled arms, flat stomach. All those years of hefting auto parts and casting fishing line, no doubt. He was vigorous and healthy and his blue eyes shamed Paul Newman.

"That's pretty much the story," June said.

"What would we do without old George?" Sam asked.

"We almost had a chance to find out. I gave serious thought to killing him." She reached into the truck and got out her purse while Sam stopped the pump for her. She pulled out a twenty and handed it to him.

The price on the pump was 16.78. He removed a wad the size of a large orange from his pocket and peeled off four ones. She saw him pass by twenties, fifties, tens, fives.

"It's your lucky day . . . I'm running a special," he said, giving her more change than she had coming. He obviously didn't want to count out silver.

"Sam, you shouldn't carry around all that money," she said. "At least, don't pull it out and count it off for customers. What if someone robs you?"

"I don't worry about that much," he said.

"You should," she said, getting into her Jeep. "This town is growing. And changing."

"I'll bear that in mind, June. In fact, I'll think about that while I'm fishing. I was just looking for a subject to think about today."

Myrna lived in what Grace Valley residents considered the Hudson family home. Grandpa Hudson had made his money in mining and banking, married a young woman late in life and migrated up to Grace Valley when his baby daughter, Myrna Mae, was born. Twelve years later Elmer came along, and by then Grandpa Hudson was well into his sixties. Yet it was his young wife who died, at only thirty-four. That left Myrna, aged fourteen, and Elmer, aged two, and their daddy, facing his seventieth birthday. But he didn't quite make it.

As things often went back then, Myrna raised her brother in the house that was their parents', even though she was a mere girl herself. She was completely devoted to Elmer, saw to his education, judiciously guarded the money that was left to them, invested with caution, kept the house clean and in good repair, and never gave a thought to herself or her own needs until Elmer was a certified doctor and married to June's mother — all of which came when Elmer was in his thirties and Myrna in her forties.

Remarkably, Myrna let go of Elmer with grace and pride. It wasn't until then that she married Morton Claypool, a traveling salesman, with whom she had seventeen good years before she "misplaced" him. Her word. The whole story of that was yet to be revealed, but town gossip ranged from him having another family somewhere, to whom he returned, to him lying stiff and cold under Hudson House. Myrna, June believed, relished the mysteriousness this part of her life presented to the town. And in her own way, she encouraged the rumors.

All those years — from the time she was a teenager, and like a single mother, through her marriage to a traveling salesman — Myrna was sustained by books. Then sometime in her early fifties, she began writing fiction — gothics, mysteries, romances, sagas. She wrote while Morton traveled, and she sold her work almost immediately. When Morton didn't return after one of his many trips, Myrna barely seemed to notice. In fact, the stories were getting racier, and definitely more grisly. In one, a wife traveled to a small, distant town to hunt for her missing husband, who was buried in another woman's backyard. In another, when a woman's cheating husband came home, she killed him and sealed him behind a closet wall. These were not uncommon themes. People whispered, but they loved her.

The Hudson family home wasn't really a mansion, but it had that Victorian, gabled look about it. And it had been built in the early part of the century. Elmer had never been interested in living there once he had a wife and medical practice, and then a child. It was natural for him to move into the simple but homey doctor's house. June, however, had loved to visit Myrna when she was little. The nooks, crannies, closets, pantries, cellar and attic of her house were priceless. Myrna had never discarded a thing; every room was a treasure, an adventure.

When June pulled up to the house, she saw from the car parked out front that one of the Barstow sisters was there. Some years back, when Myrna began to lose some of her physical stamina, she'd hired the Barstow twins, Amelia and Endeara, as maids and cooks. One at a time they came, almost every day. June wasn't sure Myrna needed them so much as looked after them. The Barstows, cranky, bitter old women, had no source of income and couldn't get along with anyone besides Myrna — including each other.

Not surprisingly, it was Myrna who answered the door. "Thank goodness you have your clothes on," she said.

"I'm going to kill my father."

"Don't be ridiculous, he's finally got a story. He hasn't had a good one in weeks."

"It's not so much fun when the joke's on you."

"Didn't *you* tell anyone?"

"No," June lied. It was as safe a lie as she could ever tell because Tom Toopeek would have his tongue cut out before he'd pass along gossip. "I wouldn't have told Elmer, but in the shock of the moment I was caught off guard. The old blabbermouth."

"It must have been quite a sight."

"Oh, I'm sure."

"Well, don't fret on it, dear. Come in. Amelia has made potato soup and I want to try a new book idea out on you."

Aha, June thought. That explained these frequent calls lately. Myrna had been building up to a new book.

"In this one," she said, "I think I'll focus mainly on dismemberment."

FIVE

Dr. John Stone was almost painfully handsome. He was six feet tall, had a thick crop of Robert Redford blond hair, clear blue eyes, a solid physique and a kick-ass smile. In addition to that, his attire of thin wool pants, Armani shirt, Versace tie and Italian loafers was worth more than June's May wardrobe. A smile came to her lips as she wondered how he would be regarded if he had to make a run out to a logging site.

They sat in her clinic office. She, behind the desk. The Boss.

"Why Grace Valley?" she asked.

"Peace and quiet for my family. Safety, wholesomeness, beauty. Just the air up here is going to make a difference. My six-year-old daughter — she's a little wheezy. Might be pre-asthmatic."

"Well, it's peaceful and quiet for some of the community, but it can get a little hectic for the doctor. Why, just this morning —"

June stopped herself suddenly. If she was going to get miffed at Elmer for spreading tales, she'd have to keep her own mouth shut.

"I heard you were surprised by a family from back in the mountains. They let themselves into your house? At the crack of dawn? And you were in your . . . what was it? Your underwear or something?"

Her mouth hung open in wonder.

"I had lunch at the café before coming over." He shrugged. "I hope I didn't offend. . . ."

She shook it off. "It was a towel, actually."

"Oh brother," he said, self-consciously trying to cover his twitching mouth with a hand. "I mean . . ."

"That's a good place to start this discussion. Country doctoring is crazy sometimes. Rough and inconvenient and unpredictable. If they don't come to your house and catch you getting out of the shower, they'll flag you down at a crossroads and ask you to look at a swollen ankle, or catch you in the bakery and ask if their rash looks like it's getting better. That doesn't even touch the accidents — falls, fishhooks, large animal mishaps, car wrecks and shootings."

"Shootings?"

"Not what you're used to, I'm sure.

Ninety-five percent of the residents here have guns. Plural. They hunt, seasonal or not, shoot trespassers, euthanize animals and have accidents. It can make an ER residency in Oakland look tame."

He leaned forward, his elbows on his knees. "What do you do when you're overwhelmed? It's just you, isn't it?"

"Most of the time. My dad is a physician. He practiced out of the house I grew up in. He's been retired about two years now, but he's still in here every week. Sometimes he's invited, sometimes he just shows up and sometimes I have to call begging. And there are other doctors around. Northern California is peppered with hundreds of little towns, and we have to help each other when there's need.

"But how can I make you understand, Dr. Stone, that much of what I do for this town, much of what I consider my obligation, isn't solely medical. I have a pantry full of food staples and a closet full of clean clothes. I keep an impressive supply of pharmaceuticals on hand, and a lot of that I pay for myself when I can't get some church or charity group to help out. I keep blood in the refrigerator, infant formula in the broom closet. I use the sheriff's office to help with pickup and delivery, patient transport and emergency assistance. I have a key to the café in case I need a large supply of ice when they're closed. And sometimes it's really hard to draw an income. I mean, the state and county will help with indigent patients, but in order to process that, you need the patient to fill out forms." She shrugged. "Fortunately I have a good working relationship with the local agencies. But more often, I just get paid in eggs." She smiled. "They're the best eggs in the west, of course."

He listened so raptly it was easy to surmise his captivation. Or perhaps it was the look of a doctor having second thoughts. . . .

"You've had a very impressive education, and come from a big-city practice," she continued. "You might think you want to be a country doctor, but your reality might be skewed by Andy of Mayberry reruns. It's a lovely life here, but not always a simple one. At least not for the doctor.

"For me it's different. I grew up in the town doctor's house. I was coloring on the floor in the corner of his examining room while he was setting a tibia. I saw my first home birth when I was seven. And though my mother tried to intercede, I rode along on more emergencies than she thought was prudent. But I was raised by this town.

When your dad is the town doctor, you see every citizen in your home at one time or another. And you end up visiting every one of them in theirs."

She stopped for a moment, trying to judge the rather awed expression on his face.

"It isn't my intention to scare you away. I just want to be sure you make an informed decision. I think you might be right for us, and there's no question we need your skills here. But are we right for you?"

"You haven't scared me," he said, relaxing into a smile. "I know a little bit about small town medicine. I paid off some of med school by working on a reservation in Arizona. Federal grant."

"Oh," she said weakly. "Now I'm a little embarrassed."

"Don't be. I purposely didn't put it on my résumé."

"Because . . . ?"

He shrugged. "It really wasn't what it might appear. . . ."

"I . . . I don't think I understand."

"I'm not so noble. I needed money. It was a contract I made with the government. Med school for rural medicine. I borrowed money to pay off the grant so I could leave the reservation early and get into private practice."

"I see. So you don't much like —"

"The desert."

"Is that *all* that drove you out of the program?"

"I was twenty-eight and more interested in a new car than serving mankind. Or in my case, womankind. I understand there will be poor areas here."

"Profoundly poor, Dr. Stone. Mostly in the outer, more rural and mountainous areas, although we have some people of very humble means right here in town. There are families who rely on me who can barely feed themselves . . . and we can have some very rough, lean winters for people who build and log and farm. So . . . what makes you think you could survive this?"

"Two things. I'm ready for a different kind of medicine now. And . . . I don't need the money anymore."

"I see." She thought a minute. Regardless of his qualifications, which were stellar, it was imperative that she be convinced he knew what he was getting himself into — and that it appealed to him. This practice wouldn't buy him any more Armani suits. "Tell me something, Dr. Stone. Why did you look so shocked when I described my work in this town?"

"It wasn't shock, it was fascination. Respect. I've never heard a doctor — anyone, for that matter — describe their work or their people or their life with such affection and pride. It was there even when you were talking about the most unappealing aspects of your role. You don't just do your work, you live your work. You *are* your work." He shook his head as he considered this. "I might as well have been listening to you sing."

"Why . . . thank you. That's quite a compliment." He's trying to get hired, she thought.

"You make even the inconvenience sound romantic."

"It can be a pretty strenuous routine for someone who 'doesn't need the money.' "

"You think I can't pull my weight?" he asked. "Just give me a go. I'm not over the hill yet."

He hasn't even *seen* the hill, she thought. How would the simpler people of Grace Valley view the pleats in his pants and the tassels on his shoes? He might be too much for them. "Maybe we should have a trial run?" she suggested. "A three-month contract?"

"How about six? I grow on people."

"Well . . . I'd like to —"

"This is your clinic. I'm not going to hang

78

around if you don't want me, but I'm no one-night stand. I'd like to start off by feeling —"

He was cut off as the door flew open and Charlotte filled the frame. "Julianna Dickson just called and said she's feeling strange."

June popped to her feet. "Damn!" She tugged off her white coat.

"I told her to stand on her head, pant through the mouth like a puppy and keep her legs closed," the nurse continued.

"Good. Get me a couple bags of O-neg!"

"Jessie's settin' you up."

"Come on, Dr. Stone," June said. "This should be right up your alley. Julianna is on baby number five, and between my dad and me, we've never witnessed a birth." She grabbed her bag and headed for the back door. She glanced at his fancy, shiny shoes as she kicked off her clogs and stepped into her boots. "I don't suppose you have any old shoes in your car?"

"No, why?"

"It's been a very wet spring. Some of the driveways around here don't qualify as driveways anymore." Jessica ran down the clinic hall with a small cooler containing two bags of blood. June grabbed the handle and bolted for her Jeep. To her surprise and approval, Dr. Stone kept up with her and jumped into the passenger seat. June peeled out.

"I was going to get ahead of her this time," she told him as they barreled down the road. "Get her in the hospital and induce labor. She's about three weeks early."

"Does she usually hemorrhage?"

"She has twice."

"What about paramedics?"

"That's the other thing about small towns. We're very spread out. Plus Grace Valley sits on the juncture of three counties — you're going to have to get your degree in geography before you go out on house calls. You don't want to go out to a farm or logging site and waste a lot of time calling the wrong rescue team or police department."

She drove with one hand and picked up the mike of her radio. "Charlotte, you there?"

"Right here," it crackled back.

"I want you to stand by for a call for the ambulance. I'm on the beeper, but I saw my dad's truck at the café if you have anything special."

"He's already here. Saw you speed out of town and couldn't stand to mind his own affairs."

"You tell him his meat loaf is riding on

Julianna's efficiency."

June replaced the mike and said to John, "We all have pagers and cell phones, but with the tall trees and mountains, it's easy to be out of range. The radio is the best emergency tool we have. If you decide to work here, you'll have to get one."

"Don't you have a midwife around here?"

"No, but we could sure use one. We have an unlicensed woman down in Colby. She does a pretty good job and takes care of a lot of women, but I have to work with her on the sly or the state board will get all up in arms. Honestly, they do so little to help us function out here. All we really want is the best medical care available, and if that's an unlicensed midwife, it's better than a squat in the fields. But the city docs are regulation crazy."

He laughed. "Those doggone city docs!" His glassy-eyed look suggested he wondered just who was crazy. And he hung on for dear life while June rounded the curves.

June pulled off the road and headed down what appeared to be an overgrown path, the space between the trees narrow and dark. "There's a back way into their orchard. I called Mike Dickson two weeks ago and told him he'd better make sure it's cleared, what with his wife being pregnant." They bounced over a deep rut and John hit his head on the roof of the Jeep.

"Ouch! And this is cleared?"

"Ah!" she said, breaking through the forest into the orchard, then maneuvering wildly among the trees. "Here we go! The Dicksons are the nicest people you'll ever meet. Big, happy family, hard-working folks, and their orchard's been in the money since the first tree gave fruit, I think. If you ever need anything, for any reason, you can count on Mike and Julianna Dickson." June came around the back of the house and pulled in front, stopping suddenly behind a tractor. "You understand, you're on your own."

Before he could reply, she was gone — out of the Jeep, up the porch steps, kicking off her muddy boots and running into the house at breakneck speed in her stocking feet. John was stranded up to his ankles in mud. Wet spring, she had said.

Mike Dickson's mother was quietly tending small children in the front room, but June whizzed past without even the formality of a hello. She knew where to find Julianna — in the downstairs bedroom with her young husband at her side.

"Sometimes I feel so left out," June complained as she snapped on rubber gloves.

Julianna's knees were raised under the bedsheet and Mike sat beside her, holding her hand. Fresh towels had been laid out; Mike had delivered all his own children — though not by plan — and knew what to expect.

"I tried to wait," Julianna breathlessly replied.

June threw back the sheet and took her place between Julianna's raised knees. "There's a doctor with me, Julianna. He's an OB, so don't get nervous when you see him. Thinking of coming here to — Oh my! Hello, baby. Please don't push, darling. Please, please, please." She ran her gloved fingers around the crowning head. "Let's see if we can let him come slowly, so I can watch that cord. . . ."

John Stone was suddenly beside her, helping himself to gloves from her bag, snapping them on and looking at the crowning head with an expression that could only be described as satisfaction. The first thing he said was, "John Stone, how do you do." The second thing was, "Ah, yes."

John plucked a clamp out of June's bag, draped a clean towel over one arm, leaned into the field of birth and said, "Let's do it!"

Before June could concur, Julianna brought out the baby. First came the head, after which June yelled, "Stop!" When she'd checked the neck for a cord and uttered a quiet, "Okay," the baby was born in one swoosh. John clamped the cord and held out the towel. June wrapped the baby and turned him over, gently rubbing his back. Cries filled the room at once; no suction was necessary.

"I'll be a son of a gun!" John said. He made eye contact with Julianna, grinned his biggest grin and said, "You're almost as good at this as me! Big, fat boy!"

He actually nudged June back a bit so he could have a better look at the birth canal. He massaged Julianna's lower abdomen. "You're doing great," he said. "Excellent. You're in such fabulous condition. With such a fast birth, you'd expect slack muscle tone, but you're fit as a boxer."

"Floor scrubbing," she said. "My mama said floor scrubbing on your hands and knees brought babies easier."

"Are you about ready to stop scrubbing floors, Julianna?" June asked.

Mike laughed and kissed his wife's hand. "I don't know that you can complain anymore, June. You finally got invited to the party."

"June, let's put that baby to the breast. It'll bring the placenta and slow down the bleeding," Dr. Stone said.

"I just hate to give him up," she admitted reluctantly passing the baby to Julianna.

The OB was right, a few minutes of newborn suckling finished the job. While John completed the examination, June went for a basin of water. Grandma had it ready for her.

When she walked back into the birth room, she saw something she would never forget. The fancy Dr. Stone stood at the side of the bed holding the newborn wrapped in a towel, the sleeves of his expensive shirt rolled up, the end of his designer tie sticking out of his pocket, his pant legs rolled up almost to his knees and his bare toes curling against the cool hardwood floor. On his face was a look of pure joy.

"June," he said, grinning, his eyes shining, "you gotta let me in on some of this."

Six

June lived in a house that Grace Valley had refurbished. It had been a rundown hovel when she'd somehow managed to buy it, much to her parents' dismay. There she was, a brand-new doctor come home, living with her parents, no guaranteed income and plenty of med school debt besides.

But she had loved that old house since girlhood. It had been abandoned for at least five years, during which time the local youth made sport of it, broke the windows, used it as a hideaway, love nest, who knew what. It hadn't been well maintained to start with, and by the time the local kids were done with it, it probably should have been leveled.

But it stood, about six miles from the center of town, on an isolated little hill. It had a wonderful porch that stretched the length of the house, a fabulous shade tree, a pleasant little dormer window in the second floor attic and a view to die for. Before it saw its first coat of paint, June had imagined herself sitting on a porch swing and looking down the road, over the rooftops of houses and buildings in town, past the steeple of the Presbyterian Church rising proudly above the trees, across the valley for miles and miles and miles. To the sides and back of the little house was forest, deep and lush. All that was missing was the white picket fence.

It had taken a very long time to complete the image, to take the house from shambles to near perfection. The plumbing was restored by a man whose ulcer June treated, the electrical work by the Stewart brothers, whose women popped out a couple of babies a year. Hardwood floors came from the Bradfords; their teenage sons were in a terrible car accident, but, blessedly they recovered completely. New windows, carpet, louvered doors, paint and spackling were the result of a long winter of bad flu all over town. The countertops were provided by five cases of measles among the Wilson boys. Her appliances came, willy-nilly, as John and Susan Reynolds's kids were treated for various maladies, Reynolds' Appliance was a staple of three small towns.

June herself supplied the furniture and ac-

cessories of needlepoint pillows and hand-
stitched quilts, being one of the town's best
stitchers. Her house was lovely and she
adored it. She found peace and solitude and
comfort in it.

Usually.

Following the birth at the Dicksons', she
took John Stone back to the clinic, where
he'd left his car, and agreed to give him six
months at the clinic. Then she went home
to make her father Tuesday night meat loaf.
She listened to her messages and was relieved to find she was not in demand. But
she moved through the kitchen chores with
nagging slowness rather than pleasure.

"Look at me," she said when her father
arrived. "I am a spinster."

"Oh boy. You held the Dickson baby for
more than four minutes, didn't you?"

"I'm thirty-seven. I haven't had a real date
in five years. I'm married to this town. Even
if I were to meet someone and fall in love,
the whole process would take longer than I
have. I'm officially past the age of child-
bearing."

"What a crock," Elmer said. "You know, I
thought about bringing wine and then
didn't. I wish I had. You could use a drink
of something. I don't suppose you have
anything alcoholic?"

"Somebody gave me some expensive brandy once . . . but I don't know if I like brandy."

"Forget it, I'll make fresh coffee."

"Oh Elmer, what have I done to myself?"

"Stop feeling sorry for yourself. It's not too late for you to think about your personal life."

"Isn't it? Where would I start?"

"You could call some of your old pals from school and tell them you'd like to be fixed up. Let the word out you'd like a date and you'll get swamped. You're a pretty girl, June."

"I'm not a girl."

"Yes, you are. As for children, no one ever knows if they're going to have them. You might have trouble having a family. You might be infertile like your mother. We never used caution and we only had you."

"How do you know it was her? Maybe it was you."

"Nope," he said. He paused to count scoops of coffee. "I sent a sperm specimen to the Ukiah lab when I was fifty-seven. They were exhausted little old fellows with beards, but they were there." He filled the coffeepot with water.

"You never told me that," she said. "About the specimen."

"I would have told you if it had come up. Like if you'd had trouble conceiving. You never wondered why we didn't have a house full of kids?"

"Mother said you preferred to fish on your time off."

He laughed, which caused him to jiggle and wheeze. "She always had a better sense of humor than I gave her credit for." He put his arm around June's shoulders and gave her a squeeze. "You have a long day, honey?"

"Long? Shoot, I got off early. Typical day. I start off by flashing the Mull family, go to the clinic to find that my receptionist is now imitating a parrot, see twenty-five patients in the morning, have a three martini lunch with Myrna and Amelia Barstow — Myrna's martinis, obviously — and listen to her new book idea." Remembering that, June stopped there. "Dad, have you heard her new book idea?"

He made a face. "I have. Hard to believe that skinny little old woman is preoccupied by that kind of violence, isn't it?"

June shuddered. "Body parts . . . that's her new theme. Dad, whatever happened to Morton Claypool?"

"He went off, is all."

"But where?"

"Beats me. If Myrna knows, she doesn't let on."

"There's talk, you know."

"Oh hell, she loves the talk. I bet she started half of it. In spite of the grisly books she writes, the woman wouldn't hurt a fly. I asked her if she wanted to hire someone to chase down Morton, find out if he was dead or alive, and she said no, it wasn't necessary. She wasn't inclined to have him back or give him a funeral."

"Don't you think that's sort of strange?"

"For Myrna? Or in general?"

"I bet she knows where he went."

"That could be. I'll never forget when she told me. It was right around the time of your high school homecoming game. Your mother and I picked up Myrna to take her, and on the way she said, "Well, it appears Morton's gone off and isn't coming back." Matter-of-fact. Your mother asked Myrna was she worried, and Myrna said not a bit, that if there was any bad news, someone would have called her." Elmer paused and then continued in a much softer tone, "I'll admit something to you if you swear to never tell her. I checked around Hudson House for freshly turned soil."

"Dad!"

"Just on the off chance . . ."

"Why, you clever sleuth!"

"Myrna's a wonderful woman, but she's a tad on the eccentric side."

"A tad?" June said. "She's a circus! I can't imagine what it must have been like being raised by her."

Elmer smiled almost wistfully. "Like being raised by a fairy princess."

They passed dinner more pleasantly then, reminiscing about childhood and Myrna, discussing John Stone and the interview, arguing a bit about whether June felt like being "fixed up." The last dish was being dried when, with perfect timing, the phone rang.

"June?" said Tom Toopeek. "I found that Mull boy. And we got big trouble."

Shell Mountain was back in the Six Rivers National Forest in Trinity County. It wasn't Tom Toopeek's jurisdiction, but he had driven around the back roads anyway, inquiring of the Mull family, and eventually someone told him the general locale of their house. When he would have knocked on the door, Clarence fired at him, so Tom sought out some other police before trying to go in. Clarence Mull now held them at bay with a firearm.

Tom didn't mention to the police he had

called upon for help that Clarence had fired on him. Shooting at people was undeniably against the law, but Tom didn't want to make a commitment to taking the man into custody until he knew more. It wasn't that he cut corners or did favors — nothing like that. It was a simple matter of always doing what was best for the individual and the community. There might indeed be an argument for letting that infraction go, as the wiser move for all concerned.

He waited for June before deciding, as he often did. More often, he suspected, than she realized.

June and Elmer drove out to the Shell Mountain area, following Tom's directions. After bouncing along an old, narrow, abandoned logging road for more than thirty minutes, they came upon several police vehicles.

"I believe that's Stan Kubbicks from the state police," Elmer said. "But who's that other guy?"

"I don't know," June said, squinting. "Forestry, I think. And Bob Manning, from Alderman Point. Jesus, what a mess this is."

She parked behind the last of four law enforcement vehicles, grabbed her bag, jumped out of her truck and went straight to Tom. "Thanks for coming out, June," he said. "Maybe you can help us with this. It appears Clarence is a vet suffering from post-traumatic stress and bipolar disorder. . . ."

"He's fucked up," Stan said, and spat on the ground.

"Poor guy," June said. "Does he say why he won't let you in?"

"I've talked to him, yelled across the yard there, and told him I'm here to give his boy a ride to the hospital. But he's delusional. He thinks if there's paperwork involved, he'll be arrested for something and put in a prison camp."

"There isn't any warrants on him, is there?" June asked.

"Naw. He's just a fucked up old vet," Stan said. And spat again.

June glared at him briefly.

"Sorry, Doc," he said contritely. June was positive he grappled with whether he'd been glared at for using the *F* word or for spitting. Insensitivity toward Clarence's condition would never occur to him.

June leaned around Tom to peer past all the vehicles. There, settled snugly back in the trees, was a little house made of a variety of woods. Logs, twigs, planks, blocks. Composed of maybe two whole rooms, it wasn't much more than a shack, really. The old pickup was sheltered by a tarp strung between two trees. There was a rail fence around a small portion of cleared yard — probably a garden area, or corral for the jenny.

"Does anyone around here know him?" June wondered aloud.

"People back in here have a community of sorts," Tom said, "but mostly they're back here because they want to be left alone. Or maybe they're hiding from the law. They're real cautious of each other. And nobody has offered to speak to Clarence on our behalf. Probably because of all the bells and whistles."

"Is there anyone from the Veterans Administration who could talk to him?"

"Charlie McNeil is a kind of liaison from the VA to some of these dropouts hiding out back here, but we haven't been able to reach him. If we can make any progress here, Charlie can follow up for us."

June nodded. "Well, I'll have to go in there and —"

"You can't, June. Clarence has a gun," Tom stated.

"Well, of course he has a gun," she said impatiently. "He had one this morning at my house. Everyone who lives back here has a gun. Just about everyone in the valley has a gun, for that matter. But he isn't going to shoot me. He might shoot you, however, if he's delusional."

Elmer entered the conversation. "I'll go in. I'm not the police."

"Oh hell, Elmer, he doesn't know that," June said. "But he does know I'm not the police. The poor man needs to be on medication."

"Then I'll at least go with you," Elmer said.

"That wouldn't work any better." She looked at Tom. "He's a huge man, Tom. And strong as an ox. His boy is about six feet tall and he carried him out of my house this morning like he was a toddler. I have some Haldol and Thorazine already drawn."

"Would that calm him down enough for us to go in there and get his boy?" Tom asked.

"It would drop him like a stone. I'd hate to resort to that, but if I have to, I could give him a shot. The most important thing to me is getting Clinton out of there and on his way to a hospital. Excuse me a moment."

Having said that, she simply walked around Tom and headed straight for the house at a nice brisk pace. For a second everyone thought she was simply moving in for a closer look, but she kept going. She did it so quickly and unobtrusively, she made a clean break. Tom made a grab for her and yelled, "June!" But she was already past him.

"Goddamn it!" Elmer ground out. "I hate it when she does that!"

June knocked on the door of the shack, while Tom, and Elmer and the others held a collective breath. "Mr. Mull? Clarence? It's Dr. Hudson. Let me come inside and look at Clinton's foot."

The door opened a crack and two dark, beady eyes peered out. She could tell right away that he was on another planet. Then the door swung open and she was admitted to the dark room lit by only the faintest glow. When the door closed behind her, the light came up, brightening the room.

There were four pallets, a table with two chairs, and animal skins lined the walls. There were open shelves for the dishes and pots, blankets strung up as room dividers, and to June's astonishment, several large stacks of books, magazines and newspapers against the wall. Clarence positioned himself by the front door and peeked through a skin-covered slit, his rifle at the ready. Jurea Mull sat at the table and operated the light, probably at Clarence's command. She nodded at June and almost smiled, but not quite. Wanda crouched in a corner, hugging her knees, and Clinton lay on the bed very still, perhaps even unconscious. A sound from the other side of the room caused June to turn and see that the jenny actually shared the house with them, right on the other side of a waist-high partition. The donkey chewed and smacked, leaning her snout over the partition and drooling onto their packed-dirt living room floor. The family was not dressed in their best today; their clothing was old and threadbare.

There was nothing about the poverty of the room that alarmed June. Having grown up the best friend of Tom Toopeek, she had learned that abundance is a state of mind. Tom was one of seven children who had spent the greater part of their childhood living in a two-room cabin with a dirt floor while their father, Lincoln, slowly and laboriously built their home one log at a time. Yet they were a happy, healthy family, generous and welcoming. June had loved staying with them. Rather than thinking they had very little, she remembered thinking they owned the entire forest.

In the Mulls' cottage, June realized, there could be that same sense of family, unity and abundance in better times, but at this moment there was only foreboding. Jurea seemed nervous and pale. Wanda was afraid; there were tearstains on her cheeks. And Clarence stood at the door with a gun, paranoid, peeking out at police.

But yet . . . they seemed to be well fed and, with the exception of Clinton's injured and now infected foot, they appeared healthy. Perhaps not educated or medicated as well as they should be, but who was she to judge? Maybe things here were okay when Clarence wasn't in a bad patch.

She knelt beside Clinton. He was feverish, his cheeks pink and dry.

"Oh Mr. Mull, what have you done?" He turned from the door and looked across the room at her. June met his gaze, but she did not see understanding. Instead she saw the paranoia in his eyes. "I told you to get Clinton to the hospital." Clarence didn't respond. In many ways, he was sicker than Clinton. "Okay," she said, turning back to the boy and opening her bag. "I'll see what I can do."

She pulled out a stethoscope and hooked it into her ears. Then, while she listened to Clinton's heart, she withdrew a syringe from her bag and, with a thumb, popped the top. She had to get Clinton help soon. Very soon. She couldn't wait for Clarence to calm down, see reason. She rose silently and prayed his overalls weren't too stiff with dirt. She approached his back on silent feet, and when she was almost there, Jurea spoke softly.

"Clarence is upset, is all. He just needs a little time . . . and for those police to get on back to their business."

June stopped suddenly and hid the syringe in the folds of her sleeve. She moved to sit at the table by Jurea. "Is he afraid of the police, Mrs. Mull?"

"Not directly so, no. He thinks of them as soldiers. Left alone, Clarence does all right."

"You mean he doesn't hallucinate?" June asked.

"Not so much, no."

"Mrs. Mull, tell me the truth now, because you know I don't mean you any harm. Is Clarence growing cannabis back here? Marijuana? On this land?"

Clarence turned from the door and barked at her so loudly she jumped. "We don't have no use for drugs in this house!"

"The Lord frowns on weeds and hemp except for the healing," Jurea said. "I did give Clinton some herb for the pain — got it from one of my brothers — but we don't traffic in that. We keep to ourselves is all. We got our reasons." She leaned closer and whispered, "You know."

June then noticed the large Bible by the lamp on the table.

"Mrs. Mull," she said softly. "I have to take Clinton out of here or he'll die."

Jurea's gaze dropped. "I don't like to defy Clarence," she whispered. "He's always been so good to me. To us."

"Well, this isn't good," June said. "Clarence," she said sharply. "Come here and listen to me. If you aren't growing pot here, those police have no interest in you! I asked Sheriff Toopeek to find you and your boy because he needs medical attention. So do you, but that's your business, not mine."

"I don't aim to be taking drugs and shots," he said.

"They gave him shots when he got home and they made him sick," Jurea said. "He just needs to be left alone. He can't take the people." She lowered her gaze, lowered her hideously scarred face. "We each have our own reasons for that, do Clarence and me. That's why we get along so nice, I reckon."

"But it isn't always the best thing for the children."

"I see that. I do."

"You have to help me with this, then."

"What little I can do, I will."

"Good enough," June said. "Clarence, I

think we understand each other. I understand why you live back here and why you want to be left alone. That's fine by me. So just let me take the boy to the hospital. You don't have to go."

"Can't let the boy go alone, Doc. He'd be afraid."

"No he won't, Clarence," Jurea stated, and she said it very strongly. "He don't have that sickness that makes him afraid of people. It's just you and me get like that."

"There you have it, Clarence. Let me take Clinton to the hospital and try to save his life. You can stay here with your wife and daughter. If you deny me this chance, he may die . . . and I know you don't want that."

"He's taking the medicine," Clarence argued.

"It's not enough. Now, do you want to carry him to my car, or should I have Tom Toopeek come in here?"

"That Tom fellow there. He's Vietnamese, ain't he?"

"Tom?" She almost laughed, but quickly cleared her throat. "Um, no. Tom is Cherokee. His family moved here from Oklahoma when he was five. I grew up with him. He's my best friend."

"He looks Vietnamese from here," Clarence snorted.

Everyone probably looks Vietnamese, June thought. "He's Native American. Indian. My best friend. Would you like to have him carry Clinton?"

Tom, Elmer, Stan, Bob and a Forestry Service officer named Warren all waited tensely by their vehicles. The door to the shack opened and June came out carrying her bag and Clarence's rifle. Behind her was Clarence, huge and heavily tattooed, who wore only a vest on his naked chest, despite the harsh chill in the forest. He carried in his arms his barely conscious son, a lad of substantial size.

"Give the boy to Tom," June instructed him.

Without hesitation, Clarence transferred the boy, then June handed Clarence back his rifle.

"I'll see that everything possible is done for him, Clarence. And I'll send someone out here to bring you news of his condition. Tomorrow, or maybe the next day."

Clarence took his rifle and looked into Tom's black eyes. They were both large men, over six feet tall. They both wore ponytails and had faces chiseled out of brown granite. "Cherokee, huh?" Clarence asked.

"Yep."

"I was in country with a Navajo."

"My wife's people."

"All right then. Keep them other Vietnamese away from here," he said, indicating the other police with his eyes.

Tom gave a brief nod and turned, taking the boy to his car. "Go to the hospital in Rockport, it's closer. I'll follow," June said. Then she turned back to Clarence. "Do you know Charlie McNeil? From the VA hospital?"

"I thought I told you!" Clarence barked. "I ain't going to that hospital!"

"I understand that, but if Charlie came out here to see if there was anything you needed, would that be all right?"

"Is he Indian? Like that guy?"

"No. I think he's Irish. Short fellow with red hair. Very nice man. Can he come?"

Clarence thought about this for a moment. Finally he said, "If he brings some books and magazines for Jurea."

Seven

Myrna Hudson Claypool's dinner parties were legendary. Not for the food served, which, in fact, was often disastrous, but for the unique atmosphere, both planned and spontaneous.

When Myrna learned that June was inviting John Stone to join the clinic, she had the perfect excuse to have a party — to welcome him. She'd invite those who would be working with him. That would be Elmer, June, Charlotte and Jessica. Charlotte's husband, Bud, was invited, but he was on a fishing trip. In fact, he was always fishing when Myrna had one of her dinner parties. Then there was the Stone family — John, his wife and their six-year-old daughter were the guests of honor. And to keep things interesting she would add her poker table — Sam Cussler, Judge Forrest and his wife, Birdie, Burt Crandall and his wife, Syl. Thirteen, all told. By Grace Valley standards, a bash.

Myrna would be the chef and would have both Miss Barstows to help, serve and clean up. Amelia and Endeara, the sixty-two-year-old spinster twins who hadn't said a kind word to each other in as many years, usually job-shared cleaning and cooking duties at Hudson House. To have them both on duty was rare and probably dangerous, but it underscored Myrna's desire that the evening be special.

Myrna used her new color printer to make up fancy invitations. She made a little menu insert to put inside that read:

> clam petit four appetizers
> shrimp salad *du bois*
> potato leek soup
> rolled candied lamb with mint
> cucumber stuffing with walnuts
> asparagus à la crème
> devil's torte supreme

When Elmer saw his invitation he said, "Yikes."

June was having a short business meeting with John after hours in the clinic, trying to put the final touches on his six-month contract. She handed him his invitation, saying, "You're the guests of honor — you, and

106

Mrs. Stone and your daughter — so you'll have to go."

"But of course we'll go! How lovely of Mrs. Claypool!" And then, "What do you suppose 'rolled candied lamb' could be?"

"I wouldn't dare hazard a guess," June replied. "Mrs. Claypool is my aunt. She's a fascinating woman, really. And kind of . . . well . . . eccentric is really too tame a description. But she is adorable and great fun. Your daughter will especially love her. Her dinner parties are famous, and highly entertaining, but I recommend you have a bite to eat before going."

"Still, it is nice of her, isn't it?"

June shrugged. "Myrna's nothing if not nice."

The night of the party, John and his wife opted for a country club casual look in linens and knits. Their daughter, Sydney, was stunning in yellow denim overalls and Doc Martens. Jessica wore a long, lean, black dress that accentuated her multicolored Mohawk, and Charlotte wore a beige, double knit pantsuit and her white nurse's shoes. "Corns," she said when she caught Judge Forrest staring at her feet. But it was Myrna, as usual, who stole the show. She answered the door in a stunning floor-length shiny black cocktail dress with enormous shoulder pads and a slit up one side. Nothing risqué, but a rather demure Bette Davis ensemble that didn't bare too much of her skinny calf. If she held a cigarette in a holder, the picture would be complete.

Susan Stone gasped in surprise and took a step backward.

"Welcome to my home," Myrna said dramatically, bowing at the waist and throwing an arm wide. "You must be Sydney Stone," she said to the little girl.

"No one mentioned this was formal," John said.

"This isn't formal," she explained. "I'm eighty-four years old. I have at least a hundred years' worth of keepsakes in this house."

Susan's eyes grew round. "Then it *is* an heirloom gown," she said almost reverently.

"Well, it *will* be . . . when I'm done with it," Myrna said. "Come in, come in, come in."

"This is going to be fun, isn't it, honey?" John whispered to his wife.

"Weird," Susan said suspiciously. "Pretty weird."

June could see the relief on John's face when he entered the sitting room and saw familiar faces from the clinic. She greeted him, met his wife, introduced him to her

108

father and a couple of the others. While they made small talk, the bell rang and the remainder of the guests arrived.

Sydney hid behind her mother's legs, staring out at Jessica, mesmerized by her hair and piercings. Jessica, smiling, bent at the waist so that her colorful plume was eye level for Sydney, and gave it a playful wobble. Sydney withdrew even farther.

Myrna had thrown her shoulder wrap over one of the overstuffed wing chairs in the sitting room, taking possession of that piece of furniture for herself. Beside the thronelike chair was a hassock comprised of a stack of three large pillows on wheels. On the hassock was a tiara.

"Miss Stone," Myrna called. Everyone turned to look at her. The Stones stared in some confusion, but those of Myrna's friends and family who knew her and had been to her dinner parties just smiled knowingly. "Miss *Sydney* Stone. Come here." Myrna patted the hassock.

John gave his daughter a gentle push and Sydney went to Myrna, but slowly.

June often wondered what it must have been like for her father as a toddler, preschooler, grade-schooler and onward, to be mothered by this slip of a girl who had never quite grown up herself. Myrna wasn't much bigger than six-year-old Sydney.

"Miss Stone, do you go to many dinner parties?"

Sydney shook her head and chewed her finger.

"No? Then you can be the princess for this one. For tonight you can wear the princess crown and tinkle the bell for the servants, and next time we'll poke around this big old house and see if we can find you a proper gown."

"But not like hers," Sydney said, pointing at Jessica. The room howled with laughter.

"It's not for everyone," Jessica said, not offended.

"No, you don't want that much jewelry," Myrna agreed. "Maybe something a bit more like Cinderella? All right then! Come, come, let's crown you." Sydney allowed Myrna to put the tiara on her head, and she sat cautiously on the cushions. The bell remained on the floor. "Very nice. Tinkle the bell one time for the drinks and hors d'oeuvres." Sydney complied, and as she did, her smile grew.

"I told you your daughter would love Aunt Myrna," June whispered to John. "When I was growing up, my favorite thing in all the world was to come to Aunt Myrna's and look through her collections. I don't believe she's ever thrown a thing away."

Amelia bore the drinks — apple cider or white wine. Endeara bore the appetizers. They wore their black serving dresses with white aprons and white caps, like clones, wearing identical frowns as they passed among the guests.

"Good evening, Amelia, Endeara," everyone in their turn uttered softly, but neither maid bothered to respond. When things were passed around, they moved silently back into the kitchen.

"Things haven't been going all that smoothly in the kitchen," Myrna confided. "But I think they'll manage to get the meal served just the same. I've been doing a fair part of the cooking myself. And tasting. I must say, it's the best I've had."

Judge Forrest bit into a crab petit four and made a sour face. Wrinkled as he was, it looked as though he'd just conjured up a few more lines. The rest of the room paused with their hands midair, then slowly returned the little square appetizers to their small plates. Myrna seemed not to notice. "I don't know if you'll like this Princess Sydney," she said. "It's very much an adult food."

"But I do like it," Sydney said, taking small bites of her square. She, too, made a face, but was having such fun, she'd never admit it tasted awful. She was a little girl; she'd eat mud pies.

"Not to worry," June whispered to John and Susan. "It might taste bad, but it's not dangerous."

"Splendid!" Myrna exclaimed to Sydney. "You're a princess of excellent tastes! I should have known!"

Sydney giggled happily.

The dinner was horrible, almost completely inedible. Judge grumbled to Sam, "You'd think she'd get a decent cook, since she can afford it!"

To which Sam said, "That'd sure take all the fun out of it." Everyone at the table was accustomed to Myrna's ghastly meals, except the Stones — and they had been warned. But no one in Grace Valley would refuse one of her invitations. Myrna was the most interesting person in the valley.

The coffee was good and the torte was passable. The conversation, on the other hand, was delicious. Judge Forrest, who still sat on the bench, had utterly no discretion and told tales of the last week's cases: feuds, battery, drunk driving, one contested will. "I think you'd call it a perfect week. It was my pleasure to put Gus Craven behind bars, with no work program and no time off for good behavior."

"It's about damn time," Elmer said.

"If there's a God, Gus'll lip off to some big bruiser in jail and get his skull cracked open," Charlotte said.

"We'll have to check on Leah," Birdie added, and withdrew from her purse a small notebook in which she kept track of her endless commitments. "Susan, if I give you a call sometime, can I persuade you to do some charitable work?"

"Of course," Susan said. "I'm partial to charities that cater to the needs of women and children."

June whispered to John and Susan, "Gus Craven has been beating up on his family for years. Most of the town has been waiting for him to get his just reward." Both Stones nodded. "I'm sure some of the women will want to get together and see what can be done to help Leah now."

"Is there no shelter in the area?" Susan wanted to know.

"Not in Grace Valley," Birdie said. "And it's a matter that could probably use our attention soon. I'd like to think Leah's the only woman this happens to, but the unfortunate fact is, she's hardly alone."

Burt and Syl Crandall had raised seven children while running their bakery at the center of town. Sam's gas station was a block away. Between the two of them they came across enough gossip to keep any dinner party going.

"Justine Roberts spends at least three hours delivering flowers to the church," Burt said. "Pastor Wickham, by coincidence, always seems to be alone there at the time."

"Do you mean to say he's finally found himself a willing woman?" Myrna asked.

Sam's eyes sparkled and his pink cheeks above his silver beard turned into red candied apples. "She looks happier coming out than she does going in. I reckon it's a spiritual thing for her."

Elmer wheezed and laughed. "It puts her in a holy mood. It always did me."

"Listen to you, pretending to remember," Judge scoffed, at which Birdie whacked him on the arm with her fan and told him to mind his manners.

"That young woman is a flirt," Charlotte announced.

"Young?" Jessica choked. "God, she must be thirty!"

All eyes turned sharply toward her and she gulped. "And Pastor Wickham is an old lech! Susan, you don't want to be bending over to help pick up hymnals if he's around!"

"I'll take that as a warning," she said. "But how are his sermons? I think we'll be attending there."

"Not nearly as entertaining as his passes . . . and his wife's futile attempts to keep him in line," Sam said.

John Stone slapped his knee and laughed. "I'm going to love this town!"

Susan Stone wore a very uncertain look.

"Let this serve as fair warning, Dr. Stone," Myrna announced. "Your every move will be watched."

"I can see that," he acknowledged. "And I'll be watching right back!"

"Now, let's retire to the parlor for the evening's entertainment!"

"Oh goodie," Jessica said, rising quickly. "I hope it's dancing!"

"I hope it ain't no goddamn charades," Judge grumbled.

June rose and moved between John and Susan Stone, escorting them toward the parlor. "Once we took off all our clothes and did body painting," she said. They stopped walking and their chins practically dusted the floor as their mouths hung open in stupor. "Kidding," she said, moving ahead of them.

"No, no, no," Myrna protested. She held Sydney's hand as they entered the parlor together. "Princess Sydney should hear the story of our angels. But first, we'll have the Barstows bring us a refill on the coffee. Princess? Will you ring the bell for me?"

By now Sydney was fully involved in her role. With gravity befitting a hostess princess, she lifted her chin and the bell simultaneously and gave the latter a jingle.

"Splendid!" Myrna said.

"I'll do it!" one of the Barstows snapped offstage. "Just get the devil out of my way!"

"You'd better mind telling me what to do. I don't work for you!" the other snapped back.

"Thank you, Endeara," Myrna said as she was served first. "No more squabbling back in the kitchen now. It sets everyone's nerves on edge, you know."

"Are they always like this?" Susan asked under her breath.

"Always. Since they were children, actually."

"Why do you put up with it?"

"Well . . . because someone has to, I suppose."

"What I mean is —" But Susan stopped. She had meant to inquire as to why Myrna didn't simply hire maids who didn't squabble, but as she looked into Myrna's large, clear, innocent eyes, she knew her question would not be understood. Myrna had not so much hired them as taken them in.

June glanced at Susan and saw that she had grave doubts about her move to Grace Valley. Hearing about the angels could either improve those doubts or bring them into specific relief.

"South of here, in the foothills, is a town called Pleasure," Myrna began. "Now it's the county seat and where Judge does his judging, but back then it was just a little speck on the map. There were prospectors looking for gold in the hills, Spaniards sailing up the Pacific Coast looking for war, homesteaders, fortune hunters, painted ladies and barroom brawls. It was a town that catered to the whims of men with loose change and low morals.

"There was a man named Clint Barker who lived there, the meanest, most low-down son of a gun you ever wanted to meet. He was probably an ancestor of Gus Craven's."

"Who?" Sydney asked.

"Never mind, darling. Just know that Clint was *mean!* He lived alone all his life, and then when he was about forty and crusty as an old dog — forty was older then than it is now — he hit a gold vein, came into a princely sum of money, and went south for a few weeks. He came back with a young wife. Young! All of sixteen, I believe. And beautiful. Her name was Miranda.

"Well, Clint was a cruel husband. He worked her and beat her and treated her like the mud on his shoe. And it won't surprise you, she soon ran away from him.

"Clint practically tore the whole county apart searching for her. When he finally found her she was living with a young widower and his small, motherless children. Right here in Grace Valley, before this was much of a town. The widower was a kind and loving man by the name of Wyatt Manchester and he was a homesteader. A farmer. He took Miranda into his home and cared for her bruises and her broken heart, and she cared for his children. I think they fell in love. I'm sure they did, they must have.

"But Clint found them, and without the blink of an eye, he shot them all. The whole precious bunch of them, Wyatt, Miranda and the children."

"Ahh, Mrs. Claypool," Susan Stone tried to interrupt.

"It's all right, it comes out well," Sam said, shushing her worries. "It's a regular Disney movie."

"Then what?" Sydney asked, trying to get Myrna back on track.

"Well, of course the law took Clint Barker away and hanged him for the murder. Not long after, the town of Pleasure sort of fell quiet. There wasn't any more gold in the hills, the Spanish lost interest and what was left here were farmers, ranchers, loggers and fishermen. It was a decent place again, without barroom brawls and painted ladies.

"Then, back in the twenties, when I was just a tot and Elmer not yet born, there was a couple passing through Grace Valley by wagon on their way to a family wedding south of here. They hit fog and ice, which around here can be so dangerous, especially on the mountain passes. Their horse and wagon slipped into a ravine and they had to climb back up to the road. They couldn't rescue their animal or possessions, and night was setting in. Freezing and lost, they went along the road, in desperate search of help or shelter before night swallowed them up.

"A man wandered into their path. He was handsome, about thirty years old, and he wore boots and a heavy jacket and carried an ax and rope. He took them back to his cabin, where his wife gave them hot soup and dried their clothes by the fire while he went back to the road and rescued their horse from the ravine. They were a beautiful young couple with two tiny children, so loving and sweet, and obviously cared so much for each other. There was such a feeling of health and wealth in their small, tidy home. Clearly the traveling couple's lives were saved by these people. On their return trip, they stopped in Grace Valley with a gift for the family who had come to their aid.

"They searched and searched, but couldn't find their way back to the cabin, so they came into town and went from door to door, asking everyone they met for directions to the Manchester home. But no one had ever heard of them. It was when they asked an old-timer who'd lived in the valley since prospecting days that they learned the truth — Wyatt Manchester, Miranda, and Wyatt's two small children had been dead for fifty years. They are angels who come to the aid of travelers who pass through this burg. They have been most often seen out on Highway 482, at a turn in the road known as Angel's Pass."

There was a moment of reverent silence when Myrna finished, then Judge said, "That story gets better every time I hear it."

"Well, it's not a story, you old party pooper. It's the God's truth!"

John was leaning forward, elbows on knees, mesmerized. His wife looked a little less intrigued. "Has anyone seen them since?" he asked.

"Oh my, yes, people claim to see them all the time!" Myrna said.

"Have *you* seen them?"

"No, I'm sorry to say I haven't. I hope I will, before I die. What a treat that would be."

"If you don't see them before, you'll see them after," Elmer pointed out.

A row from the kitchen broke the mood, and Myrna had to excuse herself to go settle the Barstows down and help sweep up the broken glass.

"John," June said, taking him aside. "When I first came here to practice with my dad after medical school, I found the people I'd known all my life were resistant to me. Small town people are slow to accept change, slow to draw newcomers in. But they're a friendly, generous and really welcoming bunch. On Monday I'll introduce a few of my patients to you, and again on Tuesday, and so on. After a few weeks, you'll undoubtedly have a list of scheduled appointments of your own. But be patient."

"I'm not worried, June," he said. "If I have a little time on my hands for now, that will suit Susan just fine. We still have a lot of unpacking and exploring to do."

Tom drove the police Range Rover slowly through the forest, along one of the many old logging roads that wound its way into the foothills of the Trinity Alps. To the men in the back seat he said, "My experience with Clarence tells me it's best if we leave the car and walk in, single file. According to his wife, it's the rush of people that brings on his delusions."

"If he's delusional, it's probably all the time," Jerry Powell said.

"Not necessarily," said Charlie McNeil. "I've found the vets have a variety of designer symptoms to accompany their PTSD. It might be that too many people around stresses Clarence, makes him feel unsafe, and the paranoia brings on the delusions. I have one vet who is being slowly driven out of his mind by the DEA helicopters. Every time they make a run over these foothills looking for the pot growers, he thinks he's back in Nam."

"Does he think they're his choppers?"

"So far. But you never know when that might change."

"Okay," Tom said. He stopped the Rover. "Follow me. Single file. Put a little space between us — it's less threatening."

Jerry and Charlie had worked together many times, though Jerry's specialty was adolescent and family counseling and Charlie was a VA nurse with a Master's Degree in counseling. They made an odd-looking couple: Jerry tall and lean, and Charlie, short and squat. But as a team, they had the right stuff to help people. And they each carried a bag of books and magazines for Mrs. Mull.

"Clarence!" Tom called from the edge of the clearing. "Clarence Mull, it's Tom Toopeek! Permission to come across the yard!" He waited. "Clarence Mull!" he yelled again.

"Maybe he's not in there," Jerry whispered.

"He's in there. There's smoke from a cook fire. Can't you smell that? Smells good," Tom said.

Charlie sniffed the air. "Wonder what he's cooking? That does smell good."

"Well, if he doesn't shoot us, maybe he'll ask us to dinner."

"If he was going to shoot you," Tom said, "you'd already be dead."

"He shot at you," Jerry reminded Tom. "You're not dead."

"There's no question in my mind that if

he had wanted to hit me, he would have. That's one of the reasons I didn't arrest him. He just wanted to be left alone. He doesn't want to hurt anyone."

At that moment there was a rustling sound to their left and Clarence came through the trees, his rifle in one hand and a string of mountain trout in the other. He stopped when he saw the three men, slowly regarded them, and nodded once to Tom. "You bring Jurea some reading?" he asked.

Charlie hefted the sack he held. "A great deal of reading, Mr. Mull. I'm Charlie Mc-Neil and this tall man is Jerry Powell. We came with Chief Toopeek to talk to you because we have information about your son."

The door to the small house slowly squeaked open and Jurea filled the frame with her tall girth. Only June and George Fuller had seen Jurea's scarred face, and though Tom, Jerry and Charlie had been warned, it took an effort for all of them not to gasp or wince or turn their eyes away.

"I guess if you have word of Clinton, his mother should hear it," Clarence said.

Charlie moved toward Jurea, shifting his bag of books and magazines onto one hip and stretching out a hand in her direction. "How do you do, Mrs. Mull. My name is

Charlie McNeil and I'm a nurse with the VA hospital. I'm glad to meet you."

"I ain't going to no goddamn VA hospital!" Clarence barked.

Both Charlie and Jerry jumped in surprise.

"I told them that," Tom said. "We're not here to take you to the hospital, but to tell you how your son is getting by. He didn't do too well, Clarence. I'm afraid he lost the foot."

"Oh Clarence!" Jurea cried. "Oh Clarence, my boy!"

"The doctor tried, Mrs. Mull, but there was gangrene. And Clinton is still very sick with fever, but his prognosis is good. He's going to be all right now, thanks to surgery and antibiotics."

But Jurea dropped her head into her hands and wept for her son. Jerry reached toward her and laid a reassuring hand on her arm. "Mrs. Mull, let us take you to see him."

"I daren't leave Clarence and Wanda," she said through her tears.

"We could make it a fast trip," he urged.

"I couldn't, sir. It wouldn't be right and it would probably only shame the boy. But could you tell him," she said, finally lifting her face, "that I cried for him?"

"Of course," Jerry said.

"And that he's ever in our prayers, all of us," she said.

"Might shoot that jenny," Clarence said.

Tom kicked at the dirt. "That'd be a shame, wouldn't it."

Jurea sniffed back her tears. "He wouldn't. He's just talking."

"I'm going to come back in a couple of days," Charlie said. "Might bring these two friends with me for company. We brought you dozens of books and magazines, but how about if I brought paper and pens and colored markers for you and your daughter? Could you draw something for Clinton? Write him something?"

At his words a remarkable thing happened to Jurea's face — the half that was unscarred lit up and she smiled. The pull of muscles caused the scar to lift away from her blind eye and for just a moment she looked almost pretty. But the more important thing was what Charlie saw — that the scar might actually be helped by plastic surgery.

John Stone showed up at the clinic bright and early Monday morning and spent the day getting acquainted with some of the patients. He had lunch with June and Tom Toopeek at Fuller's Café, and while there, shook the hand of several locals. June told him to take off early, reminding him that small town folk were slow to accept new-comers. Then she told Charlotte and Jessica that she thought he was going to work out pretty well. In due time, she suspected, patients might even ask for him.

On Tuesday morning, June drove into town and was forced to slow down for the traffic. There was no fair or festival that she could think of, no farmer's market or bazaar or homecoming game, but there were cars parked everywhere. The clinic lot was full, the lot at the Presbyterian Church had a couple of dozen cars parked there and the café spaces were full. June paused in front of the clinic, stupefied.

While she watched, Laura Robertson jumped out of her truck and dragged her son, Matt, by the wrist while she balanced a plastic container on the palm of her other hand. She walked briskly to the clinic. When she opened the door, June could see that the waiting room was overflowing with people.

Two middle-aged women exited the clinic while she watched. They stopped in the middle of the street, leaned on each other and tittered and giggled like teenagers.

June slowly drove to the café, and double

parked and went inside, still in a state of shock. Most of the regulars had moved to tables in front of the café, where they could watch the rush at the clinic.

George had her coffee ready and a bag of blueberry muffins. Tom leaned against the pastry counter with his steaming cup.

"I see Dr. Stone is taking appointments," Tom said.

"I warned him that small towns are funny — friendly on the one hand, but slow to draw in newcomers on the other."

"Hmm, you must have been talking about some other small town," Tom said.

EIGHT

That first week the handsome Dr. Stone practiced in the valley, June thought she'd have to install a revolving door, but things soon calmed. Even so, his popularity was established as phenomenal. Spring melted into summer and John had a full appointment register. And he seemed oblivious.

"Do you have to put up with this everywhere you go?" she asked him.

"With what?"

"Hordes of crazed fans, begging a moment of your time to bask in the radiance of your handsome smile . . ."

"Oh June, you're hilarious! I'm just the new doctor in town, that's all."

"I have to tell you, John, I didn't get a single cake when I came back to town."

"Probably because you grew up here. Hey, I've been meaning to ask you, about the angels. . . ."

"Yes?"

"Well, are there really angels here?"

"Tough question."

"Well," he said, "do you believe in it? Them? Whatever?"

"I don't *not* believe it."

"What's that supposed to mean?"

"It means — I grew up hearing stories about angels. There are several. Another favorite version is the sheriff's deputy who got shot by a fugitive out on 101 and some woodsman-type fellow stopped the bleeding and stayed with him right up until help came. Then he disappeared into the forest without a trace. The deputy was convinced he was Wyatt, the angel. I think the Good Samaritan actually gave that as his name."

"That's pretty convincing," John said. "I mean, a wounded deputy . . ."

"I know. Except that if I were growing pot back in the Trinity Alps and I saw a shot deputy and wanted to help him, but didn't want anyone to know who I was or why I was around, I'd say my name was Wyatt and disappear back into the trees."

"Oh." John was clearly deflated.

"By the way, *they're* real, you know. Marijuana farmers. Don't go back in the hills. Stick to parks, forestry approved trails, that sort of thing. Some of those old paths could be booby-trapped. Plus the growers have their own little wars. Drug farming is very territorial."

"You ever see a real marijuana farmer?" John asked.

"That I know of? No. We don't seem to have any trouble related to that business in town, but back in the hills it's open season. There are dozens if not hundreds of old abandoned logging roads out there. People who don't know where they're going have gotten hurt."

"Okay, fine. Tom and your dad both already warned me about that. But what about the angels? I guess you've never seen one."

"No, I haven't. And you should remember that Aunt Myrna, well, she *is* a novelist. A storyteller extraordinaire. She tends to embellish everything."

"But the whole town believes in these angels!"

"So it seems."

"And you don't *not* believe in them!"

"John," she said, giving his arm a reassuring pat. "Angels are a state of mind. Don't get so intense about it."

"Sydney is driving us crazy. She wants to know if they're real or a story. We've always told her the truth — we don't make things up. Silly things."

"Silly things? Like Santa and the tooth fairy?"

John grinned. "Well, *they're* real."

"Thank God. I thought you were going to be one of those atrocious modern parents who take away their kids' fantasy life before they outgrow their training wheels! My father is one of the most no-nonsense, pragmatic, low on bullshit parents a kid can grow up under, and he said, whether I knew it or not, whether I could see them or not, I had angels."

"I guess I can see his point," John said.

But June had stopped listening. She was remembering back to when she was seven, climbing the big tree in her yard with Tom Toopeek, Greg Silva and Chris Forrest. She was the only girl — she was often the only girl — but she was as loud and fast and strong as the boys. They were building a tree house. The base and platform had been up for weeks, anchored by Elmer and Mikos, who made sure it was safe, solid and would bear their weight. But she and her friends were always adding to it — walls, rope swings, ladder rungs up the trunk and along the huge boughs.

And she fell.

It was funny; she was completely unconscious, but she remembered every bit of it.

The long flight down, the thunk of her skull, the crack of her spine, and then hearing everyone around her but not being able to respond or move.

The boys ran into her house screaming, "Doc! Doc! Mrs. Hudson! Mrs. Hudson!" while June lay there beneath the tree, lifeless. Her mother and father and friends all came back to her, her father yelling that no one should touch her. Her eyes were open, she could see him looming over her, but she couldn't even blink. His face above hers filled the space of her vision. Then he slowly touched two fingers to her neck to get a pulse and she found her breath. She inhaled sharply, painfully, then coughed and began to cry.

She had had the damnedest headache for about a week, but was otherwise miraculously uninjured. Her mother tried to keep her out of the trees, but that passed. It had been June's only real brush with death.

"June? June?"

She blinked and looked at John. She smiled. "I've met the Princess Sydney and I believe she has angels, whether she can see them or not."

"That's probably what I'll end up telling her, but I was looking for some slightly more reliable feedback. For my own curiosity, as well. You know, if someone like Doc or Tom Toopeek had actually encountered angels. . . ."

"Have you met Jerry Powell yet?" she asked him.

"No, I don't think so."

"Dr. Powell, child and family therapist, Ph.D. in clinical psych. He moved here a few years ago from San Jose, I think. Really nice guy."

"Doesn't ring a bell. Why? Has he seen the angels?"

"I don't think so, but he's been for a ride in a spaceship."

She walked away from him, grinning over her shoulder.

"We're going to be drinking bottled water, for sure," John muttered.

Mikos Silva had a nice farm between the Trinity and King mountain ranges, south of town. It was an even, flat valley there, not too far off the highway. He had built himself a sturdy house and raised three kids — two boys and a girl. Greg Silva was the same age as June, and they had been friends all through school.

All the Silva kids had moved out of Grace Valley, but they hadn't gone far. The oldest, Maria, married a fisherman and moved to

Humboldt Bay, where she worked as a nurse and raised her kids. Greg became a policeman in Redding, and Stuart Silva, the baby, joined the navy and went career, but he was still in California. None of the kids really wanted the farm, which was a source of some disappointment for Mikos, but he was quick to say he had chosen a path unlike his own father's, and no one had complained over him.

It was possible Mikos was the sweetest, kindest man in the valley. He visited neighbors, took in sick animals, gave food baskets to poor families, wrote letters to lonely soldiers abroad. He was perpetually happy and generous. But a year ago he'd lost Mrs. Silva and since then, his very closest friends, like June and Elmer, could see that he was suffering more than grief. His health was failing. He was giving up.

He was seventy-eight and had worked hard all his life. He bore no ill will to the medical people who had been unable to save his wife from the scourge of cancer, but he wasn't likely to take his own complaints to doctors, even though they were lifelong friends.

June had noticed on a recent visit that Mikos seemed a little short of breath, had a grayish pallor, and that his hands appeared swollen. So she had taken to stopping by more frequently, but the most he would allow was to have his blood pressure checked. It was high. She gave him medication, but it was obvious he wasn't taking it.

She drove by his farm on the way home from the clinic and found him sitting on the porch. His collie, Sadie Five, stood beside his chair. She went to the porch edge and wagged, welcoming June. She was Mikos's fifth collie.

"I'm sorry you go to such trouble, but I'm always happy to see you," Mikos said.

"I'm happy to always see you, too. And Sadie." June had left her bag in the Jeep; some things were better treated with kindness and respect than with tools and drugs. "My father is always telling me I need a dog."

"He's right, of course. We all need dogs. I have such trouble understanding people who go through life without them — except maybe busy people like you. I think you wonder what would I do with a dog?"

"That's right, I do."

"Ah, but the more accurate question is what would a dog do with you?"

"And the answer?" June urged.

"She would take very good care of you, I'm sure."

Mikos sat in an old metal chair that squeaked when he moved. His legs were so short, his feet barely touched the porch floor. He might be all of five foot four, but the arms and shoulders on this little farmer were broad and hard and bore the strength of three men.

Beside him was a small table, a pitcher of tea, an extra glass. June sat in the other chair. He poured her a glass.

"Did you know I'd be coming?"

"I knew someone would be coming. It might as easily have been you. So, you have a new doctor."

"John Stone. From the Bay Area. He has a specialty in OB-GYN as well as family medicine. The day he arrived we went out to Julianna Dickson's house. It was quite an introduction to the town. He knows how we do things here now." She laughed.

"That's been two months," Mikos said.

"Yes, and in that time John's seen almost every woman in Grace Valley. He's very handsome. Very charming."

Mikos laughed. "As charming as me?"

"Not quite, but nearly."

"It seems like you made a good choice with him, June. The women could use another handsome, charming man around here. It'll take some of the pressure off me."

He grinned devilishly.

June sipped her tea. "How are you feeling?"

"Excellent," he said. "Maria phoned earlier today and left a message. My granddaughter Beth is having a daughter." He clicked his teeth and shook his head. "They can take pictures of the baby inside the mother and tell what sex it is, then phone you and tell your machine about it while you plow the fields. If anyone would have told me about this fifty years ago, I'd have called him crazy!"

"How wonderful for you! And tell Maria I send congratulations! When is the baby due?"

"In the fall. The first great-grandchild."

June touched his hand. "I wish Mrs. Silva could see."

"She will see. She will see."

June was surprised to find Christina Baker in her examining room. She was now seven months pregnant, still underweight and anemic, and should be under the care of a specialist. According to her chart, she had seen John Stone twice, but had asked for her next appointment to be with June. John had run a number of tests, probably to be certain the source of Christina's problems was simple anemia and not something more dangerous, but John had a lot to learn. Christina couldn't pay for all this blood work and the sonogram, and the county might not, either. A clinic like this could be pauperized by indiscriminate testing.

"You don't have much longer to wait for this baby," June said. "Are you getting excited?"

"Um-hmm. We set up a crib in the pantry between the kitchen and porch, but the baby will probably sleep with us at first."

"How did you like our new doctor? Dr. Stone?"

Christina's gaze instantly dropped. June wondered if she had met the first person in town who didn't automatically adore him.

"That's not much of a recommendation," June said, after listening to a few stretched-out seconds of silence. "He's been very well received here by most."

"I rather like seeing a woman doctor," she said.

"I can understand that. But Christina, your weight is still low. Are you getting enough to eat?"

"Gary says I eat like a horse."

"Are you ever hungry?"

"Hardly ever." She shrugged.

"Okay. I'm going to give you a protein

supplement. Mix it with milk and drink it twice a day. Get yourself a wire whisk and stir it up thick. It's almost like a milk shake. It'll help you fill out a little, make sure that baby has enough birth weight to go home from the hospital with you after he's born."

"Will it just put weight on the baby?"

"That's my primary concern at the moment, but you could do with a couple of extra pounds. It's normal for pregnant women to round out a little, Christina. In fact, it's your obligation to do this for your baby."

"I'll do what I can, but I've always been on the slight side."

"I was, too, when I was your age. We make the plump girls jealous, don't we?" she asked, trying to coax a smile out of this young mother. "Then next month, I'd like you to see Dr. Stone. He's an excellent specialist and —"

"Please, I don't want to be Dr. Stone's patient!"

"Christina, I understand your shyness, but the chances are better than fifty-fifty Dr. Stone or some other male doctor will deliver your baby, so it's just as well to get acquainted with him."

"I *been* acquainted with him and I don't want to see him anymore!"

She was so adamant that June sank weakly onto her stool and found herself looking up at her young patient.

"Christina, is there something you'd like to tell me?"

"I don't have anything more to say about it, except I want to have a woman doctor and that's all."

June chewed her lip. She didn't want to put words in the girl's mouth, but something was wrong here. Terribly wrong. June had checked John's references, of course, but maybe it would be a good idea to get some more in-depth recommendations. Or warnings.

She said a silent prayer before she asked her next question. "I guess I don't quite understand why you are so opposed to seeing Dr. Stone."

"I just don't like the way he touches me. Okay?"

June's heart sank. She barely found the strength to stand up and leave the examining room — which she did only after being certain Christina had nothing more to add.

Tom had to do a little parent taxi duty in the middle of the afternoon. Ursula, an eighth grade teacher, had parent conferences after school, and Tanya had a baby-sitting job following her volleyball match. Tom was to be the car service, taking her from the high school out to the Granger farm. He was early and used the opportunity to drive slowly around the high school parking lot and grounds, looking at the lay of the land, sniffing out any possible trouble. The place was nearly deserted; school had been out for two hours. The buses and most of the cars were gone except for those teachers, coaches and students who stayed late for meetings, activities, practices and games.

Another year, he thought, and Tanya can do her own driving around. In fact, she can drive the younger kids to all their stuff. And pick up a few things at the store, and run a few errands, and fill up the tank, and get Grandma to Rockport for her American Women meeting, and . . . He frowned. *And drive around the back roads too fast, park and make out, stay out too late, go to those secret teen drinking parties in the woods. . . .* He said to himself, "Don't borrow trouble. She's a good girl, just growing up beautiful and making Daddy nervous." He felt the beginning of a smile . . . that froze.

He saw the bright red of Tanya's sweat-shirt just peeking out from behind one of the school's pillars at the side exit to the parking lot. He let the Range Rover silently move forward until she came into view, and he saw that she was covered by a lanky boy who had her pressed against the pillar while they kissed. It was Tanya's sweatshirted arm holding the boy that Tom could see. And some of her long, silky black hair, which hung almost to her waist.

It wasn't just any boy, it was Tom's worst nightmare. Frank Craven. Abused and poor and angry Frank.

Tom laid on the horn with a solid long blast, startling the kids apart. Frank composed himself quickly and glared at the police chief in the Range Rover. Tanya gave her dad a wave, then put the hand against Frank's cheek, turned his face back to her and gave him a quick peck on the lips before grabbing her backpack and heading for the car.

"Well, that was pretty embarrassing, Daddy," she said when she jumped in.

"Tell me about it," he replied. "I'm glad I was alone."

"I *thought* we were alone!"

Tom drove a little. He was comfortable with quiet, but he knew he'd better not indulge too much of that. "How long, Tan?"

"What?"

"How long has Frank been your boyfriend?"

"I don't know. Awhile."

"In weeks or months, please."

"Since Christmas or so. Or I guess since Homecoming."

"Jesus."

"You praying over us?"

"Tanya, why didn't you tell anyone? Why is it a secret?"

"It's not, Daddy. Not really. It's just that the only time we could ever be together was at school. And Frank wasn't allowed to make phone calls. You know why. Because of that monster of a father he has."

"Who is now locked up," Tom reflected. "But not forever, you know."

"Oh, we know."

"Tanya, Frank is troubled."

"Wouldn't you be?" she shot back.

"It isn't good, him being your boyfriend."

"It's too late, he already is. We like each other, Daddy. He's a good guy."

"He's got issues that go back generations."

She laughed, but not really in amusement. Not meanly, either, but hollowly, as though in surprise. "Well hell, like the Cherokee have no issues! Or the Navajo!"

"I'm talking about domestic issues, Tanya, not cultural ones. I've seen the angry spark in that boy's eyes and I'm afraid of what he'll become, if he hasn't become violent already. I'm afraid he'll hurt you."

"He won't hurt me, Dad."

"You can't know that for sure."

"I do know it. I do. And if he ever acted mean to me, that would be it. It would be over forever."

"He's in counseling for fighting."

"I know. That's a good thing, don't you think?"

"Have you talked to your mother about this? About Frank?"

"No, but I think I will now. Because you obviously can't *wait* to tell her."

I dread to tell her.

"Just don't get any ideas," she said. "You know, about restricting me or telling me I can't like him or anything like that."

He sighed. "Tanya, I am filled with ideas."

"Well, you know how that works. You put the clamps down, I want him more. Right? So don't try any of that stuff. Just leave me alone about it. It's my business."

"Oh brother."

"And don't get Grandma and Grandpa all worked up about this, because you *know* how they are. Grandma's secretly working on my arranged marriage, and I don't think it's to a blond-haired Craven."

"Tanya . . ."

"If you weren't so nosey —"

"Tan . . ."

"Honestly! Sneaking around the parking
—"

Tom slammed on the brakes and skidded
quite a ways down the country road. Tanya
was flung hard into her seat belt, and when
she turned to look at her father, her eyes
were large and round with surprise. He
turned in the driver's seat and leaned over
the console that separated them. He appeared to be a little larger than usual and
she was reminded that, although Tom Toopeek seemed stoic, methodical and mostly
gentle, he did have another side. A rarely
seen side.

"Be sure your tone is respectful, Tanya.
You were cavorting in public, that's how I
saw you. It was shameful. Your mother
would have been appalled. You should be
punished for that behavior, but I'll let it go.
This time. And I will tell you this, Frank
Craven has serious problems and he needs
help to sort them out. If, during this time
that he's trying to redirect his life, he hurts
you in any way, he will have to answer to
me!"

Tanya's eyes became moist and she
touched his arm. "Daddy . . ." she squeaked.

Tom shifted and began to drive again. "I
think maybe you'd better tell Frank that,"

he said, his voice much more controlled. His rages were rare, and they were always quickly spent.

"I'm sorry, Daddy," she said softly. "I'll be careful."

"And from now on, more honest than you have been. Careful and honest."

"Yes, Daddy. I will."

"That is all your mother and I have asked of you."

The rest of the way to the Granger farm there was no more talking, only occasional sniffing from Tanya's side of the car. When Tom pulled up to the farmhouse, Tanya started to reach for her backpack, but he grabbed her wrist. This time his voice was gentler. "Tanya, you are my pride and your mother's jewel. You must respect yourself as much as we love you."

She nodded her head solemnly and left him alone in the car, alone with the burden of his fears for her. If she thought he was nosey before, she hadn't seen anything yet.

NINE

"Something serious is bothering the good doctor," said Corsica Rios.

"A woman carries her troubles in her hands," Birdie Forrest explained to Jessica.

Ursula Toopeek whispered to Jessica, "Not in her palms, but in her fingers. More specifically, her fingertips." Ursula's mother-in-law, Philana Toopeek, nodded vigorously. Philana was a woman of very few and always carefully chosen words.

The hardest place ever to be with a secret was the quilting circle. As the women worked the needles and tugged on the fabric, pulling at the edges of the quilt, they could feel the tension in each other's stitches and hands. Almost everyone in the circle was expected to use some sort of job-related discretion. But among these longtime, trusted friends, it was hard to keep quiet about a personal issue that was *longing* to be freed, to be shared.

It was an odd and fabulous quilting circle, the Graceful Women. June's mother, Marilyn, had been in it all her married years till her death of heart failure nine years ago. The oldest member now — the grande dame — was Birdie Forrest, Judge's wife. Birdie had been Marilyn's best friend and was June's godmother. The next in line of seniority was Philana Toopeek, Tom's mother. Marilyn and Birdie had brought her in about thirty years ago. Corsica Rios had joined them over twenty years ago, when she was a single mother and student. She was now a county social worker. It was June who had invited Tom's wife, Ursula, a teacher. And then, as an experiment, Jessica — an experiment that had worked.

It wouldn't have occurred to most people to invite a twenty-year-old Goth into a quilting circle of older women. But one day at the clinic, after modeling the latest in her fashion craze — a floor-length black skirt with a slit to the thigh, black sweater, black hose and Doc Martens — Jessica had admitted she'd sewn the skirt. But of course, June had thought. The girl would have to sew to come up with her many avant-garde outfits. She was motherless, and would have had to figure it all out on her own. So June brought her to the circle, where five women pitched in on the nurturing of Jessica, and Jessica stitched on something that was not quite so bizarre for a change.

Jessica had a rather special loyalty to June, and said in her defense, "It's been a very busy week in the clinic."

"It has been. But actually, I was missing my mother," June said.

Philana cleared her throat, but didn't look up from the quilt. "A woman misses her mother when she has problems with a man or a child."

"That's simple," Ursula interjected. "The handsome new doctor is drawing women patients from three counties."

"He's a strange one," Birdie said.

June had to concentrate to keep her head from snapping up at attention.

"Strange how?" Ursula asked.

"He has this oblivious nature. Always positive, always devastatingly gay."

Jessica laughed so loudly and suddenly, that her colorful Mohawk wobbled.

"He's a huge phony, don't you think, June?" Birdie asked.

"I hadn't thought *that,* really. . . ."

"I'm sure he's a very good doctor just the same, but the way he's always so charmed by everything . . . It's nonsense. Maybe he's covering something."

"Oh please, as though it isn't possible for a man to be amused and charmed? He has a very developed feminine side," Corsica argued.

"No, Birdie is right," Jessica said. "He's covering something. It makes him come off very dorky."

They all stopped stitching and stared at her.

"Really," she said. "You think you have Robert Redford or Brad Pitt or something, until he opens his mouth. Birdie says it better, but what I mean is, he's a dork. He's not very with it. His wife, Susan? Now, she gets it. She's totally sharp. But John? He's pretending not to notice or take seriously the fuss all the women are making, and it makes him look stupid, but he's not. He's, like, way too positive. Oh, and Birdie, I've told you before, stop calling things that are happy 'gay.' "

"Yes, dear, you must remind me, mustn't you? By the way, I love what you're doing with your hair these days. Must have Charlotte positively out of her wits."

"She's coping very well, actually. I'm going to shave it off soon. Maybe next week. That should put ten pounds on her."

"Wicked, wicked girl!"

"If she wouldn't pick on me so relentlessly, I wouldn't do nearly as many artful things with my hair. Doesn't she understand? My father is an *artist!* It's not likely I'll run out of avant-garde ideas! She has a nerve, too. She must never look in the mirror."

"I know I shouldn't be tacky and mean, but I've always wondered how she manages that dye job of hers," Ursula said. "The color is rather extraordinary, but that half inch of gray at the hairline is simply remarkable. It always looks as though she did it three weeks ago."

Philana reached across Corsica to touch the top of June's hand. "Is that what makes your fingers tight tonight, June? The handsome new doctor?"

It was maddening, she thought, how everyone referred to him as the Handsome New Doctor. She wished her challenges with John Stone were limited to his good looks or dull personality. Even though she had trusted friends in whom she could confide, and could most often trust Elmer's discretion if the subject was vital enough, she was keeping her own council for the time being. At least until she had a sense of whether John was worse than dorky, or whether her pregnant young patient was either a troublemaker or hysterical or both.

At the moment she had utterly no idea.

"You were almost right, Philana," June said. "I was wishing I could talk to my mother about something . . . about not having a child. I'm feeling such regret."

There, she thought. That will get them off the scent.

All fingers went still and all eyes focused on her face.

"What?" June said. "I'm thirty-seven. Did you think I hadn't noticed?"

Ursula swallowed. "Who do you regret not having a child *with?*"

"Just because I haven't had a date in about a hundred years doesn't mean it was my choice! There's no one here to date, for goodness sake!"

"There are plenty of handsome young men around."

"Oh really? They must all be healthy as horses because I don't know any of them."

"They happen to be, and that's the good news," Ursula said with a laugh. "You wouldn't want a sick one, would you? Now let's see, there's Larry Richards, the vet. He's a great guy. And so handsome."

"He's fifty!"

"True, he might find you too old. And how about Bill Sanderson at the Humboldt County Sheriff's Department? We're all crazy about him at my house. He's available."

"I had this teacher in high school, Mr. Larkin," Jessica added. "What a hunk."

"Lou Larkin's married."

"Not anymore. And there's always Greg Silva."

"He doesn't live here anymore."

"He visits his father every week and would probably move back in a second if he had the slightest reason to. But Jessie, what about your father? Is he seeing anyone?"

"Believe me, June wouldn't want to get involved with my father. His art comes before everything. Sometimes it's like talking to a brick."

"Really? I never thought that of your dad," Ursula said. "He always seems so articulate and funny and —"

"When he's out in public, he can do that, but at home he's a whole other —"

"Wait a minute," June protested. "We're off the subject here. I'm not having any regrets about not dating. It's not having a child I'm lamenting!"

"Oh mercy, forgive us," said Birdie. "Here we were thinking you'd have to do that with a *man*."

"To tell the truth, I don't think I'd want to do it that way," June said.

"What was that?" Birdie asked, cupping a hand over her ear and staring off into the distance. "Ah," she said. She looked back at June. "That was your mother. Shrieking."

Jessica howled joyously. "Oh Birdie, I love you. What did my dead mother say about my Mohawk? Did you ask her?"

"She said you were just going through a little stage, darling. Now, June —"

"I haven't done anything, Birdie, but I've given it some thought. If I were to meet a man I liked, it would probably be years and years before we got to the parenting stage. Wouldn't you suppose? And I'm not saying I wouldn't be interested in meeting, dating and marrying someone. That would be lovely. But I don't have to do that to be a mother. I could be a single mother. Women do it all the time. Actresses, particularly."

"Would you want to, you know, have a pregnancy? Or would you adopt a child?" Ursula asked.

"Selfishly, I think I'd like to be pregnant, to give birth."

"Have you run this by Elmer?" Corsica inquired.

"Not exactly," June admitted. "But you remember when Julianna —"

"Ahh," all the older women said, and looked back at their stitching without even

155

letting June finish. Because of her youth and inexperience, Jessica didn't know what had transpired, so she continued to stare at June, puzzled. But June knew what had happened. Philana, Ursula, Corsica and Birdie were all mothers, and knew the magic of holding a newborn. Added to that, the Dicksons were a storybook family — young, beautiful, strong, healthy, happy. They lived in the midst of their voluptuous orchard in their large Victorian home, nurturing each other and the children. Their lovely country home smelled of lemon polish and apple pies. They grew their own food, home schooled the kids. Grandma Dickson lived with them; Grandpa Holmes lived next door. A couple of hours in their home and all you wanted from life was to have children and polish furniture and bake.

"I think it's a great idea, June," Jessica said protectively. "And if you go through with it, I'll be happy to baby-sit."

The quilting circle always met at Birdie's house because she and the judge lived in town and the others lived in a wide circle around Grace Valley. Also, Birdie was the senior member and was privileged to choose. As she got older, seventy now, she chose not to do too much night driving or fussing, so she picked her house and provided only the coffee; the others all brought plastic-wrapped and Tupperware-encased goodies. Afterward, it was not uncommon for June to stop by the clinic, a mere two blocks away. She'd check the messages, maybe look at charts, do a little paperwork, jot out a to-do list for the next day. Or maybe just sit peacefully in her office.

She was so proud of the place. She'd dreamed of it her whole time away at med school and during her residency. When she got back to Grace Valley she'd begun hounding Elmer. There were doctors' offices and clinics and hospitals up and down the coast, but not much inland where they were. There were easily a dozen small towns around them, not to mention rural farms, orchards and mountain homes whose residents would find the trip to the valley more expedient than going all the way to one of the coastal towns.

These were her people; she was their doctor. She'd grown up in their homes, just as they had come to hers in times of need. She was committed to giving her life to them, so the clinic was a capital idea. Elmer thought so, too, but he didn't think the town could shoulder the cost, and he knew the doctors couldn't; they might take vegetables and eggs for payment, but building contractors liked real money.

It was Myrna Claypool who'd come to the fore. She'd built the clinic and paid for it. With cash. June wanted to call it the Claypool Clinic, but Myrna refused. She said too many people already thought she was dead; it wouldn't help things to go naming buildings after her.

Myrna might wear funny hats and write graphically violent novels, but she was from the old school and thought it vulgar to discuss money. No one had any idea how much she was worth, not even Elmer, or whether she had boundless bundles of money and chose to drive a thirty-five-year-old vehicle, or had shot her whole retirement fund on the clinic. As to that, no one knew whether her money had come from the Hudson legacy or from her books, which seemed to enjoy widespread popularity. Perhaps she had done business with one of the San Francisco banks and mortgaged the clinic; her house and land had to be valuable. Whatever her means, the clinic — ten rooms — and its accoutrements cost one-and-a-half million dollars. She had hardly blinked an eye, and she would not even discuss repayment from June and Elmer. "The town's been good to me," she had said, her final word on the subject.

June sat at her desk. The folder she looked down at was John Stone's employee packet and contract. If he had compromised the integrity of the clinic or any of the patients, he would live to regret it. This was her silent oath.

She closed the file before she got too stirred up. When she looked up, she almost jumped out of her skin.

A bearded man stood in her office doorway. He leaned on a gun that was almost his height, as if it were a staff.

"Jesus, Cliff," she hissed. She fell back into her chair to catch her breath. It was only Cliff Bender, a farmer and woodsman she'd known her entire life — which might be the same length of time he'd grown that matted beard and worn those filthy overalls.

"Little jumpy tonight, Doc?"

"You better not have tracked dirt in here, Cliff. I don't get the floor washed again till Friday night."

His boots were a sight, but he turned one foot up and peered at the bottom. "I reckon I wiped 'em good enough."

"What's the problem?"

"It's the toe. Again."

"Shoot. I thought we had it licked."

"I'm thinkin' about loppin' it off, save us

both some time and trouble."

June laughed. "Don't get drastic, I still have a little fight left in me. Go on, you know what to do."

He gave a nod, turned and went to the treatment room down the hall, where he would soak his infected toe. June had told him on previous nocturnal visits that she wasn't about to touch that filthy foot. He would take off the old boot and sodden sock, roll up the crusty pant leg and soak his foot in a basin of soapy water — just as he'd done before. *Then* she would deal with the toe.

Cliff was diabetic, and just getting him on an insulin schedule had been challenge enough. Helping him take care of his body's special needs was going to be the end of everyone in the clinic. He'd smashed his toe uprooting a stump a few months ago and he just couldn't beat the infection. Lopping it off might indeed be the final answer.

As June put away John's folder, she thought about the irony of the day. Here was Cliff Bender, a farmer they were all so used to he didn't even frighten children, but damned if he didn't look like a psycho. He had beady eyes and was always sneaking up on her. That big old gun was not for show, he'd shoot a trespasser in a heartbeat.

He had no family, and worked a small piece of land at the base of the mountains. He might be scary looking, but he had never given anyone in Grace Valley any cause for concern. Cliff was safe as a puppy.

But was the handsome and charming new doctor someone to worry about?

Jesus, she thought in frustration, even I'm thinking of him as the Handsome New Doctor!

June gave Cliff twenty minutes to make sure his foot was clean. Then she slipped on gloves and trimmed back the nail and any necrotic flesh. She lectured on cleanliness, soaking, resting, and all of it. He wasn't likely to take her advice any more seriously than in the past, but she was honor-bound as a doctor to push the issue. She then gave him a butt full of antibiotic, being every bit as careful as she would if he were a small child. He complained bitterly just the same. She packed up a parcel of Epsom salts, salve, sterile gauze and tape, and six brand-new pairs of socks.

"I think we'd have fewer problems with this toe if you'd just invest in a pair of new, waterproof boots, Cliff."

"I'd hate to do that, Doc. These are just now broke in good."

"Well, I tried. Come on, I'll let you out

the back and clean up."

"You want me to hang around a little? Till you get your stuff put away?"

She looked at him in confusion.

"Seems like maybe you're a little het up."

She smiled and shook her head. "I was. I was worrying about . . . a patient. But I'm fine. I'll just lock the door."

"Must be a bad patient if you're lockin' doors now."

"I should have had it locked before. Then you wouldn't scare the pants off me."

As she opened the door and held it, he gave a slow, deliberate look at her bottom half as if to check for pants. And she laughed. There was a lot of character to the old coot.

"You ought to have a dog, Doc. To look after you now and again. Keep you safe from scary old codgers like m'self."

"Go on, now. And keep that foot as dry as possible, you hear?"

"Yes'm. I'll do that."

June locked the clinic's back door and went to clean the treatment room. She chuckled as she did her chores. There had been no discussion of fees and there wouldn't be any invoice. She didn't ever charge Cliff. He would find any figure unreasonable, and would argue and grouse and threaten to lop off the toe. Truth was, he probably had a pile of money stashed at his house. Elmer remembered Cliff had once had a lot more land than he currently did, and Lord knew he wasn't wasting money on clothes or boots. Sometime in the next couple of weeks June would find vegetables or eggs or some slaughtered animal on her doorstep. Vegetables could be washed and eggs cracked, but she was never sure about meat. Elmer always threw it out, so she did, too. Elmer said it could be road-kill, coming from Cliff. Once, when Cliff was hunting wild pig, he'd come upon a mother and ten piglets. He said he just couldn't kill a mama pig and leave those babies without anyone to take care of them. So he'd killed the piglets. Such was a woodsman's logic.

It was nearly eleven when June was leaving the clinic. As she opened the back door she found herself face-to-face with two enormous men in plaid flannel shirts, jeans and long, heavy, fake beards.

"Clinic is closed, gentlemen," she said, trying to keep her voice steady.

"Ah, we're going to have to keep it open awhile, Doc. Got us a little problem here," the nearest one stated.

"I said —"

"We just need you to take out a bullet, Doc. Won't take you five minutes."

"Okay, let me just make a quick call to —"

"To Chief Toopeek? I don't think so." And with that, he pulled out a very mean looking gun and pointed it at her. "Like I said, this shouldn't take long."

"And like *I* said, come on in, boys."

TEN

June's patient sat on an examining table with his shirt and fake beard removed — an absolute necessity if she were going to treat his injury. She cleaned, anesthetized and numbed the area of his shoulder where the bullet had entered. Unmasked and irritable from pain, he reminded her of an ornery, oversize two year old. And thus her fear began to yield to annoyance. How *dare* they abuse the privilege of medical care!

"Are you sure you wouldn't rather lie down?" she asked him tersely.

"Ummff," he grunted, looking away and remaining upright.

His partner sat on the stool in the treatment room, watching.

"You might as well take your stupid beard off, too," she said to him. "It's not as though there's going to be a lineup."

"You never know," he said.

"Fine, suffer. See if I care. But put that

stupid gun away. I mean, really. Look at you, look at me. You think I'm going to make a break for it or something?" She then tapped the injured area of the man's shoulder with a scalpel. "Feel that?" Again he grunted. "Okay then, here we go . . ." She opened the area with her knife and held up a gauze wipe as the fresh red blood flowed down the man's chest. She reached deeply into the fleshy wound with a hemostat, and her patient moaned loudly. "You make as much noise as you want . . . but just don't move. Just about have it, hang in there. . . ." The moans became louder and the blood flow thicker. "Touching it, touching it, ahh. . . ." And despite his loud growl of pain, she pulled forth a slightly squashed bullet. With one hand she put pressure on the wound, while with the other she turned the clamp to and fro, looking at the bullet. "Good deal. It's in one piece."

Behind her there was a loud *thump.* She and her patient turned as one to witness the huge, gun-toting bearded man lying on the floor. He had fallen right off the stool in a dead faint and his big ugly gun had slid across the floor out of his reach.

"Oh, for Pete's sake," she muttered. She gently pushed on her patient's chest. "You're going to have to lie down now, pal.

I have a lot of sewing to do here and it looks like I'm also going to have to make sure that big dope who brought you in didn't crack his head open." She sighed deeply. "You know, you didn't have to put on such a show about it. All you had to do was ask me to get a bullet out for you," she said peevishly. "This isn't Oakland. People accidentally shoot themselves all the time around here. Why, just last fall Rob Gilmore shot himself in the butt, or so he says. If you ask me, he was probably being his usual asshole self and Jennie shot him. Which she should have years ago. But for now, just relax a little . . ." All the while she talked, she gently eased the big man back. Uncomfortable and weakened, he offered no further resistance. "Here," she said. "Press down on this gauze." She positioned his fingers on top of his own wound.

June dropped the bullet and clamp on the sterile tray, snapped off her gloves, washed her hands in the sink and grabbed an ammonia capsule from the drawer.

She stepped over the gun, stooped to the man who moaned and struggled for consciousness. She lifted his head slightly, deftly pulled the fake beard off his face and tossed it aside. His eyes were pinched closed and twitchie. She watched him; his eyes opened, saw her, closed. She held his head and waited. He opened his eyes and winked at her, slamming them shut again.

What game was *this?* She cracked the capsule and waved it under his nose. His *handsome* nose. He coughed and sputtered and choked and opened his eyes. "Big tough guy," she said, but she smiled in spite of herself.

He very gingerly came to a sitting position. "Whoa," he said.

"How's your stomach?" she asked. "I want to be ready."

"My stomach's okay . . . but my head is floating off into space."

She was gazing into completely lucid, deeply blue eyes. The big faker. He obviously couldn't put down his gun without his wounded partner becoming suspicious, so he had faked a faint. "We have beds in the room by the back door. . . ."

"Naw, I'll just sit right here. I'll be okay. That's never happened to me before."

"You've seen a lot of bullets get pulled out of shoulders?"

"I've seen one or two shooting accidents."

"You're a Vietnam vet?"

"Me? Hell no. I'm too young to have been in that war."

"I guess you are." She tilted her head and

studied his face. He had a rich tan for someone who lived in the woods. High cheekbones, a square jaw and nice ears. His nose had a crook in it, probably from a fight. He had one of those heads of too much thick, unruly hair. His eyebrows were bushy and became knitted as he began to regard her fiercely, but she ignored his purposely scary look. Who was he trying to kid? "What's your name?"

"Just call me Jim," he said.

"Okay, Jim. Let me tell you something. If you're ever hurt or sick and need my help, you just ask. Okay? If you ever come into my clinic pointing a gun at me again, I'll take my revenge. And you'll never see it coming."

"Hey," the man on the table called. "Anybody going to sew up my shoulder?"

June rose to her feet. "Oh, you *do* speak. Fancy that."

She got out a clean pair of gloves and opened the surgical kit that sat on the tray. With a sterile hemostat, she poked around the open wound. "How are you doing? Should I numb this again?"

"I'm okay," he said, looking away from the wound.

"I'm going to have to pack this. It's going to give you some trouble. Pain. Possible infection. Actually, much as I hate the thought, you should come back and see me in a week or so. But by appointment."

"That ain't gonna happen," he said. "Gimme some pills. I'll see someone about it if I can . . . but not around here."

"Fine by me," she said.

Jim came slowly to his feet, reminding her how large a man he was. Monstrous, really. This was a place full of very large men — loggers, farmers, fishermen . . . drug growers.

"You've been a good sport about this, Doc," he said.

"Yeah, yeah, that's what all the guys say. I'm a good sport."

"I really didn't mean to scare you," he apologized.

"Yes you did, you big jerk. That's exactly what you meant to do and I resent it. I've lived in this town my whole life and I know what's going on. I have a pretty good idea where you're from. But I also knew that you were really afraid of me, afraid that I'd call the police or something. I was actually going to call my dad or my nurse — either one could have been here in five minutes and it would have made this whole procedure quicker and cleaner, not to mention easier on me. Easier on all of us. Of course,

I would have had to insist there be no weapons." She pursed her lips and looked him over. "Costumes optional."

"You would have called the police," he said, though his voice was not accusing.

"Eventually. But it's not in my job description," she said as she pushed sterile, medicated gauze into the hole where the bullet had been. "Tom Toopeek has been my best friend since childhood. We work together in every possible way, but we're real careful to keep our roles clear and our lines drawn. I don't compromise his upholding of the law and he doesn't compromise my work as a doctor." She looked up and made eye contact with Jim. "I consider myself a healer first. It's more important to me that this man get treatment than that he get punishment. I don't care if you believe that."

"I see," he said, the temptation of a smile tugging at his lips. "And would that line ever blur?"

"Sure," she said, looking back to her work. "You just about blurred it. You pushed a gun in my face and became a threat. If you just ask for help, you'll get it."

She finished dressing the wound, then used an Ace bandage to bind the man's arm to his chest. She covered the tray with a towel and pushed it aside, dropping her gloves on top, then she went to the cupboard and pulled out some pill bottles. "One of these every four hours till they're gone. These are for pain, take as needed, but not with anything else, like any other pain killers or alcohol. And —" she extracted a very large syringe from the drawer, a vial from the drug cupboard "— bottoms up."

"Aww," he complained.

"I could find a bigger needle. . . ."

Jim laughed and the other man struggled off the examining table, presented his backside and opened his jeans.

"Just drop them to about —"

"I know, I know, I've had shots before."

She finished her job, handed him his pills and helped him shrug one arm into his shirt. "That's about all I can do for you."

Jim pulled a wad of bills out of his pants pocket and peeled off a couple of hundreds. "This should —"

"Get that out of here," she snapped. "I don't want that money!"

He looked confused. "I'm sure you could use it, Doc."

"It stinks of green marijuana, for God's sake! There are a lot of people who think it's just a little plant, maybe ought to be legalized, but I'm not one of them. I consider the consequences far-reaching and tragic! I couldn't disapprove more completely if it were straight-out murder!"

"But you've — ?"

"I choose my battles, that's all. I thought I was clear."

He put his money back. "Well, I guess we're real lucky you chose the battle you did. Thanks."

"It's what I do. Now get out of here." She followed them to the door, fully intending to call Tom once they were gone.

The injured man went out the door, but Jim lingered. "Maybe you should have been a little more afraid of us, Doc," he said, frowning.

She smiled at him. "You don't know anything about being a doctor, do you?" There were lots of times she was afraid, yet had learned how to perform in spite of that. And with confidence. Besides, once these men were in her treatment room, they hadn't scared her. Not at all. After she realized Jim had pretended to faint so he could remove his weapon from the scenario, she had begun to feel almost safe. A little pissed off, but almost safe.

"You have a gun in the office?" he asked.

"Not as of yet, but I've been thinking about getting a dog."

He grinned. "Lock the door."

"Believe me, I intend to."

She opened the clinic's back door fifteen minutes later and let Tom in. "Sorry to bring you out, but there's no way I can leave here alone tonight without someone knowing what's been going on here."

"Of course," he said. "Unfortunately, I don't know how much I can help. I do have it on good authority that there's a camp back in the Alps known as Triple Cross. A compound. A small town, maybe. It's all hybrid cannabis, and the DEA has had it staked out for months. Very few people know about it and you'll have to keep this strictly to yourself. I assume they're planning a raid — maybe tonight was the night."

"If they did raid it, my patient could have been a casualty. Can you find out?"

"I can ask the question, but the DEA is not obligated to answer. I would have expected anyone who got away to head toward Redding. Or the Oregon border. And based on what I was led to believe — that it's a large camp — I would have expected much more than one gunshot wound."

June thought about this. "Then these two who came in tonight could have been involved in some infighting, perhaps."

"Maybe. It's a very territorial business. I'll call the DEA from here," he said. "Then follow you home . . . unless you'd like to come out to my place for the night?"

"No, I'll be happier at home. They're not going to give me any trouble. I think I made peace with them. I told them I'm a healer, not a cop."

"That was kind of you. . . ."

"Kind? That jerk had a big gun! I don't think I've ever seen a revolver that size."

"Maybe the DEA will ask you to look through some mug shots tonight, while it's fresh in your mind."

"Oh God, I hope not. I'm so tired."

"Fear can take its toll. . . ."

"Is it possible at least one of them was working undercover? The one with the gun — Jim — he didn't seem very . . . I don't know . . . criminal."

"Don't be naive. They've busted little old lady Sunday school teachers who have whole rooms full of indoor gardens! You'd be wise never to trust anyone with a pocketful of money that smells of freshly cut cannabis. Anyone who's been that tight with the stuff is bound to at least have questionable relationships."

"Well . . ." She paused and chewed her lip. She wasn't going to mention the pretend fainting just yet. "I hate to sound self-righteous, but I'd never be —" She stopped herself. She was about to say she'd never be *attracted* to a criminal. "I'd, ah, never be as comfortable as I was with a dangerous person. Especially one with a big gun like that." She shrugged. "I have excellent instincts."

One corner of Tom's thin mouth lifted, along with one finely arched eyebrow.

"Stop trying to read my mind," she demanded.

Tom called the DEA, read them June's description and reported the gunshot wound. He also informed them that the men tried to pay June with money that carried the distinct skunklike smell of green marijuana.

"They don't have to see you tonight, June."

"Good. So, did they have a raid?"

He shrugged. "I asked if there had been any arrests tonight and was told no. We have to assume we still have a major DEA drug raid in the mountains to look forward to."

"Well, I hope no one gets killed," she said. And meant it more deeply than she could admit.

ELEVEN

June didn't have time to ponder drug busts and handsome gun-toting mystery men, for the next morning, though tired and unsettled, she had to pursue the matter of John Stone. It couldn't wait.

As though Murphy had planned it, John Stone was standing in the corridor of the clinic when Jessica said, "June? There's a Dr. David Fairfield on the phone for you." Fairfield was the chief of the women's clinic in which John had worked before getting his second residency.

He stiffened; it was unmistakable. He was facing an examining room door, paging through a patient's chart, and June could only see his back, but she saw him freeze. It was brief, but he had definitely heard who was calling for June. He didn't turn to look at her, but went into the examining room and closed the door. She felt a twinge of guilt for checking him out behind his back.

But why should I? she asked herself. It was her responsibility to do so! It was her duty! She shouldn't feel the least bit guilty. So why did she? Maybe because all this checking should have been done *prior* to their agreement. John must wonder, and rightly so, if she planned to check his references indefinitely. Well, she was stuck now. There was nothing to do but proceed.

June sidled close to Jessica so that no one would overhear. "Jessie, I know it's tough scheduling, but have you been able to free up Charlotte to stand in with John during his pelvic exams? Being a woman doctor, I hardly remember that he needs company."

"Well, *he* remembers," Jessica said. "I've had to fill in a couple of times when Charlotte was busy."

"He's sensitive to that?"

"Sensitive? I think it's his strict protocol — big city doc, you know." She smiled and whispered, "Or maybe because the women swoon over him so much. He's extra careful, even though he *pretends* not to notice all the attention he gets."

"Hmm," June nodded. She wanted to ask, "Every single time?" But then she realized she needn't have asked at all. It wasn't necessary for a woman to have her feet in the stirrups to be vulnerable. Just being in a small room with a closed door could be perilous if you were with a bad person.

"I like it when he asks me to help," Jessica said.

"Oh?"

"He explains everything so thoroughly. He gets you involved, you know?"

"But you think he's a dork!" June whispered.

"He's not a dork all the time," she whispered back. "When he's talking about medical things, he's very thorough, very involving. It's fun. I got to put a stitch in Bobby Randall's cut foot. Cool," she said, twirling away. "Ah, June? Dr. Fairfield?"

"Oh!" June skittered down the hall to her office. "Dr. Fairfield, hi," she said, a bit too cheerily, trying to mask her nervousness about this situation. "Sorry to have kept you. It's busy around here to —"

"Yes, I'm busy as well. What can I do for you, Dr. Hudson?" She immediately heard two things in his voice. He was an older man, perhaps Elmer's age, and he was cold.

"I operate a clinic in Grace Valley, Dr. Fairfield, and have recently invited Dr. John Stone to see patients here. We're a small town without an OB, and since he's added family medicine to his credentials, I think he's tailor-made for us. But of course I have to check his references."

His first response was a condescending laugh. "Grace Valley? Do you have a prestigious country club there? An upscale yacht club, perhaps?"

"Why . . . no. Nothing even close."

"Well, I confess I'm confused. I wouldn't have expected John to turn up there."

"Here?"

"In a, well, a little bend in the road without a five star resort."

"Ah . . . and would you care to enlighten me, Dr. Fairfield? Explain why?"

"Oh, the Dr. Stone I knew was extremely upwardly motivated. He required a lot of attention, in the forms of money, prestige and recognition. The Fairfield Women's Clinic suited him perfectly. Our patients are among the Bay Area's most prominent."

June didn't know what to say. Not only was that contrary to what she thought she knew about John, it had nothing whatever to do with her current problem. When she'd seen John delivering Julianna Dickson's baby she had been convinced he had the stuff of a small town doctor even though he dressed out of *Gentleman's Quarterly.* He seemed fancy, yet comfortable with Grace Valley's simplicity. She didn't really care about his taste in restaurants; she only cared

180

whether their ethics matched. She was only looking to dispel suspicion of improprieties in the examining room. It took her a long second to respond. "Well, that certainly doesn't describe Grace Valley. . . ."

"And family medicine? I would have put him in cosmetic surgery . . . or cardiology. Something more . . . visible."

"Then you haven't been in touch with him since he left the Fairfield Clinic?"

"Hardly. We didn't part on the best of terms."

"Do you mind telling me why that was?" she asked.

"It's very simple, my dear. Dr. Stone not only wished to leave us to pursue a private practice of his own, but he also wished to sell us back the partnership we so generously gave him. At a handsome price, naturally."

John? Greedy? She might describe him as pretty, maybe even superficial, but greedy hadn't come to mind.

"And his rapport with his patients?" June asked.

There was a long silence followed by a heavy sigh. "A reasonable number of people asked for him specifically. As for his ability, I'd have to say he met the requirements. Met the minimum standards."

"You'd *have* to say? That doesn't sound like a glowing recommendation."

"Young woman, you must certainly be aware that I'm not obligated to speak to you at all, much less to cast aspersions on the name of a qualified doctor who, as far as I know, practiced adequate medicine." Aha, June thought, there's a doctor trying to avoid a lawsuit. "I'll go out on a limb, however, and tell you to watch your back if you're cutting him in for half," Dr. Fairfield finished.

My dear and *Young woman,* he'd said. The man was a superior jackass. This was a waste of time; she didn't have the least confidence in his opinion. She rested her forehead in her hand. "Is there anything else you can tell me about Dr. Stone? I assure you it will be held in the strictest confidence."

"Yes, he's a good golfer. Plays to a four handicap. Perhaps that will come in handy in your Grace Springs."

"Valley," she corrected. "Thank you so much for your time."

He didn't say goodbye. The phone simply went dead in her hand. She stared at it in amazement. He must be mighty secure to be so rude, she thought.

There was a tap-tap-tap and her office

door opened. There stood Elmer. Her mouth was still open, the receiver still in her hand. "Your best friend just drop dead?" he asked.

She closed her mouth, replaced the phone and motioned him inside. She didn't speak until the door was closed and Elmer sat in the chair facing her desk.

"Dad, I was trying to do a routine check of John's references and just spoke to the head of the women's clinic where he was a partner some years ago. Dr. Fairfield of the Fairfield Women's Clinic."

"I know of the place," Elmer said. "Has an outstanding reputation. They do a lot of community service work. Free clinics for poor women and the like."

She sat back. "Dr. Fairfield is an insufferable ass."

His eyebrows lifted. "Maybe that best explains John's departure. . . ."

"He doesn't have much nice to say about John," she said. "Apparently they didn't part on the friendliest of terms."

"Ah, I see your problem. You don't know what to believe."

"Exactly!"

"June, you should try to talk to an office manager. Or someone who worked alongside John, like one of the nurses. His

'Charlotte.' An ideal resource."

"Of course," she said, relieved, reaching for the phone. "You never know how little you know about things like this until it's upon you. I'm used to knowing people half their lives before I consider them for employment."

"Haven't you waited a little long for this? The man's been seeing patients here for a couple of months."

"Hmm," she said. "Been busy." But Elmer was frowning. He knew. He didn't know what he knew, but he knew she was far more efficient than this.

Before she could lift the receiver, the phone rang. "June Hudson," she answered.

"June, dearest," came Birdie's high-pitched and lilting voice. "Are you very very busy?"

"Oh . . . no more than usual. Are you all right?"

"Oh perfectly. But I was wondering if you'd do me an enormous favor."

"If I can."

"There's a large box on my porch. It has a couple of rugs, a couple of pictures, some fabric, miscellaneous stuff I picked up at a thrift shop in Rockport . . . and Judge has the little truck. Would you be a darling girl and put that box in your Jeep when you're done with work and bring it out to Leah's farm?"

"Leah's?"

"Yes, dear. A couple of us are out here helping her get organized, and that box of stuff is meant for her."

"Sure," June said slowly. "Anything else I can bring?"

"Well, these boys do love their sodas. Regular Coke, if I'm right."

"My pleasure."

"You're an angel. Bye."

Again June was left staring at the phone. "Birdie," she said to her father.

"Yes, that's why I came over. There are some neighbors out at Leah's, getting her farm straight. She's darn near missed planting. She won't be able to do as much, but we can't have her miss seeding altogether. So I'm taking that big barbecue grill from out behind Fuller's Café and I'm going to cook some burgers and weenies a little later to feed the whole bunch. You're welcome for dinner, if you're in the mood."

"Wow. Who's organizing this?"

Elmer stood. "I don't rightly know. You know how these things happen."

Gus Craven had isolated his family on their farm at the edge of the valley, and the whole town knew he abused them. His benders were legendary and his violence terrifying. Since no one could seem to do anything about it, people got used to it and left them alone. It always seemed more dangerous for Leah and the boys if neighbors tried to intervene, so they held back, soft-pedaled and prayed for the best. But for a few visits from the police, that old bad seed was left to do his trouble. That was the worst of small town life — that everyone knew and no one could do a damn thing about it.

And this was the best of small town life — that there were people present at Leah's farm, trying to help her get back on her feet, trying to set right what Gus had for too long mishandled.

Gus had been behind bars for just two months; by now the bruises were healed. What money Leah had, if any, had been used up several weeks ago. June knew that Birdie had looked in on Leah to see if there was anything she needed, though it was well-known she and the boys needed everything. Women from the Presbyterian Church visited her, took some rummage sale clothes and gathered up nonperishables. But what June saw as she drove onto the Craven property took her breath away. Smoke billowed from a large picnic grill where her dad and George Fuller turned burgers and hot dogs. Trestle tables had been set up in the yard along with folding chairs she recognized from the high school cafeteria. She saw her aunt's old Cadillac in the yard beside the Barstow sisters' car, and thanked God they weren't cooking. Sam Cussler was up on a ladder, painting the house. The bakery truck had pulled up to the back porch and its doors stood open; Syl and Burt were unloading fresh buns.

June parked the Jeep and carried the box to the front porch. There she found Tom Toopeek's father, Lincoln, methodically stretching new screen over the front door. She could smell the fresh paint, lemon oil, vinegar and cookies. She put the box on the porch and stepped through the portal to the living room, where the activity became still more exciting. The old carpet had been stripped away and a new one, rolled, lay against the wall. At another wall Susan Stone and Julianna Dickson were consumed with laughter as Julianna tried to peel a runaway sheet of wallpaper off Susan's back. "Um, I think that goes on the wall," June said, and they almost fell to the floor in their hilarity. The fumes of too much wallpaper paste, maybe?

She was nearly knocked over by some little

ones racing through the house. It turned out to be Sydney Stone, little Stan and one of the Dickson kids. "Syd!" Susan shouted. "Slow down!"

"They can't slow down," Julianna said. "Too much sugar."

Leah and Birdie were smoothing a table linen over a dining room table. June barely recognized Leah. Her color was rich, her hair clean and silky, and she wore khaki slacks, a collared shirt and hiking boots instead of her usual limp and colorless housedress. She looked years younger. She smiled at June, who realized Leah was only thirty-three. Life with Gus had made her look haggard. His absence had brought back her natural vitality.

"June, look what Birdie found for us! We've never had dining furniture before. And a hutch, too! And enough chairs for everyone to sit at one time."

"It was Rakinstock's old piece," Birdie said. "You know how they're always trading out furniture faster than Judge changes socks. They were just going to donate it anyway, and I said, I've got just the place. Now I guess we have to be on the lookout for some special glass and china pieces to fill up that breakfront."

"There's a time I didn't want glass in the

house, but maybe now . . . I never imagined anything so . . . so beautiful," Leah admitted.

Another shriek of uncontrolled laughter made June turn to find Susan and Julianna on the floor, holding each other up, crushing a huge snarled piece of wallpaper underneath and between them. June couldn't suppress a smile of envy; they made cute girlfriends.

She recognized her aunt's hat slowly descending the stairs, the wide brim seeming to float. "Birdie . . . Oh, hello dear," Myrna said. "Birdie, we're ready to start painting the master bedroom, but we need another tarpaulin. Will you send one up?"

"I'll get Judge to bring it up. He's on the back porch fixing the kitchen window. Be just a minute."

As the sun slowly sank westward, June saw a transformation take place at the Craven farm. The house was redecorated and furnished, clothes were hung in closets and folded into new chests of drawers. The cupboards were filled with food and dishes, the fields closest to the house were planted and everything that needed repair was seen to. There was a smile everywhere she looked. The police chief who had carted Gus off was sanding down a porch rail so it could be painted, and the judge who'd locked him up was installing new doorknobs and water faucets.

People kept coming through the afternoon, and George Fuller kept dragging more and more meat out of a huge cooler in his truck. There were sodas and chips and potato salad and pickles and cookies galore.

When the sun went down, a bonfire was lit. Tired workers dragged folded lawn chairs out of car trunks and truck beds, coffee and cocoa brewed, children roasted marshmallows and Burt Crandall passed out huge slices of pie and cake.

June had no idea when this barn raising had been planned, who had done the calling or how the chores had been divvied up. She supposed Birdie was at the helm of this project, but people around Grace Valley caught on very quickly. They dug into their basements and attics, sheds and barns for items that would be needed. They were resourceful and giving by nature. And trusting, usually . . .

"June?" John Stone sat on the ground beside her. "Isn't this the best thing you've ever seen in your life? This is what I've always wanted. This is what I thought I might get close to when I made that deal with the government to practice a little rural medicine."

"It was a little too rural for you, though, was it?" she asked.

"The reservation isn't the same as a quaint small town," he admitted. "I know my limitations. I'm not gritty enough for that work."

"John, you still have creases in your jeans, tassels on your shoes. . . ."

"What can I say? I'm a fashion plate."

"Right out of *Esquire* . . ."

He laughed. "Grace Valley won't be ruined by a little style." He reached into his shirt pocket and pulled out a folded piece of paper. "Here are the names and phone numbers of a few people who I worked with at the Fairfield Clinic. I'd have given this information to you sooner if I'd known you were going to check references that far in my past. Here's the office manager, medical assistant, OB nurse. You would get a more accurate picture of what I was like to work with from any of them. Dr. Fairfield hates me."

She was momentarily taken aback by the force of his words. As she took the paper from him, she asked cautiously, "Mind telling me why he hates you?"

"June, it's strictly personality crap, absolutely *nothing* professional. The old man and I didn't see eye to eye on anything. Don't worry, I didn't break any laws or anything. I left the Fairfield Clinic over six years ago, and I left because of the stress of working in an environment of almost constant haranguing and disapproval. This place is a fresh start for us. I think Susan and Syd are going to be really happy here. I can't tell you what it felt like to hear that Dr. Fairfield was waiting on the phone to talk to you. It was like that old man's animosity was going to follow me around forever." He stood. "I left all that behind me a long time ago — and gladly. Fortunately, almost everyone else at the clinic respected me and liked working with me. But don't take my word for it. Call some of these women. They'll vouch for me."

"Okay. I'll be happy to."

"Thanks. I appreciate it. I'd better get Princess Sydney and Susan home."

"I'm heading out myself, still have a couple of stops to make."

"Anything I can help with?" he asked.

This was so hard. What was not to like about this guy? "No thanks, John. Just a couple of people I like to check on on the way home most nights."

"You're good to this town, June."

"This is a good town, John." She hoped there hadn't been a warning tone to her voice, but it just may have crept in.

She was surprised that Mikos hadn't come to the Craven farm. She was glad he hadn't, but surprised. As she turned down his drive, she could see that the house was dark. It was early for him to have turned in. As her headlights strafed the front of the house, she saw his silhouette sitting in the chair on the porch. She also saw the table, the pitcher of tea and Sadie Five at the porch edge, wagging. "Oh no."

But then she knew this was what she'd always expected — and the reason she stopped regularly. Because he was not interested in medical intervention, and his symptoms could certainly have been life threatening. He had the stoic acceptance of a man ready to cross over. She thought it was partly because he missed his wife so much. When she reached the porch and greeted Sadie, massaging her neck, she found something she had not expected. There was a ribbon that attached a note to Sadie's collar. It said, *June, take care of Sadie Five. You girls need each other. Mikos*

TWELVE

June made three phone calls from Mikos's phone — one to Mikos's daughter, Maria, one to the funeral director in Garberville and one to Tom Toopeek, still out at Leah's farm. That last brought Tom and Elmer.

June was accustomed to her father's feistiness, to his nosiness and high energy. But as Mikos was lifted onto the gurney to be taken away, Elmer seemed to shrink and age. It jolted June to see it. Even though he was past seventy, she was nowhere near ready to accept losing him.

"Do you think he gave up too soon?" Elmer asked in a small voice.

"Yes! Don't you?"

"I don't know, June. He was satisfied with his life. He missed his wife. He knew his heart was giving out. . . ."

"Yes, he knew, and there was still a lot we could have done, if he'd only let us get involved!"

"He didn't want to mess around with it. He was pretty much done, I guess."

"Well, there might be children and grandchildren who will take that decision a little personally!"

"Don't get mad at Mikos, June. I'm not going with him."

She let out her breath. She was sorry. She didn't mean to be so abrasive, but it suddenly threw the fear of God into her. Just the thought of losing Elmer was more than she could bear.

The sharp edge of her anger gave way to tears when she saw her dad clutching Mikos's hand and leaning over him, saying goodbye. "It was a mighty good time, old boy. You were always the best part of the journey. Thanks for everything."

Elmer let them take his old friend away, and went to stand beside his daughter.

"I will never be able to say goodbye to you in that way," she said. "Is that clear?"

"Come on, June. Let's go to George's and have another piece of pie. He's probably got a little something under the counter to help get the bug out of your ass."

"Just so you know," she said stiffly.

She had to collect Sadie's dishes and food and put them in the Jeep, and though she looked around for a leash, she knew she wouldn't find one. "Things will be different when you're not on a farm," she told the dog. "You'll have to be very well behaved if you're going to stay with me."

Sadie made a yowling sound that closely resembled, "All right," causing June to do a double take.

June should have expected the old guard, the official mourners, lined up at the lunch counter with coffee cups and pie plates in front of them: Sam, Lincoln, Judge, Burt, and Bud Burnham. George was behind the counter. Sadie came in beside June, wagging happily at all the old men, and June gave George one of her dishes. "Sadie will have a water, straight up, and I'll settle for black coffee." She sat on a stool at the end of the bar.

George reached under the counter and brought out a bottle of Jack Daniels. With coffeepot in one hand and liquor bottle in the other, he passed down the line. Sam tapped his coffee cup twice, with two fingers. Lincoln waved a hand over his cup for coffee only. Judge held up one finger, Burt made a gun out of his thumb and index finger and shot it into the cup, Bud indicated an inch level and June had already asked for black coffee only. "Give me hers," Elmer said, and his cup was generously

196

laced with bourbon.

"He was a good man, lived a good life."

"May he sleep well tonight and every night. . . ."

". . . And may the streams be full where he fishes . . ."

". . . And his friends and family happy to see him . . ."

"Good night, old friend," Elmer said, lifting his cup.

"Good night," they all chorused. And drank to him.

June was awakened in the middle of the night by the sound of Sadie squeaking and pawing at the back door. June was accustomed to being jolted out of bed by the phone, but this was a new sound, so she came awake slowly, trying to make sense of what she heard.

When she got to the kitchen, she said, "I bet you're used to having your very own door at the farm, aren't you? We might have to do something like that if you're going to stay with me. I'm not sure it's a good idea for you to come to the office with me."

Sadie craned her neck to look up at June, and made a sound of agreement, a pleasant yowl. June liked the sound and smiled down at her new roommate.

"Okay, try not to be long. It's been a hard day and I'm ready to get back to sleep."

Sadie stepped out onto the back porch and stood, sniffing the air. She was motionless, nose up, concentrating.

"Remember to put it on the grass, Sadie," June said.

Sadie was not distracted. She continued to sniff the air, and the only thing that moved was her twitching nose.

"Well, I guess there's a process to everything," June said aloud. She hadn't had a dog since she was sixteen, the year her old terrier, Lucky, died. She didn't get another dog because she was going away to school, then because she was working long hours, then because it had been so long since she'd had a dog she didn't feel that pull anymore.

She went to get the coffeepot ready for morning while Sadie did her thing. June glanced out the window and saw that Sadie was now standing in the yard, sniffing the air. "We're going to have a real problem if you have to get up at 2:00 a.m. to go outside and look around, have a smell. This is a little, you know, inconvenient." She scooped coffee into the basket, filled the pot with water, and then it hit her. She had not had a dog because she was afraid of the emotional bond. She always knew she could love another dog as much as Lucky, and love it deeply. But she wasn't sure she could take a pet's death again. It was too much. It was astonishing how horribly that could grieve a person, how much pain could come with that loss.

She looked outside but could no longer see the dog. She went to the back door, out onto the porch and called, "Sadie! Come here, girl!" As she whistled, it all come back to her — the sounds, the calls, the *feelings.*

But Sadie didn't come.

June left the door ajar just a crack so that when Sadie came back she could nose it open. The porch light was on, and June sat on the living room couch. She began to nod off almost immediately, waiting for Sadie to return, then suddenly she was wide awake, as though struck by lightning. She glanced at her watch; it was 4:00 a.m. She'd slept sitting up for two hours.

"Sadie?" she called, but her house was silent.

"June, you are so stupid!" she said to herself, jumping up. She grabbed her keys and got in the Jeep, only much later thinking about the fact that she hadn't even taken her cell phone or pager and could have been out of reach for an emergency. She didn't realize till she was halfway to her destination that she was wearing a fairly thin nightgown and no shoes.

She drove up the long dark drive to Mikos's house and when her headlights strafed the front she could see the chairs, the table, the pitcher of tea they had neglected to put away. And there, on the porch, lay the furry mound patiently waiting for her master and friend to return. June left the lights on her and stepped out of the Jeep. Sadie lifted her head and thumped her tail a few times.

"Come on, Sadie. He's not coming back. Come on, sweetheart."

Sadie stood and sniffed the air.

"It's okay. Come on."

The dog slowly walked down the porch steps, squeaking a little, then stopped and looked back at the porch once more.

June crouched and grabbed the thick fur of Sadie's neck and kissed her long snoot, dropping a tear onto Sadie's fur. "Didn't he tell you that it would be just you and me now? Well, you're not going to see him again for a while . . . for a long while, I hope. Come on, old girl. I need someone to watch over me so I don't let myself be too much alone."

The very next morning, June phoned from the list of references John Stone had given her, this time *before* going to the clinic.

"Hello, this is Dr. June Hudson calling for Lisa Rapp."

"This is Lisa."

"Hi, Lisa. I was given your name and number by John Stone. I understand you are his former OB nurse."

"That's right."

"I'm calling from Grace Valley, upper Mendocino County. I have a small general practice here. Our population is about fifteen hundred and John is going to see patients in our clinic. I'm calling you for a reference."

"Well, you've got it. He's the best OB-GYN I've ever worked with."

Now we're getting someplace, June thought. "Really? Tell me what makes him so special, if you don't mind."

"Everything about him is special. He's ethical and kind, he has a great sense of humor, he's highly skilled and has super instincts. Besides, the patients love him."

"Would you have him for your doctor?"

"I did have him for my doctor! He's a miracle worker with infertility. My husband and I had a baby seven years ago, after trying for years. Thanks to John, we squeaked one out just in time. I'm now forty-six and perimenopausal. I have a feeling that if I hadn't met and worked for John Stone, I might never have had a baby."

Thirty-nine. June mentally calculated. I could do that.

"Now that's the kind of endorsement I've been looking for," she said.

"Well, everyone loves John."

Not everyone, June thought. "I did get very high recommendations from the doctors he worked with in his family medicine residency. But there's this one sticky wicket — maybe you can help me out."

"I'll try."

"He spent years at the Fairfield Clinic, yet Dr. Fairfield clearly despises him. And I have no idea why."

"John and Dr. Fairfield disagreed often, and I have to say, through absolutely no prejudice, it was John who was usually right. They tangled on issues ranging from when to schedule a C-section to John's divorce. . . ."

"John is divorced?"

"You didn't know?"

"No, he never said. I assumed Susan —"

"Second wife. But if you want to know more about that, I really think it's up to John to tell you. Wouldn't you agree?"

"I suppose, but —"

"Dr. Fairfield was very clear that he

believed marriage was forever, and disapproved of divorce. He can be so . . . so . . . *antagonistic!* He's done a good thing with that clinic, you know? But he didn't do it alone. There have been some outstanding doctors there who have contributed to its growth and reputation, one of them being John Stone. But if Fairfield decides he doesn't like you . . ."

June could imagine; she had talked to the man. He was arrogant and insufferable. "And that's all there is to it? Dr. Fairfield is a difficult man?"

"Not all. Look, Dr. —"

"June. Please."

"Look, June, I don't think I should be telling you this, so please keep it between us. I love John Stone and I don't want him to feel I've betrayed him, but I'm pretty sure I know why Fairfield despises him."

"Okay. Go ahead. I won't say anything." And I need to know, she thought.

"John was invited into the partnership and he made a modest investment to enter. He was their darling boy and they were thrilled to have him. Older doctors who had been there since the day Fairfield opened began to retire, young doctors were brought in as associates, and just by pure timing and luck, John was attaining seniority and voting power. Then he and Fairfield started to tangle, John filed for divorce, the pressure got worse and he decided to leave the clinic. His original investment and voting power had grown — it was his single ace in the hole. He offered to leave quietly, give up his vote and pension for cash. And he inflated the price."

"Inflated?"

"He was pissed. The partnership had allowed Fairfield to unfairly harangue him. And the partnership got stuck with the bill." She paused. "Partnership meant loyalty to John. He stuck his neck out for them, but they. . . . Some of the other doctors, nervous about what Fairfield could do to them, turned their back on John."

"So he hit them all in the pocketbook, Dr. Fairfield and the partners."

"Exactly. And June? I think if Dr. Fairfield had been the least bit civil, John would probably have stayed. But he made it unbearable. I quit, too. I've worked for three different OB's since . . . and none can hold a candle to John."

"I don't think I've seen John mad," June said.

"It's a rare and beautiful thing." Lisa laughed. "Mess with his patients or his family and you'll see him flare."

"Or his money, obviously . . ."

"No, no, no, you don't understand. Oh Jesus. Please, ask John for the details, but it was this godawful mess about his divorce. He'd been separated for at least a couple of years, his wife was dragging her feet on a settlement, Fairfield was riding him constantly. John was already involved with Susan, who was very young, and I think she might even have been pregnant at the time, and he wasn't legally free to marry her even though they'd been living together and he hadn't been with his wife for years, and — Oh God, John's going to kill me . . . if Susan doesn't get to me first!"

"Okay, okay, I see where this is going."

"You can't imagine how awful it was at the time. The stress was terrible!"

"The fodder of every contemporary talk show. The wife was there during the hard years of becoming a doctor, dumped for the younger woman. Susan wasn't a nurse or anything, was she?"

"Why yes, as a matter of fact. But June, it really wasn't like that. It wasn't that old wife-put-him-through-med-school thing or —"

"You don't have to explain, Lisa. It's none of my business. I think I get the basic gist of things. It would be hard to dislike Susan anyway. She seems like such a lovely person."

"Believe me, she's a huge improvement over the first Mrs. Stone. I mean *huge!*"

June ended the conversation by telling Lisa she'd been a big help. She tried to get the other two people on John's list, but ended up leaving messages on machines. She doubted she would ask John about his divorce. It was always better to have people volunteer things of such a personal nature.

So what do I know? she asked herself. That John was hated by Dr. Fairfield because of partnership money. That he was loved by his old nurse and, according to her, his old staff and former patients. That he could get mad when pushed too far. That his second wife was probably as nice as she seemed.

So what about Christina Baker? June wondered, and decided that in the absence of any more detailed information, she might just have to ask John about that. It was a very delicate matter; a person could be easily offended by the question. But she would eventually have to ask it. When the time was right.

THIRTEEN

Time off was something June just didn't have . . . until John Stone came to town and began to share the load. It was yet another reason she wanted so desperately for him to work out. This was what she had been waiting for — a Sunday afternoon to call her own. She started off the day by going to church and ended it with Sunday dinner at her dad's with Myrna.

Sunday dinner at Elmer's had gone unchanged since June's mother had died. He seared a roast on both sides and stuck it in the oven with vegetables, then went to church and let it do its magic. When he returned with June and Myrna in tow, he poured himself a cabernet, Myrna a martini, June a cup of tea in case there was doctoring to do, and they sat in the small living room that June's mother had furnished far too many years ago.

On this day, June had said to her dad, "I'll

have a glass of that cabernet, Dad. John Stone is taking care of the town."

"Well, hell's bells and hallelujah!"

The afternoon waned and the late spring sun settled over the trees and rooftops. Mellowed by the red wine, June rocked on her porch, Sadie comfortable at her side. This was the life, she realized, though it took willpower to just sit there, to examine the tense feeling of doing nothing with her hands. She thought about her needlework, untouched for months; she considered the novel she'd been reading for weeks. There were at least ten videos she'd purchased and had yet to watch. But she sat idle for a change. The entire evening was hers. There was no reason to hurry, no reason to stay busy.

Christina Baker is probably just overreacting, she thought for the hundredth time. John Stone is probably one of the best doctors in California, and I've got him. These were her thoughts, maybe prayers, as she idled the time away.

He came up the long drive from the road, though June didn't see a vehicle. He probably could have approached from either side of her house, out of the trees, but instead of surprising her, he gave her lots of time to get used to the idea that he was coming to her house. Unarmed.

He was clean shaven and freshly groomed. The sleeves on his red-and-black plaid shirt were rolled up to right below the elbow and he wore an oversize belt buckle. His shoulders were as broad as she remembered, his thighs hard in his crisp blue jeans. As he got closer, Sadie perked up and sat at attention. She made a throaty sound of greeting and whacked her tail on the porch floor a few times. He smiled at the dog. He braced one foot on the top porch step, leaned down and reached a callused hand out to Sadie. "Good idea. A dog."

Sadie licked his hand. Sadie knew what she was doing.

"Not dressed in drag today, Jim?"

He chuckled.

"How's your friend?" she asked.

"I don't know. Haven't seen him since that night."

"Ah, that makes sense. I wouldn't hang around a place where I'd taken a bullet either. Lemonade?"

"Thanks. You sure it's okay?"

"I guess so. Anyway, what if I said it wasn't?"

He spread his hands. "I'd have to try to talk you into it."

That was a relief. She didn't want him to

leave, but she wouldn't mind if he thought she had control of this situation. She went in the house and put the pitcher and two glasses on a tray.

Suddenly, she had a hard time remembering when she'd had feelings like this. A rush of excitement. Light-headedness. Her ears were hot. There was a giddy weakness behind her knees. How silly.

"So, what brings you out of the woods?" she asked, placing the tray on the porch table.

"I just wanted to thank you," he said. He smiled devilishly, still scratching behind Sadie's ears. Sadie's eyes were closed and she strained toward him dramatically. She was in ecstasy.

"You thanked me the other night."

"All right then. I wanted to see you."

"Well, I guess you can never be too grateful. Make yourself comfortable."

"You didn't call the police while you were inside getting the lemonade, did you?"

"Of course not. I think you probably are the police."

He was about to ascend the porch steps and came up short, a rather stricken look on his face. "Talk like that could get me killed."

"By who? The good guys or the bad guys?"

"By all of them."

"I probably won't say anything to anyone." Then she smiled a small sly smile. "If you behave yourself."

"You shouldn't make assumptions about people, Doc." He drew his heavy eyebrows together and made his scary face. "You don't really know anything about me."

"I know you pretended to faint . . . and you winked at me. And don't call me Doc. It makes me crane my neck looking for my father. It's a family business, you know."

"You know why I fainted?" he asked.

"So you could lose the gun without looking suspicious to your wounded friend."

"Phew. They should hire you to write *Dragnet* episodes." When he came up on the porch, the boards protested. He stood in front of the swing and judged the chains that held it to the ceiling. "Think she'll take me?"

"Man about your size put it up. Let's see if he's any good."

"I like the way you think," he said, but he sat slowly, gradually letting his full weight rest on the swing. That's when she saw he'd polished his boots. That was also when she wished she had some sewing in her lap, though she wasn't entirely sure why.

"You said you've lived here all your life,"

he began.

"The year I was born, there were 798 people in the town called Grace. We were incorporated years later as Grace Valley. There was a big fight about it. Some people wanted to pay homage to my grandfather — who I never knew, who my dad barely knew — and call the town Hudson Valley."

"But they didn't?"

"No. Funny thing, the surviving Hudsons — my dad and my wacky aunt Myrna — couldn't have cared less. Myrna finally gave the town a thousand dollars toward a statue of Grandfather Hudson so they'd move on. Nothing gets a town moving like money."

Jim frowned. "Where's the statue?"

"Oh, there isn't one. Probably never will be. Besides, my grandfather didn't settle the town. It was already here. All he did was make money in the Bay Area, marry late in life and build his young wife a big house on a hill. I think he threw a few bucks at the town in the decade he lived here. And I think it was my grandmother, his young wife, who called the place Grace. She said people got here by the grace of God and angels."

"A religious woman," he said.

"Not really. More likely a grateful woman. She was a pretty but poor girl and married a man old enough to be her grandfather. People probably thought she was a gold digger, but if you ask the only living person to know her, Aunt Myrna, she'll tell you her mother adored her father. She was kind and gentle and helped people whenever she could. She died in her early thirties. My brokenhearted grandfather followed soon after."

June didn't tell him about the resemblance. Erma Hudson had been reed thin, fair-skinned and with what they once called dishwater blond hair, like June. She'd been freckled like June, Myrna said, which of course didn't show in the oil portrait. The moment little June Hudson saw the portrait of her long-deceased grandmother, she'd claimed her as her angel. Until her mother, Marilyn, died. Then she had two. Angels were a very big thing in Grace Valley.

"My aunt Myrna was only fourteen when her parents were both dead, and her little brother, my father, was two. She raised him."

"Alone?"

"Uh-huh. Seventy years ago a girl that age might have married and had her own children, so it wasn't exactly an oddity. But Myrna didn't marry until my father was through medical school and married himself."

"This seems like a good town. It would be good to be from here," he said.

June told him about the legend of the road angel at the pass; about Morton Claypool, who Myrna had misplaced twenty years ago; about how the town rebuilt Leah Craven's house and seeded her south field.

"Not all small towns have that kind of compassion," he pointed out to her. "Sometimes they're cruel and crazy and unforgiving."

"We have more than one face, you know. We have our problems, our bad seeds. Leah's house was fixed up and her field planted by folk who are so relieved her abusive husband, Gus, is finally behind bars. And have you ever been out to Dandies? I wouldn't mind if that place accidentally caught fire. Tom calls me out a couple of times a month to stitch up brawlers from there.

"But, in general, it's a well-meaning town. I remember a particularly crazy period . . . about the bear."

"The bear."

"A black bear in a bad mood. A logger on the northeast rim was mauled . . . we almost lost his arm. The next day a rural woman just south of town spotted a bear tearing her laundry off the line, so we knew it was on the move. The woman shot at the bear and sent it into the woods, then she sent up the alarm.

"For a few days you could cut the tension around here with a knife. Women carried guns in their pails and laundry baskets, people drove their kids to school, Tom Toopeek sat on top of his Range Rover with a rifle near the schoolyard and the café was empty. Instead of meeting there for coffee, the local men were seen at various crossroads around the valley, exchanging information about where the bear might be found. I remember we kept our garbage inside, closed our windows and doors tight, and ate mostly cold food. It wasn't a good time to cool a pie on a windowsill or have the aroma of freshly baked bread wafting through the woods.

"Forestry held a town meeting right away and asked the locals not to hunt the bear — they wanted to trap and remove it. They might as well have asked them not to take a breath. Bud Burnham accidentally shot out Ray Gilmore's knee. That was a god-awful mess. He still has a peg leg. Never got mad at Bud though — which is another thing about that period. They took it as a perilous time and knew there would be risks, what with every jittery person in town carrying a loaded gun and jumping at shadows.

"They got a black bear. Shot her dead. Some Forestry people backtracked her trail and found two cubs that had to be transported to a game refuge. One of Mama's paws was deformed — she was missing two claws and pads. She might have had an accident or fight years earlier and she was fully healed. But see, her claws didn't match the injury. She hadn't mauled the logger. They got the wrong bear."

"Did they go back out?"

"Nope. Blood lust satisfied, they all went home. Then they told their families that no matter, they should always be on the lookout for a bear that comes this far down into the valley. You never know."

He leaned on the swing, head back, thinking through the logic. Then he came forward and said, "You remind me of my grandmother."

She smiled. "You old sweet-talker."

"She used to talk to me while she ironed, and she ironed all the time. She ironed everything. That's when she'd tell me stories from her childhood."

June realized she'd been talking for a couple of hours. It was dusk and would soon be dark. She shivered as the chill crept into the air, and she wondered what she was to do with him after dark. Invite him in for dinner? Offer to drive him back to wherever he'd left his vehicle?

"Tell me something about yourself," she said. "Anything."

"Hmm. Well, if things were different, I might ask you out to a fancy restaurant for dinner."

"That's really not about you, now, is it?"

"That's about the best I can do right now."

"Okay. . . . How different would things have to be?" she asked.

"Very." He laughed. "I'll bet you look incredible in — what do they call 'em? A little black dress?"

"That's what they call them, and I don't have one. I used to, but —" *But I stopped having dates.* "We don't have a fancy restaurant around here anyway."

"But things would be different, remember. Do you dance?"

"I don't remember."

He laughed again. "We could get us one of those floor maps with the feet on 'em. Or fake it."

"There's no dancing around here, either."

"You look like a dancer. Long legged and skinny."

"Great come-on, Jim. Skinny. You should throw in flat chested for good measure."

"I like skinny girls. . . ." he murmured.

"Fortunately, I like stupid guys. . . ."

He began to glower, then slowly a broad smile took over. "I'm smarter than I look. I just don't want you to notice . . . I'm seducing you."

"Well, lucky you, I didn't notice. At all."

"So, what have people said about you?"

She thought for a minute. "That I'm sturdy. And plain."

"Plain?" he repeated, shocked. "Gimme a break!"

"In fact, it was Arlise Cruise, the mother of my childhood rival and nemesis, Nancy Cruise — no relation to Tom. She used to say things like, 'She does real well for a plain girl.' God, she hated me."

"You must have gotten all the good-looking boys."

"I got at least one, who played touch tag with me and Nancy all through school. If I ever see him again I'm going to sedate and torture him."

"There's nothing more pure than a woman's revenge, now is there."

"You don't want to cross me," she said threateningly. She shivered again.

"We'd better decide," he suggested.

"Decide what?"

"If I'm going in or going away."

"I'd like to shiver for a few more minutes, if you don't mind," she said. "I haven't made up my mind yet."

"Take your time," he said. But he stood, reached out a hand to her and drew her slowly to her feet. "Take all the time you need," he said, pulling her closer.

"Inviting you in might be moving a little too fast, even for us. After all, I only know you by way of a criminal gunshot wound."

That made him laugh, but low in his throat. She moved closer to him, just as he moved his hands to her hips, drawing her. It was better . . . warmer against him. He slipped an arm around her waist, and with his other hand, lifted her chin. In the twilight, he looked down into her eyes. "You're beautiful . . . for a skinny girl. . . ."

"You're not that bad looking . . . for a dope. . . ." she answered.

He bent his head, his lips just barely touching hers . . .

The phone rang.

His head immediately snapped up as though the sound were a signal. He scanned the tree line but held her against him. "It's okay," she whispered. But still he searched his surroundings, his eyes narrowed, his body tense. "We'll let the machine get it," she said, but she couldn't seem to recapture his attention. It was the only time she'd ever seen a man appear to prowl while standing completely still. "Oh, hell," she said, reaching up and plunging her fingers into the thick hair at his temples, pulling his mouth down to meet hers, where his initial surprise melted into unmistakable appreciation.

June's first thought was that it had been too damn long since she'd been kissed like this, then that she'd *never* been kissed like this. As she opened her mouth under his probing tongue she said a quick silent prayer that she was right about this guy, that he was really a good man. Because whatever he turned out to be, she was already locked in pretty tight.

The phone's final ring was cut in half by the clicking of the answering machine as it picked up. Then there was the familiar beep. And then John Stone's voice, a breathless, frantic edge to it. "June? June, if you're there, pick up! June, I'm on my way out to 482. There's been an accident! We have injuries."

"Damn!" June said, pulling out of Jim's embrace. "Why *now?*" She nearly tipped over her wicker rocker trying to get into the house to grab the phone. "John! I'm here!

Go ahead!"

"Four-eighty-two, about three-tenths of a mile past Old Mill Road. Mike Dickson found them and is administering first aid. He called Tom Toopeek, who called me, and I'm calling you. You should radio Elmer from the car."

"Paramedics?" She was so accustomed to calling Elmer for help, she didn't even question this order, though a third doctor on the scene was a crowd.

"Tom radioed for them. According to Tom, we have two victims, one unconscious and one conscious but disoriented, possible internal injuries but no apparent compound fractures. Stable pulses and respirations, but that's the extent of vitals Mike Dickson is capable of reporting."

"One car?"

"Yep. Off the road at a curve. Right at dusk. How far are you from there?"

"Ten minutes, maybe less."

"I'll beat you there, so drive carefully. Isn't that the bad spot where . . . ?"

"Angel's Pass. Do we know the victims?" she asked reflexively. She almost always knew the victims. There was the sound of air, almost as though John keyed the mike on and off, but he was calling from a cell phone, so there was no mike. "John?"

"June, it's Judge and Birdie."

"Oh Jesus."

"Just drive carefully."

FOURTEEN

June's head was empty but for the repetitive urgent prayer, *Dear God, let them be okay, dear God, please . . .* She drove too fast and knew it, but couldn't seem to slow herself down. She forgot all about Elmer. When she arrived at the scene everything stopped and she shifted into an eerie slow motion, she entered a sluggish dream state. The lights from Tom's Range Rover and John's BMW illuminated the scene — rising smoke and dust, the steaming wreckage of mangled metal ground up against the tree line.

There, crouched in the headlight beams, John and Tom hovered over a backboard. June couldn't make her legs move; her feet were leaden. It seemed like hours before she got to the others. And when she did arrive, she couldn't quite make sense of the situation. Birdie lay supine, a collar on her neck, a reddened rag on her brow, her beautiful, thick, wiry silver hair matted and stained with blood.

June heard muffled voices, but couldn't make out the words.

Beside Birdie, sitting on the ground, looking ancient and vulnerable rather than imposing and authoritative, was Judge. Dazed. Hunched. A trickle of blood and spittle dripping down his chin. He resembled a nursing home patient more than a judge.

Again she heard the muffled sounds. She saw that the noise was coming from Tom and John, but she couldn't quite hear them. They were shouting at her, but sounded as though they were underwater. Their hands on Birdie, faces turned toward her, they garbled incomprehensible words.

Then, like a vacuum, the fog was sucked away and both her vision and hearing became suddenly acute.

"June! I need an IV set up and Ringer's solution!" John shouted.

"June! We need oxygen here!" Tom yelled.

Instantly she knew. They were using the collar, backboard and first aid equipment out of Tom's Rover and John's medical bag, but June carried the bulk of the ambulance supplies in her Jeep.

Mike Dickson came out of nowhere and was at her side, prodding her. His voice was calm, steady. "Come on, June, you can show me what John needs. Let's get the stuff out of your Jeep."

She came back to herself then. Birdie and Judge became emergency patients and she became a functional doctor. If anyone had noticed that she'd been stunned senseless and temporarily useless, they didn't say anything.

Many hours later, as dawn was breaking, June examined Birdie for the tenth time. They were safely admitted into a hospital room and no longer on the ground beside devastating wreckage.

"Did you see any angels, Birdie?" June asked, flicking the light rapidly across the elderly woman's opened eyes.

"No, but I saw stars."

"I'll bet. Pupils are equal and reactive. You had a nice clunk on the head, and a long rest. Slept like a curled up kitten all night long."

"She never left your side," Elmer said.

"Judge?" Birdie wanted to know.

"He's fine. He's having some X rays, then he'll be back."

Birdie gripped June's wrist. "It's Judge, June. He had a stroke or something."

June frowned. "There's no evidence of a

stroke, Birdie. He was a little disoriented after —"

"He was disoriented *before!* I tried to get his attention, but he had that glazed-over look on his face, like he gets when he's thinking about some complicated court case or baseball, and he doesn't hear a word I'm saying. But instead of snapping out of it, he veered right off the road. Right at that sharp curve. Something's wrong with his head. I mean, more so than usual."

"It's okay, Birdie," June said calmly. "That's exactly why we're keeping him. We'll get some blood, take some X rays. I think I'm going to have Elmer drive him down to Ukiah for an MRI, and maybe, based on what you've said, we'll have him see a neurologist."

"June, you need to check him for a brain tumor. And Alzheimer's. And —"

"Birdie, slow down. Don't get yourself too excited. You're a patient, too. A patient who's been unconscious all night. Now, I'll get the nurse to bring you a pen and paper, and when you think of something you want me to check, you write it down. For the time being, I need for you to be calm."

Birdie took a deep breath. "I know you'll take good care of him, June."

"And of you." She patted her hand reassuringly. "Think you can relax? Or should I get you a little something?"

"I'll be fine, once I see Judge again."

"He should be up in a little bit. And I'll be back shortly."

June left the hospital room and leaned wearily against the wall just outside. It was barely after dawn, but she hadn't so much as dozed all night.

By the time the ambulance had taken Birdie and Judge away and she'd had a chance to really look at their demolished car, she'd felt a huge surge of panic. They shouldn't have come out of that mess alive, much less in the condition they were both in, which was stable. The car had been crushed around a thick tree and there was no windshield or front seat. And if Mike Dickson hadn't come across them, they could have both died, or wandered off, or who knows what. Mike usually avoided 482 going to and from his orchard, for exactly that reason. It was a touchy stretch of road. They hadn't had any fatalities there since June had returned to Grace Valley, but they'd had a few serious accidents.

She remembered too clearly her reaction when she'd seen the wreck, when the fear of losing Birdie had hit her. Some things you just never prepare for. She loved Birdie so, depended on her so — two things she took completely for granted. At that moment, fear had ripped through her like a hunting knife. Birdie had been her mother's best friend for thirty years or more, June's godmother, the mother of June's high school sweetheart, and finally, June's replacement mother after Marilyn's death. But June wasn't alone in her love for Birdie. The whole town adored her.

June closed her eyes. Just the memory of blood on her dear friend's silver pin curls was enough to bring her to her knees. She said a little prayer of thanks that they were, so far, all right.

"She's going to be fine," Elmer said, sneaking quietly out of the room. "I bet that old coot she's married to has a carotid occlusion. Bet he got dizzy and confused and hit some soft shoulder right there at that turn."

"Good guess," she said tiredly. "Dad. I froze."

"I would've, too."

"No, Dad. I froze. I couldn't get out of the car. Then I couldn't breathe, couldn't walk, couldn't hear John and Tom shouting at me."

"I bet. I would've been worse."

"Dad, you don't —"

"June, I *do!* Don't overthink this! They're family! You had a panic response. It happens . . . even to doctors."

"It's never happened to me before."

"Lucky you," Elmer said.

"Are you saying it's happened to you?"

"I can remember once or twice, but not the circumstances. I *do* remember thinking I'd lost my ability to be functional and objective. As time went by I realized I was only in shock for seconds, but seconds that seemed like minutes. You need some rest."

"I'm fine. I'm fine now, I mean. I'm not leaving till I'm sure they're okay. And I have patients."

"You do your early rounds and I'll take your patients. Me and John. Besides, I'd like a chance to work with him, see how he functions around there. Based on your —"

"Oh Dad, I'm sorry! I meant to tell you, I talked to his old nurse. She was with him for several years and sings his praises. Apparently he went through a nasty divorce, had an ex-wife who wouldn't let the divorce proceed and got into a nasty conflict of ideas with Fairfield. But as for skill and patient rapport, he is supposedly a minor god."

Elmer chewed on this a moment. "He's sort of goofy for a god, don't you think?"

"Sometimes." She laughed and confided conspiratorially, "Jessie says he's a nerd. Or was that dork? But a good doctor. She likes working with him."

This made Elmer smile. "Little bald girl can sure call 'em, can't she?"

"That aside, I would appreciate it if you'd take some of my morning patients, Dad. John would be glad to, but if you could just help out, I should be in by —"

"Take your time, honey. I know pulling Birdie and Judge out of a ditch just about took ten years off your life."

"At least. And if you don't mind, I'd like to go by my house, take a shower, let Sadie have a pee — that sort of thing. Poor Sadie . . ."

"She's going to have to learn how to be a doctor's dog."

June looked in on a few patients, then got herself a cup of coffee. She stood in front of the nursery window, holding her steaming cup. Musing. Nothing could replace newborns for musing.

When John's call had come the night before, she'd rushed out of the house only to find the porch deserted. Jim had gone. She'd called out to him, but there had been no answer, and she'd had no time to wait. Sadie just looked toward the road. June had put Sadie in the house and jumped in her Jeep, making tracks. He hadn't been walking down the long drive, nor had she seen any vehicle. There wasn't any time to think about him again until dawn.

Now it seemed as if he were some apparition. She wouldn't mind, as long as he made regular visits. Maybe that was how Mrs. Muir felt. But could you still taste the apparition's kiss long after you'd licked your lips clean? Still feel the ghost's arms around you? Smell his hair?

"Any of these yours?" a voice behind her asked.

She turned. "Blake! I was waiting around to see you, I was trying to get out of making a proper appointment. Aren't you here awfully early?"

"I had a delivery. A stubborn one."

"Everybody okay?"

"We are now. What are you doing here at the crack of dawn?"

"There was a car accident. An awful experience. Two old friends — Judge and Birdie Forrest. But they're doing well now. I need to speak to you, Blake, if you have a few minutes."

"No better time than now. The office doesn't open till eight, I've already made my rounds and no one is in labor."

231

"It's a personal favor I'm asking. . . ."

"Whatever you need, June."

"If we could find an empty room some-where, or maybe even a stall in the ER . . ."

"Why don't you tell me what you —"

"A diaphragm," she whispered.

Blake Norton was a handsome bachelor in his late forties, one of the many professional transplants from big cities. But he was ahead of his peers and had opened his Rockport family practice almost twenty years earlier. He was, therefore, well acquainted with both Elmer and June. June used Blake as her primary physician.

Behind the curtain in a birthing room on the labor and delivery wing, with her legs up in the air and her butt hanging out, her doctor said, "I admit, I'm flattered. With the arrival of the esteemed Dr. Stone, I didn't think you'd be needing my services anymore."

"I'm not ready to make him my doctor," she said.

"I guess I can understand that," Blake said. "He comes with an amazing reputation, doesn't he?"

"You've heard of him?"

"I asked about him when I heard you were bringing him in. I need a good OB now and then. I still have a number of colleagues I keep in touch with in the Bay Area. He practiced there, right?"

"Uh-huh. The Fairfield Women's Clinic."

"Then he must be good."

"Why do you assume that?"

"Because that clinic, from a physician's point of view, is just about the best place to practice reproductive medicine in all of northern California. Excellent reputation. The best doctors available. Neonatology, infertility, gyno-oncology, everything. One-stop shopping. I've heard that celebrities actually travel from afar for the services of that group."

"My goodness," she said, having had no idea word of the place was so well traveled. But then Elmer had said he'd heard good things about that clinic. The environment must have been sheer hell to make a good OB leave a clinic like that.

Blake gave her a fitting and an exam for good measure, then backed away, snapped off the gloves and handed her a nice little ivory case in which her new birth control device was now stored. "Thank you, Blake," she said.

"And may I say one more thing?"

"I really thought I'd get out of here without you saying 'one more thing.' "

"I'm delighted to provide you with this service, June. At long last." He winked.

"Did you just *wink?*"

He winked again.

"Jesus. At least you didn't say, 'Anyone I know?' "

"I don't dare," he said. "Unless I hear rumors of your frequent travels out of the area, the odds are excellent that I do know him."

"Ha-ha on you. Now get out of here and let me dress!"

It was now 7:30 a.m. and she was fairly certain she had just protected herself against the future offspring of a ghost.

Did it all seem unreal because it had been so long since she had had any kind of romantic interest? Because he was a stranger? Because of the chaos of the accident?

All the same, she took her little ivory case, slipped it into her bag and checked on Birdie and Judge one more time before leaving the hospital. Birdie was sitting up and Judge was grumbling that he wanted to go home — excellent conditions for both of them.

There was no welcome quite so pleasurable as that of a pet. Sadie almost wiggled herself into the floor, she was so animated. She yelped and pawed and licked June's face, making her drop to her knees and laugh. "Okay, okay — I bet you're about to explode," she said. "Let's go!" They went out on the back porch together; June didn't let Sadie take solo trips anymore. She watched her closely, lest she run pell-mell back to Mikos's farm. But June had to throw the ball to get Sadie out on the grass. Finally, on the third throw, Sadie paused to water the lawn, but only a dribble. Then she bounded back up on the porch with the ball in her teeth, her heavy golden tail swishing wildly through the air.

"Maybe later, sweetie," June said. "Right now I have to get cleaned up. And you must want breakfast, huh?"

June thought her an amazing dog — she'd lasted almost twelve hours and hadn't even made a mistake. Plus she had not depleted the food and water from last night. She must have been saving herself.

But when June got to her bedroom she realized she had misunderstood Sadie's appetite and apparent comfort. Sadie had been fed and let out — that's why she was in such great shape. And there, on June's pillow, lay a bunch of miniature daisies from the forest, tied at the stems with a white ribbon.

At lunchtime the next day, June wandered across the street to the café. Elmer and Sam were sharing a booth, while Tom leaned against the counter. June slid in next to her dad. "Aren't the fish biting today, Sam?" she asked.

"I heard the catch of the day was here," he said.

"Oh?" she asked. Before she could get him to elaborate on the statement, Leah appeared beside her table and stood poised, pen and pad in hand. "What's this? Leah?"

"It's been a while since I've done this, but it didn't take long for it all to come back to me," she said. Her face was as bright as her smile. It was amazing what the absence of stress and fear could do for a person; her skin glowed a healthy pink and her eyes were so much larger and clearer than June remembered. "Do you need to see a menu, June?" she asked.

"After all these years? Is there anything new?"

"Besides me? Just Frank." She inclined her head toward the lunch counter, where Frank, in a white shirt and cap, stacked clean cups and glasses. "George says if he does a good job at bussing and washing up dishes, he'll teach him to cook."

"Who's gonna teach George?" Elmer asked.

"Dad! You're going to get yourself thrown out of here!"

"Naw, George expects me to complain. Leah, bring me another piece of that awful blueberry pie, will you please?"

"My pleasure, Doc. And a coffee refill?"

"Yes, ma'am, if you will."

"Leah," June marveled, "I don't know that I've ever seen you looking better. This job must agree with you."

"It's like a new lease on life. I told Frank he should start saving for a car, but he insists all his money will go in the family pot to keep us whole. Jeremy, Joe and Mack are going to tend little Stan and the garden this summer, while school is out, and if things go right for them, they should be able to have a vegetable stand by the road come harvest."

"You tell those boys if they can bring in a good crop, I'll cart them over to where 101 meets Highway 68 south of Piercy," Sam said. "They can catch that traffic coming out of the redwoods. Make a ton of money."

"That's awful nice of you, Sam. That'd help out."

"I'll get over there and see they get a little

fishin' in, too," he said. "Boys can't pass summer without fishin'."

Leah's eyes began to mist up. "Well," she said, her composure failing her, "let me get your pie and coffee. And June?"

"Chicken sandwich on a sourdough bun, whatever salad George made up and iced tea."

"It's macaroni salad today. Be right back."

When Leah had gone back behind the counter, June said, "That was a wonderful thing George did. He must have made up the job for Leah and Frank — it didn't seem like he needed anyone."

"He may be soft in the head, but he's soft in the heart, too," Elmer added.

"Can you believe how vibrant she looks? My gosh, I didn't know she *could* look that good!"

"Gives you a hint of what that useless Gus saw some years ago, doesn't it?" Sam asked. "What I'd like to know is how a bad apple like Gus hangs on to a woman like Leah. She's good as gold."

"You know how. He beat her into submission and scared her to death."

"Well, he'd better look out. If this dose of independence and self-esteem gets her a little gumption, she might find the strength to finally be through with that old sauce."

"Who's this? Mrs. Stone?" Elmer asked.

June craned her neck, looking toward the door. It was Susan, absent of husband and child. She was a picture of youth in her jeans and clogs, blond pageboy swinging across her shoulders. She had a tiny figure, peaches and cream complexion, and head-cheerleader disposition — always positive, always upbeat. "Don't the two of them together remind you of Barbie and Ken?" Elmer demanded.

"You're getting awful hard to shut up these days, Dad."

"Matter of fact . . ." Sam began.

Susan looked around the café and in the process gave June a halfhearted wave. She obviously didn't see who she was looking for, and the expression on her face seemed one of complete distraction. She finally made her way over to where June and the old boys sat.

"Susan, come here and join us. I need help keeping these two in line."

She slid into the booth beside June. "I was hoping to run into John over here — he's not at the clinic. Jessie said he might be having lunch."

"He might be, but he's not having it here today. He had a surgery in Rockport this morning and made rounds for the both of us. He hasn't gotten back yet. Did you try his cell phone?"

"No," she said wearily. "I only just decided I was looking for him. June . . ." she began, then trailed off while she thought over what she was about to say. "June, have you been very involved with the Presbyterian Women? Or any of the Bible studies?"

"I'm lucky if I make Sunday church," she said. "Why?"

"It's a damn shame," Susan said. "There are a lot of good people around here, and the pastor of the biggest church in town is nothing but a sleazy lecher."

"That's our preacher," Elmer agreed.

Leah returned with their food and coffee refills. Susan was convinced to order lunch and supply the story.

"I guess I thought it was a joke, the way everyone talked about him."

"He didn't hurt you, did he?" June demanded.

"As in assault? No, nothing like that. But does it hurt to have your minister proposition you? I couldn't believe my ears!"

"What did he say? I mean, if you feel comfortable —"

"He said he found me attractive, that I'd tempt the very saints, and if I needed any private counseling, he was available. I asked him if he'd just made a pass and he said, 'No! Of course not!' But there was no mistaking it."

"Did you tell him so?" June asked.

"I absolutely did," she said. "But I got the impression he couldn't care less."

"He couldn't," Elmer said. "He does it all the time."

"He's gotten a slap or two," Sam told her. "Wouldn't hurt for him to get a few more."

Susan's expression became dark. "Slapping is too good for him," she said. "He needs to be *removed.*"

June bit into her sandwich and chewed slowly, considering Susan's remark.

"June, do you know the names of some of the women who have also been sexually harassed by Pastor Wickham?" Susan asked.

Sexually harassed? She hadn't thought of his actions in those terms, but there it was. She nodded. She wasn't quite prepared to name herself, but if it came to that, she'd step up to the plate with Susan.

"If you wouldn't mind, I'd like to talk to some of them. I know this is a small town, and some things are just quirkie and eccentric and all in good fun, but I don't think this is funny. And I don't think he should get away with it."

"I agree!" June said. "He's met his match

at last! For now, why don't you ask Julianna what she knows. She's lived here a long time."

"Uh-oh," Elmer said. "It'll be like shutting down the movie house for some of these folks. We've been watching Pastor Wickham get himself burned for almost a year now."

"Understand," Sam said, "it's not as though anyone really approves of him. He's been a nuisance, but I don't think he's actually dangerous. He's kind of stupid, you ask me."

"You just never know what kind of harm an attitude like that can do to a woman," June lectured. "Especially if he stumbles on a woman who is vulnerable. Needy. Spiritually hungry. Or maybe just gives him too much credit."

"Who'd put any stock in what that pretty boy with the hair plugs is peddling?" Elmer asked in disbelief.

"You never know," June said. "Right, Susan?"

But Susan wasn't listening. She was staring off into space, sucking on her straw absentmindedly.

"Susan?" June said, nudging her.

"Hmm?" she asked.

"Where *are* you right now?"

"Oh, sorry, June. I was just thinking about Jessie . . ."

"Jessie? What about Jessie?" June asked, intrigued.

"You know, what she does on her lunch break."

"No, I don't know. What exactly does she do?"

"Well, she brings a lunch to the clinic, and while she eats she reads your clinical and science textbooks."

"My Jessie?" June asked in surprise. "She didn't even finish high school. What interest could she have in those textbooks?"

"I don't know, but she was so engrossed, she didn't even look up until I stood right in front of her and cleared my throat. Then she tried to cover the book with her napkin."

"Why would she do that? I don't care if she reads them."

"I can't answer that, but just so you know, the book was microbiology, and there were no pictures on the page."

"Well, I'll be damned," Elmer muttered.

FIFTEEN

For just a while, until medical tests were completed and until Birdie's constant headache disappeared, the quilting circle was suspended. The women still dropped by her house, of course, bringing things like casseroles and flowers, teas and even newly collected fabric scraps, to be stored for next time.

June looked in on her daily.

"There's something different about you," Birdie said.

"Yes, there is. I almost lost you. I'm completely changed. Forever."

"You won't be rid of me for a while yet, but that's not it."

"There isn't anything else," June said.

Birdie cocked her head, taking June in in a sidelong glance. "It's not like you to lie," she said matter-of-factly.

June couldn't lie to Birdie because she was too busy lying to herself. When she stretched her neck to look down her long drive toward the road at dawn or at dusk, she would firmly tell herself she wasn't looking for *him.* When she drove extra slowly on her way home, it was only to enjoy the scenery, not to catch a glimpse of a red-and-black plaid shirt. And when she stayed at her clinic a little late, door unlocked, it was not in hopes that someone might have shot one of his friends. God, no.

At Fuller's Café, where she took morning courage and carbs, she asked Tom, not once, not twice, but three times total, "Have you heard anything about raids or busts or anything in the Alps?"

"Those things can drag out forever, June."

"But you would hear?"

"I have made it a point to be informed."

"And would you tell me?"

He frowned. A Cherokee can look particularly serious when frowning. "June, it has crossed my mind that maybe you should look through some mug shots."

"Whatever for?"

"To see if you can identify the men who came by your clinic that night. To see if either of them is a known criminal."

"Have they asked me to? The DEA?"

"No. But maybe for your own good . . ."

It wasn't until that exact moment that she

realized she'd been hounding him for information. And that he was probably onto her.

Didn't anyone understand what it was like to be her? To be thirty-seven and have your best friends be a married cop and your seventy-year-old father, your most exciting evening out be the quilting circle? To not even own a "little black dress"?

She was *dying* to look through pictures! To ask Tom what he could find out about this ghostly figure called Jim. It had been just over a week. Nine days, to be exact. And she wasn't yet angry that, after all that sweet talk and the best kiss she'd had since high school, he hadn't come back. He's out there in the woods, saving the world, she told herself. Bringing justice to the forest. Surely.

She sat in her clinic with Sadie, her new and constant companion, sorting patient files, making notes and setting up her patient roster for the next day — all things that could wait for morning or be done some afternoon during a lull in the schedule. Waiting. Foolishly hoping.

"June?"

She jumped and Sadie came to attention. "Justine? I didn't hear the door!"

"I'm sorry to bother you. I saw the light, and, well . . ."

"Come in. What's wrong?"

"Everything. Everything is wrong."

"Are you sick? In pain?"

The answer must surely be yes for Justine crumbled. She crossed her arms over her stomach and stumbled to the chair in June's office, overcome with sobs.

"My goodness!" June gasped, moving quickly around her desk to help the distraught woman into the chair. "There, there," she said. June began delivering tissue after tissue as Justine wept copiously. Sadie licked Justine's elbow for a little while, then got bored with the lack of appreciation and found a quiet place to lay under June's desk. A good ten minutes passed before Justine even began to settle down.

"Sooner or later you're going to have to blow your nose, dry your eyes and tell me what has you so upset. If I'm to help you, that is," June said.

On cue, Justine made a final noise into a tissue, one that sounded remarkably like a train whistle. She sniffed loudly, blinked tightly, and straightened her spine. "I'm pregnant," she said.

If June looked surprised, it was more by the timing than the actual event. Just days after Susan Stone made an oath to see

Pastor Wickham dealt with on the issue of his flagrant womanizing, here came Justine. There had been copious talk. Justine owned the little flower shop at the end of the street and delivered the flowers for the Sunday service to the Presbyterian Church every Saturday afternoon. She was said to take a suspiciously long time in making up the arrangements and also to leave the church with a rather satisfied look on her face. It was Elmer and the old boys who talked that way, and it annoyed June no end. But if there was anything harder to stop than Pastor Wickham's roving eye, it was idle gossip. Gossip, and the disaster before her. This was just what June had feared.

"Oh dear," she said to Justine.

"I'm sunk," Justine stated. "My father will never speak to me again if he finds out."

Justine was a roundish young woman of twenty-six, but she wasn't large enough to conceal a pregnancy. June didn't like where this was going. "Well, he will eventually find out. Won't he?"

"I'll need an abortion, June. Right away."

"One thing at a time," June said. "Are you absolutely sure you're —"

"I drove over to Fort Bragg and got one of those little tests. It was very positive."

"They're not all that accurate. You should

have an examination. And then —"

"I *know* I'm pregnant! I'm not stupid!"

"Okay, okay . . ."

"Sorry. I've been a little testy lately."

"Well, that's understandable. But before we —"

"Can you even imagine how pissed off I am? All that sweet talk! All that business about having spiritual conflict because he couldn't *help* himself where I was concerned! That his passion overcame his ethics, and even his commitment to *God* couldn't stop him from loving me! That I'd tempt the very saints!"

"Does he say that to every — ?"

"What bullshit! He probably got all his spiritual conflict from being scared shitless that his bully of a wife is going to kill him!"

"Justine, really, you don't have to tell me all —"

"That's probably a big fucking lie, too! That he hasn't had sex with her in six years!"

"Really, this is none of my . . . Don't they have a five-year — ?"

"Do I look stupid?"

"N—" June tried to reply, with shaking head.

"Would I have let him if he hadn't promised me we'd be together forever? That he wasn't in love with her anymore, that he hadn't been in years, and if it weren't for the children —"

"Oh, famous last —" June began, in spite of herself.

"I should have known! He's just another duplicitous, horny, groping son of a bitch! And I'm pregnant!"

With that, she melted into more helpless sobbing, and June resumed handing off tissues.

Was this the only person in Grace Valley who didn't know Jonathan Wickham came on to practically every woman who crossed his path? June frowned as she patted Justine's back. Justine, as far as she knew, didn't have girlfriends. She lived a fairly isolated life as the youngest daughter of her widowed father. Standard Roberts owned the flower fields east of town, where he grew many of the flowers Justine sold, and Justine still lived in his house. She had since her mother died when she was sixteen, ten years ago. She probably cooked his meals, did his laundry and cleaned the house. He was a hard man, bitter and unfriendly. Shoot, maybe Justine *didn't* know about Jonathan! Who was going to tell her?

Here it was. Here was how his shenanigans could hurt.

"Justine, we can deal with this situation, but you're going to have to get a grip. And we can't solve this whole thing tonight. I'll see you first thing in the morning and —"

"Can you believe how he *used* me?" she sobbed.

"There's a lot of hysteria about this event right now," June said. "Let's try to maintain a —"

"The bastard! Man, what a guy will say to get laid!"

"I realize you're overwrought, but —"

"I wonder how Mrs. Wickham will take the news. I bet she'll kill the little dickhead!"

"Now just hold it!" June shouted. Justine's head snapped up and June's eyes blazed. "I realize you're very angry," June said.

"Totally pissed," Justine corrected, but she did so with some control.

"Whatever. Just get a grip before someone gets hurt."

"Someone *has!*"

"Let's concentrate on resolving this rather than making it worse. Shall we?"

Justine slowly and perhaps reluctantly nodded. June let out her breath in a sigh of relief. Boy, this could get ugly. There was not only a wife, a girlfriend, a bunch of offspring and a pregnancy here, but a *congregation.* A small-town congregation that was heavily populated with women who were more than ready to pull the plug on the womanizing preacher. The shit could really hit the fan.

"What I'd like you to do, Justine, is try to get some rest tonight without doing anything more to escalate this drama. Then first thing in the morning, I'll meet you here for an exam, okay? Let's get the facts right before we go in search of a solution. Then, once we know exactly what we're dealing with, we can —"

June was cut short by the ringing of the phone. She reached for the receiver. "I'm sure you'll make a good decision once you've heard all the facts and all the options, hmm?"

"I guess," Justine said, not entirely mollified.

"Excuse me," June said. "Hello, June Hudson . . . yes . . . yes . . . okay, please take a breath . . . you administered mouth-to-mouth? Uh-huh? He's breathing again? Okay, look at his nail beds. Okay, how about his mouth? Tongue and gums? Pale, blue, rosy, bright red? Okay, here's what you do. Run the shower hot and get a good steam going in the bathroom. Go sit in there with the baby. No, you hold him, Julianna. No, he's going to be fine. We don't know yet, do we? But if it's croup or bronchitis or some-thing like that, you might as well get started loosening it up while I drive. No, he's going to be fine, just do as I say. I'm on my way. I'll be on the cell."

She put the phone down and looked at Justine. "You heard," she said. "It's Julianna Dickson's baby — wasn't breathing and is now blue around the gills. I have to hurry. Sadie!"

The dog came to her at once, ready for a house call.

"Of course," Justine said. She'd grown a bit pale.

June was standing in her office door, fingers on the light switch, Sadie at her side. "Now," she said.

"Oh!" Justine said, jumping up. "Sorry. Sorry. Sorry to have bothered —"

"No bother. See you in the morning. Sadie, let's go!"

June had the lights out, the clinic's back door locked and the engine started in the Jeep in less than twenty seconds. And Sadie, learning to be a doctor's dog, was in the passenger seat beside her in a flash. *This* was how she normally moved — like her pants were on fire, not like she was slogging through wet sand.

Route 482 was faster. It never even crossed

June's mind that it was the site of the accident. All she could think of was getting to Julianna and the baby. They were excellent, resourceful, educated parents; they would do everything right. But the reality was that sometimes everything was not enough.

Julianna had called earlier in the day to report that the baby had a sniffle, but no fever. June had told her to "nurse the baby through it," for there was no sign of the infant developing worse upper respiratory symptoms. The steam room June had suggested was a shot in the dark, plus something to keep them busy and close to the baby. Julianna had just found the child lifeless, bluish, and had brought him back with resuscitation. It could be SIDS and have nothing to do with a cold or upper respiratory infection.

June, Oh God, June, he wasn't breathing! I don't know how long he'd been without oxygen!

In all these years and all these babies, June had never heard that kind of panicked call from the Dicksons.

She flew around the curve known as Angel's Pass and there, in a flash of light, she met the headlights of an oncoming car. She pulled hard right, felt the scrape of rocks and logs as she went off the shoulder.

She pulled hard left, seeing no sign of the other car, and attempted to correct her mistake, but it was too late. She fishtailed in the gravel, hit a tree hard enough to bounce off, and the Jeep spun crazily around. Her head broke the glass of the door window as the vehicle skidded into a row of pines. Sadie squeaked in either pain or fear, tossed around the inside of the Jeep like a rag doll. Everything went black.

The underside of the Jeep scraped over metal refuse left from the earlier accident. There was a spark. Then a flash. Then a hot glow as the belly of the Jeep caught fire.

June felt strong hands in her armpits, pulling her free. Her legs snagged on jagged metal and scraped over broken glass, but she couldn't open her eyes. She groaned, feeling the heat of the fire on her legs as she cleared the wreckage. Then she was aware of being lifted into capable arms and carried away from the fire and over the road. She could hear Sadie yapping at their side. "Good girl," the man said. June didn't recognize his voice, but Sadie calmed and only "talked" in her sweet, throaty way. June was overcome by a sense of well-being even though she could hear the crackling and popping of her Jeep burning behind her.

As he carried her down the road, she sank into his arms. At peace. He had a leather and wood smoke smell about him. At least it wasn't marijuana, she thought distractedly. With a blast, the Jeep exploded behind them and she flinched. "It's okay," he murmured, and immediately she felt safe again. The Jeep erupted in yet another huge blast and she thought of the oxygen she had been rushing to the Dickson's.

"The baby," she whispered, her hand searching her bloody head for a cut.

"Is there a baby in the car?" the man asked, surprised.

"No . . . the Dickson baby," she said. "I have to . . ."

She felt him gently lay her on soft, velvety grass. Her hand was pulled away and replaced with a cool, damp rag. "I didn't think I saw anyone else in there," he said. "Your dog — she has a cut, but she's okay I think."

June pressed the rag against her head wound and blinked the blood out of her eyes. That was why she couldn't see; she wasn't blind after all. Even through closed eyes she could see the glow coming from the burning Jeep. "Oh no," she cried. She could not take care of the town without the Jeep. She began to quietly sob.

"But you have your life," he said. Had she

expressed that thought aloud, she wondered? "Here, hold still." He pulled the cloth away and rinsed it out in the shallow stream beside her. He wiped her eyes clean, then placed it again on her head, stifling the bleeding.

The next time he took it away, she could see clearly. He was a handsome and muscular man, but young. Not even thirty. He wore a homespun, collarless shirt. His hair and beard were dark, and the beard was real. His pants were held up with suspenders made of rope and his boots looked a hundred years old.

"Thank you," she said weakly. "Who . . . who —" She was suddenly overcome with nausea. He must have seen the signs because he quickly raised her back and leaned her over to the side. She lost her dinner on the ground.

"Just relax. You're going to be okay," he said.

"Where did you come from?" she asked him.

"I live around here."

"But where? I don't . . . Who are you?"

"Just a neighbor, ma'am. Good thing I happened by. Here," he said, taking the cloth again and rinsing it one more time. She saw then that he had an ax. He followed her eyes and smiled as he returned the rag to her cut. "It's good I had it with me. I had to use it to get you out of that tangle."

"You opened the Jeep with an ax?" she asked dumbly.

"There weren't too many choices," he said. He stood and hefted his ax. "I think you'll be okay now. The fire is going to bring your friends to you."

"You're leaving?"

"No, I'll be right over here," he said, crossing the road in the direction of the burning Jeep.

Then someone was patting her cheeks to rouse her. "Doc," he was saying. "Come on, Doc, this ain't no time to play possum." When she came to again she was looking into the beady eyes and matted beard of Cliff Bender. "Hey, Doc, hey! Come on, Doc!" She shook her head to clear her vision. She must have lost consciousness after the man had left her.

"Where . . . ? Cliff?"

"Can you stand, Doc? Be a good idee t'git further away from that fire, you know what I mean. Just in case the trees take spark. Want me to carry you?"

Her hand was still pressing the rag against her head. "Did you do this?" she asked, lifting the rag.

"Naw, you must'a done it yourself. Took a nasty whack, did you?"

"Oh man," she moaned. "Sadie?"

"She's right here, Doc. Up we go. . . . On your feet now."

With a hand under her elbow, he brought her upright. The world swam and she swooned against Cliff, nauseous again.

"Easy does 'er," he urged.

Before they'd taken twenty steps, June could hear sirens. "Cliff, did you see that man?"

"Who's 'at, Doc?"

"The man who pulled me out of the Jeep. He pulled me out and put this cloth on my head. Did you see him?"

"I got here right off, Doc. I was on the road when the Jeep blew. I reckon I'd a seen him if he was here."

"He was here." Or, she thought, I could have been hallucinating. She pulled the cloth off her head and studied it. It was not hers; it didn't come from her medical bag or her Jeep. "He rinsed the rag in the stream," she said.

"What stream is 'at, Doc?"

"Why, the stream right over . . ." But she didn't know where it was. "Do you think I might've crawled out?" she asked Cliff.

"Or maybe got throwed," he suggested.

259

"Yeah," she said. "Throwed."

Tom was the first to arrive. He merely glanced at June before applying his fire extinguisher to the Jeep and surrounding brush. Cliff didn't wait to be asked — he pulled a second extinguisher from the Chief's Rover and gave assistance. They hadn't made much progress when the volunteer fire department arrived with the only truck. Sam Cussler drove, and when he came to a stop Rob Gilmore, Scott Wiley, Chuck Burnham and Lee Stafford leaped off, dragged hoses and splattered flames. Soon after them, from both directions, came pickup trucks filled with men, sand, shovels, extinguishers, picks, pails and axes. A runaway fire in this part of the world could leave the mountains looking like the face of the moon. Firefighting was not only serious business, it was everyone's business.

Tom crouched down in front of her. "What happened?"

"A car," she said. "There was a car coming right at me."

"Out here? There's no car."

"But I saw lights . . . coming at me . . . and then —" She pulled the rag off her head. "Oh brother, wait till I tell you what happened next." There was a loud blast from the direction of her Jeep, now little more than a black cinder. "Oxygen tanks! Tom, I was on my way to the Dicksons. The baby had stopped breathing!"

"Okay, let's go," he said, helping her to her feet.

"Uh, Doc?" Cliff said. "It weren't no car. Look there." He pointed down the road a bit, to where the ground was freshly graded from the cleanup after Judge and Birdie's accident. Pushed off to the side, barely visible from where they stood, was a rear windshield, whole and undamaged, leaning against a tree. Someone must have meant it for salvage, then overlooked it, clear and nearly invisible in the daytime. The reflection of flames and headlights bounced off it eerily.

She'd been nearly killed by her own reflection.

And saved by an angel?

SIXTEEN

June felt as though her head were caught in an ever-tightening vise. The morning light from the window was no help. She groaned and tried to sit up.

"Good morning, sunshine," John Stone said.

She looked at him through swollen slits. There he was, jauntily dressed in his starched percale shirt, pressed pleated pants, tasseled loafers. In a town full of loggers, farmers, vintners and ranchers, John really stood out. This morning he carried a cup of tea and had a dish towel tucked into the waist of his slacks. My very own Mr. Jeeves, she thought.

"Wow," she said weakly. "I must have really tied one on."

"I have some Percodan for you," he said. "After you've had a bite to eat."

"What are you doing here?"

"What do you remember?"

She closed her eyes briefly and it was all there. "Accident, fire, the Dicksons, the hospital. . . ." Sadie lay beside her on the bed; a piece of scalp about the size of a silver dollar had been shaved and about a dozen stitches applied. In sudden panic June reached into her bedside table for a mirror. The cut on her forehead stretched into her hairline. It had been neatly stitched and discolored from the antiseptic, but her hair was all there.

"I wouldn't shave your head there. You'd look pretty stupid if I had."

"Whew. I figured your sense of style would come in handy eventually."

"Your X ray was clean — no fracture. Mild concussion. Major head pain. I gave you some analgesic and brought you home. I thought I'd stay and make sure there were no complications. I guess you're going to have to take the day off."

She accepted the tea. "What about the baby?"

John reached into his pocket and brought forth a dog biscuit for Sadie, which she politely accepted. "His chest was clear, but the emergency room doctor thinks it's possible they're looking at a mitral valve stenosis. Julianna and Mike are taking him to a pediatric cardiologist today."

"Oh dear. That's going to be tough. That could mean heart surgery."

"Maybe. But at least they caught it — that was a very close call. All kinds of close calls last night. Be right back," he said. He returned with an English muffin on a tray.

"As valets go, you're pretty good," she said. "But I don't know if I can eat."

"You have to if I'm going to give you something for pain. It's your only chance of keeping it down."

"I guess. Where's my dad?"

"I told him to go home and get some sleep. He's going to have to take some of your patients today. I can cover most of them, but I'll need some help." He sat down on the edge of the bed. "June, think maybe we need another doctor?"

A little huff of laughter escaped her. "What did I do before you came along?"

"The Jeep, June. Total toast. What are we going to do about that?"

"It'll have to be replaced. I'll have to lease something and call a medical supplier to load it. I don't think Tom and the deputies can get us through much more than a couple of days without a medical vehicle. Talk about your headaches."

"Count me in on that expense."

"I'll get reimbursed over time," she said.

"Great. Then we can both get reimbursed over time. This is my town now, too, you know."

"John, I don't want you to take on too many of these responsibilities until you're sure you're going to stay permanently."

"I'll make a few phone calls today, get some prices," he said, ignoring her. "And, if your head lets up, call your insurance company."

"All that stuff is at the clinic. . . ."

"Better yet, I'll have Jessie do it. The girl's a paper genius."

June took a small bite and chewed. "John, you have no idea how much I appreciate all this."

"Sure I do. And you're welcome. But you'd do the same for me."

I would now, she thought. As she ate her muffin, let John fluff her pillows, and accepted some pain pills, she wondered how she could ever have doubted this guy. With a wife like Susan, how could he get by with anything? And if Susan and Julianna were friends, there was another vote of confidence, because Julianna was not only one of the nicest people in Grace Valley, she also had the best instincts — the single thing that had probably saved her baby's life last night.

Besides all that, John had stitched up June and her dog and stayed the night to be sure she was all right. Could somebody that sensitive be bad?

She made up her mind. She couldn't condemn him based on the nervous indictment of a young patient who wouldn't even explain the circumstances of her complaint! She sighed deeply, at last convinced in her own mind.

"These will knock you out," John said, shaking out a couple of pills. "That's about the best medicine right now. Stay in bed . . . sleep it off. You'll feel much better tomorrow."

"Thanks, John. I'd be lost without you."

Sleep she did. And dream — bright, vivid dreams about the forest, filled with animals and angels. There was a brightly colored parrot diving at her from the highest branches of pine trees, screeching and cawing. She finally realized the phone was ringing insistently.

She rolled over and checked the clock first: 3:00 p.m. She was groggy from the pain medication. She grabbed the phone. "Hullo?" she said thickly.

"Dr. June Hudson, please," a woman's voice requested.

"Who's calling please?"

"Dr. Wendy Feldtbrow," she said.

June almost said, "Not really! Dr. Felt Brow?" But she caught herself. "Um, this is June Hudson. How can I help you?"

"I understand you've been doing a background check on Dr. John Stone?"

She sat up unsteadily, groping both physically and mentally. "Well, I wouldn't exactly call it a background check. John is seeing patients in our town clinic and I've been checking his references. Strictly routine stuff."

"Hmm. Well, it's a good thing I called. You wouldn't refer to his references as *routine* if you knew."

"Knew?"

"About the sexual assault charges."

June literally swooned. Next to murder, there couldn't possibly be anything more serious to allege against a physician, especially an OB. She repeated the charge back into the phone, her voice breathless. "Sexual assault?" she asked weakly.

"I can tell you had no idea."

"Do you think he'd be seeing patients in my clinic if I knew?" she asked incredulously. June got out of bed, carried the cordless with her to the kitchen and started making coffee. She wasn't sure if the dull ache in her head was a result of the accident or the phone call. "Can you be more specific, please?"

"Well, let's see. . . . I ran into one of the staff of the Fairfield Women's Clinic. That's how I learned you'd been asking about Dr. Stone. You must have talked to someone at the clinic."

"David Fairfield," June said, giving the coffee an extra scoop. She wished she could take it as an IV push. "But I assure you, he never —"

Wendy Feldtbrow laughed softly. "Well, there you go. He might have mentioned to one of his staff that you'd inquired after Dr. Stone's reputation and it wandered through the grapevine to me. I am a surgeon and at one time had privileges at some of the same hospitals as Dr. Stone. We knew each other. Pretty well, actually."

"And? What are the details of this assault?" June pressed.

"If I could, I'd like to start at the beginning. I also knew his wife and we had several mutual friends. John was a good doctor, but he started having professional problems. He was faced with a patient lawsuit, he was reprimanded for dating another patient while he was still married to his wife, he was drinking too much, incurred terrible debt troubles, began making mistakes, generally screwing up.

"For example, he missed a delivery entirely because he didn't answer his page even though he was on call. Fairfield suspended him, he was evicted from his apartment, his car was repossessed, and there was even some talk about prescription drug abuse. That was just gossip, of course, but if you could have seen him at the time . . ."

"Jesus!" June stared at the coffeepot, willing it to brew faster.

"I felt so sorry for him, Dr. Hudson. His friends were bailing out on him left and right. I should have known better. After all, I am a doctor. But I offered moral support. As I said, I knew him to be a good doctor at one time. I found myself alone in his company and he became . . . well, amorous. And insistent. When I was adamant that we not get involved romantically, he assaulted me. He attempted to rape me."

"My God." June thought of John, passing her the cup of tea, the dish towel hanging like an apron from his waist, the dog biscuit for Sadie. His lovely wife, darling little daughter, his dopey handsomeness. She couldn't put this all together. But if he had been in trouble and addicted to pills and alcohol . . .

"I called the police, naturally. I was ready to push it, to file charges and take it all the way, but the deputy prosecutor didn't think it would fly in court. You know the drill — John's word against mine. But he was fired from the Fairfield Clinic not long after that."

"Fired? He didn't say he was fired!"

The doctor snorted impatiently. "Why would he? I'm sure there are a million things he's covering up. I felt pretty stupid, I can tell you. After all, I'd heard the nurses talk! He was a known flirt. He was accused of sexual harassment on several occasions. I'm sure one of the reasons the Fairfield Clinic couldn't wait to get rid of him was his known problems with women."

"Dr. Fairfield didn't say he was fired, either!"

"Well, I can't explain that. Nor can I tell you the outcome of all his other problems. Everything was kept very hush-hush. I mean, the Fairfield Clinic is awfully prestigious. They wouldn't want it to get around that one of their doctors —"

"Yes, but surely there was talk! You must have heard something about the lawsuit? Dating a patient? Drug abuse?"

"I think I might have heard things, if I hadn't been the one to accuse him of sexual assault. That kind of took me out of the loop, if you know what I mean."

"I would think that very fact would have your colleagues running to you with each new tale!" June said.

"Well, it seems to have had the opposite effect."

"And all this happened . . . when?"

"Let's see. Summer. Seven years ago. He left the Bay Area soon after the trouble started, and I was a practicing surgeon until last year. Now I'm doing some research."

"My God. You'll have to forgive me, Dr. Felt Good —"

"That's Feldtbrow."

"Oh dear, sorry. You've caught me at a double disadvantage. First of all, the shock of this story has me speechless. And, if I seem a little dense, it's because I was asleep when you called. I took a big whack on the head last night. Car accident."

"Oh, I'm sorry."

"So I need a little time to digest this."

"Of course you do!"

"This is very unsettling, to say the least. Do you have any documentation I might look at? Your police report, perhaps?"

"I might have that somewhere . . . filed away. I'll look around for it. Of course, there is one place I know you'll find the documentation you'll need. The police department.

This is all a matter of public record. Unless he's somehow managed to get the records purged."

"I suppose," June said, wondering how she could find out. "And could you give me a phone number? I have to think this through . . . decide what I'm going to do next . . . and I may want to talk to you again."

"Absolutely."

June scribbled out the name and number and they said their goodbyes.

John Stone was a roller coaster ride. Boring nerd? Deviant? Sweet caretaker? Abuser?

June called the clinic to see how the day had gone. Apparently Elmer and John had managed very well; even Charlotte was in a good mood. "Just like old times," she said. "Having your dad take charge of the office again."

"Well, I hate to upset your routine, but I'm planning to come back tomorrow."

"Isn't that a bit soon?" Charlotte asked.

"For you, probably. For me, not at all. And tell me, how is Dr. Stone holding up? I believe he was up all night, sitting vigil over my split skull."

"He's starting to wilt," Charlotte said. "Looks like he should call it a day pretty soon. But he said he wants to go out to your place to check on you before going home."

"No!" June looked down at the tablet on which she'd written Dr. Wendy Feldtbrow and a phone number. She ripped the page off and folded it in half. "I mean, that's not at all necessary." She couldn't see John now for she wouldn't be able to conceal her concern and confusion and anxiety about him. "Tell him to send Elmer out here. I'm perfectly all right. I don't even have a headache. But I do want to borrow my dad's truck. I have a couple of errands."

"You shouldn't be driving."

She didn't feel like arguing with Charlotte. "Fine, I'll let my dad drive. And maybe have him take me out to dinner. But I don't need John tonight."

"You sure?"

"Oh yes. I'm sure."

Elmer arrived at six. He gave two sharp taps on the front door to warn her, then opened it. "June?" he called. "You see this out here?"

"See what?"

"You better come look."

Sadie bounded out the front door ahead of her. When June got to the porch, she gasped. It was covered with gifts. There were flowers, plants, casseroles, cakes, pies, cookies, cards, stuffed animals, embroidered pillows, bows, bells, an ice chest filled with tea and lemonade, a daisy afghan, a stack of paperback novels tied up with a ribbon, videos, playing cards, a get-well poster — everything but a side of beef. She had never heard a single car engine; Sadie had never raised an alarm.

"Looks like the whole town has been here," she said, stunned.

"A long way from a dozen eggs or a basket of fruit, eh, June?" he asked.

"I've never seen anything like this," she said.

"Makes a body feel it might've been worth it to take a sick day, after all," Elmer suggested.

She realized then that perhaps they never had. Either of them. Oh, they'd had the occasional day off, even that rare case of the flu or a sprain. But neither of them had ever been seriously ill or hurt. The people in town must have been terrified at the mere thought they might lose their doctor.

With that, she smiled. Hadn't she just been thinking, with all the fuss the women made over John Stone, that she'd never had that kind of welcome? Come to that, she'd had to live with the fact that there were still people who sought out her father first.

So this was what they really felt, she

thought with secret satisfaction. They loved her. They valued her, after all.

"Good thing you weren't hurt bad," Elmer said. "You'd have to rent a Quonset hut."

SEVENTEEN

June knew with reasonable certainty that Tom could be found at the café in the morning. In fact, it was typical for their paths to cross several times a day, whether as they were catching a meal or a coffee break, or when some medical emergency threw them together. Like the accident. But with a sense of urgency, she decided to see him at once.

"I'd like to run out to the Toopeeks," June told Elmer as they were clearing the front porch of gifts. "And . . . let's take some of this stuff out there. Much as I appreciate the gestures, there's no way I can make use of it all."

"Goody," Elmer said. "I haven't had a piece of Philana's pie in weeks. You know, she makes a new pie every afternoon. Puts George Fuller and Burt Crandall completely to shame. As I remember, she could make 'em that good even back when she was working with nothing but a campfire and mud-pit oven."

Back when . . .

When June was small her favorite thing in the whole world was to spend the night with the Toopeek family. They had a fire in the yard and slept in bedrolls on the hard-packed dirt floor of their dark, musty little house. It was more of a lean-to than a cabin. The family had moved to the valley when Tom was three, the fourth of what would be seven Toopeek children.

Their barren camplike life-style was not some Native American custom, but due to poverty. By almost anyone's standards. But June never remembered a time that she considered the Toopeeks poor. She didn't even realize they'd *been* poor until junior high, when they weren't anymore. And she was nearly grown before she learned that a few Valley people had had to fight against their neighbors to support Lincoln's right to settle where he had. Elmer, Judge — who had not yet been a judge but had always been called one — Sam, Myrna, Bud Burnham, old Cliff Bender — who had been old since June was a kid — and Mikos Silva . . . They were an odd lot. It seemed some of the people in the area had a problem with Indians living off the reservation. What they didn't understand was there was no reservation in California for Lincoln and Philana; they had left their people in Oklahoma. But apparently there were a number of white townspeople who would have run the Toopeeks off if they hadn't been stopped. Many times June wished she could have witnessed that battle.

Marilyn Hudson not only defended the Toopeeks' right to homestead, she also befriended Philana. The women took to each other at once; they shared their philosophies and customs regarding domestic arts, child rearing and marriage. But the idea of June sleeping overnight there horrified her. "They sleep on the *ground,* Elmer," she had complained.

And Elmer countered, "They sleep on bedrolls and keep each other very well. Let her go. She'll learn something."

June didn't learn the things her mother had envisioned. She didn't learn how lucky she was that her family had a Maytag washer and Frigidaire refrigerator. Instead, she learned the names of all the stars, how to cook fish on a stick over the fire, how to track a deer by its droppings, how to make an herb plaster to cure poison ivy and oak. She ran wild with Tom and a couple of the other Valley boys. She went home dirty, exhilarated and smelling gamey.

Lincoln and Philana had been in their twenties when they'd hobbled into town in a dilapidated old pickup with four little kids and a fifth imminent. They'd had some sort of disagreement with their families and left them, using the last little bit of their money to buy a small parcel of land from an aging farmer. They lived first in tents — a state of affairs that drove some Valley people crazy — then they built the little cabin with trees they cleared and cut with primitive tools. That cabin was still the anchor of the current house, the house Tom and Ursula had built to hold their own brood of five. Lincoln and Philana still lived in the original cabin, though they shared the rest of Tom's house.

Ursula was Navajo. She and Tom had met when both were students at Sacramento State University. She often joked that she had to get him quick before he went all the way back to the Cherokee Nation for a wife. Tom, of all the Toopeek children, was the one most interested in preserving some native customs; he even took his degree in history. But then law enforcement drew him, first in Sacramento and eventually back home. Most of Grace Valley welcomed him back gratefully, in need of an experienced lawman, but there were still those who didn't think he and his should even live there, much less hold a position as authoritative as chief of police. They were probably the same ones who wouldn't use June as a doctor because she was a woman.

It was from Ursula that June learned how ethnocentric the tribes were. You weren't simply Native American, you were Cherokee or Sioux, Navajo or Cheyenne. And despite the fact that the Toopeeks had left their reservation and taken land among the whites, they clung to old ways and were not quick to change. Recently, within the past year, June had heard Lincoln say to his daughter-in-law, "That may be the way the Navajo do it, Ursula, but the Cherokee do it so."

Of all the things June learned from the Toopeeks, the most important was their sense of abundance. Even when they had next to nothing, they always seemed to have a little left over to share. Whereas Elmer would grouse at June, "Turn that damn light off — you think we're made of money?" Lincoln would say to her, "Our table is your table, and bring your mother and father."

When Elmer and June arrived at the Toopeek house, there was a light on in every window and the glow from a campfire behind the house. There were strict burning regulations in northern California, but the old father of the police chief would have his ritual fire whenever he pleased.

"June!" Tanya Toopeek said in surprise when she answered the door. "You're just in time. Grandfather is praying for you."

"Good deal. Get your brothers and sisters to get some stuff out of the truck, will you?"

"Sure. What stuff?"

Ursula came to the door, a dish towel in her hands. "What stuff?"

"The town came to my house while I was sleeping off my knock on the head. They left their get-well gifts. More than I will ever eat or use, I'm afraid."

"If you're looking for people to help you eat, this is the place. Let me see," Ursula said, leaning close and squinting at the stitches in June's hairline. "Ouch."

"Doesn't hurt much anymore," she said. "But damn, did I have a headache this morning."

Elmer reached the front door with laden arms. "Ursula, you have coffee?"

"For you, I'll make fresh. June, I feel guilty. I didn't bring any gifts to your porch."

"Thank God. Really, you can't imagine all the stuff. . . ."

"But doesn't it make you feel wonderful? To know the town values you so highly?"

"It's a little staggering," June said. "I've never felt unappreciated, but . . ." She stopped. Five Toopeek children led by Tanya pushed past her to the front drive. "I can't remember anything like that ever happening in Grace Valley. Do you?"

"Birdie had a nice kitchen full of casseroles," Ursula said. Her eyes grew round and astonished as her children, aged eight to fifteen, begin to reenter the house carrying covered dishes, plastic containers, boxes, bags and pans filled with goodies. "My God," she whispered, aghast. "June, this qualifies as an outpouring!"

"This isn't even the half of it," June said. "The porch was covered. I had to leave Sadie home because we nearly filled the truck bed. And now that she's gotten used to going everywhere with me, she was expressly unhappy to be left. You should have seen the look she gave me."

"Well, come in. We'll have coffee and start packaging and freezing your goodies and casseroles."

"I'd like that, but actually, I have to see Tom about something. Shouldn't take a minute."

"He's out back, whittling while Lincoln

chants. He's praying for you, you know."

"Tanya said that," June said, surprised anew. "Do you suppose his prayers had something to do with all my casseroles and desserts?"

"There were many times he managed to cover his own table and feed seven children when their means were slim. I suspect he has great influence."

Wish I could get him on a special project, June thought. But she kept silent.

June carried two cups of coffee into the backyard. Tom crouched on one side of the small campfire and Lincoln sat cross-legged on the ground on the other side. She shivered slightly inside her wool jacket. The late spring afternoons had begun to be warm and humid from the rains, but in the evening the temperature dropped, and the night air was crisp. The fire felt good. "I brought coffee," she said.

"June," Tom said. "I didn't know you were here."

"Long enough for Ursula to brew a fresh pot." She held out a mug toward Tom, who accepted, and toward Lincoln, who held up a hand to decline.

"I'll go inside for some in a few minutes," Lincoln told her. "You have that one."

"Thanks. And Elmer is inside, Lincoln. Probably sitting behind a big slice of Philana's pie."

Lincoln smiled. "Today would be rhubarb. The favorite of the house."

Then he seemed to withdraw into himself and resume meditating, shutting them out.

"I want to talk to you about a couple of things. I need your help with something," June told Tom. "A very delicate matter."

He straightened up and waved a hand toward the picnic table. "Step into my office."

"I still can't believe this is happening. It has to do with John Stone. . . ."

"John?"

"I did a routine check of his references. He graduated from medical school with honors, did a residency in OB-GYN and later went back east, to Boston, for a second residency in family medicine. He gave me a list of doctors to talk to for character references and they recommended him highly.

"Then I had a young, pregnant patient refuse to see John again. She panicked at the suggestion, and she needs a specialist. She implied he was improper with her."

"Did you speak to John about it?" Tom inquired.

"No. And in waiting, I waited too long. At

a loss, I called the founder and CEO of the OB-GYN clinic he was a partner in before his second residency. This doctor was not on John's list of references, and for good reason. He appears to despise John, but wouldn't be specific about his reasons. He would only say they parted on bad terms, something about John wanting to be bought out of the partnership his clinic gave him. It was easy for me to brush off — economic differences have nothing to do with me. Besides, that's not so unusual. John would have built equity into his share by investing his own time and work, patients he would have to leave behind.

"But John realized what I had done, who I had talked to. Assuming I wanted a list of references from that California clinic, he gave me a new list of names — his old OB nurse, an office manager, a physician's assistant. I talked to the nurse, who sang his praises."

"Back and forth, back and forth," Tom observed.

"You don't know the half. After John stitched up my head, spent the night looking after me, saw all my patients so I could rest, I wondered how I could ever have doubted him. He's a good guy, Tom, I just know it. But this afternoon I got a call from a woman, a doctor who knew John well some years ago just before he left the Fairfield Clinic. She gave me a laundry list of personal problems John suffered. Then she topped it off by telling me she had him arrested for sexually assaulting her."

Tom was frozen silent by the allegation, the quick shrinking of his black pupils, barely visible, the only outward sign he was stunned.

"Now I don't know what to think. I really can't talk to him about it, not until I get some information. The only place I can think of to look is public records. Police records."

"That's easily done," Tom said. "And . . . if there's no record of this assault . . . ?"

"Why wouldn't there be?"

"Any number of reasons. He could have been picked up and not charged, in which case certain baseless records are expunged regularly to make room for real arrests. Or he could have been charged and dismissed. Or —"

"But will you check?"

"Of course. My advice, however, is that you speak to John about these allegations. And look closely at his eyes as he explains."

"Yes, you're right. But not just yet. First let's see if we find anything."

Tom smiled. "We?"

She smiled back. "You. Thanks in advance. I'm going to do my best to put this from my mind until I hear something about your investigation."

He took a sip of coffee. "You said there were a couple of things."

"Oh! I nearly forgot." She reached into her pocket and pulled out a bloodstained rag. "When Cliff woke me, this rag was pressed to the cut on my head. When John stitched me up, I instinctively stuffed it into my pocket. Look at it."

He did so without touching it. Folded, it was about six inches long, three inches wide and a triple thickness. "Cheesecloth?" he asked.

"More like homespun. Or maybe muslin. It isn't mine . . . didn't come from my bag."

"Cliff?"

"Nope. Cliff thinks I was thrown out of the Jeep, but I wasn't, Tom. I was pulled out of the burning Jeep by a thirty-year-old man who kept his pants up with rope suspenders and carried an ax. In fact, he said he used the ax to open the Jeep and get me out. He put this on my head and rinsed it out in a stream that wasn't there."

"I get the impression you haven't told anyone about this," Tom said.

"It was him, Tom. Wyatt. There's no question in my mind."

"Wyatt is a very prevalent folktale. It's possible you dreamed him."

"And this?" she said, eyeing the rag still resting in her palm. "Did I dream this?"

"There are a number of possible explanations. It could have been lying on the roadside."

"Except for the blood, it's perfectly clean! I'm sending it off to a lab. I'd like to know what kind of fabric this is and how old it is."

"I'll be anxious for the results as well, but if I may, you might wish to limit the people you share this story with."

"You think no one will believe me?"

"Oh, I don't know. Some would, some wouldn't. I'd just hate to see them lift an eyebrow, the way they do at Jerry Powell's spaceship ride."

"Well, maybe he really did have a ride in a . . . Okay, I see your point."

"By the same token, June, I think I'll take a run out to the salvage yard and look at the Jeep. It's burned to a crisp, but if the driver's door was opened with an ax, I'll know it with one look."

Jessica pulled up to the Stones' house in

her little Toyota truck, ready for some baby-sitting. Susan had called earlier and asked if she would mind. John had been putting in so many hours, the couple never had any time to talk. Tonight they would just grab a bite at the Vine & Ivy in town and have a real conversation, while Jessica tangled with Sydney over a video game or two before bedtime.

The door opened before she could even knock and there stood Susan, looking a bit sullen. "Bad news," she said. "John just got a call. Vintner by the name of Hank Bryant cut his leg on some binding wire, badly enough that he doesn't think he should try to drive to the hospital. . . ."

"I know Hank," Jessica said.

"I guess our dinner out is probably off. I'd hate to ask you to wait around. What if it takes all night?"

At that moment John whisked through the doorway with his bag. "Sorry, Jessie," he said, moving quickly toward his BMW. "Susan will pay you anyway. Lost wages."

She looked longingly at his back as he went. "It's not important," she said, because the money meant nothing to her. She just longed to see what had happened to Hank, and to see what John would do.

"John?" Susan said, stopping him. He

looked at his wife and Jessica over the top of his car. The young girl looked so forlorn, he tilted his head to one side in some confusion. Susan, standing behind Jessica, pointed at her, but John didn't get it. "John, do you need any help on this house call?" Jessica's eyes lit from within, and slowly it dawned on John.

"Ah . . . ah . . . yeah! Sure. Jessie? You want to ride along?"

"Is it okay?" she asked excitedly.

"As long as you don't try to take over the sutures," he said.

Like a bolt, she was beside him in the car. "This is great," she said. "Really great!"

When Elmer drove June home from the Toopeeks, she was forced to make an immediate decision — one she hoped she would not live to regret.

"Good of you to leave a light on for Sadie," Elmer said.

But she had not.

"Well, I have to think like a dog owner now," she said.

"I'm sure Sadie appreciates it. You'll be okay?"

Oh, she hoped so. She prayed so. But she said, "I think so, Dad. And in case I didn't say so already, thanks for everything you've done. I sometimes forget to tell you how much I appreciate you."

He laughed a little bit. "Sometimes I forget to do things for which I can be appreciated. Get some rest."

She climbed onto the porch and approached the door slowly; she could hear Sadie squeaking on the other side. June let herself in, closed the door behind her and let Sadie welcome her. First things first. Then she said, "I'm alone." And that brought him out of the shadows and into the light. "You've got some nerve, you know."

He smiled as though he knew. "I wanted to see that you were all right. And I brought you something."

"Flowers? Candy? Believe me, I'm all stocked up."

"No," he said. "This." He held out his hand and there, on his palm, in an opened leather sheath, was a badge.

EIGHTEEN

"I've heard that undercover police officers who are investigating narcotics and such have to occasionally partake. You know, to prove to the people they're investigating that they're really okay. This is true?"

"This is true," said Jim. "But I don't find myself in that particular situation. So don't worry. Worry about something else if you have to worry."

"Should I worry about you being killed?"

"I don't know that you should. It's optional. My mother, for example, worried about that a lot. Before it was really even an issue, she worried it like a hangnail."

"Does she still?" June asked.

"I hope not. She's on the other side now."

"Oh. My condolences."

He smiled and drew her near. "It was quite a long time ago. She worried herself nutty when I was a street cop."

"You can't imagine how grateful I am for

the badge, Jim. I didn't think it was possible I'd be attracted to . . ." Her voice trailed off. She hadn't intended to be quite so transparent. "Well, that's out," she said in disgust.

He laughed heartily, stretching out his legs and relaxing against the sofa. "I knew you'd fallen for me."

"Must be the pain medication — loosened my tongue. As I was saying, I believed I would know if you were of a criminal bent. I believed my instincts would direct me. But I worried about it, because my instincts have been a little jostled lately." And she frowned to herself, thinking how she'd frozen when Birdie and Judge needed her, how she'd been rescued by an angel, how she'd investigated John. Phew, it had been a rugged week. "Jostled doesn't even touch it."

After finding him in her house, she'd brewed a pot of coffee for him, a pot of tea for herself, and they'd settled onto the sofa together. He explained that he had been aware of the fire, and learned that it had been her Jeep. "I hadn't expected to see you again this soon," he said. "I'm not the best kind of boyfriend."

"What makes you think I'll let you be my boyfriend?" she countered.

Ignoring her question, he continued, "I

don't get away often, and if you ever happen to see me in public circumstances, you should pretend you don't know me. Whether anyone likes it or not, I'm going to do this kind of work for about three more years. And then I'm going to retire."

"And who besides me wouldn't like it?"

"I have a sister who took over worrying when my mother passed on. She's not exactly sure what kind of work I do, but she knows I work for a federal agency, and suspects the worst."

"Just so you don't have a wife, or even an ex-wife. . . ."

"Whew! Even an ex-wife would disqualify me?"

June thought about it. "Yes, I think it would. Today."

"God, you're tough!"

"I am. I don't like crowds."

"No intimate partners. No kids. No girlfriends. I have a couple of ex-girlfriends, but even you couldn't be that picky. . . ."

"Just out of curiosity, when you 'get away,' as you put it, where do your buddies think you're going?"

"To get laid."

That put a rod in her spine; she came stiffly upright, eyes wide, mouth open in shock.

"What're they going to understand? Huh?" he asked.

"Where do you say you're doing this? You don't say you're coming to my house, do you?"

"Of course not. We have a halfway house. A safe house. A friendly little brothel down the road where one of our own takes clients. Her clients are insiders. It gives us a little break from the action."

"So, what exactly are you doing right now?" she asked curiously.

"Come now, you know better than that. I've already told you too much. But as my doctor, you have to maintain confidentiality, don't you?"

"So, are you saying if I let you be my boyfriend, you're going to have to be kept totally secret? For three years?"

"Unless my territory is changed. In which case it will be even harder to be your boyfriend."

"Then why would I even entertain such a notion?" she asked him.

"Well, I'm counting on you not being able to help yourself," he said.

She settled into the crook of his arm, leaning against him very comfortably. "I'm going to be able to help myself tonight. I have a headache."

■ ■ ■ ■

June wasn't going to rush into anything. Despite a crippling attraction, despite unmistakable desire, she did not pop open the ivory case that held her brand-new diaphragm. She would, at the very least, get to know him better. Her secret man. It brought a smile to her lips just thinking about him.

For one thing, he had the bluest eyes she'd ever seen. Positively deep wells. And she loved the way his cheeks became hard and round like little apples when he smiled. And that dimple right under the left one, at the corner of his mouth. Oh, and there was the hair, thick and unruly. He was forty years old and there was no evidence he'd ever lose his hair.

Her headache had not prevented her from at least completing that kiss she'd started a few days before. She'd been right about that much — it was a wonderful kiss. He was a powerful kisser. A hungry kisser. Of course, his hand had strayed to her breast and she'd said, "Not yet. You're going to be patient. And I'm going to get more comfortable with this idea."

He'd said, "Okay." But he'd kissed her in

a way that suggested she might not want to force too much patience on him. Which just added to his allure. There was nothing quite so sensual as impatience, nothing so titillating as a man with a weak grasp on self-control, as a lover just *dying* to possess.

She had pushed him out the door at midnight and he'd disappeared into the trees. "I might as well be having an affair with Robin Hood," she told Sadie.

She dreamed about him that night and in the dream he became Wyatt and Wyatt became Jim. When she tried to hold either one of them close, she found her arms empty. But in the early hours of the morning, as she woke for the day ahead, she was snuggling dreamily into the down comforter, nurturing a fantasy that was rich and deep. With flushing anticipation, she knew that before terribly long she was going to have a man in her life again.

Her distraction was so acute, she actually forgot she didn't have a vehicle to drive to work in. When she popped out onto the porch in the morning, Sadie by her side, she stopped short at the sight of Tom leaning against his Rover. "Hiya," he said.

"Jeez, I must be losing it," she answered.

"You weren't expecting me? Who were you expecting?"

"You're not going to believe this, but I forgot I don't have a Jeep to go to work in this morning. I —"

"I believe it." He straightened up. "His name is Jim Post, and you're right about what he's doing."

"You *know?*"

He opened the passenger door for her. "I know. But be advised, very few people know who he is or what he's doing. And I don't know where he's working, okay? We probably shouldn't talk about this again after today."

"God, I can't believe it," she said. "Right here in Mayberry."

"Not exactly," Tom said. "Mayberry is Mayberry — pretty quiet most days. With Gus Craven in jail, my only worry is whether I'll have to break up a fight between the Barstow twins. But right up the road is Gomorrah."

"Our neighbors," she said grimly.

"They don't bother us much, we don't bother them much. Well, County Sheriff tries to bother them, DEA tries, Forestry tries . . . but me? I live in peace with my enemies."

Yes, she thought. This is true. That stuff going on back there, the drug farming, they tried to stay aloof from that. Because they couldn't stop it or cure it or make it go away. If the Justice Department couldn't get the best of it, then how could one Cherokee cop?

"But *he's* okay. I told you," she said.

"If I were you, I'd think twice."

"Because?"

"Because of what he does for a living. Not only does he mingle with pretty unsavory characters, that kind of work tends to rub off on people. Makes them pretty cynical. Dark."

"No, he's not. He talks about his grandmother. He likes to hear the stories about the town."

"What if someone from back there follows him?"

"What if?" She shrugged.

"That could put you in danger."

"If he were sneaking out to *your* house, there could be danger for *you*. I'm not a cop. I'm no threat. I'm not even a girlfriend yet, though the thought beckons. Besides, we met innocently. I think we could get away with it even if his cronies knew." She smiled and she lifted her chin in a challenge.

"Don't even think that!" Tom snapped at her. "God, don't even think that! Those men back there, they aren't fraternity brothers. They aren't gentlemen. They have no respect for proprietary relationships. There's no honor among thieves. There are those, back in the camps, who, if they knew he had a woman, might follow him to your house, wait for him to leave and —"

"Okay! I knew that!" She and Sadie got into the Range Rover, and he drove toward town in silence. "He's good at what he does or they wouldn't let him be doing it. He wouldn't put me in harm's way. He wouldn't."

"I assume the same," Tom said more quietly. "Or I'd ask his boss to pull him in to keep you out of danger. But please, don't get romantic and stupid. He's in a serious job . . . and it's nothing to play around with."

"Did you warn Ursula that she shouldn't get involved with a lawman?" June asked.

"It's not the same thing, and you know it. And speaking of her, you can't confide in Ursula. In anyone. When Elmer eventually finds out, it's going to upset him."

"Now stop that! You act as though I'm going to marry this guy, and so far I've only let him in my house a couple of times. Are you spying on me?"

"June, you gave yourself away. You kept asking about the men who came to your clinic. You had that twitterpated look in your eyes."

"*Twitterpated?*" she asked, bursting into laughter.

"I have seen that look in Tanya's eyes. Boys don't get it."

"Oh. Boys don't get it. Oh brother. So, you saw this look, and I asked too many times, and you did what?"

"I asked the right question of the right person because I had personal concerns. What happens with their operation is out of my hands — except that I'll be ready for any fallout. What happens with my friend is a matter of importance to me."

"Tom. How sweet," she said. "Well, thank you, I guess . . . But I already knew he was all right. And even though he might be doing something very risky, he makes me feel safe. He makes me feel —"

"June, please. Don't tell me too much. I'm not good at this sort of thing."

She leaned forward in her seat, staring at his stoic profile. "It's hard to tell when a Cherokee is blushing."

"Blushing is not a Native thing. We don't blush, we glower." He turned his fierce expression on her, then looked back at the road. "You understand, for his safety, as well as your own, no one can know about him."

"I know how Mrs. Muir must have felt," she said.

"You can always decide this is a bad idea," Tom offered.

"No I can't," she said, because she couldn't.

"The thing is," he said, "not being able to talk to anyone, not being able to share . . . it could be lonely for you."

"Lonely?" she asked with a laugh. "Oh Tom!" She looked at him; his puzzled frown was directed to the road. Lonely? What did he think she had been? Because she had six hundred friends who loved her enough to sneak get-well gifts onto her porch, he thought she was never lonely? Because she had Elmer for Tuesday night meat loaf, the Graceful Quilters on Thursday nights, medical emergencies, town fairs, dinner parties at Aunt Myrna's. . . . Did he think she was never *lonely?* My God, it had been years since she'd been kissed, much less held and stroked and told she was beautiful. Maybe a secret man was the best kind for her, the way people were always in her business.

"We speak as though this is fait accompli," she said. "But Jim and I haven't done anything that could possibly bond us as a couple." No need to tell Tom about the best kiss since junior high. "Who knows if he'll even show up again?" she said, though upon parting the night before, he had promised.

"Maybe this won't last long, in that case. Let me gas up here at Sam's, then I'll run you by the café for your coffee."

"Sure," she said absently. It was good to back Tom off the trail, get him thinking about something and someone else. June would prefer to manage her own romance without the chief of police's help.

Sam came out of the filling station as Tom gassed up the Rover. Funny, June thought. Fish must not be biting yet . . . or maybe he was already fished out for the day. He and Tom exchanged a few quick jokes while the pump ran, and Sam pulled that wad of cash out of his pocket so he could make change.

Her eyes were drawn to a flash of color in the window of the station. Flowers? Not just flowers, but an exquisite floral arrangement in spring pinks, yellows, peach, soft orange, lavender. . . .

"Oh my God!" she gasped. "Justine!"

She opened the Range Rover's door and, grabbing her bag and whistling a command to Sadie, took off down the street to the Flower Shoppe.

NINETEEN

"Justine!" she called.

Justine came from the back room carrying a beautiful carnation arrangement formed around a small carousel. "June? Hi. How are you? I heard about your accident. I was worried sick. I brought some flowers to your house — the porch was already covered with gifts."

"Ah, yes. Yes, thank you." She stretched her memory for which flowers came from Justine, but she hadn't gone through each item as she should have. She silently berated herself for not making a proper list for thank-you notes. Birdie would be appalled. "Justine, I'm so sorry. I missed our appointment!"

"Well June, that seems reasonable. You were in a car accident, after all."

"I can see you this morning if you like. We'll just have Jessie make a dent in the schedule and you come in whenever you want."

Justine laughed rather brightly. "Now June, don't go crazy over this, there's no rush. I'll make an appointment for sometime next week. I don't even know how soon a person should have a first checkup. When's the earliest I need to be seen? Since I already know my condition."

First checkup? June thought, frowning. This was a new twist. Far different than the panic of a couple of nights ago, along with the demand for an immediate abortion. Plus Justine looked fabulous, not just better than the other night, when her face had been splotchy from tears and her hair and clothing in disarray from general neglect. This was more than an improvement, this was a whole new Justine. Even her usually ruddy complexion looked rosy. And instead of looking chubby and unpretty, she looked pleasantly roundish and *sensual.* Maybe it was her posture.

"Well," June said, "that all depends on how you're feeling."

"I feel just great," she said, flashing a bright and healthy smile.

"And . . ." June faltered. "You're not very far along, are you?"

"No. Just a month or so. But I can already

tell. You know?"

"No morning sickness?"

"Well, at first I felt just ill all over." She laughed. "At first I wanted to *die!*"

"And you feel better about . . . things now?" June asked. She'd known some people to blossom with pregnancy, but never like this. If she didn't know better, she'd think Justine had just spent a couple of months in a health spa. But it had been less than forty-eight hours since she'd seen her. And then Justine had been distraught.

"I'm feeling better about everything, thanks."

June suddenly believed Justine must have worked something out with Jonathan, which she immediately felt would be a mistake. Either that or she'd successfully murdered him.

"Well, if you're not in crisis and you're feeling well, come and see me by six weeks. That should be soon enough."

"Okay. I'll call Jessie."

"Justine, I must say, you're looking wonderful. Pregnancy must agree with you."

"Yes, I think it does. I'm hoping it's a girl."

"You've changed your mind, then? About the —"

"Oh God, yes! I was a little crazed when I came into the clinic the other night. Plus

I'd just barely left Jonathan. I had only just told him about the baby. Needless to say, he was in a state of shock. And probably didn't handle himself very well."

"Ah. And have you had a chance to work things out with him? A little more rationally?"

She frowned. "No. I don't plan to ever speak to that big jerk again."

June leaned wearily on the counter, resting her head on the heel of her hand. Sadie nosed around the store, squeaking. "Nonetheless," June said in confusion, "you certainly appear born-again, if you don't mind my phraseology."

"Born-again! How funny!" She laughed.

"It's none of my business, but I'm sure curious about the change, your about-face."

"I owe it to Sam. When I left your clinic the other night, I was still so upset, I didn't want to go home. I was afraid my dad would know something was wrong and somehow find out my problem and — you know — kill me. So I came here. Between crying jags, I got a little flower arranging done.

"Then after the fire — your Jeep — Sam brought the fire truck back to town to gas her up, saw the light and came over to see if I was all right. Well, I was *not* all right! I don't know what it is about Sam. You can just talk to him, you know?"

"You can?"

"He's so understanding. So gentle. So *wonderful!*"

"He is?"

Justine nodded, but her eyes were rolled skyward. "Oh God, yes! First of all, he made me see that this problem was not a problem at all, but a gift. Anyone who doesn't see it that way has no respect for humanity. For life. For motherhood.

"Then he told me about how beautiful and sexy and remarkable pregnant women are! How all the curves and padding just makes a woman that much more womanly. Even my complexion has already gotten healthier! Even through all those tears, he could see that."

"He could, could he?"

"There was really a lot to talk about. I was so hurt and confused and upset, and I was desperate for a clearheaded perspective. So yesterday I closed the shop and went fishing with Sam. By the end of the day I was a new woman. I'm having this baby, June. I'm raising her, I'm going to be a good mother, and at least I'm going to be responsible for my actions. In a loving way." Then her expression changed to a more bitter twist. "Unlike some pious people I know!"

"Well," June exclaimed. "If you're happy, I'm happy!"

"Oh, I am! In fact, I don't know when I've been happier! I'm thinking about asking Sam to be my childbirth coach!"

"Really? I wouldn't have cast Sam in that role, but —"

"He'd be perfect. I just need to be sure I'm around positive people now. People who are happy for me. People who really care about me."

"I certainly can't argue with that. Good for you. You come and see me in a couple of weeks, unless you have a problem — in which case you should call me at once. Okay?"

"Okay. Are *you* feeling all right now?" Justine asked, touching her own head in reference.

"Huh? Oh yeah." June touched the spot. "It itches. Sadie, come here!" The dog immediately turned and came to June. June crouched, bringing Sadie's head next to hers. "Look. Twins."

"How cute," Justine said.

"See you later, then," June said.

"Sure, hon."

Hon? This was a very strange transformation. But, June had to admit, it was better than what she'd see before.

"Um, Justine, I was just wondering. . . . Have you told your father?"

"No. Not yet. No hurry on that, I guess. It's only going to get him riled up, so I'd as soon wait till I *have* to. You know?"

"Oh, I do know! Good luck!"

Still shaking her head in bemusement, June went to the café. Tom was already there, along with some of the old locals, including Elmer.

"Everything all right?" Tom asked.

"Uh-huh. I had forgotten, Justine left me a beautiful floral arrangement yesterday. A get-well thing. I wanted to thank her."

"It appeared to be an urgent thank-you," Tom observed.

But June's attention was drawn to her father, who glumly stared into his coffee cup and hadn't even muttered "good morning."

"What's the matter with him?" she asked Tom.

"Poker's been called off."

"Really? Judge isn't up to it yet?"

Elmer turned toward them. "Judge is still out, and Sam isn't coming. That doesn't leave enough of a table."

"Oh, too bad. You can come out to dinner if you like. Why isn't Sam playing?"

"Damned old fool," Elmer said. "He has a

date. Taking Justine to dinner and a movie in Fort Bragg. For God's sake," he said in disgust.

"Oh Dad," June said, laughing. "Sam's just trying to cheer her up. She was kind of, I don't know, down in the dumps."

"Shows what you know," Elmer said.

"Dad, he's seventy! Justine is a twenty-six-year-old girl!"

"He said if things go right, he'll be missing a lot of poker . . . and he'll be buying a ring!"

Justine was the youngest of five girls; her mother had died when she was sixteen. Justine suffered her loss just a year before June's own mother died, and though they had nothing else in common, June had always felt a kind of bond with the girl because of that. Except it never seemed Justine felt any such bond with June.

Justine's older sisters married early and left Grace Valley with their husbands in what almost appeared to be a frantic exodus out of the valley, away from the grumpy, shortsighted, widowed Standard Roberts. Stan, as he was called by the locals.

Stan didn't mix much. He was always a presence at town doings, from fairs to meetings, but he had to be because he owned a large flower farm between the town and coast. He had to protect his interests and sell his wares. Justine got most of her flowers from her father's farm, and June assumed Stan had helped finance the shop.

Standard was a known grouch and had been even when his kindly and tolerant wife had been living, but he was not a cruel sort, like Gus Craven. Stan was just morose. He'd always had an impatient and gruff tone with his daughters, but June had never known him to be abusive. She made a mental note to be extra observant. If Stan didn't take well to this pregnancy, she wanted to be a support for Justine.

She wondered how Stan would like the idea of having a seventy-year-old son-in-law. Such a situation might require far more support than even June could muster.

"He didn't really say that!" she said to her father.

"He did. Said he always thought Justine special."

"Lord above! You think he'll ask Standard for her hand?" June asked.

"You think he'll ask me to pick Standard's bullets out of his backside?" Elmer retorted.

"This town just keeps getting more eccentric!"

"Eccentric? That what you call it?" Elmer

asked. "I would have said psychotic!"

They were both distracted then by the sound of screeching tires as a beige station wagon with one of those Christian fish slapped on the bumper careened through the town. Past the church, the clinic, the café, the police station. It fishtailed to an abrupt stop in front of the Flower Shoppe. Mrs. Clarice Wickham got out. Four bobbing heads remained in the station wagon as Clarice slammed the door and stomped up the steps to the shop.

"Uh-oh," June said. "Hell hath no fury . . ."

"Now what's that about?" Elmer muttered.

But June didn't answer — she just left her cup on the counter and bolted. She wasn't even aware of Tom and Elmer following her. "Stay in the car, kids," June said to the Wickham children as she ran past Clarice's parked vehicle. By the time she got in the shop door, Clarice was in high gear.

"If you think I'll stand by and watch you strut and humiliate my family, you're sadly mistaken, young hussie!"

"Young *hussie?*" Justine said. "Have you any idea what your —"

"I have a reputation to protect! I have innocent children who don't deserve the kind of cheap, nasty gossip your behavior is bound to bring down on them, and I could be forced to dramatic measures if you don't agree to just go away quietly and —"

"Go *away?!*"

June's mouth hung open; she was mesmerized by this display. Clarice's fists were clenched at her sides and her whole head was red. Her cheeks flamed and her scalp burned through her thinning blond hair. Elmer whispered in June's ear, "So it's true then. The pastor and Justine."

"*Was* true," she whispered back.

Tom Toopeek was not mesmerized. He was activated. "All right, Clarice, that's enough. Let's step outside and talk about this."

She snatched her arm away angrily when he would have led her. "There's nothing to talk about — except maybe the way this tart has tried to ruin my husband's career through lies and blackmail! Arrest her!!"

"Blackmail?" Justine asked dumbly.

"We should talk about your driving first," Tom said patiently.

"Blackmail?" Justine repeated.

"Slut!" Clarice screamed. "Whore! Tramp! Bawd! Harlot!"

"Bawd?" Justine asked in confusion. "Blackmail?"

"All *right!*" Tom shouted. He grabbed Clarice's upper arm more forcefully and began to pull her away from Justine's counter. But the woman started sobbing, covering her face with both hands and wilting before their eyes.

June was astonished. While Jonathan Wickham had managed to piss off a bunch of town women, he definitely had a power over others. That Justine and Clarice could be so swayed by the pastor was shocking. June wondered just how he managed it, and then had a fleeting regret that he'd never been a patient of hers or she might know.

From the back room, Sam emerged. Calmly. He held a cup of steaming coffee in his hand and had a look of anger in his steely blue eyes. Justine didn't turn to look at him, but smiled as he came up behind her. He slipped an arm around her shoulders, and as he did so, Justine seemed to grow taller and straighter. Her facial features reflected confidence for maybe the first time in June's acquaintance with her.

As for Sam, he was stunning. A handsome and powerfully strong man with a tan face, thick, snowy white hair, broad shoulders, flat stomach and remarkable height of at least six foot two, he made Jonathan Wickham look like a wimp by comparison.

Everyone in the room stood fixed and silent as Clarice spent herself on sobs. At long last she looked up, only to find Sam beside Justine. "You!" she said with viciousness. "I might have known *you* would consort with this whore! I told Jonathan it probably isn't even his! I told him he was being used and —"

June didn't even see Sam wind up, but his fist came down on Justine's counter with such force that the glass covering the top cracked into a million veiny lines. Clarice jumped and gasped, and Sam leaned over the counter and squinted his shining eyes. "That's *it!*" he shouted. "Don't let me ever hear another foul word come out of your mouth! You and your husband treat this young woman with respect, you hear me? Or you'll answer to me!"

Clarice sniffed back indignant tears. "You take her part then?"

"Oh yes," Sam said. "I'll be taking her part from here on. So watch out."

By the time June got to the clinic, the morning was wearing on. She made her apologies as she flew down the hall. "Sorry," she said. "Sorry to be late. Sorry."

"Slow down," Elmer said.

"You're okay," John said. "Not a bad

morning. Yet, that is."

"I can move a couple of things around and you can take some of the load off these men . . . or you can go back home and rest another day," Charlotte said.

"Thanks, Charlotte, but you're stuck with me." June hung her sweater on a peg inside the back door. She didn't hear a word from Jessica, who was usually bright and chipper. "Jessie?" she asked.

The girl turned slowly from her filing. "Hmm?"

"Everything okay?"

"Yeah. Fine." And she turned back.

Charlotte pushed June down the hall toward her office. "She's been like this the last two days. Moody. Cranky."

John sidled up beside them. "Y'know, she's been like this since she was out at our house. We asked her to baby-sit so we could go grab a quiet dinner. Alone, you know. But just as she pulled up, I had to run out to Hank Bryant's place to stitch up a laceration. He cut himself on baling wire. Took twenty-six stitches."

"And she was fine then?"

"She was absolutely fine. Excited. Happy."

"About baby-sitting?"

"Oh no, I took her with me out to Hank's."

"You did?"

"Well, she didn't have anything else to do. And she wanted to go. Then when we finished, it was too late to go out to dinner, so the three of us shared a frozen pizza. But honestly, she was fine."

"She's depressed," Charlotte snorted. "I bet her father's finally come down on her about the way she looks."

"Oh, I doubt that," John said. "She said she and her father have a great understanding."

June peered at him suspiciously. "You and Jessie are getting pretty close, are you?"

"Certainly," he said. "She's my best girl." And with that, he sauntered away. And June gulped.

Later in the day, June stopped by Jessica's desk in the front of the clinic, when no one was around to hear. "Jessie, are you feeling any better?"

"Oh, I'm sorry, June. I know I'm moody. I just have a lot on my mind."

"You can talk to me about anything, you know. Absolutely anything."

"I know. And I'm going to do that. Just give me a couple of days to think this through. Then I'd like to talk about it."

"Sure thing, pet. I'm here when you're

ready. Day or night."

Jessica smiled. "I appreciate that."

TWENTY

The phone rang and June pulled the towel tighter around her, wondering why no one waited until she was dressed anymore. "Hello?"

"What's this I hear about Sam and Justine?" Birdie demanded.

"Well, what did you hear?"

"I heard that Sam fancies himself in love with Justine, who is pregnant with Preacher Jon-Boy's baby."

"Good Lord!"

"Oh, don't play dumb with me. How much of that could possibly be doctor-patient confidentiality?"

"I did happen to be in the Flower Shoppe at the same time Sam mentioned he intended to stick by Justine from now on, on the off chance anyone wanted to give her any trouble. Other than that, I can't comment."

"Is it true Clarice Wickham called her a

lot of dirty names?" Birdie lowered her voice when she asked this.

June gave a huff of irresponsible laughter. "You should have heard her mouth," she whispered back. "It was unbelievable."

Birdie cackled. "Well, it's a shame. That poor Justine suffered a lot of naiveté by losing a mother at a vulnerable age. Was Standard going to teach the girl about men?"

"I agree it's a shame . . . but, Birdie, I have to run. I'm in an awful hurry."

"I didn't really call you about that. I just got very excited. We haven't had a good scandal around here since Morton Claypool went missing."

"Then why did you call? Are you feeling all right?"

"Oh fine, really. But there's someone I need for you to talk to. I made a new friend at the hospital, someone with special needs. Will you go there with me? This morning? Please?"

"Birdie, I *can't,*" June fairly wailed. "Oh God, I want to. You know I'd do anything for you! But I have to try to rent a vehicle this morning. I'm going to push my earliest patients off on Charlotte and John and see if I can find something in Rockport or Garberville. Can't Dad help you out?"

"Oh no, it has to be you. You have special talents, you know. Plus this is a job for a younger doctor."

"Birdie, let me do it another time, maybe later in the —"

"Good grief, don't sound so desperate! Come with me to visit my new friend, who happens to be in Valley Hospital in Rockport, and afterward I'll take you to dealers to shop for a truck. If you find one, you can drive it back to the valley. After all, I was just forced to rent a car. I can help you get the best deal."

"Oh Birdie . . ."

"June, this is important," she said in that firm, implacable tone. "I wouldn't ask you if it wasn't."

And I wouldn't say I was busy if I wasn't, June thought. But she didn't say anything. She relented, which in the end she always did, but she was unnerved. Why was it that whenever she said she was too busy, too pressed for time, her friends felt they could still press her to do what they wanted? Did no one consider that she would have to stay up a bit later, work a bit more over the weekend, or maybe have even less time to grab a meal?

She was still bristling when Birdie pulled up in her rented red Taurus. June decided to bring Sadie Five along, at least subconsciously hoping to annoy Birdie. "Excellent idea!" Birdie exclaimed. "My friend will love the dog. Love her!"

"I hope you realize I don't have much time to spend with your friend. What's the matter with her anyway?"

"I guess you'd call it an orthopedic problem, but that's just the beginning. I'm going to clam up about it and let you see for yourself. And hear for yourself."

"Well, then, how's Judge?" June asked.

"He's a nutcase. He is not the same since the accident and he annoys me more than ever!" Judge was still at home, recovering.

"Is he wearing his collar?"

"Only when someone is looking. The rest of the time he takes it off and complains. I don't think there's any point in keeping him home any longer. We really must send him back to the bench soon. I was not made to share such a small space with such a grumpy old man."

"He'll stop grumping soon," June laughed.

"I don't know why he would. He's been grumpy since he was seventeen," Birdie said. "Say, Myrna's got a new murder mystery out right about now. There's an autograph signing down in Westport on Saturday. Will you be going?"

"She never mentioned it!" June said, surprised.

"Two o'clock at the Bookworm. I'm going down if you want a ride."

"I wonder why she never mentioned it?"

"She may have forgotten. She's getting a little that way, don't you think?"

"What way?" June demanded.

"June, darling, there's something you're going to have to get used to. There's a lot of us just shy of going over — me and Judge, Myrna, Doc, Sam, Lincoln and Philana. . . ."

"Just shy of going over?" June repeated.

"Well, think about it," Birdie said. "It would no longer be premature for any of us. And a little late for some."

"All right, that's enough. I'm not going to talk about your impending death all the way to Rockport. That would definitely be asking too much."

Birdie had only been in the hospital for two nights, and the first was spent semiconscious with a terrible headache. But she was still able, as only Birdie could, to get around the place and stick her nose in a lot of business.

Birdie had to stay in the lobby with Sadie because her friend was on the third floor — no pets allowed. She told June to go to room 328. June expected to find a woman in her seventies, a woman much like Birdie. This indicated she didn't know Birdie as well as she thought she did, because the person Birdie directed her to was a sixteen-year-old boy. An amputee. He was sitting up in his bed and he wore knit running shorts, a T-shirt, his stump elevated and wrapped in white gauze. There was a trapeze over the bed so he could move himself around, and when she entered the room he appeared to be doing pull-ups on it. His young arms were muscled and tan.

"Clinton!" June said in instant recognition. "My gosh, you're looking an awful lot better! The last time I saw you —"

"I was almost dead," he said. "But I lost the foot."

"Yes. I was so sorry to hear that."

"I guess I'll be careful where I put the one I got left."

"Have you tried any prosthetic limbs yet?" June asked.

"Not yet, but I been up on crutches. I guess Miz Forest passed on that I wanted to see you."

"You wanted to talk to me?"

"Uh-huh. Miz Forrest said she knew you. You was friends."

June sat on the edge of Clinton's bed. "Well, yes. We've been friends forever, but she didn't tell me you *asked* to see me. She just brought me over, that's all. I was in a wreck a little after Bird— after Mrs. Forrest and Judge. See?" she said, pointing to her stitches. "Stripes. Now I have to go find a vehicle. What can I do for you?"

"We gotta do something about my folks, Doc. You gotta help me."

"What's the matter with your folks?"

"You have to ask?"

"Well, I mean . . . Why don't you explain what you want. Specifically."

"I don't know what I want. All's I know is I'm sixteen years now, Wanda's fourteen, and we ain't never been to school. We hardly ever get off that mountain, and if it wasn't for my mama's people on the other side of Shell Mountain over Paskenta way, down by Potter Valley, we'd hardly ever see anyone. Doc, you know my dad's sick, don't you?"

"Clinton, why don't you tell me what you know about your dad's sickness."

"I just know what I gathered from Mama talkin' to Granny an' her brothers."

"That's good enough," June said. "In fact, that's a good place to start. Your parents visit with your grandmother and uncles?"

"Yes, ma'am. She, Mama, has Granny and six brothers. She was the only girl and took the back end of a hammer in the face when she was about six years old. The claw end. My granny hid her because of her face." He shrugged. "Then my daddy was livin' alone in the forest, more or less hiding after he'd been to the war he calls 'In Country,' and he met my uncles and Mama. He took her off my granny's farm and brought her up to Shell Mountain where she had us — me and my sister."

"And you've always lived there?"

"Yes'm. Where Daddy needs the light to be dim and the air cool and not so many people about. Mama wouldn't mind being around people at all. In fact, she calls herself sociable, but she's afraid people would be put off by her scars. I expect she's right. That's their problems. Daddy gets het up somethin' terrible if there's a lot of people around and Mama worries that she'll put off people with her scars. That's why we're in the woods and ain't never seen a television set 'cept at my granny's house."

"I see your problem, Clinton," June said. "The good news is there's medication that can help your father, allow him to be more comfortable around people and so on. But the bad news is he's absolutely against the idea. I think he had some bad experience with drugs meant to help him."

"Yes'm, I heard him say so."

"Do you think your mother might help to convince him? That medicine has improved a lot in recent years?"

"I ain't never seen Mama go against him. Never."

"Maybe you can convince her, Clinton."

He gave a short laugh. "Doc, have you seen my daddy? He's a mountain unto himself."

She smiled. "He is that, Clinton. And you love him just the same."

He dropped his chin, looking down.

"I'm going to send Charlie McNeil to talk to you, Clinton. He's with the VA hospital. He's the man who went to see your parents to tell them how your surgery came out. I think between the two of you, you might come up with an idea or two that can help your parents."

"Do you think it possible, Doc?"

"There's always hope, Clinton. Tell me, if you could have any wish regarding your parents, what would it be?"

He only had to think a moment. "I'd just like to get them off that mountain. Before they get any worse."

When June got to the clinic, it was nearly lunchtime and the waiting room was still full; John and Charlotte had not been able to keep ahead of the crowd. She found her father seeing a leisurely few patients an hour, also. Doc was from the old school and couldn't be rushed.

"Things moving a little slow, Jessie?" she asked.

"Not really, it's more like an epidemic. We had twice as many people as we had appointments. And this is for you," she said, handing her a message slip. "The tech says they can't proceed without talking to you."

The message slip informed her that Justine Roberts was waiting for a pelvic sonogram at Valley Hospital and the technician questioned the order, which was written by Dr. Stone. "Can I have the chart please?" June asked.

"On your desk," Jessica said as she simultaneously dived for the phone. "Grace Valley Clinic," she said.

June went to her office and opened the chart. Justine had come in first thing in the morning, complaining of a little cramping and "heaviness" in her lower abdomen. John had used a urine test for pregnancy, and while it was positive, he drew blood to rule it out. "Normal fundus," he had scrawled. The uterus hadn't grown at all? An OB of John's experience would be able to detect even the slightest enlargement due to pregnancy. But he'd also recorded a normal cervix. Then why the sonogram?

June called the front desk. "Jessie, will you ask Dr. Stone to give me a minute when he's between patients, please?"

"Sure thing," she said.

It was only a few moments before John gave the door a couple of taps and stuck his head in. She held up the chart, Justine's name pointing toward him, and lifted her eyebrows in question. "I'm surprised by this," she said.

"Which part?"

"Not pregnant?"

"I don't think so. Possibly, if she's under a couple of weeks. . . ."

"She thought she was further than that, but still early. Why the test?"

"A hunch," he said.

"What kind of hunch?"

"I hate to say. . . . Let's do the test and then talk about my hunches."

"That's just it, John. The tech at Valley is waiting to hear from me. They don't want to do the test. She's asymptomatic, insurance won't pay."

"The ovaries," he said. "It's just one of those things you get a sense for over time, but she's feeling pelvic heaviness on and off, slightly crampy, period's late but the uterus is small and firm, she had minor discomfort during coitus, and I'll give you odds it's at least a small cyst."

"That's not good enough," June said, putting down the chart.

"Hey!" he protested. "It's good enough for me!"

"John, we don't do expensive tests on hunches!"

"Bull! You operate on hunches all the time! Your dad sets minor fractures without X rays!"

"That's different. He has those old country-doctor hands."

John leaned against the door frame, crossed his arms over his chest and smiled. "These are old pelvic hands, June. My hunches are usually good."

"Yeah, I appreciate that, but what about insurance?"

"Try 'rule out ovarian tumor,' and if that doesn't work, I'll pay for the test and her insurance can reimburse."

"You must feel strongly," she said. Or you're independently wealthy off that partnership sale, she thought with secret snottiness.

"I never do anything without strong feelings. You going to second-guess every order

I write?"

"This question comes from the tech. I told you there'd be a settling-in process. You don't walk into Grace Valley and get the key to the town."

"All I want is a picture of this nice lady's ovaries," he said patiently. "And a minimum of crap about it. I've seen a million blocked ears and runny eyes this morning. Twenty kids have coughed in my face and drooled on my shirt. Justine threatened to sue me —"

"What?"

"Oh, nothing." He waved June off. "She said something about feeling like a fool if she's not really pregnant. Any idea what that's about?"

"It's a long story, one I'll be glad to share after we clear out the waiting room. I'll call the technician and okay the test."

TWENTY-ONE

Only in Grace Valley's worst nightmare could it happen. Judge Forrest was at home recuperating from the car accident when Gus Craven's public defender took a petition for early release to the court. Gus had been good, he said. Had served a third of his sentence without getting into any trouble and should be released on his own recognizance. Besides, the jail was crowded.

The sitting judge obliged, with a stern warning that if Gus appeared again, he would go to the state penitentiary for a minimum of five years. Gus was released from jail.

"What?!" Tom Toopeek shouted into the phone when the director of corrections called to warn him. The bad news was repeated. "Well, for God's sake, don't let him leave till I get there!"

Tom called three people before he jumped in his Rover and sped to the County Corrections Facility. He called Corsica Rios and told her to get to Leah and the boys at once to warn them, then he called Judge to relate what had happened in his absence from the bench, and asked him, if he was up to it, to provide Leah with a little legal paperwork to help her protect herself. Finally he called Ursula and told her to keep an eye on Tanya, then he went to pick up Gus.

He parked outside the double-gated fence and leaned against his car, waiting. When Gus exited the facility, Tom was the first thing he saw.

"Sheesh! Just what I need! Goddamned Indian cop!"

"How about a ride, Gus?" Tom asked.

"How about you shove it where the sun don't shine. I'll call Leah from the next phone."

"I heard Leah isn't taking calls. Besides, how you going to get to the next phone, Gus?"

"My thumb!"

"Get in the Rover," Tom said, his patience waning.

"Anything say I have to?"

"No. It's only me inviting you, so we can have an important little talk about what you do next. But if you continue to decline the offer, I'm sure the nice guards in the patrol towers will be happy to look the other way while I help you into the car."

"Police brutality!" Gus yelled, then looked around. He hadn't roused anyone's attention. "Police brutality," he screamed again.

Wet brain, Tom thought forlornly. It just didn't seem possible one man could be so ignorant. He must have lost too many brain cells in the years he'd stayed pickled. "Come on, Gus. I'm getting bored with this."

Gus got a little red in the face, but he knew it was hopeless. He let himself in the passenger side with jerking, furious moves. He huffed onto the seat, crossed his arms over his chest and pouted. Tom had to reach all the way across the console to fasten his seat belt for him. Then they were underway.

"I'll be honest with you, Gus," Tom said. "I tried to convince Leah to file for divorce, but she hasn't gotten around to it yet. You getting out right now, well, it's a surprise and inconvenience to everyone. Especially Judge Forrest."

"That woman ain't getting no divorce! We're married till the death!"

"It isn't going to work out that way. I'm going to drive you to the farm so she can tell you herself, and then I'll help you find a place to stay."

Gus started to laugh, it was a mean and

mocking laugh. " 'At's my farm, Chief, and no Injun cop is gonna take it away from me."

"This has nothing to do with me. While you and I drive out there, Leah's getting herself a separation agreement that allows her to stay on the farm and take care of the boys until a divorce agreement can be reached. That's when you'll have your property settlement. And at the same time, we're getting her a protection order. In case you don't understand, Gus, it means that if you go near her or the boys, I get to arrest you again, and Judge gets to put you in jail again. And next time it will be on a more permanent basis."

Gus continued to laugh through Tom's explanation of legal procedure. He seemed to be shrinking into the seat as he curled forward in hilarity that was wholly contrived. But when Tom was done speaking, Gus stopped laughing and stared at him with squinty, mean, pinpoint eyes. He bared his rotting, yellowed teeth when he spoke. "Ain't gonna be no agreements and no orders. 'At's my farm, my wife, my young. 'At's where I'm going and 'at's where I'm staying." Then for emphasis, he socked his balled fist into the palm of his other hand.

Tom hit the brakes and put the Rover into

a hard spin. When they stopped, Gus's eyes had opened up considerably and he was hanging on to the door and the dash to steady himself. The Rover rocked to a stop sideways in the road, blocking any oncoming traffic. There didn't seem to be any, but the road curved around and over hills, and the shoulders were thick with trees and brush. At any moment a semi could round the curve and plaster them.

Tom leaned toward Gus. "Listen to me, you insufferable little jackass. Things are different at the farm now. The house is fixed and it's clean and the field is planted and your family is safe and happy. Leah's got a job, she's going to keep that job, she's paying her own bills, and she looks good for the first time since she met you."

Gus was shaking his head to and fro, craning his neck to see out the sides of the Rover. "Get out of the goddamned road, you ignorant Injun!"

"Look at me, Gus," Tom said slowly. "You hear what I'm telling you? With you gone that family of yours can live a decent life at long last, and I am not going to let you go back there and destroy that again. Look at me!" Tom shouted.

Gus stopped swiveling his head and looked at Tom. Tom glowered as only Tom could, and Gus's voice got a bit smaller. "You're gonna get us kilt, you goddamned fool," he said, but he looked at Tom as he was told to.

"You're going to stay away from Leah and the boys. I don't care what you do or where you do it, but you stay away from that farm, Gus."

"Just pull off the road, Injun," Gus begged nervously. "Could be a car or truck coming any second. Pull off the road, say whatever you want. I'll even go a few rounds with you if that's what you're looking for."

A slow smile spread across Tom's handsome face. "I don't think you understand, Gus. If I were to lay my hands on you, you'd never stand up again."

"You threatening my life, Chief?" he asked skittishly. " 'Cause if you —"

"Don't ever make me come after you, Gus. You wouldn't live to tell about it."

"That's what I thought I heard. I heard you saying —"

"Get out of the car," Tom said.

"You got it, you crazy son of a bitch!"

Gus opened the door and virtually leaped from the front seat of the Rover.

Tom slowly turned the car around and drove down the road. Just as he started off a large produce truck came barreling over the hill and passed him going the other direction. In his rearview mirror he could see Gus standing in the middle of the road, jumping up and down, shaking his fist at him.

Tom didn't get much satisfaction out of the whole event. He was pretty sure Gus was too damn stupid to take any of his advice seriously.

When Tom got out to the Craven farm he felt a swell of pride just driving up to the house. It had gone from a hovel to a pretty little farmhouse. Someone had taken the time to plant flowers all along the front walk and hang a couple of baskets of geraniums from the porch roof. Since the last time he'd been out there a rocking chair had been added.

Leah must have heard him drive up, for she stepped out onto the porch, drying a bowl with a dish towel. She had probably just gotten home from the café. Even after a long day of being on her feet, she still looked better than Tom had ever seen her while Gus was around. But there was no mistaking the worried look she wore. Behind her a couple of the boys peeked out of the door.

"Tom," she said when he approached the porch.

"Hi there, Leah. I just left Gus, not far outside the jail. He's on foot. Looking for a phone, I suppose."

"I think maybe he found one. It's been ringing, but we're not answering."

"Just as well. Did you hear from Corsica Rios?"

"Yes, she was here. Brought me a restraining order." She laughed. "Maybe I should try waving it in his face as he's pummeling me and the boys."

"Here's what you do. You lock everything up tight and you keep a real close eye on the road. And the very second you see him or hear him, you call me, because once he violates that order of protection, I'm taking him away. Next time it will be longer. I gave him a warning. As powerful a warning as I'm able."

"What if I don't see him coming?" she asked.

"He's a pompous little bully, Leah. If I know Gus, he'll be shouting and swearing from the road."

That brought a smile to her lips, but it was wan.

Frank stepped out onto the porch behind his mother. Unlike his father, Frank was going to be a big man. He was already over six feet, and once he filled out a little, he would be a powerful figure of a man. Tom almost smiled.

"Frank."

"Chief."

"You heard the advice I gave your mother?"

"Yes sir."

"Good. I have some more. I think for the time being you shouldn't leave the younger boys out here alone when you go to work. Take 'em someplace. Take 'em with you to the café if you need to — George would put 'em up in a booth with some coloring books or puzzles. Just till we get the lay of the land."

"You mean just till the sorry old bastard shows his face and gets himself carted away again?" Frank asked.

"Pretty much. And just so you know, I'm going to insist that Tanya keep a distance for now. Till things settle down again."

Frank made a sound of disgust and looked away. Leah tried to quiet him with a pleading look and a touch on his arm.

"If you care anything about Tanya, you don't want her in the middle of this," Tom said. "Am I at least right about that?"

"I wouldn't let anything happen to Tan," Frank said, but he said it with sarcasm and a measure of disrespect.

Tom had nothing more to say on that subject. He fairly dreaded the conversation he was obligated to have with Tanya about it. "Lock up," he said. "And call me at once if you see him. Lee, Ricky and I will take turns driving by the farm through the next few days, but we can't keep you covered all the time."

"Tom, when you talked to Gus, how'd he take it?" Leah asked.

Tom tapped his foot in the dirt and ground his teeth a little. It wasn't like him to squirm at a question. He finally muttered, "Just how you'd expect."

John still wore his scrubs as he wrote in the patient's chart. He looked at his watch — 10:30 a.m. He'd have time to go back to Grace Valley, see a few patients and still get back by early afternoon when Justine would be resting in her room.

June came into the recovery area, pulled off her surgical cap and hovered near John's chair. "How did you know?" she asked in a whisper.

"Instincts. Good guess. Family history. I don't know."

"Family . . . ? Justine's mother died of cancer, but an entirely unrelated type."

"You'd be amazed how often we see a

reproductive cancer pop up when the only family history is cancer of another type."

"You probably saved her life," June said.

John sat still as a rock, deep in thought. They had found a malignant tumor, found it in just the beginning stages, and they would soon know whether or not it had spread anywhere in the pelvic cavity. But it had been an ovarian malignancy — the most dangerous of all reproductive cancers. The conservative response was a total hysterectomy. But because Justine was only twenty-six, he had left her the other ovary, fallopian tube and uterus.

"I'm not sure we did the best thing," he told June.

"It's not up to us," she said.

John turned and looked at her for the first time. "Then you agree with me?"

"If it were me, I'd say pull it all," June said.

"Yeah, but that's different. You're different. Your age, for one thing. And your particular disposition toward childbirth."

She was quiet a long moment. A lot of people just assumed she didn't want children because she didn't have any. Finally she said, "We're not that different." John thought about that, but didn't reply. "Do you want me to talk to her about it?"

"Yes. No. What I mean is, I'd like you to say something to her about the surgery, about it going well, and tell her whatever you want about the cancer. Tell her I'm going to be around to have a longer conversation with her about her treatment and prognosis later, when she's wide awake and more alert. When she can take it all in."

"Have you told her anything yet?"

"Just that we took one ovary and left the other."

June clapped a hand on his shoulder. "Good job, John."

It was four in the afternoon before John could make his way back to Rockport, to Valley Hospital. Justine was sitting up, and beside her, also sitting on the bed, facing her and holding both her hands, was Sam. John gave a couple of polite taps on the open door. Sam edged off the bed and stood at her bedside.

"How are you feeling?" John asked.

"All right. Considering."

"We have to talk about your treatment. About this disease."

She gasped at the word and looked up at Sam.

"It's a curable disease, Justine," John said. "And we caught it early, which means your

344

odds of beating it are even better. First of all, there's no reason to be afraid." He paused, then asked cautiously, "Do you want to have this conversation together? Or shall we talk and fill Sam in later?"

"I want Sam to stay," she said.

"Ah, tell you what, Justine, let me run downstairs for a cup of coffee while you talk to Doc Stone. I won't be gone too long," Sam said.

"Please, Sam, come right back," she begged.

"I will, I promise."

He kissed her forehead and she grasped his hand, letting go of him reluctantly. The minute he was out of the room, large tears gathered in her eyes and spilled over. John sat where Sam had been on the bed and handed her tissues from the bedside table.

"I can't believe I was never going to have a baby," she said. "I was angry about it, then happy about it, then it was over!" She gripped the tissue and turned watering eyes up at John. "I was happy for such a short time! It's not fair! I just want to die again!"

"Some of this emotionalism has to do with the ovary and the surgery and — well, it's like a huge dose of PMS. Justine, I have to refer you to an oncologist, to treat the cancer. And I'm going to tell you right now that, even though we caught it early, in the very early stages, an oncologist is likely to recommend a complete hysterectomy."

She shook her head violently. "I won't do it. I want another chance."

"To have a baby?" he asked.

"That's right. I'm young. There's plenty of time."

"On the one hand," John said, "if you had lost that ovary to anything but ovarian cancer, there would be plenty of time. But your other ovary is like a time bomb, Justine. To anyone with a strong family history of reproductive cancer or an experience with it as a patient, doctors usually recommend a clean slate. Get rid of the cancer catchers."

"You going to get rid of my breasts, too?" she asked, filling her hands with her own breasts.

"No, no, no," he said, shaking his head. "But we'll check them often. You can detect lumps in breasts, even feel lumps in the uterus. But ovarian cancer has no symptoms, and we can't feel or see your remaining ovary."

"What about that blood test? Dr. Hudson said there's a blood test!"

"It helps, but the problem is that, by the time we can detect a growth by means of an ultrasound or blood test, the cancer can be advanced."

"I won't do it!" she insisted. "I'm going to have a baby!"

"Okay, settle down and let me explain something to you. You can't conceive while undergoing chemotherapy. You'll have to wait till that's well behind you. And then the increased hormone level of pregnancy will put you at risk. But if you're absolutely determined, you should have your baby as early as possible, and then count yourself lucky to have gotten that far, and follow up with surgery so you'll be around to raise him."

She turned her face away and looked off into space. "Her," she murmured.

"I'm sorry?" John said.

She looked back. "Her. It will be a girl."

"Oh, I see." He cleared his throat. "And Justine, don't eliminate adoption as an option."

A slow smile spread across her face. "Adoption? Do you think anyone would let us adopt a baby? A woman who's had cancer and a seventy-year-old man?"

"Justine, you should talk to your family. . . ."

"My *family*? My father? He won't speak to me because of this scandal! And my sisters think I've lost my mind."

"Then you've told them that —"

"I didn't have to tell anyone anything! Everyone knows! That I thought I was knocked up by Pastor Wickham and now I have Sam and cancer and —"

John came abruptly to his feet. "Pastor Wickham?"

"You didn't know?"

"Well, *you* didn't mention —"

"I would've thought June —"

"We have so many patients —"

"Yes, it was Pastor Wickham, the shit-head."

"Whoa."

"But that doesn't change anything. I still have cancer, want a baby, am in love with a seventy-year-old man and have my whole family pissed off at me." She sighed and added, "Well, it changes one thing."

"What's that?" John asked.

"Where I go to church!"

Leah had been bringing the younger boys to the café with her when she and Frank came to work in the morning, and from there they fairly scattered. Birdie took them home with her for lunch one day, they went off with the parents of friends from school another, and Ursula Toopeek took them home to play with her kids once. But the day came when Leah and Frank arrived at the café alone, not looking so good and having hitched a ride with Lincoln Toopeek.

"Uh-oh," Tom said when he saw his father's old pickup pull up to the front of the café. "This doesn't look like good news."

Leah and Frank jumped out of the back of the truck, brushed down their pants and headed around the café for the employees' back door. Tom, on the other hand, went out the front door to the truck to speak to his father.

"What's up?" he asked Lincoln.

"They were walking. It must be six miles. They could have called and I would have gone for them, but they were walking. I think things must be bad again."

Inside, George Fuller was the first to see them. Leah had a large purple bruise rising on her cheek and Frank had a black eye and fat lip. "Oh God," George said. "He came back, didn't he?"

"What was your first clue?" Frank asked thickly.

"Anybody else out at the house hurt?" George demanded.

"No. We ran him off. We shot at him and he took the truck. So —"

"Did you call the chief?"

349

"No. We just wanted him to go."

"But Leah, you were supposed to call the chief! Get him arrested again!"

"I know, I know, but —"

Tom burst in the back of the café where Leah and Frank were just pulling their aprons off the shelf. "Leah! I told you to *call* me! At once!"

She whirled and looked daggers through him. "He came in the dead of night, broke down the door, knocked us around a little, ripped the phone out of the wall and took the truck. I was hoping to hear he'd had a bad wreck . . . but no such luck."

"Where are the younger boys?" Tom asked.

"Home. Watching the road. Jeremy has the rifle on the door."

"I'll call Corsica, have her pick them up. And get your phone repaired. You two go across the street and get checked over by June before you work."

"Forget about it," Frank mumbled.

"No," Tom said. "I want you to get something to bring down that lip and help the eye . . . or Tanya won't give you a second glance. Jesus, Leah, I'm sorry about this. I should've taken better care —"

"What can you do? He's bent on destruction. He's a mean cuss, and he won't rest till he kills us all."

"Well, I've got him now. He violated the order and can go back to jail."

"In and out, in and out . . ." She looked not only battered, but defeated. "He'll just get to us again. One way or the other."

"Not this time. This time you'll have up to five years to get yourself together. I'll hunt him down, and in the process, get you your truck back."

"You know, Tom," Leah said, the sound of tears in her voice, "maybe you ought to just let it be. He said all he wanted was his truck and to be free of our aggravation. I can live without a truck . . . and he can go drink himself to death somewhere else."

TWENTY-TWO

June had a headache, unrelated to the injury she'd had in her car accident. Well, maybe not completely unrelated — she couldn't seem to find herself a vehicle. Her insurance company, which was always johnny-on-the-spot when nothing was wrong, was acting like a miserly mistress now that she wanted to collect on a fully loaded Jeep, complete with ambulance gear. She was using a rented Nissan truck with a first aid kit, portable oxygen tank and her medical bag until she could work something out. And on her clinic desk she calculated over and over, and over again, how much this whole thing was going to cost.

She rubbed her temples. There was a knock at the door.

"What?" she said tersely. Sadie, who preferred to sleep under the desk and underfoot, squirmed out at the testy tone in her voice.

John peeked into the room. "Got a minute?"

"No. Why?"

"Well, let me know when —"

"Come in, come in, I'm just in a foul mood. I'll get over it. What's on your mind?"

He entered and closed the door. He sat in the chair facing the desk, facing her. "Something you said the other day . . . when we were wrapping up after Justine. I said you were older, didn't want children, and you said something. Remember?"

"I remember."

"You want to talk about that?"

"Why would I?" she countered.

"It's one of my functions," he said, shrugging. "This is something I'm used to talking to my patients about — their choices regarding parenthood. Birth control, et cetera."

She leaned toward him. "I'm not your patient."

"Whew, you are in a foul mood. Maybe we can do something about that PMS while we're at it."

"I repeat —"

"All *right!* Jesus. I was just trying to be friendly. But if you don't want to talk . . ."

Want to talk? Boy, did she want to talk! About the way the town had gone a little crazy lately. About the fact that she was impatiently awaiting word from Tom on what he was finding out about John, but Tom was a little busy, considering Gus had gotten out of jail, beat his wife and kids and was now on the run. Or how about the fact that she hadn't heard a word from the illusive Jim Post, and she was positively *aching* for him? But she settled for, "I'm sorry, John. I'm having trouble with the insurance company and I need an equipped vehicle for this clinic. In fact, I'm thinking I need two vehicles."

"Why is that?"

"I need an emergency vehicle to make calls in, and now that we're working together and sharing the on-call duty, we should share an emergency vehicle. Which means the clinic should have an emergency vehicle and each doctor should have their own car." If it wasn't John in the clinic with her, it would have to be someone. She couldn't handle it alone anymore. "I've talked to the dealers in the area and no one is going to work with me until I get some positive feedback from the insurance company."

"I thought you were going to lease something?" he said.

"I did. I leased a little truck. That was about what I can afford on my income."

"But when the insurance pays off the Jeep — ?"

"I'll still be a little short. It's pretty expensive to get the largest sports utility vehicle and load it with ambulance gear."

"What's pretty expensive?" he inquired.

"Around ninety thousand," she said.

John whistled and said, "That's gonna take a bake sale or two. June, I don't mean to be presumptuous, but I heard through the grapevine that Mrs. Claypool funded the clinic. Had you thought of asking her for a little help? Or maybe a loan?"

"Sure I've thought of it. But, the price of the clinic notwithstanding, I have no idea how well fixed my aunt is. She might be well off, she might be struggling to get by. The cost of the clinic might have wiped her out. It can't have escaped her attention that I have no vehicle . . . and I'm sure if she could help, she would. But damn it, John, the cost of taking care of this town shouldn't always fall to Aunt Myrna. There are plenty of other people around here with money, too."

"Are you sure it's just a tension headache, June?"

"I'm sure there's enough tension around here to account for it."

He stood and rubbed a hand on the back of his neck — a helpless gesture. "If you think of any way I can help . . ."

"Thanks, John," she said, at once feeling the inadequacy of the word. He had done so much! He'd served well beyond his role in taking care of her, most certainly had saved at least one life in diagnosing Justine, and was already dearly loved by the town — by a town that didn't love anyone too soon. June's gratitude should be overflowing. Flooding! She should give him a damn party! But she held back in wait of a final word. A verdict of not guilty.

He left her office and *she* felt guilty. He seemed so guileless. She should have talked to him, should have told him about Dr. Feldtbrow.

But she hadn't. And now it seemed the only thing she could do was wait.

School was out, the sun set later and later, the moist heat of late June settled over the crops and the mountains, and Tom Toopeek spent a long day combing the roads near the Craven farm, looking for clues about what direction Gus might have traveled. Or a spot where he might have camped, close by, in wait for his middle of the night attack. Tom finally went home for dinner with his family, but decided to go out again after dark.

Lincoln read a paper in the living room, the children were roaming or doing chores, and Tom sat in the kitchen with a cup of coffee while Philana and Ursula put the finishing touches on dinner.

"You should see what he managed to do to the house in the short time he was there," Tom said. "Aside from sweeping up glass, Leah doesn't plan to make any repairs until I can find him and lock him up."

"Knowing he's going to jail for a long time, don't you think he's gone?" Ursula asked.

"I would prefer that scenario, even though it would cost Leah a truck. To think of him gone . . . Easy on the temper, in my case."

"You have no temper," Ursula said with a laugh.

"I have a foul temper, it turns out. I had serious homicidal thoughts while driving Gus away from the jail."

"Aren't there four kinds of murder?" Ursula asked. "And isn't one of them praiseworthy?"

"I am drawn to the Craven house," he said. "They are so broken. Despite all our efforts — mine, Ricky's and Lee's — we couldn't keep them safe from him. How did we fail so miserably?"

"Tom, he must have hidden on the land

and waited," Ursula said. "It wasn't what you expected him to do. Poor Leah. Will she never escape?"

Tom looked out the kitchen window and saw Tanya ride up on her bike, which she walked into the shed behind the house. "Where has Tanya been?"

"Baby-sitting."

"They don't drive her home?"

"She volunteers to ride. For the exercise. Young girls are vain about their figures."

There was something not right, and it all seemed oddly connected. Her hair was loose; it was hard to ride a bike with long hair loose and whipping in the wind. And there was the trouble at the Cravens — the broken glass, the missing truck, the family's stoic acceptance of their lot.

When she entered the kitchen Tom bolted to his feet with such furor that his kitchen chair fell over.

"I fell!" she said defensively. "Off my bike!"

"Oh Tanya, let me see," Ursula said sympathetically. She pushed the girl's hair away from her face and saw her blackened eye. "Goodness," she said, wetting the dish towel to put on the bluish spot. Tom glowered blackly and Ursula didn't know why. "You'll be —"

"Save me something," he barked. "I'll eat later!"

He whirled away angrily, letting the back door slam behind him as he left the house. Tears coursing down her cheeks, Tanya fled after him, crying out for him to stop. "Daddy! Daddy!" He waited at the opened door of his Range Rover. She stood before him, all five-foot-two of her. Petite and beautiful, flawless but for her blackened eye. "Please, Daddy, don't make trouble for them now. I'm never going to be around him again, I swear."

"You defied me and your mother," he said.

"I did. I'm sorry. I was foolish to think I knew more than my parents. And I won't defy you again. But Daddy, there is nothing you can do but make things worse. Please."

He crouched down to look closer at the dark bruise, to look into her tearing eyes for final clarification. "He hit you?"

She nodded miserably. "He didn't get his way," she said.

"Did he do anything else to hurt you?" Tom asked.

"No, this was hurt enough. And now I see that you're right. He is not of my culture, and by that I don't mean Native or tribal. I know that now, Daddy. Please don't do anything to him."

Tom put a large hand under her chin, lifting her face. He turned it to and fro, examining her for marks. Though it didn't show on his face, he felt a deep sense of satisfaction in hearing her wisdom. He knew, because she was fifteen, that he couldn't count on it being a long-lasting wisdom, but a father would take what he could get.

"Go inside and tell your mother the truth about your bruise. And don't lie to her again, Tanya. Those things are so hard to repair."

"I know. Daddy, please don't —"

"Don't what, Tan? Hurt him? Arrest him? What do you think I would do?"

"I don't know," she said skittishly.

"Do you think I have no wisdom of my own?" he asked her.

"I know you do. I just want it all to go away."

"For you, it already has."

June was just putting away the last patient chart she'd been working on when Jessica came running into her office, jumping up and down frantically. "June, June, they're fighting in the street! Come quick!"

"Who?" she asked as she ran down the clinic hall to the front door. But Jessica didn't answer; she just bolted. And there they were, as advertised — Pastor Wickham, Standard Roberts and Sam Cussler. It was a little hard to tell what Sam's role was in this fisticuffs; he might've been trying to hold Stan off of Jonathan Wickham. But just as June thought that, Pastor Wickham delivered a mean right hook to Sam's cheek. They fell in a pile of bodies and a cloud of dust. Sadie barked in protest, but stayed firmly at June's side.

"Call Tom," June told Jessica.

They must have begun their argument in the church and spilled out onto the street because they were at the bottom of the church steps. Sam was the oldest of the three, but probably the strongest. Stan must be nearly sixty, and Jonathan, though considerably younger at about thirty-eight, was the trimmest in muscle and least likely to sustain any damage. But if someone didn't separate them soon, the pastor might get his clock cleaned.

Jessica came back out to the clinic's front stoop. "Tom's gone home to dinner, but Ricky's coming down."

"If he doesn't hurry, we're going to have to stitch and mend all through our dinner," June said absently.

"Oh great! I'll help!"

She cast a suspicious glance at Jessica. Help?

Ricky drove down the block with his lights flashing and siren whirring. It was his clever way of drawing attention to the fight so that anyone left in the café could come help him pry these men apart. Indeed, he managed to alert George and his oldest son, two hearties who came instantly to Ricky's aid. One man each.

June crossed her arms over her chest and looked at the threesome in disgust. *Children.* Sam was cut on the chin, Stan had a nice lump growing on his forehead and the pastor was spitting what might have been teeth. Their knuckles were damaged and their clothes rent. "All I can say is I'm glad Justine isn't around to see this. You ought to be ashamed of yourselves!" June declared.

"Ashamed?" Standard echoed. "I see two men who can share the shame, but me? That's my daughter they tinkered with!"

"I haven't tinkered a damn, you old goat," Sam said. "I'm the only one's been there for her in her time of need. You weren't anywhere to be found!"

"I'm not likely to be sharing the waiting room with a white-haired old man who has designs on a girl a third his age!"

Jonathan Wickham spat blood on the

ground. "There's no pregnancy! It's all just a slander! Ruining my good —" Sam and Standard looked at him first in shock and then furiously pulled against the restraints of their respective custodians.

"Stop it!" June shouted. They obeyed at once. "What is the matter with you? Ricky, boys, get them in the clinic so I can patch them up. And mind, you make one aggressive move in my clinic, I'll sedate you! You won't wake up for a month!" She turned on her heel and angrily strode back inside.

"Jessie," she said, "set up the treatment room with a suture kit and get yourself some gloves." Jessica smiled briefly and brightly before going to do as she was bidden. "Ricky! Bring them all back here. Line 'em up on these stools." When her order had been carried out, June added, "Okay, you can leave them. But wait up front, will you? If there's any trouble back here I'll need some help holding them down while I fill them full of Thorazine . . . or some other equally powerful tranquilizer. I think I might have some veterinary tranks on hand."

"You sure, June?" George asked worriedly. " 'Cause if you want me to stay right here —"

"I'll take it from here. I want to talk to these idiots alone, if you don't mind. But don't leave the clinic just yet, huh? Hang around till I'm done?"

Three men echoed, "Sure thing, June."

She washed her hands, put on some gloves and smacked a chemical ice pack against the counter to get it started. The ice went on Stan's head, she pressed a gauze pad against the cut on Sam's chin and moved his hand to hold it in place, and then told the pastor to open his mouth.

"You know, Jonathan, you would test the patience of the very saints." His eyes jerked up to hers in surprise. "Ah, so you recognize your tag line? You've created serious trouble for yourself in this town. Your credibility is shot — at least with the women, that's for sure."

He began to mumble something and June pulled her gloved finger out of his mouth. "There's no evidence that I —"

"Oh shut up," the room said in unison. Even Jessica.

"There, you see?" June asked. "Just in case you think people don't know, you can rest assured everyone is onto you. And it's your own damn fault. But that's not even the worst of what's going on here. Have the three of you ignorant jackasses forgotten that Justine is in the hospital, recovering from cancer surgery?" June wadded up a gauze strip and stuck it between the pastor's teeth. "Looks like you just lost a bridge, Jonathan. It could have been so much worse. Bite down on this. It'll help you keep your mouth shut.

"Jessie? You want to help with the stitches?" she asked, discarding soiled gloves and washing her hands before donning new ones. She had never seen her clerk's eyes shine more brightly. Jessica nodded and held up her own gloved hands. "Okay, first the anesthetic." Jessica pointed to the lidocaine syringe that lay ready. "Well, you appear to be up to speed. Sam, you don't mind a little on-the-job training, do you? It's the least you deserve." He nodded bravely.

June watched closely as Jessica, in an experienced manner, popped the top off the syringe with a thumb and began to inject tiny bubbles of anesthetic along the cut on Sam's chin. When she finished and stood back, June regarded her with raised eyebrows. "Let me start, and if you're very good, I'll save you a couple."

Jessica glowed.

While June stitched, she lectured. "I have a patient lying in a hospital bed, facing treatment for a disease that could kill her. She's alone, afraid and has been betrayed, and the three of you are acting out your own anger and hurt pride."

"You'd have your nose a little out of shape if —" Stan began.

"Shut up, Stan, you're a little late," she snapped. "If you wanted a say in that girl's life you might have started sooner. Maybe added a little something to her self-esteem with praise and affection instead of sticking her with all the chores and the family business. That girl lost her mother! And all you're worried about is your pride!"

"Amen," the pastor muttered.

"If I were you, Jonathan, I'd start at the beginning of that prayer, not the end, and include a little humble pie. I'm sure the number of people you should beg for forgiveness exceeds even my imagination, but you might start with Standard Roberts, the father of the girl you betrayed. Then you can move on to your wife and any other woman in Grace Valley you've offended."

Sam couldn't help but let out a satisfied whoop of laughter. "You tell 'em, Junie!"

"You'd better hold still or I might accidentally sew your mouth shut, which, now that I think about it, isn't such a bad idea." She stood back from her handiwork. "You want to try a couple, Jessie?" she asked.

"Yes, ma'am," the girl said, reaching

anxiously for the hemostat and needle. June stood at Jessica's shoulder and watched her make four absolutely perfect sutures. Again she lifted her eyebrows.

"Put a butterfly and gauze on that, Jessie." She snapped off her gloves and took a seat in front of the three men. "Sam, I know you think you're the one with the sterling motives, but look at you. I'm not saying you're not a good catch, but the girl is twenty-six. And she has cancer. And she is, for the moment at least, refusing further reproductive surgery because she wants a baby. If she succeeds, and something happens to her, who's going to raise that baby? You? Being there for her, giving her love and affection and loyalty when she's needy, is a wonderful gesture, as long as you're sure you don't compromise her at the same time. Her basic human need right now is health — health *first* — so she can live long enough to enjoy the rest.

"The three of you ought to think, just for a moment, about someone besides yourselves. It seems that you have either exploited her affection or withheld affection from her or misguided her — or all of the above. What Justine needs right now is support and *respect*. Stan, call her sisters home to see her. Sam, be absolutely sure you don't mislead her. And Jonathan . . . Oh Jonathan, I don't know about you. Maybe you'd better keep your distance from Justine and ask Clarice if she'll ever forgive you.

"Now get out of here. And don't you *dare* fight again."

When they were gone, Jessica went about the business of cleaning up the treatment room. She put the instruments in the sink for sterilizing, disposed of the bloody rags and gloves, got out the mop and pail, all the while keeping her head bent down.

"Jessie, what's all this about?" June asked.

The girl slowly raised her eyes, and in them there was a light. "June, I think I want to be a doctor," she said.

"Is that so? Well, you might have to graduate from high school first."

For Tom, everything came together once he saw his daughter's bruised cheek. Suddenly, he knew what was missing — besides Gus. He had sent Lee around to all the old haunts where a man like Gus might take a drink, but the man hadn't been seen. He had called the sheriff's departments in three counties, but the truck had not been spotted anywhere. They had searched the farm and woods nearby as well, to see if the old sot was staying close, biding his time and waiting to pounce again, but he was not found. And Leah, who had been surprised in the middle of the night by her wildly abusive husband, was leaving the younger children at home alone when she went to work. They were devastated, but unafraid. Tom had thought they seemed *resigned.*

Then Tanya rode up on her bike, her face marred by yet more Craven rage, and something clicked.

The bike. How far could you ride a bike in a couple of hours, along country roads?

Tom went out to the Craven farm, drove up the drive and saw Leah in the rocking chair on the porch, the rifle on her knees. He stopped and asked if everything was all right, then he drove down the drive and went west, taking side roads when they came up. But he stopped and turned back when he reached fifteen miles. He then traveled east from the Craven farm, again going off on deserted side roads or abandoned logging roads, but always stopping and turning back before going farther than fifteen miles.

It was after eight o'clock and the sun was low when he drove slowly along a third road, which wound through a stand of redwoods. He was about twelve miles from the Craven farm. He parked, got out his flashlight and walked among the trees, directing the beam. Though there was still light along the road, the huge trees blocked the sun. It was dark and eerie in the woods at that hour.

The flashlight bounced off a fender. It looked as though the truck had careened through the trees, over a berm and down a shallow ravine. The front of the truck was plunged headlong into a narrow, dry creek-bed, and Gus was slumped over the wheel.

As Tom got closer the smell of whisky got stronger. There was little doubt alcohol would be found in his blood, but in the days he'd been missing the smell would have waned. Unless his clothing had been soaked in liquor.

He called the county coroner and the sheriff's department crime lab. It took them two hours to set up, after which he left them. He drove out to Leah's and knocked on the door. She came, holding her old chenille robe closed.

"We found him, Leah. And the truck."

Her chin quivered. Tom thought she must be relieved it was over.

"Was it you? Or was it Frank?" he asked.

She lifted her chin somewhat defiantly. "What are you talking about?"

"My guess is it was you, while he was pummeling Frank. He was such a pompous little ass, he didn't realize that in two short months you'd grown strong enough that he shouldn't turn his back on you. And I'll bet it was the shovel that you whacked him in the back of the head with. But I'd bet you really didn't mean to kill him, even then. Why didn't you just call me, Leah?"

"Because it was true, what I told you — that he pulled the phone out of the wall. And I guess we just got so scared. It seemed like where Gus was concerned, everything always came back and got us. Gus was the one always seemed to skate out of things, while the boys and me, we just walked around all bruised and tattered."

"So you put the bike in the back of the truck, drove out a back road and pushed the truck into the ravine. Then rode the bike home. If you had been on foot you would have had to hide the truck too close to the farm, or if you drove it far, it would have taken you too long to walk home. And you both had to work in the morning."

"Yes, I thought —"

"No, it wasn't her. That was me."

Tom turned and saw Frank coming from the kitchen. At any other time he would have had a piece of the youngster's hide for hitting Tanya. But as he'd already told her, that matter was finished. It was time to move on.

"Frank, don't say another word!"

"It's all right, Mama. The whole family knows, Chief. Sooner or later you'd get Jeremy or Joe or maybe little Stan to tell you. Daddy couldn't break up the house without the little ones getting it just as bad as Mama and me." He took a step closer. "See, there just wasn't anything anyone could do to stop him."

"What's going to happen now, Tom?" Leah asked.

"Well, I'm going to call Corsica and have her send someone from social services out here to pick up the children, and then I'm going to take you and Frank to the sheriff's office to make a statement."

TWENTY-THREE

Sam put a Scarlet Eagle fly on his line.

"You'd do better with a Nasty Cat in this stream. Fish are on the bottom here. It's a little on the muddy side," Stan said, casting out.

"I'll take my chances," Sam said, a competitive edge to his voice. Across the river a large trout jumped. "Not too close to the bottom, I reckon."

"You just know everything, don't you?"

"Not everything. Most things." Then he laughed.

They fished in silence for a half hour. The morning sun was just making its mark on the valley, taking its time coming fully across the mountain range. It was Standard who spoke first. "Been so long, I hardly remember Peggy."

"Forty-two years ago. She was twenty-eight."

"I guess I forgot we had that in common.

Both lost wives to cancer. Georgia was in her fifties, gave me five daughters before she died."

"Georgia was a fine woman, don't you think? She put up with the likes of you for a long time. Never complained."

"Oh, she complained plenty," Stan said. "But since she's been gone she gets more perfect by the day. They were different cancers though, weren't they?"

"Whose?" Sam asked.

"Our wives'. And Justine's."

"Oh, yes. Peggy had blood cancer. Fought it since college. Once or twice we thought we had it licked. That's the reason there weren't kids for us."

"You never married again after her," Stan pointed out, as though Sam hadn't noticed.

"Nope. Never came up."

"Around here, there aren't that many different people to marry."

"Peggy herself came from San Diego. I was in the navy when we met."

Sam hooked a large fish and played it for a while, so they fell silent. When he finally pulled it in, Standard netted it for him. "I might've been wrong about the Nasty Cat lure. Seems you know your business around a stream, after all."

Sam smiled. "It takes a big man, Standard . . ."

"You think we were wrong to beat the tar out of Pastor Wickham?"

"Not in the least way!"

"Me neither."

"But I think June's right about Justine, that we should leave off vengeance and hurt pride and think about what Justine needs."

Stan switched lures, going for one of his favorite reds. If it worked for Sam it might work for him.

"I don't expect Justine will be inclined to take much goodwill from me," Stan said. "After her mother died, I was just too closed up in myself to be any kind of father. The other girls, they married off and hardly even call."

"You just be patient, Standard. She might come around, if she senses you're sincere."

"I'm never good with words, you see. Never have been. Her mother complained of that, too."

Sam cast again. "Well, take her a nice big fish then. See if that doesn't cheer her."

"I just may!"

Sam whistled low. "Standard, you poor old bastard, you're right. You're just not so good."

"What are you talking about?"

"You don't take a twenty-six-year-old

woman a fish!"

"Well, you said —"

"I was just pulling your chain!"

"Well, pull your own goddamn chain!"

Sam was about to give more back to him when a rustling caused them to turn and see Elmer Hudson standing behind them. "Good," Sam said. "It's not a bear."

"If I hadn't seen this with my own eyes, I'd never believe it," Elmer said.

"You think it's strange to see two men fish?" Stan said, casting again.

"These two I do, but never mind that. I was looking for you. You won't believe it — or maybe you will. They found Gus. Slumped over the steering wheel of that old truck, in a ravine, in a redwood reserve, dead as a doornail. Looks like Leah whacked him in the head."

"Not soon enough," Stan said. "I saw her in the café the other day and heard tell Gus had come back and knocked her and the boys around some."

"She should'a whacked him about ten years ago. Would have saved her some bruises and the chief some gas for that Rover."

"Well, on that we can all agree. But they've gone and arrested her just the same."

"What for?" Stan and Sam asked in unison, and the looks on their faces suggested the question wholly sincere.

"For killing Gus!" Elmer nearly shouted.

Sam and Stan looked at each other and shook their heads. "Don't some things just defy understanding?" Sam asked.

Birdie knew Judge was not ready to go back to work, but she couldn't help that. It was seven in the morning and he sat in his favorite chair three feet in front of the television, sound blasting, wearing his neck brace, his toast and coffee on an old metal TV tray. Before the accident he'd have been gone to work by six, put in a twelve hour day, brought work home, taken a long walk after dinner, then read till eleven. Except on poker night, when he'd get home late and read till twelve.

Now he sat in his chair most of the day and dozed. He hardly read at all.

"Judge?" she said.

"Hmm?" He didn't take his eyes off the television.

"Tom called. He found Gus Craven last night." Judge turned his head and looked up at her. "Dead. In his truck, nose down in a creekbed in the forest. Whacked on the head with something hard, like a shovel."

Judge turned in his chair as she spoke, and by the time she was finished, he was standing. "They arrested Leah."

"Holy Jesus," he said, pulling off his collar.

"She confessed," Birdie said. "What are you doing?"

"Getting a shower. Lay out my suit, old woman. I have to get to work."

"I don't know that you're going to be much help now," she said, shaking her head.

"Doesn't matter. I'm not letting anyone else have that bench while one of my own is coming through. That's how old Gus got out, if I recall."

"But Judge, you haven't been yourself. Your head still pains you. You nod off at the worst times."

"I'll get some drugs from the old doctor. He's not as persnickety as his daughter."

Charlie McNeil drove, Jerry Powell sat in the front seat and Clinton Mull sat in the back, his crutches leaning beside him. "Are you sure there's no other way?" he asked the men in front.

"Absolutely sure. Are you ready?" Jerry asked.

"I'll never be ready, but I'll do my best."

Charlie parked outside the Mull house in

the woods, and Jerry helped Clinton to get out and upright on the crutches. By the time the car doors closed the whole family was standing outside, waiting. Jurea twisted her hands in front of her, anxious to be released from some inner bonds so that she could run to her son and embrace him. Wanda yelled to him right away. "Clinton!" she called, dashing forward. He stopped when they faced each other and she bent at the waist to study his bandaged stump. "Does it hurt?" she asked.

"Not as much now. But I'm trying out fake feet — now that ain't the easiest thing. Mama," he said. She cautiously came to him and carefully embraced him, crutches and all. "Daddy," he said, and Clarence nodded, crossed his arms over his chest and frowned suspiciously. "I can't stay long. I have to go back to the hospital and keep trying to get a foot I can walk on. This kind of thing doesn't happen quick," he said. "So can we go inside and sit at the table awhile?"

"Clinton, I think you grew while you was away," Jurea said. "Is that possible?"

"You were just missing him, Mama," Wanda said. "She was missing you so much, Clinton, it was terrible. Every night at supper she wanted us to tell Clinton stories."

"That so?" he asked.

"We had to entertain ourselves somehow," Jurea said. "Usually you're the one entertaining us all through evening till bed. . . ."

Charlie and Jerry looked at each other. What they had learned in their visits to the Mull house over the past weeks was that this was a family that suffered, but loved each other deeply. They endured illness and poverty, but clung to each other to get by. In fact, to some degree the clinging was keeping them from resolving the other two problems.

"I have to tell you all something," Clinton said right off. "Both Jerry and Charlie think it's really important that I tell you this truthful thing. Daddy, I tried to get various people to kidnap you for me. I met the wife of a judge, and she offered to help me, but she wasn't enough. I asked the doctor — Dr. Hudson, you know — and I asked these two guys, Charlie and Jerry." Clarence's expression didn't change at all. "No one would do it. But do you want to know why I tried to get someone to kidnap you?"

Clarence didn't answer.

"I think you should tell us why, Clinton," Jurea said.

"Because the only way I want to come back here to live is if I can have permission to leave the mountain sometimes. To go to school. I want to go to school and maybe play a sport, even with a missing leg. But I can't get permission to leave the mountain while Daddy's sick with his paranoia and war injuries. So I thought if . . .

"Daddy, do you know that in all the years since you been back from Vietnam, the drugs they have to treat sickness like yours have gotten to be so good, they're like miracle drugs? It's like you don't even know you're taking 'em — except you get to feeling normal."

Clarence shook that off in disgust and turned his back.

"It's true, Daddy. They have drugs for hallucinations, for anxiety, for compulsiveness, for phobia. All kinds of things they weren't using before. And you could start taking medicine now, here at home, and see how it suits you. You don't have to go to a hospital."

"That so, honey?" Jurea asked.

Clinton turned his attention to his mother. "Mama, Jerry and Charlie think you can find some help for your scars. They think it's worth . . . Charlie, tell her. Please."

"Jurea, there are a couple of foundations set up by the Veteran's Hospital that help the dependants of veterans who don't have other medical coverage, and there's a plastic surgeon from southern California who visits up here twice a year. He's got a team that does surgery all over the world, surgery as challenging as yours would be. He's due here in a couple of weeks. You could see him. He could evaluate you. Tell you if there's anything he can do."

"I can't think there's any help for this," she said, raising a hand to her face. "You ever in your life see anything as awful as this?"

Charlie reached in his shirt pocket and pulled out a picture, passing it to Jurea. Wanda jumped up and looked over her mother's shoulder at the face of a woman without a nose. Jurea's hands went directly to her own, touching it tentatively as if to be sure it was still there. He then produced a picture of the same woman with a perfect nose, and Jurea almost gasped in shock. "It's pretty complicated," Charlie said. "Took several surgeries and the doctor had to build a nose out of flesh and muscle and even plastics. But the result is there."

Clarence, arms still crossed over his chest, turned back to the group and looked suspiciously over his wife's shoulder at the pictures. They lay on the table — the noseless woman on the left, the perfect nose on the right. Before and after. He reached a hand down and reversed the pictures so that it looked as though the woman had been photographed after her nose was cut off.

"No, Daddy, that ain't how it was. Besides, no one even knows if Mama's face can be fixed, even a little bit. And no one *will* know unless she goes to the hospital when the plastic surgeon is in Eureka."

"We should let them think," Jerry said.

"Yeah," Clinton agreed. "That's what you should do — Mama, Daddy. Talk it over and think about it. Daddy, Dr. Hudson, that nice lady doctor, she'd come out here and give you a physical and try you out on some drugs that would help you feel less scared all the time. And Mama, you should think about seeing that doctor in Eureka. Because wouldn't it be nice if Wanda could go to school in town? And maybe go to a football game, like you did when you were a boy, Daddy?"

Wanda shrunk back a little, looking at her parents with pity. "I don't need to go to no football game, Clinton," she said quietly.

"But wouldn't it be nice if you could?"

Much later that same day, Jurea touched her husband's hard shoulder with a gentle hand and said, "I always wanted more for them kids than I wanted for myself."

"What about your face?" he asked.

She shrugged. "I want it to be fixed, but more for them than for me. And for you."

"This is a great way to spend a Friday night," June groused, leaning over a cup of coffee.

"My wife would agree with you," Tom said.

Tom and June sat in a booth near the window in Fuller's Café while, at the counter, a bunch of people gathered and George cut pie. There was an occasional outburst from one old man or another.

"They're going to make trouble," June predicted. "My father has notified everyone in three counties that the prosecutor is determined to bring Leah to trial on murder charges. I honestly don't know if they're planning to protest or bust her out."

"I think they're focused on bail for the moment," Tom said. "June, there are two things I've been meaning to tell you. First, I looked at the wreckage of your Jeep. It appears the metal was rent at the driver's door by a sharp object. If the Jeep rolled, a sharp rock could have done the damage. If it didn't roll, it was probably an ax."

"I knew it! I knew he was there! He was real!"

"Have you traced the type and age of that

cloth?" he asked.

"It'll take weeks, but it doesn't matter," she said, giving her head a shake. "We have an angel at Angel's Pass, and he saved my life."

"We may indeed have an angel, June, but the man who saved your life left his ax in the woods, twenty yards from the road. The blade was badly dulled by its work against the metal of your Jeep."

"But —"

"I don't know what his business was in that part of the forest, so near Grace Valley farms and orchards. Might be he had a truck nearby. Might be he had reason to leave the scene. . . . But whatever the circumstances, he was a flesh-and-blood angel with a Black & Decker ax."

"Jesus . . ."

"I'm sure when you get the report back on that cloth, it will prove to be no older than what a man carries in his pocket nowadays to blow his nose on."

"Well, hell. . . ."

"The other piece of news might suit you better. I got a call back from San Francisco this morning. My contact there checked four Bay Area police departments. There is no record of charges of any kind ever being brought against John Stone. Nor lawsuits."

June looked suddenly deflated. "I don't understand," she said. "He's wonderful, then he's suspect, then how can anyone think that, then the very woman who brought charges calls me, then —" She stopped talking as a BMW came up the street and pulled behind the clinic. "Speak of the devil."

"You really should talk to him about this. Perhaps there's an explanation."

They could see the light in her office flick on.

"Wonder what he's doing?" she thought aloud. "Well, no time like the present. I'll go over there now, while Elmer and his cronies are stirring the pot. We can talk about this tonight, since we won't be interrupted by patients."

As she was leaving, she heard Elmer's voice rise up in passion. "There's a couple of things fundamentally wrong with this town lately, if a woman can't defend herself against a violent man, yet we all sit in church and take spiritual advice from a womanizing preacher!"

"I vouch for that! It's been wrong long enough," someone said.

When the men as well as the women have had enough of that, June thought, maybe the town will have the courage to change it.

She walked across the street to the clinic, ready to have this issue with John resolved once and for all.

TWENTY-FOUR

June and Sadie walked across the street and went in the back door. John didn't hear them enter because of the noise he was making while rifling through her desk drawers.

"Looking for something?" June asked.

He looked up in surprise and his face was rigid with anger. She actually jumped back at the sight. Indeed, had she ever seen that look before, she'd have been more worried, and much sooner. He slammed a hand on the desk. "What the hell are you trying to do to me, June?"

"What?" she asked dumbly. "What do you mean?"

"I mean, are you the one having me investigated, for chrissake? People from the Marin County Sheriff's Department have been calling the house, asking about sexual assault charges against me, scaring poor

Susan to death! What the hell's going on here?"

"Shoot," June said. "How's that for discreet?"

"June?" he asked. "God, why are you doing this to me?"

"John, I got a call. First I talked to Dr. Fairfield, who was less than complimentary. Way less, let's be honest. And then, despite the good recommendations I got from others who had worked with you, I did get this call. This very damning call." She cautiously moved around his side of the desk, opened the top drawer and pulled a piece of paper out of a small notebook. She unfolded it so that the name and number lay exposed. "From this woman, saying she had had you arrested for sexual assault."

He frowned. "I don't know this woman."

"A surgeon? From San Francisco?"

"Feldtbrow? Is that some sort of Indian . . ." He scratched his head. "I don't think I've ever heard of —" He stopped. His frown deepened. Then he picked up the phone and dialed. The voice mail came on the line. "You have reached five-five-five . . ." He held the phone away from his ear, smirked, shook his head. "Jesus Christ," he swore.

"What? You know her?" June asked.

"Oh yeah. Carolyn. My ex. Just when you think you can relax —"

"Your wife did this? But why?"

"My *ex-wife* created a circus at the time of our divorce! I left the practice because of the upheaval she put us all through, the pressure she applied to the other doctors to get rid of me. But I can swear to you that there were never any accusations like *that.* None! Have you talked to any of the other staff at the Fairfield Women's Center?"

"Just one of the names you gave me," she said. "And of course, Dr. Fairfield."

"I *know* how Dr. Fairfield feels about me. Anyone else?"

There was a pounding at the front door of the clinic, which had been left locked. "Someone must've seen the light and thinks we're open for business. I'll go see." She started down the hall, John following. "Him being the founder and chairman of the clinic partnership, I figured Fairfield would —"

"He's my ex-wife's goddamn *father!*" John stormed. "I'd like to think I could have landed a partnership in a clinic that respected me without anyone's help, but the fact is, Carol's father headed the most prestigious OB-GYN practice in Sausalito. I *married* into it, for chrissake. And I divorced out of it."

June was stunned. "No wonder Fairfield had bad feelings about you cashing out your partnership. It was divorce settlement angst!"

"Exactly! And they're crazy besides. And obviously still pissed off."

"John, I've never heard you swear so much."

He dropped his chin, contrite. "We try not to . . . with Syd, you know. But Jesus, June, she makes me so goddamn furious with this —"

"Why would your ex-wife make trouble for you after all this time?"

"It's her hobby, June. She's obsessed. She's hired detectives, leaked inflammatory lies to the press, tried to sue me for everything from fraud to breach of promise. She's been restrained by the courts. And that's just what she's done to *me!* You can't imagine how miserable she's made Susan's life. She has harassed us for seven years! She's a spoiled, rich little psychopath who would do *anything* to —"

The pounding on the front door resumed, with Tom's shout added to the mix.

"June!"

Tom's cry of panic, something almost never heard, caused June to turn and struggle to get the door unlocked and opened quickly. Tom was supporting Christina Baker — the very patient who had refused to see John Stone because she found his examination "too personal." She was barefoot, wearing a sundress or perhaps nightgown that reached midcalf. Her eyes were swollen, tears streaked her cheeks, and there was an impressive contusion on her forehead. Dark streaks of blood ran down her legs.

"Christina," June exclaimed, joining Tom in supporting her. The young girl was trembling with fear, her small body vibrating.

"The bleeding," she murmured weakly. "I hurt. This isn't right. This isn't . . . right. . . ."

John muttered, "Dear God," before he brushed June and Tom aside, swept Christina up in his arms and carried her to the back of the clinic.

"Get my dad and Charlotte, and take the dog to the café," June ordered Tom. "Sadie! Go with Tom!" Then she went to the file cabinet, pulled Christina's file and ran to catch up with John.

John took their patient directly to the treatment room rather than an examining room, anticipating an emergency delivery. June snapped on a pair of gloves and held a pair toward John, who accepted them before continuing, though he'd already been exposed to all that blood while carrying her.

Christina lay whimpering on the table. John had slapped a blood pressure cuff on her arm. He palpated her uterus and got her vitals while June pulled out the emergency delivery kit kept in the treatment room and withdrew sterile sheets, gowns, gloves and other paraphernalia from the cupboards. Neither of them paused for even the seconds it might take to appreciate how well they worked together.

"Christina," John asked. "Did anything happen to cause the bleeding? Did you get hurt?"

"Fell. I just fell. I drove myself here as soon as . . . I drove myself here when the blood started."

John made eye contact with June, and for the second time that night, she saw fury there — but this time she didn't understand.

"We need an IV here, angio catheter, sixteen-gauge, Ringer's. And an ultrasound, stat."

"We've got an ultrasound at twenty-six weeks," June told him, flipping open her chart.

"That'll do for me," John said. "Emergency transport?"

"Fifteen minutes. One way."

"Damn small towns," he muttered. "Call. Tell them to put a doctor on, and a baby transport unit. First, the IV, then draw me some blood. We need to know if she's in DIC."

June immediately knew this wasn't going to be an ordinary rushed delivery. John wanted blood drawn that would show, within ten minutes, if she was clotting. "Disseminated intravascular coagulation" was the blood's inability to clot, not particularly rare in the case of placental abruption. The patient could bleed to death during an emergency C-section. John was prepared to open her up right here in the Grace Valley Clinic, where the most serious surgery performed was a simple lumpectomy.

June drew the blood and was hanging a bag of Ringer's on the IV stand when the front door slammed. When Elmer appeared at the treatment room door, she shouted, "Call medevac and have them bring a doctor and a baby transport unit. Possible abruption."

"Probable abruption," John corrected. "Her pressure's dropping and we have fetal distress. Baby's heart rate is sixty. Where's that ultrasound?"

June passed him the folder that held the

precious record of Christina's test. He took a very fast look at the report. June already knew it showed the placenta was not in the way of the birth canal.

"What have we got here for a surgical procedure?" he asked.

"Brevitol . . ."

"Nope. We can't reverse the effects of Brevitol on the baby with a Narcan injection. What else?"

"Only morphine. It probably won't knock her out but it will calm her down and help with the pain. Lidocaine, Narcan, surgical kit, emergency delivery kit, oxygen, the bare essentials."

"Spinal needles?"

"Yep."

"Hemostats? Clamps? Retractors?"

"Hemostats," June repeated, cautiously opening the sterile kit. "Ten. Eight clamps. Four retractors."

"We'll be retracting with our hands for the most part. We going to get some help around here?" he shouted. "Drain the bladder and set her up. Throw a wedge under her left hip — a rolled up towel should do it." He locked his hands on the hem of Christina's dress and gave it a rending tear. June lifted the patient's knees and got to work on the catheter.

"Christina," John said, his voice calm and confident and silky. "It looks like your baby is ready whether you are or not. We're going to deliver the baby, Christina, and you're going to have to be very still and brave. Hold on to these hand grasps, here, but don't move or wiggle. Can you do that for me?"

"Are you mad at me, Dr. Stone?" she asked. June snapped her head up from her chore, confused, but neither John nor Christina paid her any attention.

"Of course not, Christina. Just do as we tell you now, and try not to worry."

"I'm so scared. . . . I'm so scared. . . ."

"It's okay, sweetheart, you're going to be just fine. We'll give you something for the pain. We're going to have to do a cesarean section."

"I wanted to see my baby born. . . ." she whimpered.

"Not this time, honey. Not this time."

June recognized the voice John used — the gentle father voice he usually reserved for Sydney. She finished with the catheter and drew the morphine to put into the IV. She draped the patient, propped her left hip and prepared a large, sterile bowl filled with lidocaine. She dropped a sterile syringe out of its package into the bowl, then drew spinal syringes full of everything she could think of.

"How long on that morphine?" John asked.

"Two minutes, tops."

Elmer came back. "Charlotte's on her way. Tom got her."

"You've got the patient until the nurse arrives, and I hope she gets here fast because you're getting the baby, Elmer. You'll need a Narcan injection."

For just a split second John stopped to stare at Elmer. Perhaps he was impressed by the way this seventy-two-year-old doctor calmly turned to the difficult task of preparing for this birth. He put out sterile sheets, towels, a suction bulb and drew a syringe of Narcan. Elmer didn't tremble or stop to think. June smiled, her pride evident.

John wanted to get to the baby as quickly as possible. There was very little time; they could lose them both.

Christina made a weird, gagging sound and Elmer whirled around instinctively — the patient's head was his area. He snatched a bowl from the cupboard with record speed, and leaned Christina over so she could vomit into it.

"I love it when we get that out of the way before we zonk her. Good girl. Doc," John said to Elmer, "there's no way we can intubate or ventilate her, so set up the suction nearby. Someone has to stay at her head in case she does that again and starts to aspirate. You'll pass her off to Charlotte when she gets here so you can concentrate on the baby. Ready with that morphine, June?"

"Ready."

"Take her down, nice and easy. Doc, watch that pressure." John threw Betadine solution on the protruding mound that was the site of his operation.

"I don't believe we're doing this," June whispered. "Morphine is running. Want to follow that with an antibiotic? Ampicillin?"

"Excellent idea," he muttered, turning around to the countertop to quickly suit himself up in sterile gown, mask and new gloves.

Assisting in such a situation was far more exhausting and nerve-wracking than being the cutter. June was flying into cupboards, preparing the patient, catheterizing her, drawing up the syringes full of meds, tearing open and dropping instruments onto sterile trays, laying out sponges and supplies, stopping this to do that, stopping that to do this. She had no idea what sutures he'd call for and got out everything she had.

Her hands moved like lightning, her mind racing ahead of John's every request.

I can do a lot of things, but I couldn't have done this, June thought. She knew she held people together pretty well, all things considered. But without John, she knew she wouldn't have had a fighting chance of saving Christina and her baby. Even now, though she had confidence in John's skill, she wasn't sure they'd make it. She hoped Christina wouldn't rise off the table from the pain; there was nothing to strap her down with. John turned his back to June and she tied his gown.

"Almost ready, Doctor?" John asked.

"Soon, soon," she said. She reached for the tube of blood she'd drawn and quickly rolled it between her palms. "She's clotting," she said.

"Thank God for little favors. It's show time, June. Shake a leg."

June was literally out of breath, trying to get herself gowned and gloved. Suddenly Charlotte flew into the room, and with her, the dusky aroma of those extra long cigarettes. June glanced at the clock. Eight minutes. "Welcome aboard," John said. "You going to faint or anything?"

"No way," Elmer promised.

"You'll faint first, young man," Charlotte

gruffly replied.

"Then let's go," John urged. "Here's where we cut and pray."

Without the tiniest briefing, Charlotte tied the back of June's gown and replaced Elmer at the patient's head. John took a spinal needle filled with lidocaine and he began injecting the local along a line from Christina's naval to her pubis. "Doc, come under this drape and hold her thighs. And be ready for your precious burden, which is coming in about one and a half minutes, if I'm worth my salt."

Christina began crying and muttering, either through narcotic-induced hallucination or pain. She sounded like an animal, forlorn and caught in a painful trap. "Don't, please, don't," she sobbed. "I won't do it again, I won't . . . please . . . don't. . . ."

June knew Christina wasn't begging her doctors to stop, but rather, was caught in some terrifying nightmare.

"We won't tie off the bleeders on the way in," John was saying. "Use sponges for retraction with your hands, June. And be sure to keep that lidocaine coming. Squirt it in, generously. We pour and cut, pour and cut. . . ." His hands moved deftly and quickly. "Pressure?"

"Sixty over forty. Pulse, one-twenty and

thready."

No one heard Jessica enter the clinic, but her voice came from the doorway, clear and curious. "Holy smoke! I'm here if you need anything!"

"We'll be okay, unless you happen to have an emergency helicopter in your purse."

"Not tonight, John," Jessica said. "Wow."

"Just stay outside the door, Jessie," he said. "Lidocaine. Pour it on. Her husband did this to her. Son of a bitch beats her." June stopped moving and looked up. "*Pour, I said.*"

June accommodated him. Christina yelped in pain and began shaking. Elmer applied more pressure to her thighs and Charlotte held down her shoulders. Charlotte, as June had long suspected, had nine arms. She held the patient, watched the IV, kept track of the blood pressure and pulse, and softly crooned to Christina that everything was going to be okay.

"Get ready, Doc," John said. Christina became still; perhaps she momentarily lost consciousness. Elmer eased away from holding her thighs and he turned to lift a sterile sheet from the counter. "Give me fundal pressure, June," John instructed, and while June pressed down on the uterus from above, John slid the baby out.

"Hang on," he told Christina, though she was just barely conscious. The baby, a boy, was lifeless and not breathing. "Here you go," he said, turning to place the baby in Elmer's capable hands. "Bring him back, Doc. Got your Narcan ready?"

"Got it," Elmer said, and whisked the infant away.

From the door came another, "Wow!"

"I need twenty units of pitocin to the IV bag," John ordered. June looked at Charlotte and directed with her eyes to the opened delivery kit. Like a flash, the sixty-year-old nurse moved.

"We're not messing around with cord blood. No fringe benefits, no extras, no specials tonight. Come on, sweety, come on," John murmured, massaging the uterus. He finally delivered the placenta manually. "Very nice," he said, pleased with himself. "The placenta was roughly fifty-percent attached, which kept our baby alive. We have a Couvelaire uterus, and she's responding to pitocin. We'll be able to close here in a minute. Now that the hard part is over — how's our baby?" he asked.

The sound of the suction was replaced by Elmer's CPR, which mingled with Christina's whimpering and Charlotte's cooing. John stood frozen. Then, knowing he could not afford to wait for the baby to respond, he called for the first of a series of sutures. At last there was a feeble whimper from the baby. "Ahh," John said, "gimme that suture, June, no horsing around here."

John's sutures were fast, neat and strong. Even under such harrowing circumstances he did a beautiful job. "Let's tie off these bleeders. Stat, stat, stat, suture, suture, suture, scissors." And then, remarkably, he started singing. "It must have been a beautiful baby, it must have been a beautiful child . . . stat, suture, scissors . . . I bet you drove the little girls wild. . . ." Every time he tied off a bleeder, June cut the suture and removed the clamp.

The baby's cries strengthened. They heard the helicopter overhead and glanced at the clock. "Opened and almost closed in twenty minutes, start to finish," June said. "I'm soaked to the skin."

John laughed. "What? You don't do this all this time?"

"Here they come!" Jessica announced when the clinic door opened.

"Well, finally, our emergency team. What am I giving them, Charlotte, darling?"

"She's stabilizing, Doctor. She has a bel-lyache."

John laughed and continued with his sutures.

"Gorgeous," June complimented. "He can join our quilting circle anytime, can't he, Jessie?"

"Absolutin-tootin," she said. June stole a look. Jessica leaned in the door frame, arms crossed over her small chest, and the light in her eyes was almost otherworldly.

"Her husband did this to her," John said, using his 3-0 silk to make simple interrupted sutures. "I knew it the first time I saw her. She had bruises on her buttocks and thighs. She denied he beat her so I did a blood profile on her, ruled out all the bad stuff that might've caused bruises — leukemia, aplastic anemia . . . All negative. The little creep beats her. I want him locked up."

"That's why you did all the blood work," June said, realization dawning.

"I'm sure I wrote it in the chart. It was the bruises."

"Oh Jesus," June muttered, getting his dressings ready. "How the hell did I miss that?"

"What do you mean, missed it?"

"John, Christina told me she didn't want to see you anymore because she didn't like the way you touched her. That's what started all the trouble. That's why I called the Fairfield Clinic to ask about you. Fairfield obviously told his daughter and . . . Jeez."

The medical team from Ukiah came down the clinic hallway, gurney wheels squeaking. "Stay out there, please," John shouted. "We're almost ready in here. Doc, you can give them the baby if he's stable enough for you. Yeah," he said to June, "she didn't like my touch, all right. I told her I knew she was getting knocked around, and if she wanted me to, I'd help her get away from her abusive husband. Otherwise, her pregnancy was in jeopardy. She said he never hit her in the stomach. Guess he forgot himself, huh?"

"Oh, John . . ." June moaned, fully and totally chagrined. "If only I'd talked to you in the first place . . ."

"Don't be too hard on yourself," he said. "I should have mentioned I had a case of spousal abuse — it's your clinic. But we got so damn busy. And then I should have told you why Fairfield hates me. We could have saved ourselves some misery. But this? This amounts to attempted murder, as far as I'm concerned. I mean it, I want him locked up. I'll press charges if she won't." He wiped the blood off his gloved hands with a sterile towel and applied a bandage to Christina's sutures. "Charlotte, how's she doing?"

"She's 106 over 66 and pulse and respirations regular. She's doin' real good, Doctor. Real good."

June stepped aside and did some very fast scribbling in the chart while the paramedics and doctor came in to transfer the patient. John briefed the M.D. quickly. "Sorry we couldn't wait for you."

"Ukiah radioed us that you did an emergency section here. That's a first."

"And a last, I hope. Given the circumstances, I'd say it was smooth. How's the baby look?"

"He looks good, considering."

"Christ a'mighty, who's got cleanup tonight?" a paramedic asked.

"I think you're looking at 'em. She's stable and gonzo. June's got it all in the chart for you. She's all yours. Take her away."

John snapped off his gloves. He held Christina's hand and walked beside her as she was wheeled to the door. He murmured that she had a baby boy even though she was not fully conscious. June followed the team and the gurney out the front door of the clinic.

A number of people stood around. For Grace Valley, this was a dramatic and unusual sight — three bloody doctors in surgical garb, the police chief and Ricky and a helicopter taking away the patients. Everyone watched while the copter rose into the sky, lights flashing. It veered left and shot away. In moments, the chopper noise gradually gave way to crickets. Perhaps thirty people stood in a wide circle around the vacant space in the street where the helicopter had been only minutes before. John dropped an arm over June's shoulder. "All this trouble, all the investigating and looking for references . . . ? This was all about Christina Baker?"

"Yeah. She wouldn't explain why you made her so nervous. All she ever said was that she didn't like the way you touched her. I'm the dope who didn't question the notation about bruises. I couldn't imagine what she was referring to."

"But you thought the worst," he said.

"I'm sorry. I'll make it up to you somehow."

"You already did. Good assist. I couldn't have done it without you."

"Well, I couldn't have done it at all," she admitted. "Ex-wife, huh?"

He sighed. "She can be found in Sausalito, standing over a cauldron, stirring — my bane and my pocket drain. I don't pay alimony or anything — she's a very successful surgeon. But she costs me anyway. I have to pay my lawyer every six months or so, get restraining orders, call off detectives, clean up messes she creates just to make my life a living hell. Like this mess. I'm sure she hoped I would eventually call that number she gave you, so I'd know it was her. She likes to know she's made an impact. But never fear. Your county detectives will have no trouble verifying that the only thing I did wrong was to marry Dr. Carolyn Fairfield, daughter of the great Dr. Fairfield."

There was an eerie stillness, a bizarre quiet. Spectators lingered and whispered to each other. They stood around in a night that had become suddenly calm and motionless.

"Quite a dramatic end, I'd say," June said. "The thing about medicine that amazes me most is the frequency of coincidences. Had we not been at the clinic tonight, Christina and her baby would have died. Even with all your skill, John, if I'd called you from home to meet me here, you would have barely beaten the helicopter. 'Another five minutes, and you wouldn't have made it' — such a commonly uttered phrase in our line of work."

Elmer stood facing John and June. "I can't believe how much of this we let happen," he said. "I apologize, June. Even I laughed at how often Pastor Wickham flirted and groped, and thought how funny it was when he was slapped. I never really thought about the harm he could do. I never approved of what Gus did to Leah, but I *knew* what he was doing . . . and we all might have done more than we did to help her. Still and all, even I might not have caught the fact that Christina was being battered! This is the country! Our women work hard — they get bruises!" He stepped toward John. "We're awful lucky to have you here, son."

"Thanks, Doc," John said almost shyly.

First the growl of an engine and then the headlights of a battered truck came into view. Gary Baker screeched to a stop in front of the clinic, right behind the old Datsun in which his hemorrhaging wife had driven herself to find help. He jumped out and looked at the odd gathering in confusion. "My wife around here somewheres? Christina Baker here?"

"Why you little . . ." John lunged down the steps toward Gary. June grabbed at the back of his scrubs, but he tore away.

"John! No! Your *hands!*" June screamed, but she was too late. John was on top of Baker. He had him backed over the hood of his truck and was holding him there.

"You beat her, didn't you, you worthless little worm!"

"What? What?"

"You *hit* her, didn't you?"

"Hit her? Naw. I might'a slapped her, maybe —"

June was tugging at the back of John's gown, trying to pull him off Gary Baker, screaming at him to stop, when he pulled back his right arm high over his shoulder to smash Gary in the chops. Tom, fortunately, came up behind them and grabbed John's arm, stopping him from throwing the punch.

With one hand Tom accomplished what June couldn't do with both of hers and all her strength. "Ricky!" he called. "Get one of the boys to help you and come here!" Then in a gentler voice he said to John, "Can't have you breaking your knuckles now, can we, Doc?"

"I want this little animal locked up," John hotly demanded.

Tom kept a tight grip on him. Ricky jogged over with big old George in tow. "Good idea. Ricky, I think we need to keep Gary with us awhile."

"What about my wife?" the young man demanded. "What about Christina?"

Ricky grabbed one of Gary's arms while

George took the other as if to escort him away. "Looks like she's going to be all right, no thanks to you," Tom told him, finally releasing John. "Medevac took her to Ukiah," he added. He made no mention of the baby; Tom had his own way of punishing offenders.

"You takin' me to Ukiah?" the young man asked Ricky as he was led away.

Gary Baker was neither large nor mature; he stood about five foot eight and was perhaps twenty years old. He'd been drinking and was totally confused about what had happened there tonight. He was only a tough guy when up against his petite, easily intimidated little wife. He went along with Ricky and George very docilely.

John could have killed him.

"We wouldn't want that doctor hittin' you, Gary," George said.

"No way, man. What an asshole."

"You hit that little wife of yours, didja?" Ricky asked.

"Might'a slapped her once. You don't know her. Christina can be a real —"

Gary's sentence was cut off by the sound of Ricky's fist making contact with his jaw. His knees buckled and Ricky and George hoisted him upright again.

"Like that? That about how you slapped her?"

"Hey, man . . ."

"All right, Ricky," Tom said in a patient, paternal tone. "He better be in perfect condition when I get down there."

"Aw, come on, Chief," John said.

"Okay. Once more for Doc Stone."

The next sound was of knuckles sinking into bone and flesh. John brushed his hands together and nodded as if to say it was a job well-done.

"How about that? That about how you slapped her, maybe? Huh?"

"Thanks," John said as he turned to walk back inside the clinic. "I needed that."

"Cleanup time, children," Elmer announced, opening the door. "Charlotte, Jessie, you can go on home if you want to. We can manage."

"I'm not leaving you alone to clean up my treatment room! I'll be looking for things all week!"

"Me, too, I'm staying," Jessica said.

John held the door for June. "Did I mention I don't do windows?"

This was the John June had gotten used to — this quiet mannered, sort of silly guy with the drop-dead grin and the oblivious nature. He looked ridiculous with a mop in his hands and bloodstains on his fashionable yuppie clothes, unsure what to do with himself. But he was a different person when he was thrust into emergency surgery and faced with the slim prospect of saving a life under unbelievably difficult conditions — then he could be downright commanding. Powerful.

It took two hours to put the clinic right again. John disappeared while Elmer, Charlotte, Jessica and June put away the last of the cleaning supplies. Suddenly he was standing in the middle of the hallway, nearly filling it with his handsome bulk, a grin the size of the Grand Canyon on his mouth and the unmistakable wetness of humility shining in his beautiful blue eyes. "They're doing great," he announced. "Christina and the baby. Both stable and in guarded condition. And," he added, puffing up his chest, "best stitching anyone's ever seen."

At midnight, they stepped outside. The air was cool, the sky clear and there was the sound of approaching helicopters. It wasn't exactly a rare sound; the DEA made regular passes over the hills in search of drug farms and camps. What was unusual was the number of helicopters — four or five, maybe more — and the flashing of Tom's emergency lights as he came speeding toward the clinic. He squealed to a stop at the back door and addressed the cleanup crew.

"I think you better keep the clinic open awhile. There's a major bust going down in the Alps right now, and I think this is the closest medical facility we have."

"Okay," June said. "Let's get some emergency vehicles on their way."

"You got it," Tom said, picking up his radio. "And we'll get some sheriff's department people here to provide security."

"And some ice from the café," she said to her dad.

"I'll go," Charlotte offered. "Come on, Jessie."

Muttering, maybe grumbling, everyone went back in the clinic to get ready for a possible emergency. Everyone except June. She stood on the back step and looked off into the starlit sky as the sound of choppers faded away. She said a prayer. "Please, God, let him be all right."

TWENTY-FIVE

Grace Valley saw an event unlike anything it'd witnessed before, and hoped never to see again. Dawn found Main Street resembling a bivouac, an outpost. There were army helicopters, the Forestry Service, a SWAT team, sheriff's deputies, federal agents of every stripe, and a variety of law enforcement personnel from surrounding towns and counties. George opened up the café and hauled his three sons and wife out of bed to help.

June, John and Elmer tended only minor injuries from a raid deep in the Trinity Alps that netted the law over forty criminals and ten thousand plants. According to one officer, these criminals had erected a small town in the forest, inside of which there were actually civilian residents who had come along as support industry. There was a bar, a convenience store, a hardware store. All the money in these businesses carried the skunklike stench of green marijuana.

The growing was done indoors and out, and it was still early in the season. One way to find illegal growers was to find their equipment — PVC tubing, generators, solar panels. It wasn't unusual to see what appeared to be a miner's shack built out of logs with a solar panel in the roof, and out back a gas-powered generator large enough to run a hospital.

The DEA came in to take away and dispose of the plants, ATF was there to take inventory and possession of firearms, and Forestry was there to reclaim the land. Along these gloriously beautiful mountain roads, there had been grave danger. Heavily armed men had guarded their own little pot plots, and marijuana thieves, also heavily armed, had stalked them in an effort to take over their plots. The gunshot wound that brought Jim into June's life had been the result of a minor struggle for land and plants.

While they'd made forty arrests, twice that many growers had made it into the woods and away. If they tried to come back they'd find their equipment and supplies had been seized, including vehicles, appliances and personal possessions, and the Forestry Service had replaced the little pot-growing town with an outpost of armed law enforcement officials. And dogs.

The dogs nearly drove Sadie crazy. She finally had to be put in June's office with the door closed; she couldn't stay at the café anymore. There were so many cops and dogs and uniforms, she was a nervous wreck. Being put in the office didn't help either. She whined at the door and scraped her heavy paw against it whenever someone walked by.

Once, when June was called into the street in front of the clinic to look at a suspect's arm, she saw there were easily a hundred armed men in the street, parking lots, café and clinic area. It was chaos. There was no way to tell how close they were to clearing out. The raided camp was twenty miles up the road into the mountains, but took an hour to reach by car. Soon the residents of Grace Valley who had business or appointments in town would be straggling in, and this was what they'd see. An army had landed and was taking prisoners.

There was one prisoner June didn't see, however. She craned her neck and studied the faces of those officers and suspects on Main Street, but he wasn't there. Tom's Range Rover was parked across the street in front of the café and he leaned against the passenger door, hat pulled down, his arms crossed over his chest. She could just barely see the glitter of his dark eyes under the brim of his hat. She made a gesture with a tilt of her head, a question. He responded with an elaborate shrug, lifting his palms upward. *Haven't seen him.*

By late in the morning, the street became crowded with locals who wanted to see what was going on. Law enforcement held them back, wouldn't let their trucks through and denied them entrance to the café, but word had reached the populace that the hills had been cleaned out of growers. Residents watched the circuslike atmosphere in quiet awe. If it hadn't been summer, school might have been canceled, June thought.

She called her friend and doctor, Blake Norton, from Rockport, and Dr. Lowe from Fort Seward to help man the clinic. The Red Cross sent out a couple of nursing volunteers to assist. The feds promised army medical officers and supplies would be forthcoming by early evening. The arrested had been taken away, but the clinic had to be kept open and staffed in case injured stragglers came in or law enforcement officers got hurt in the cleanup. And, of course, there were the regular patients.

But June, John, Elmer, Charlotte and Jessica had been up all night and most of the day. They were knee-walking tired. Charlotte, in addition to being tired, was in a state about the condition of the clinic, which had been tromped through by soldier-type clods. "Come on, Charlotte," Jessica said in an affectionate tone. "Let's just not worry about it now, and when they clear out, I'll help you get things back in order if it takes all month."

Charlotte was shocked and amazed by Jessica's gesture, but June just smiled.

"Thank you, Jessie," Charlotte said. "And I like that you're growing your hair again."

June was so tired that she wasn't sure she could fit in a shower before bed. As she entered her little house, all she could think about was getting out of the scrubs she'd been wearing for almost twenty-four hours. Cool sheets beckoned.

But that would have to wait, it seemed.

"I hope you brought your bag," said Jim.

He looked terrible, but his injuries were not — one gunshot flesh wound that only required a butterfly. But in his great escape, he'd taken a wild fall down a hillside, hitting every rock and stump in his path. He was bruised, scratched, scraped and cut. He wore only his stained and torn T-shirt, underwear and socks, and was wrapped in a bath towel from June's linen closet. His clothes and boots were on the back stoop, under an overturned wheelbarrow so no one would see. "I was pretty careful not to get mud or blood on anything," he said.

One whole side of his face was red and raw and would form a terrible-looking scab. "Tree bark is the worst," he said. And there was a contusion on his thigh that was frightening in its size. "Stump," he said. Both palms were scraped. "Never try to stop yourself on asphalt."

"You know, you're not going to like this, but the best thing for you, before I treat any of these cuts and abrasions, is a shower."

He winced visibly.

"I know. It's gonna sting. But really . . ."

"Do you have any liquor?"

"No. How about a Darvon?"

"I don't know. Think that'll help?"

"It's gonna sting," she said. She leaned back and looked him up and down. "I'll give you a couple of Darvon. But it's, well —"

"Gonna sting," he said, then drew himself up bravely, though bent like an old man, and hobbled off in the direction of the shower. When they got to the bathroom, she shook out a couple of pills for him and ran the water, just barely warm.

"Use soap where you can bear it, but just stand under the spray where you can't. And when you're done, put on my robe. This terry one."

"June, I'll never get into that robe."

"Or wrap up in this bath sheet," she said.

"You happen to have any men's underwear around here?" he asked.

"What size?" she asked, then smiled and left him alone in the shower.

He came to me, she thought. There must have been plenty of places he could have sought refuge, but he'd come here.

When he exited the bathroom, she was waiting in the bedroom, a towel spread on the bed and her medical bag open on the floor. She patted the bed where she wanted him to sit.

"You should see the town," she said. "It's a zoo. I didn't know there were so many different police departments. And the army is there —"

"The Guard," he corrected. "Out of Oakland, I think."

"Now that it's over, are you going to tell me about it?" She knelt on the floor, her hands gloved, and examined the cuts on his calves. He must have shredded his jeans.

"I knew approximately when it would happen . . . within a few days anyway," he said.

"When the first shots were fired, I hit the ground and waited. If I had to fire at law enforcement to protect my cover, it was going to be straight to the torso where a vest would stop the bullet."

"*You* weren't wearing a vest, however," she said, rising to sit on the bed beside him. She turned his face away so she could look at his facial wounds.

"No, but as it turned out, I never had to fire on officers. I got out clean."

"Clean?" she asked, applying a medicated salve to a face scraped so badly he looked like he'd been burned.

"Well, I got out. Fell all over myself down several hills to the road."

"You look like you were dragged behind a truck."

"Thank you. Those ballet lessons didn't help, I guess," he said.

"What are you going to do next?"

"After my vacation?"

"You get a vacation?" she asked.

"Let me back up," he said. "First, I debrief. I'll leave here in a day or so, go to Eureka for some meetings, back to the East Coast to check in, and then vacation. Unless something comes up and they need me somewhere else."

She was very quiet, thinking about one

thing he'd said. *A day or so.* "Does anyone know where you are?" she asked.

He turned his face to meet her eyes, which left the hand that had supplied the medicated salve suspended in midair. "Not yet," he said. "But . . . I should call in."

"You'll do what you have to do," she said. She turned his face away and resumed medicating.

Again he turned back and looked at her. "We'll find a way, June. Yes, we will."

She took a deep breath. "For right now, you have to go to bed," she said. "Give this embattled body of yours a rest. Could you eat a little soup first, if I fixed some?"

"I don't know," he said, wearily leaning back against the pillows of her bed, his eyelids noticeably heavy.

"I'll make you some soup and you'll sleep. Then you can explain how you're going to give me a day and then how we'll find a way."

It might have taken only five minutes to microwave a bowl of chicken noodle soup and put it on a tray with a few crackers, but when she returned to the bedroom, he was under the covers and sound asleep. The towel was on the floor.

She sat in the overstuffed chair in the corner of her bedroom, tray on her lap, and

423

slowly ate the soup, watching him breathe in slumber. His feet, probably size twelves, had ripped the top sheet from its mooring and hung over the end of the bed. His hair, curly and moist and dark, left a damp blot on the pillow. The reddish-brown hair on his muscled chest seemed to ripple like waves with each breath. He was lost in deep slumber and she was lost in him.

She finished her soup and showered, then dried her hair and pulled on soft knit pajamas — boxer shorts and a sleeveless top. She stood in indecision beside the bed, looking down at Jim. He was naked under there. Finally, she picked up the pillow from her side and headed for the couch. But in a second she was back beside the bed. She lifted the sheet tentatively, then slipped in.

In a moment her soft short jammies lay in a heap on the floor.

The last of the raiders and their arrested growers had pulled out of town and were gone in the wee hours of Sunday morning. Tom Toopeek went home to his family, but not before posting Deputy Lee Stafford in front of the clinic in his truck. Should anyone try to get help in the clinic, Lee was to radio first Tom, then John Stone. Tom did not want June to be disturbed, he said.

By seven in the morning, the street was deserted except for a couple of familiar cars at the café and Lee's truck at the clinic entrance. Elmer, Sam, Burt and George sat at the counter with coffee.

"Here he comes," Burt said, and they all turned as one to see Pastor Wickham walking across the parking lot from the parsonage to the church, his Bible tucked into one hand.

"Right on the dot," said Elmer, looking at his watch. "George, you feel up to scrambling some eggs?"

"Sure thing, Doc. Sam? Burt?"

"Over easy, bacon," said Sam.

"Pancakes on the side," said Burt.

"How you think this is going to go?" George asked Elmer.

"Wouldn't dare hazard a guess," he said. "But we've been through a lot just lately, this old town, and —" He stopped when he saw his sister's car come slowly up the street. "Now what in the world is she — ?" He didn't finish. They watched Myrna park the old yellow Cadillac.

"You gotta wonder how she can drive with that hat. The brim is damn near big as the steering wheel," Sam observed.

Myrna backed herself out of the driver's door, butt first, purse looped over her arm, wide-brimmed hat last. She wore her favorite lace gloves and had applied her bleeding-red lips. When she entered the café and saw them, she broke into a grin. "I thought I'd find you here, watching."

"Watching what, Myrna?" Elmer said.

"Don't play dumb with me, Elmer. I know you're at the top of this scheme."

"I don't know what you're talking about," he said.

"Fine, fine, deny it to the grave for all I care. I brought a deck of cards, if any of you old goats can remember how to play."

By nine-thirty Myrna was up fourteen dollars and fifty cents, Burt threw the party, Sam was even and Pastor Wickham was standing out on the front step, checking his watch. The street was empty; not a soul was out.

The pastor went inside, and momentarily the bells began to summon a congregation, but no one drove down Valley Drive. He didn't usually play his own bells, so they weren't very well done.

At ten, thirty minutes past the first service, which no one attended, Pastor Wickham walked in the door of the café. He approached the table where Myrna and the old boys played poker, looked directly at

426

Sam and asked. "Are you responsible for this?"

"For what, Pastor?"

"There's no one in church. No one. It's a conspiracy!"

"Nonsense," Myrna said. "See your twenty-five and call you. Jonathan, care to sit in for a hand, since you don't seem to have any other . . . ah . . . engagements?"

"Mrs. Claypool, how can you sit there, on the Lord's day, and gamble, while our church is in crisis?"

"The church will be fine, Jonathan," she said. "But there is a crisis, and I think it's yours. You must have a lot of people angry with you. Maybe you need to ask some humble forgiveness for being such a womanizing pain in the ass. Full house," she said, laying down her cards, raking in her quarters and looking up at Jonathan in all innocence.

Jonathan huffed and puffed. "Lies! Exaggerations! I'll call the church council this very second!" And out the door he stomped.

"That oughta keep him busy for a while."

"How's he going to explain this to the council?"

"I suppose in the usual way — those women just threw themselves at poor Jonathan."

"If the council has been awake . . ."

"How could Jonathan say that with a straight face?" George demanded.

"Myrna," Burt said. "Syl read your new book and —"

"Well, that's a relief. There was no one at my signing yesterday. No one. Not even Birdie. Have a little drug raid in the town and everyone is too preoccupied to support a local author in her time of promotion!"

"The town was full of feds and helicopters! The only thing we were missing was tanks!" George protested.

"Such carrying on. So, what did Syl think of my new book?"

"Well, I think she means to ask you something. Syl said you've done the missing husband plot again, she said you do that about every tenth book. . . ."

"Is it really that often?" she asked. "You know, as you get older, you forget how often you tell the same story all over town."

"Anyway," Burt continued. "Syl said this was the most terrifying yet, and —"

Before he could go further, Myrna yelped a happy laugh and clapped her hands together. "Oh, thank her for me! Please!"

"I will, but I wasn't done. The most terrifying and *realistic* yet," he said. "This one had the heroine go in search of her missing husband, find him with another woman, lure him home with the promise of a nice divorce settlement — because she was pretty wealthy, you know — and when he was unaware, she killed him."

"Yes, that clever witch!" Myrna declared proudly.

"And chopped him up in little pieces and buried him all over the garden. Front, back and sides of the house. And her garden flourished but she'd gotten a taste for killing, and —"

"Oh, Burt, don't tell the ending!" she begged. "You'll ruin everything!"

"Myrna," he continued, "are you ever going to tell what happened to Morton Claypool?"

"Why? You think he's in the garden?"

"Your irises have been legendary since he went missing," Sam said.

"Why Sam, you give Morton more credit than he deserves!"

When the little Sunday morning party was breaking up and Elmer escorted Myrna to the yellow Caddy, he said to her, "I wouldn't be surprised if your garden gets raided. You tempt fate."

"Oh Elmer, no one really thinks that. They have fun with the idea, that's all. Now tell me what you did to set up this boycott."

He shrugged. "I called Birdie and Susan

Stone and Julianna Dickson. I said that in light of what had happened to Leah and to Justine, and to a young anonymous patient who was abused by her spouse and almost killed, I was taking a stand against the poor treatment of women. I said that I was sick of Jonathan Wickham's behavior and excuses, and that I wasn't going to church again till the town, and its women, got either a heartfelt apology or a new preacher. Who called you?"

"The Barstows. But I'm so surprised that *no one* showed up this morning. I thought there was a core group that supported him."

"I thought so, too," Elmer said. He turned and walked across the street to the clinic, his hands in his pockets and his gait sluggish. He had thought the preacher had a core group of supporters, and was chagrined to know it was probably him and his cronies — the old men who didn't take seriously what it was like to be sexually harassed.

June felt a finger drawn down her spine, from her neck to below her waist, and her eyes came slowly open. In the distance she heard the unmistakable sound of Sadie slurping up her food in great hungry gulps. He had gotten up and fed and watered the dog. She felt the gentle caress of his hand, lifting the hair off her neck. Then his lips there, kissing.

She turned over. His eyes were clear and rested, but his face was scraped raw on one cheek.

"This is no way to play hard to get," he said, his hand stroking, starting at her shoulder, down over a bare breast, across her rib cage, over a hip, ending at her thigh.

"I must be out of my mind," she said. "You're only going to leave me."

"I have to go back to work, but if you say yes, I'll come back."

She touched the side of his face that was unhurt with the palm of her hand. "Yes," she whispered.

TWENTY-SIX

June thought maybe Elmer guessed what was going on because of how readily he did as she asked. She called him on Sunday afternoon and told him she'd overdone it and needed a couple of days to rest and recover. "But if you have an emergency, please be sure to call. Otherwise, John said he'd cover for me."

"If that's what you want," Elmer said. "Do you want me to come out there and cook something for you?"

"Um . . . no! I'd rather be alone . . . and get some rest."

"If that's what you really want," Elmer had said, but June had never asked for a day off in her life. Nor had she ever overdone it or been too tired to work.

So Elmer called Tom Toopeek and said, "My daughter wants to take a couple of days off to rest."

"Oh? And can you spare her?"

"I can and the clinic can. John Stone is there and I'll gladly help out tomorrow. What I want to know is this — is it at all possible a pot grower from the mountains has escaped the law, found her and is holding her hostage?"

"Did she sound nervous or upset?"

"A little, yes."

"Then let me just check on that for you," Tom offered.

Tom let a little time go by, then called June and said, "Your father wants to know if you're being held hostage by an escaped grower."

She glanced at Jim, who leaned against the pillows, the sheet drawn to his waist. She smiled. "Well, if you must know . . ."

"I'll tell Elmer you're perfectly safe and need some rest."

"What we really need is some men's underwear, size 36."

"Shall I pass that on, or . . ."

"It was a narrow escape, you see."

"Goodbye, June."

Jim's undercover work in the Trinity Alps was over and his next assignment would be in another part of the country, but it was still necessary to keep him a secret. There were escaped and missing growers, business connections these criminals had in California, and connections that had connections. Jim could not drop his cover and emerge as a law enforcement officer. Not yet. In time — and he couldn't say how much time — he could reappear under a new cover of some kind, without bringing unsafe attention to himself or June.

"Do you have any idea where you'll work next?" she asked.

"I doubt they have a spot for me yet. Finishing the reports and debriefing from this raid will take time. Months."

"Months?" she asked weakly.

"Say about three. Maybe four. I'm sorry."

"It must be grueling work."

"It has its challenges, but when that's done, I'm due a couple of weeks off. Is it possible you're due a couple of weeks about then?"

"I haven't taken a vacation in twelve years."

He pulled her against his bare chest. "What great news. Then you're due. What do you think about a sandy beach somewhere? You could pack everything you need in a coin purse."

She got a stricken look on her face. They had been together for two days. They had hardly bothered with clothes. And for the first time she remembered that little oval case — the color of pearl, compliments of her doctor — that would *never* fit in a coin purse. Not only had she not used it, she had not even opened her dressing table drawer where it was kept. She swallowed hard.

"June?" he said. "It doesn't have to be a sandy beach. . . . It could be —"

"Shoot," she said.

On Tuesday morning June accompanied Sadie outside at dawn. She carried her steaming cup of coffee and meant to sit on the porch steps and wait. Even though she and Sadie had bonded, and Sadie had stayed a constant at her side, she was afraid to let her roam, afraid she would have to go find her at Mikos's farm, which was still vacant and now up for sale.

But while Sadie found a comfortable place to squat, June found a package on the back porch steps. "Jim," she called into the house. "You'd better come see this."

He came out of the bedroom in his new uniform, a pair of cut-off pink sweatpants that were oversized for June and fitted like hose on Jim, and a big T-shirt that she often wore to bed. The shirt had lace around the neck and sleeves, and ballet-dancing bears on the front. He was scruffy and unshaven, his scraped face being too sore to touch with a razor, his hair wildly curly and sticking out everywhere. Every time she saw him in that lacy shirt and bursting sweats, she had to use control not to laugh out loud. He looked like Attila the Hun in a tutu.

"What's this?" he asked her.

"I don't know. I didn't dare touch it. What if it's a bomb or something?"

He crouched down and studied it, then pulled the string that held the brown paper closed. It came apart easily. It contained clothes — underwear, socks, jeans, shirt. He looked up at her. "Well, I guess it's time."

He said he'd never before felt such a deep stirring of the heart; that it hurt to say good-bye. He would call when he could, but she should understand that over the next few weeks and months he would be working and probably traveling. Before the next assignment came, however, they would have a getaway — a distant and quiet and private time together. This was important work he did, and he was good at it, but it wasn't the kind of work a person could do forever. A couple more years and this would end; he would settle down. Grace Valley was nice, he said. Just the kind of spot he'd had in mind.

"What if you're just playing me for a fool?" she asked him.

"June, anytime you think this arrangement is not what you want, you say so. But this is all I have right now."

"I'm perfectly fine with this arrangement," she said stiffly, "until you go."

He said, "I don't know why I met you when I did, but I'm going to assume it's meant to be. I think I'm in love with you."

"Aw," she said with a hiccup of emotion. "I bet you say that to all the girls."

"I'm not kidding," he said.

"Don't drag this out, please," she said. "This is awful."

He kissed her once more, then walked across the porch, down the step and down the long drive, disappearing at the road. As she watched, tears ran down her cheeks. When he was gone, she felt as though a plug had been pulled inside of her and all emotions had been cruelly drained out, leaving her empty.

Sadie licked her hand. June looked down at her new best friend. "We have to go back to work anyway," she said. She sniffed loudly. "Just call me June of Arc."

■ ■ ■ ■

He didn't call her. As each day passed, she sunk a little deeper. Her fear was twofold: that he'd been hurt or even killed; that he'd only been passing through her life because she was convenient.

The days turned into miserable weeks.

"Elmer, what's wrong with our girl?" Myrna asked. "She's been so morose."

"I don't know. I think the Jeep burning up took it all out of her. Or maybe it was that drug raid. She took a couple of days off for the first time since she's been back in the valley. She's gotten very moody."

"It seems more serious than that. She's brokenhearted."

"I know. I don't know what to do for her."

"We'll have to think of something," Myrna said.

After four disappointed weeks, Pastor Wickham put a lock on the church door. A moving van stood in front of the parsonage. He had called many parishioners, one by one, insisting he had nothing to atone for; he'd been maligned and slandered and completely misunderstood. He never uttered an apology to anyone in town, least of all Justine. Angry and hurt, he would not say any goodbyes. But Birdie Forrest wouldn't let it pass. Someone had to defend Grace Valley; the town was not to blame. She took a plate of cookies to the parsonage as the movers were loading them up.

The children were cross, Clarice's eyes were puffy and red, and Jonathan wore a look of sullen indignation. "I wanted to wish you a safe move, Pastor and Clarice," Birdie said, presenting the cookie plate.

He wouldn't take the offering. "It would have been far more charitable had you wished us a safe *stay* by showing some support," he said.

"You know, this could have been all different," she said.

"This is a mean little town," Clarice said. "And I'm glad to be leaving it!"

"It's not a mean town," Birdie argued, but without ire. "But it's become an angry town now. Mad at itself, you know. For standing by and letting people be hurt. For thinking there was nothing it could do. For not wanting to interfere, while knowing everything that went on in everyone's life. You can't have it both ways. If you *know*, you have to *act*. Isn't that what being a neighbor is about?

"I think this town is working on forgiving itself now, but it's going to take a while." And then she left, leaving the plate of cookies on the hood of the Wickhams' car.

She went back at five that evening and swept up the shards of glass from where it had been angrily smashed on the parsonage drive.

By the first of July, the crops in the Craven garden had grown thick and healthy. The corn was high, the squash plump, and it looked like a good pumpkin crop was coming. Sam, Elmer, Lincoln, Burt, John and Susan and some of the other neighbors managed to tend the yard and garden while the boys were put in foster care in Pleasure, just down the road. Corsica Rios visited them every week and reported back that they seemed to be thriving.

Except for Frank, who might not be thriving, but he was improving. He wasn't with his younger brothers, but in a group home for teenagers that Jerry Powell had put together, in a place where he could learn that he wasn't the only abused child in the county. Nor was he the only one who had a problem with rage. There was more hope for him now than there had been in the past.

Corsica and her son Ricky took the Craven

boys to see their mother every Sunday. Her prison was of another type now — walls and bars and guards. And still it was not as bad as it had been with Gus. The boys could see that in her eyes. Even Frank. No matter how bad things seemed, they didn't have to fear Gus's violence ever again.

"My lawyer says he thinks I have a good case for self-defense, and I'm going to come home to you soon," she told her boys.

The only problem, which she didn't want to share with her vulnerable sons who missed her so much, was that the prosecutor was building his case around the fact that Gus was killed by a blow to the *back* of his head.

In a hospital clinic in Eureka, Dr. David Cohen sat on a low stool with a sketch pad while Jurea sat higher, on an exam table. June stood behind Dr. Cohen, looking over his shoulder as he sketched, trying to keep all expression from her face. A couple of times she leaned too close and Dr. Cohen slowly turned and glared over his shoulder at her — but then he smiled. It was hard to wait.

At Jurea's side stood Clarence, whose appearance had changed remarkably in just a few weeks as his medication brought a new and barely familiar calm to his mind. His features were relaxed, which was the greatest change, but he'd also traded the ponytail for a close-cropped haircut, and he wore a shirt with a collar, compliments of Charlie McNeil's trip through piles of second-hand clothes donated to the disabled vets.

Jurea had been through several examinations, beginning at the clinic with June and her staff and culminating at the hospital where the visiting plastic surgeon evaluated her. There had been lots of probing of her face and eye and ear and neck, and an MRI — which really tested Clarence's newfound stability, watching his wife being pushed into that dark, clanking tube. Now she waited tensely, squeezing Clarence's hand.

Dr. Cohen looked up at her face, down at the sketch, up and down, up and down, charcoal moving, and when he looked at her, he wasn't really looking at her but at her scars, which would become his canvas. "Despite the appearance of damage, Mrs. Mull, it's all surface scar tissue and not as deeply destructive as it might seem. There are only a few tiny old fractures of your cheek. Your cranium and jaw are completely intact, and, although it's difficult to get an accurate test right now, I believe you're sighted in that eye." He sketched some more. "It's remarkable. Claw hammer, you say?"

"Yes sir. I was only six. Caught it off my daddy's backhand while he was hammering away. Sent me through the air ten feet before I landed."

June winced every time she heard that injury described.

"I'm sure it was a frightening injury at the time, but most of the scar damage came later, as your skull and face grew and the old injury didn't have much give. Had you seen a doctor at the time, you might have been helped."

"Mountain people don't put much stock in doctors and hospitals," she said.

"It would be nice if someone could work to effect change in that thinking. It could save lives, make lives easier." He stood and showed her the sketch. Her mouth dropped open. "It would take a minimum of four surgeries, over a year or maybe just a little longer. We'd be removing scar tissue, doing some abrading. There would be a skin and tissue transplant, and I think it will be necessary to implant a small plastic disk under your skin at the top of your cheek to make it symmetrical with the other side. That's the bulk of my challenge, right there," he said, moving his charcoal from side to side across the drawn face, then up and down from forehead to chin. "Making all sides and quarters equal. We're going to find it difficult to replicate the eyebrow, but you can always correct with cosmetics, and you might find a slight droop at the lip, here. But the cheek, eye, nose and jaw will smooth out and look perfectly natural about a year post op."

Jurea stared at the charcoal drawing in disbelief. This was what she'd look like if she hadn't been hit with the back end of her daddy's hammer? This face, this woman was almost beautiful. A tear gathered in her good eye and slowly traced a path down her cheek.

Dr. Cohen started to pull the tablet away and her hand shot out, grabbing it. She wasn't going to be done looking for a long time.

"You can have copies," June said. "Several copies. You can give one to each of your kids, take one to your mother. . . ."

"I'll keep the original in your chart and medical records."

"They won't believe this," she said, her hand trembling as she touched the scars on her face.

"They can believe it. I'm very good at what I do," Dr. Cohen said. "Before you leave today, we want to get a photo that we can keep. And you can sit in the lounge and look through our scrapbook of before and after pictures of work we've done all over the world. This is a wonderful team."

Clarence cleared his throat. "Charlie Mc-Neil says you're obliged to do this without pay? I like to pay my way."

"Good, I'll take you up on that. I'll do the surgeries, you and Mrs. Mull do some work for the vets and other disabled groups. There are people suffering everywhere, and it helps them to hear the success stories of people who got help. More people will be made well and happy if they only know where to go and what to do, and have someone like you to tell them not to be afraid. But I warn you, Mr. Mull — if you make yourself available to help, you'll be overwhelmed by work."

"We could do that, Doctor," Jurea said.

"When can you do the surgery?" June asked.

"First one in September. We'll be back up here then. We hope to schedule about twenty operations in the local area."

"Twenty people have scarred faces?" Jurea asked, aghast.

"No, no, Mrs. Mull." He laughed. "This team of doctors includes internists, orthopedists, gynecologists, pediatric surgeons . . . a wide variety of medical personnel. We just want to help."

"You are a godsend, Dr. Cohen," she said with reverence.

"Only a craftsman, Mrs. Mull. But maybe God brings us together at the right time."

June walked with them to the lobby of Valley Hospital. "I can't believe this is going to happen," Jurea said for the hundredth time.

"Believe it," June said. "Medicine is a world of miracles." She stopped to say goodbye to them at the hospital entrance. She shook Clarence's hand. "I never thought I'd say this, Clarence, but finding you in my living room that morning not so long ago turned out to be one of the happiest days of my life."

Clarence could hardly speak. He bit on his lower lip and looked briefly away, collecting himself. "Doc, I didn't think I'd ever see the world through clear eyes again. I got you to thank."

"Not really," she said, shrugging it off. "I think it was your son who made all this happen for you. I just came along for the ride."

When June arrived back at the clinic, the last patient of the day was just leaving. John was leaning over the front counter, writing in a chart, and she slid a copy of the sketch of Jurea in front of his eyes. At first he frowned as he looked at it, then slowly the dawning came and his eyes widened. Within seconds Charlotte and Jessica were leaning over John's shoulders, looking at the drawing.

"Is that really Mrs. Mull?" Jessica breathed in wonder.

"Is that really possible?" John asked.

"Isn't it amazing?" June concurred. "Four surgeries over the course of twelve to eighteen months. And Dr. Cohen thinks her eye may be fine, too."

"They must be thrilled," Jessica said, just as the office phone began to ring.

"A little overwhelmed, I think. But adjusting very nicely. They're moving into town and Clarence is going to do some janitor work around here. I would never have guessed how nicely this —"

"June," Jessica interrupted. "A Dr. Jim Stump, from Eureka?"

She frowned. "Can't place him," she said, shaking her head. "Can you get a message? A number?"

"Sure," Jessica answered, going back to the phone.

"Anyway, I never would have believed all these things could come together —" She stopped short. Jim Stump? "Jessie! I'll take that in my office!"

By the time she got to her phone, her heart was hammering. She lifted the phone carefully, afraid to even hope. "June Hudson," she said.

"Hello, sunshine, Dr. Stump here."

She burst into delighted laughter. "Dr. *Stump?*"

"I couldn't say Post, now, could I?"

"Is this your new emerging identity?"

"I'm not good enough for you," he said. "I haven't been able to call, to come down. It's been chaotic. These things sometimes take longer to clean up than to get busted."

"I thought you'd forgotten me — and all your wild promises."

"I'm a lousy boyfriend. You must regret the day you met me."

"Not one call?" she asked.

"I went to jail," he said. "Just for a few weeks. I had to follow up, you know. You can check if you want. Get that cop friend of yours to look into it. You should be sure you're not involved with a liar. I mean, I'm a liar all right, but I don't lie to *you.*"

"Jail?"

"As a captured grower. They had phones, but there was no way I was dialing your number from jail. So June . . . ?"

"Hmm?" she said, smiling, leaning her head into her hand and beginning to get that silly, girlish feeling all over again.

"If you say this is too much, me and you, too ridiculous, too sporadic, too —"

"Oh, it is too much. Too good to be true also comes to mind," she said softly. "When will I see you again?"

"You sure? Because I know how hard it was on you to say goodbye, and there will be a lot of those for a while yet. . . ."

"I'm sure," she said. "I may change my mind later, may kick myself for getting into this with you, but for right now, this is what I want."

"When I leave here, in a week or so, I'm going to make an invisible pass through your little town. I'll give you as much notice as I can."

"Okay," she said.

"I'll call you later, at home."

"Okay," she said again.

She had thought about this in the weeks since he'd left. She knew she'd been down, her heart hurt. Tom had noticed, and she suspected Elmer had, also. It was the ache of having had something that felt so right and was gone too soon. But she had come to realize that it was not better to be alone. It wasn't better to have no one. Illusive as he was, he was exactly who she wanted.

"Having you there, knowing where you are, feels so right to me," he said.

"Then it must be," she agreed.

While driving home, Sadie in the cab of the little Nissan beside her, she saw a woman in the middle of the road, flagging her down. June slowed, and as she got closer, she recognized Mikos Silva's granddaughter, Beth, at the end of the deceased farmer's long drive.

"Beth?" she questioned.

"Oh June, come quick. It's Matt. We came out here to pick up some of the old baby things Grandpa had stored in the attic. One of the rungs on the attic ladder cracked and Matt fell. I think he's broken his leg. And there's no phone! And —"

"Jump in, Beth. Let's go have a look."

Matt was lying on the bed in the downstairs parlor that Mikos and his wife had both used in their final months on earth. June cut his jeans up to the hip and saw that his thigh had a kinked and unnatural crimp in it. "Yep, very little question about that. But it's not a compound fracture."

He groaned loudly, gritting his teeth, and twisted the bedspread in one hand.

"I'll give you something for the pain first,

and then I'm going to call the paramedics."

"Can't I just take him in the car?" Beth asked.

"He needs a splint and a lift, Beth. And maybe an IV. If I had the Jeep, I could load him in the back, but I've just got a little truck. I don't think you want to drag him out to the truck bed and toss him in." All the while she talked, she filled a syringe with Demerol, then quickly administered it. "That will begin to take effect soon. Beth, sit with him. I'm going to call from the front porch. And don't worry, he's going to be all right."

When she stood on Mikos's porch, she saw Sadie way across the yard at the tree line, wagging her tail fiercely. A short, stocky man, bent at the waist, was petting her. June squinted. *It couldn't be. Couldn't couldn't be.* It looked like Mikos. He was wearing the overalls that Mikos had always worn and the soft, faded blue chambray shirt, rolled up at the forearms. And his dark curly hair was spun with silver. He stood, looked across that wide yard toward her, lifted his arm in a wave and turned away. He disappeared into the forest.

June was frozen. Sadie sat on the ground, her back to June, staring patiently into the trees. Then she got up, slowly turned and started toward June at a nice trot. It actually looked as though Sadie was smiling.

"Phew. Who says we don't have angels here!"

TWENTY-SEVEN

Jim had gone to jail with some of the captured growers to see if he could gather any more information about escaped suspects, other encampments, and anything that would enable the law to make more arrests and convictions. The Trinity bust made national news — not because of the size of the cache, but because of the difficulty of pulling it off and reclaiming the land.

"But," he told June in a long evening phone chat, "there will always be a problem with growers back in those mountains. It's just the best place in the world to hide and grow."

"Will you go back there?"

"No, I'm done with that crowd. On to bigger and better things."

"Aren't you getting tired?"

"Of the work? No. Of the way I sometimes have to live to do this work? There are times.

There are times. Lately, all I can think about is you."

"Don't let yourself be distracted," she said, surprising herself.

"Are you afraid to operate, since we've become a team?" he asked, not really expecting an answer.

"My father thinks I've become moody. Distant."

"Is it true?"

"It's not your fault, but it is true. I've had so many things on my mind lately. The town is going through a big change. We've grown, maybe too fast. Birdie, my friend, says the town is less tender than it was, that we're not taking very good care of each other these days. I think she might be right."

"You take good care of the town," he said.

"But lately it's been hard. Since my Jeep burned up and I haven't been able to replace it, I've been having terrible worries about money. I never worried about money before — not that I ever had any — but we always managed to keep the town, medically speaking. And I have a new doctor in the office who was trying to help a young, battered wife. Instead of realizing it and supporting him, I became suspicious of his motives, like my instincts, usually good, were cracked. I had him investigated! I'm surprised he's forgiven me.

"Then we were able to help this disabled vet and his morbidly scarred wife with medical aid, and that's good, but in the same month, we ran off our preacher! I don't know, Jim. . . . I always thought of our town as small and old-fashioned, but I think it's getting a little wacky. Am I just getting old?" she asked.

"Would you like to go dancing?" he asked out of the blue. She felt a warmth flood through her and all her worries briefly disappear.

"I wish you could come to the Fourth of July parade and picnic," she said. "My aunt Myrna is in charge of the parade. She organizes the young people and they create floats out of cars, bikes and wagons, wear costumes, play kazoos. And then comes the greatest Fourth of July picnic in the world."

"Don't go to the kissing booth," he said. "If you do, I'll know."

The best part about the parade was the excitement that preceded it. Bleachers were brought out from the high school and erected on Valley Drive between the clinic and police department, across the street from the café. The Presbyterian Women, undaunted by the absence of the preacher, set up trestle tables in front of the church and sold baked goods and lemonade. Behind the café and church was a park that stretched all the way back to Windle Stream, where Sam sometimes fished if he had loaned out his truck and couldn't get far. There George and the other men would set up the huge grills that had been brought to Leah's farm.

At two o'clock sharp the high school band, or what was available of them with so many on vacation, would strike up a marching song and lead the parade.

June arrived early and parked behind the clinic. She saw that the bleachers were already starting to fill up with parents. John and Susan were down in front, sitting beside the Dicksons. Julianna held the new baby in its knapsacklike carrier.

"Well, I assume all the children are with Mrs. Claypool and her entourage?" June asked.

"This is our first parade," John said, beaming. "Princess Sydney is going to be pulling the float."

"Ah yes — that would be the yellow Caddy at the end of the parade," June said.

"Oh, you ruined it!" Mike Dickson said. "We wouldn't tell him!"

"Oops. So, how's our newest Dickson?"

"Perfectly all right, as far as we know," Julianna said. "There's no explanation for what happened to him. When I do put him down, which isn't often, he sleeps on a monitor. I usually enjoy these baby months, but now I can't wait till he's two and *completely* out of the woods."

"Did the pediatrician think it was a SIDS episode?" June asked.

"That's his best guess."

"How terrifying, Julianna. Can I hold him?" she asked.

June reached for the baby and cuddled him against her chest. She breathed in the talcumy smell of him and felt herself melt around him. She had not felt this way at thirty or even at thirty-five. What was happening to her?

Elmer, Judge and Birdie joined them on the bleachers. "She's going to get strange again if she holds that baby for very long," Elmer said.

June looked up and was completely surprised by who she saw on the other side of the street. "Dad, John, look who's over there! It's the Mulls. Julianna, do you mind if I carry the baby with me to go fetch them? I promise not to give him up."

"It's okay, June. I think you can be trusted not to kidnap him."

"Don't be too sure," Elmer said. June gave him a glare and went to get the Mulls. Elmer leaned toward John. "She's been acting pretty strange ever since she delivered Julianna's baby. Emotional. Funky."

"She's at that age," Birdie said. "She should have someone in her life who isn't an old man or a married woman."

"I bet it's her clock," Susan said. "Tick, tock, tick, tock . . ."

"Well, I think it would be good if June had a man in her life," Julianna said. "John, isn't there someone you can fix her up with?"

"I'll think about it — but shush, here she comes. Make room for the Mulls, everyone."

It was a remarkable thing to have them come out in this way, and far more than anyone ever expected to happen. It was one thing to get Clarence to try drugs and get Jurea to see a doctor, but this — the whole family joining with the town. It was more than any of them had ever dared hope for.

By two o'clock, when the first clumsy strains of "Yankee Doodle Dandy" were being coughed out by the Valley View High School Band, June was seated on the bleachers between Jurea and Julianna, and Jurea was holding the baby. Jurea had mentioned how amazed she had been when her own babies had not cried at the sight of her, and Julianna had told June to pass Douglas to her. Also near were Jessica, Ursula and Philana watching for the Toopeek children in the parade, Charlotte and Bud and some of their grown children, the Gilmores, the Crandalls, and Corsica Rios, who had brought the Craven kids to participate.

June looked around her and saw all the faces, all the happiness and anticipation, and felt blessed. She touched Jurea's hand, the one that held the baby, and said, "Jurea, it means so much that you're here, that you trust us enough to be here. You and Clarence. You've made us all very very happy."

"I ain't done the tenth of what you all have done for us," she answered shyly.

The band came, then Tom Toopeek in the decorated Rover, with kids hanging off the sides, crepe paper and balloons blowing in the wind. He ran the siren when they passed the gallery, and everyone whooped and laughed and yelled at him. He cleared the way for the teenagers in their decorated cars, then the younger kids on their decorated bikes and skateboards, then the little ones marching along holding hands, waving banners and pulling decorated wagons or riding decorated tricycles.

Then came a sight that would never be

forgotten in the valley.

The tiniest of the children held crepe paper streamers that seemed to pull along a big, red-and-white, oversize ambulance, complete with flashing lights on top. There sat Myrna Hudson Claypool in a white nurse's dress and cap, her skinny, aged legs dangling on the windshield. Sam drove the ambulance, and beside him, waving out the window, was Justine.

It didn't sink in at all. June thought it was just another of Aunt Myrna's elaborate costumes and dramas. "She usually has the children pull streamers, and at the end is the yellow Cadillac," she said. But no one responded. All her friends around her just wore knowing grins because, as happened all the time in Grace Valley, the word had leaked. "This is awesome," June said. And she was thinking, *Man, that is exactly what we need — a real no-shit ambulance, loaded.* But she would never say so because it was simply impossible.

The ambulance stopped in front of the gallery of spectators, and someone from the band handed Myrna Claypool a microphone. Into the mike she said, "Dr. June Hudson . . . Come on down!!!"

June's heart skipped a couple of beats. She looked around at her friends and they all

460

met her gaze with knowing eyes. She began to tremble. "Not really," she said. "Not really."

On shaky legs, she descended the bleachers and walked slowly to the ambulance. Sam had jumped out and lifted little Myrna down from the roof so she could meet her niece. And behind June, everyone in Grace Valley applauded. Did they all know? Had this been an elaborate surprise just for her?

"Aunt Myrna?" she asked when she reached her. "What have you done?"

"Well, it's overdue," Myrna said. "The town is growing, we need this vehicle and your Jeep is a sadly burned little critter."

"Oh Myrna," she murmured with tears in her voice. She embraced her tiny aunt and whispered in her ear, "You must be loaded!"

"Pretty much," the little old lady replied.

Later that week, June gathered the staff together before the start of business. "I'm not coming into the clinic on Monday — I'm going to Pleasure. Jury selection is beginning for Leah's trial. It's up to you all what you want to do. I'm not opposed to closing the clinic."

"I'll call all our appointments," Jessica said. "I can't imagine that anyone will insist on coming in that day."

"Are a lot of people going to Pleasure?" John asked.

"I don't know," June said. "But my dad is going, Judge Forrest is presiding and Birdie will be there for sure. George said he's closing the café after breakfast. I just want Leah to know she has friends."

"I'll go," Charlotte said. "I'll tell Bud."

"Well, count me in," John said.

On Monday a sign was put on the clinic door — Closed for Court.

It wasn't unusual for the town to have a consciousness and for things to happen in sync. In this case, the whole town felt they had let Leah Craven down. They would not again.

June and Sadie drove John over to Pleasure in the ambulance so they could go by way of Valley Hospital and make their rounds. That put them there a little later than the majority. June had told John to expect a good, solid showing, but even she was stunned by the throng, and among them were a few reporters with notebooks open and even a news van from a San Francisco station.

"God, who do you suppose called *them?*" John asked.

"It's hard to know. Maybe everyone. We're

going to have to park and walk," she said.

"No, keep going. They'll let us through. Susan is going to *kill* me for not bringing her along!"

"Ohh, I don't think so," June said. "Look over there — see? Mary Lou Granger, Julianna Dickson and —"

"Susan! How did she know?"

"How did *we* know?"

"But she didn't say anything."

June smiled. "I'll bet you anything she thought you'd try to talk her out of it."

They parked and locked the ambulance, then slowly made their way through the throng of people, friends and neighbors, some of whom were carrying signs, trying to get to the front of the courthouse. There were easily a thousand folks present, not counting the media. As John and June edged through the crowd, they passed interviews taking place, reporters asking townspeople how close they were to Leah, whether they thought Leah guilty of some crime, what they thought the police should have done with her.

Unsurprisingly, they came upon Elmer, deep in an interview.

"So, you're saying she should not have been arrested?" an attractive young woman asked him.

"I'm saying she wasn't arrested by our police chief, the same man who discovered the body of Gus Craven. Our chief was called out to that farm dozens of times, to cart old Gus away before the drunken fool killed his wife and children. I guess he knew Leah Craven hadn't premeditated any old murder. She was just trying to save her own life and the lives of her kids."

"And the town is here because . . . ?"

"The situation should never have come to this. If we were any kind of community, we'd have taken turns sitting out at that farm till Gus got the clear message we weren't going to let him hurt his family anymore. We should have run him off years ago — and since we didn't, Leah had to. In all innocence, Leah had to run him off before he killed her."

"You advocate vigilantism?"

"Get out your *Webster's,* young woman. Vigilantism is lawless, violent action that supercedes the law. Vigilantes would have chased Gus down and strung him up. What I regret is that we didn't protect one of our own, and left her to protect herself as best she could. That she should go to trial for that is a travesty!"

"Travesty!" someone shouted. "Let Leah Go! Let Leah Go!" The chanting began.

"June?" John asked. "Do I smell what I think I smell?"

She whiffed the air. "Barbecue?"

They followed their noses and found what they were looking for. George, Burt and Sam had brought and set up the picnic grills. And seated at a small folding table downwind of the grills sat Myrna, selling tickets for hot dogs and chips.

"There you are, darling," Myrna said, rising enough to kiss June's cheek. "John, be an angel and go find your wife — tell her it's her turn to spell me."

"Aunt Myrna, did you phone all the television people?"

"I might have called in a marker or two. Have you seen Birdie, dear? Or the Barstows? Someone must have news of what's going on inside!"

The courtroom didn't have space for spectators because it was packed with prospective jurors. John Cutler, Leah's public defender, and three lawyers from the prosecutors office interviewed them one by one. The three prosecutors were led by Marge Glaser, a righteous young woman with a stiff face who had not appeared before Judge Forrest before. Ms. Glaser was moved by the letter of the law, and obviously convinced that if Leah Craven had held the shovel that hit Gus Craven in the back of the head, she was guilty of a crime. But Ms. Glaser was having a little trouble.

John Cutler was young, fresh faced, quick to smile and anything but rigid. While Ms. Glaser was impeccably groomed, lint free with every hair in place, Cutler's shirttail kept creeping out of his pants, his hair was longish and floppy, and he might have slept in his suit.

But he was having better luck, and the jury hadn't even been selected.

"Do you have any history of domestic violence in your family, Mr. Schuck?" Ms. Glaser asked a prospective juror.

"No, ma'am," he answered.

"Have you ever been called on to intercede in a domestic argument that had gotten, shall we say, rough?"

"No, ma'am."

"And let me ask you one more question. Do you think it's the job of law enforcement officers to make arrests in the event of a domestic situation? A family fight?"

"Yes, ma'am," he said.

"Thank you very —"

"If they can get there in time," Mr. Schuck said. "If it was me, I don't know if I'd wait on the police. Know what I mean?"

"That's all, Mr. Schuck."

"If anyone laid a hand on my daughter, for example, I'd likely beat him to a bloody pulp and take my chances."

"Your honor!" Ms. Glaser pleaded.

"You're dismissed, Mr. Schuck," Judge said. Then he looked pointedly at Ms. Glaser. "Would you like to try again?"

"Yes, I would!" she shot back.

John Cutler slowly smiled. He hadn't been able to ask very many questions so far.

Ms. Glaser quietly conferred with her legal team while the bailiff called another potential juror to the stand. This was the fifteenth interview in an hour, and it was clear that the prosecutor had not yet selected one juror she was completely satisfied with.

"Your name please?" Ms. Glaser asked.

"Mrs. Melba Leaver."

"Good morning, Mrs. Leaver," Ms. Glaser said, trying to be pleasant, but her smile was strained and her patience was thin. "I have just a couple of questions for you this morning. First, have you or anyone in your family ever been arrested for a felony?"

"No."

"Do you work outside the home?"

"No, my husband wouldn't like that."

"I see. And you've been married how long . . . ?"

"Thirty-six years. Five children."

"Who would you say is the final authority in your home? You or your husband?"

"Oh, my husband, most definitely."

"Thank you," Ms. Glaser said, looking pleased at last.

John Cutler stood. "Mrs. Leaver, has your husband ever, in anger, struck you?"

"What? No! He wouldn't dare! I'd shoot him in his sleep!"

Marge Glaser dropped her head heavily to the table in utter frustration. "Mrs. Leaver works for me," Cutler said, sitting down again.

"Your *honor!*" Ms. Glaser begged.

"All right, all right. Ms. Glaser, Mr. Cutler, my chambers. Leave your entourage here, if you don't mind. It's a small chamber." Judge stood and left the bench, followed by the lawyers. He took off his robe, hung it on the rack just inside his office door and sat behind his desk. He waited for them to take their seats. Cutler was all loose and goosey, trying not to grin too wildly, while Marge Glaser was clearly miserable.

"Mr. Cutler, may I suggest you wipe that silly grin off your face? Your apparent success in this case has nothing whatsoever to do with your skill as an attorney." Judge Forrest hoped that would make what he had to say to Ms. Glaser go down a little easier.

"Ms. Glaser, by the same token, you are undoubtedly a brilliant attorney and I would say your boss was a thinking man when he sent you to take on this case. The problem is, I don't see any way you can make it work."

"But your honor, if we had a change of venue —"

"You could move this trial to Australia and you would still have these facts to deal with — you have a woman who was, for better than sixteen years, severely beaten by her alcoholic husband. Her children were beaten. He was repeatedly locked up for violence directed at his family. And only after sixteen years, countless arrests, endless bruises and dozens if not hundreds of witnesses to the abuse, she whacked him in the head as he pummeled her child."

"And hid the body!"

"Then charge her with unlawful burial without a permit! Ms. Glaser, there is no doubt she killed him out of fear for her life and the life of her child. Half the town saw their bruises the next morning as they both showed up for their jobs in the café. Your witnesses amount to sheriff's department investigators and a county coroner, while Mr. Cutler here has a witness list the size of the Grace Valley phone book."

"Your honor, I've offered to plead out with Mr. Cutler, and I'll go as wide as manslaughter —"

"He can win this, Ms. Glaser, and I'll tell you why. Self-defense is not against the law. Not here, not anywhere. But here's an offer I'll make you both. If you can agree to involuntary manslaughter, I'll give Leah Craven a probation and community service sentence that will allow her to go home and take care of her family."

"Your honor, this is most irregular. It's clear judicial prejudice. It's grounds for a change of judge."

"Ms. Glaser, are you stupid or just stubborn? I'm giving you a break here! Leah Craven's supporters are having a barbecue on the courthouse steps! If you manage to lose, and cost the county an extraordinary amount of money, do you think you'll be in the same job next year? Now think about this, you two. You have thirty minutes to decide what to do. Out. Out!"

An hour later Leah Craven walked down the courthouse steps with her young attorney and wept openly as she was cheered by a riotous crowd. From coast to coast her face was seen on television, and her quavering voice heard as she said, "I hope Gus is finally at peace . . . because I am."

Part of Tom Toopeek's job was to drive around the back roads of Grace Valley and be familiar with every old abandoned logging road, farm path, orchard access road, crossroad and highway. If he ever had to chase someone, he'd better know every possible route of escape. And not just in daylight.

He was making a routine survey of the area to the east of town when he happened upon a darkly painted late model Ford truck parked off of an old abandoned road not far from June's house. He parked his Rover down the road, got out his flashlight and rifle and had a look around.

He was an expert tracker, but he simply followed a footpath from the truck's parking place to June's backyard. He saw a flickering in her kitchen window and heard something squeaking. As he got closer he saw the flickering was candlelight and the squeaking was music.

He shouldn't have, but telling himself he just had to be sure, he peeked in the dining room window. The table was set with candles and china; there was wine in glasses, an opened gift box with ribbon, tissue paper and bows spilling out. June was wearing a slim, sexy black dress with a slit up one thigh and she danced in the arms of a large man in a flannel shirt. She laughed and tossed her head seductively as he lifted her off her feet and twirled her around. Tom had never seen her like this.

Dancing?

He shook his head in bemusement and escaped to his Rover as quietly as possible.

ONE LAST THING . . .

"Sadie!" June called. "Hurry up, we're late!"

The dog came running up the back porch steps, and if a dog could smile, this one was smiling. June, in her nicest summer dress, crouched down and fastened a flower wreath around her best friend's neck.

In Grace Valley, at that moment, someone took a metal cutter to the padlock on the Presbyterian Church and opened it up. In through the large double doors flooded people — men, women and children dressed in their finery, smiling and greeting each other, laughing, joking, even singing.

June and Sadie rode to town in the ambulance. Whoever was "on call" had the ambulance and stayed with it. Today was her day, since John had another commitment.

When she got to the church, she had to park across the street at the clinic, there were so many cars. "Damn," she muttered. "I bet they've started. Now, you remember to be very good."

June and Sadie jogged across the street and into the church. Music filled the air, candles glittered at the altar, and flowers, more flowers than she'd ever seen in a church at one time, were displayed everywhere.

She and Sadie slipped into a pew at the back of the church, right beside Jessica. "Have you ever seen her more beautiful?" Jessica whispered.

June looked up the aisle. The church was full to bursting, so it wasn't easy to see everyone, but by craning her neck she could get a wide-angle view. There stood Sam and Justine before Judge Forrest. Elmer was the best man, then Burt, then George, then John Stone. To the bride's left were her four sisters. And standing behind her, having just given her away, was Standard Roberts. Witnessing was the town. And when Judge said, "Dearly beloved, we are gathered here together . . ." all that came to June's mind was, *Yes, we are gathered here together.*

All together.

ABOUT THE AUTHOR

Robyn Carr is a RITA® Award-winning author of over twenty-five novels, including the critically acclaimed *The House on Olive Street*. Robyn and her husband live in Las Vegas, Nevada. You can visit Robyn Carr's Web site at www.robyncarr.com.